KING OF WRATH

PIPER STONE

Published by Stormy Night Publications and Design, LLC.
www.StormyNightPublications.com

Stone, Piper
King of Wrath

Cover Design by Korey Mae Johnson
Images by iStock/Lorado and iStock/AerialPerspective Works

PROLOGUE

Somebody died today, someone who had a family and friends, a job they loved and plans for the future. Their life was cut short by fate, a cruel moment where a slight alteration in timing or a different decision could have prevented the tragedy. There would be sadness and tears, anger and frustration, so many demanding answers.

But they wouldn't come.

Yes, somebody died today.

I think it was me…

CHAPTER 1

 arah

Darkness.

Even though the blindfold was soft, preventing even a tiny amount of light, I wasn't afraid of what he would do. Seconds later, I sensed his presence, his scent permeating my skin, yet he remained silent.

But there was no doubt he was there, watching me. Waiting.

Hungering.

I was amazed how heightened my other senses became when he slipped the blindfold over my eyes, awakening the dark, lust-filled needs he'd exposed the first time he'd touched me. I'd already realized that the single event had pulled me into his world, the man able to capture my soul before I'd known it had gone missing.

There was a profound need shared between us, a thirst so intense and electrifying that a single touch could light the fire between us. I lost myself when I was with him, incapable of focusing and I couldn't understand the reason why. He'd taken me, used me, forced me to surrender to his darkest needs and still I hungered for more.

Now, as I remained in the same position where he'd placed me almost two hours before, my senses heightened to the fullest extent, I thought I'd go mad if he didn't brush his fingers across my arm or whisper the sordid, filthy words that kept me fully aroused.

I wanted to hate him. No, I needed to despise him in order to break the spell, but every time I believed I'd found the strength, he destroyed my resolve with nothing more than a look from his dark eyes. He was a monster, a predator, an evil man, but all I could see when I was with him was the man I'd fallen into an abyss for.

Maybe I was crazy, but my mouth watered to have his cock inside, to drown in his cum.

My arms ached, the rope he used to tie my wrists tighter than normal. Every time I shifted, the thick strands chafed my skin. I was naked and bare, waiting for him to provide a command. How had this happened? How? Why?

You know the answer.

Yes, I did, although at times it was difficult to accept.

When I moved, trying to take the pressure from my knees, I finally heard a sound. Then a deep rumble, a growl of disappointment that I'd moved at all. As he walked closer, the rustle of his trousers trickling into my ears, I held my breath.

"You're still the bad girl I met. Aren't you? My perfect little submissive." His deep voice resonated inside, creating a wave of desire that was almost overwhelming.

"Yes, sir."

When I felt the strands of a strap tickling my back, I shuddered, wetness penetrating my inner thighs as my pussy clenched and released. He reached down, fondling my breast, flicking his finger back and forth across my nipple. Then he pinched it without reservation, twisting until I cried out.

"My beautiful pain slut. You do know I love that about you. Yes?"

"Yes, sir."

This was our game, one of many. His dirty words had exposed another part of me, releasing her from invisible chains, even if physically I was his prisoner. But the two sides remained at odds, my rationality fighting the inevitable.

"Mmm... Bend forward," he directed, still brushing the ends of the tawse back and forth across my bottom.

I did as he asked, doing everything I could to keep from placing my hands on the carpet.

"Legs open wider."

Again, I obeyed him even as the strong woman inside tried to convince me otherwise. The man had been my undoing, his method of seduction like a maestro finessing a beloved instrument. And I'd fallen for it.

He'd stripped away my innocence, using a terrible moment in our lives to weave us tightly together. I was nothing but his possession, but there was no place I'd rather be. We were toxic, passionate, and totally incompatible. I'd taken an oath to save lives.

He'd promised to destroy them, issuing blinding pain for his amusement.

"Good girl." He touched my shoulder, squeezing as if providing me with some comfort. Then he cracked the strap against my naked skin. The pain was instant, my pussy aching. What had started as a plan of revenge had turned into a twisted fantasy that neither one of us could control.

Now he wanted more from me, not just my full surrender.

He wanted everything.

Including my heart.

And what disturbed me was that I was ready to give it to him.

Every sound from the crack of his wrist to the whooshing made by the thick strap was amplified, prickles dancing across my skin. As he delivered several strikes, one coming right after the other, I bit back a moan. He adored when I cried out in anguish from his actions.

Today, I refused to give him what he wanted.

After a few additional strikes, he seemed to know what I was doing. He fisted my hair, yanking me back into my original position. "You're going to deny me?"

"Yes, sir."

He laughed as he twisted his fingers around my long strands, teasing me by brushing the tawse across my nipples. "Don't taunt me. You know what happens when you do."

His deep voice was different, darker than usual. He'd changed in only a few weeks, losing himself in a world he'd told me he'd never wanted.

Even though he'd said I was the only light to his darkness.

Whatever the case, the man would be my ultimate destruction, the loss of my freedom as well as my soul.

What terrified me was that he'd already captured a portion of my heart.

When he whooshed the strap from one breast to the other, I shivered. Then he did it again, only this time cracking the strands gently against my nipple. I bit my tongue to keep from crying out until he repeated the move a third time, shifting from one hardened bud to the other. I was electrified by the anguish, ecstasy rolling through me.

"Oh. Yes. Yes…"

"That's my girl." He released his hold on my hair, pressing his hand against my back then resuming the round of punishment.

I wiggled, my heart racing as pussy juice trickled down my legs, the scent of my desire floating between us. I'd never wanted a man to be dominating, but he was all consuming.

My lover.

My master.

Gabriel.

Just thinking his name brought another tickling of desire even as anguish exploded through my bloodstream. I no longer cared, the pleasure my body would receive worth every second. He issued six more then tossed the tawse aside, gently pulling me to my feet and against his chest. As he cupped my breast, caressing with the rough pad of his thumb, I couldn't stop trembling. He had that kind of effect on me, allowing me to let go completely.

I was lost in the sea of ecstasy as he guided me to the bed, easing me down then pushing my legs wide open.

"Your pussy is beautiful, my sweet Sarah. Perfect in every way, swollen and glistening. And I'm going to gorge myself on your sweetness." He pressed my legs wide open, allowing his hot air to flow from one leg to the other, his husky growl setting the tone.

I wanted to reach out and touch him. I craved ripping off my blindfold, able to watch his face, but he wasn't ready to allow me the privilege. He rubbed the insides of my legs, continuing to tease me, infusing the explosive heat with more need than I'd felt before. He was a master of playing my body, pulling me to the moment of sweet release then stopping. He wanted me to beg for his touch, to scream out his name when I came. He craved me needing him above everything else. My friends. My job. The world I'd left behind.

I already did, the realization never far from my mind. He barely darted the tip of his tongue across my clit, and I bucked up from the bed.

Chuckling, he repeated the move then slid his wide-open fingers down from my breastbone to my stomach, concentrating on rolling a single finger around my bellybutton.

"What do you want, my beautiful Sarah?"

"Your mouth. Your tongue."

"Yes, I have both of those."

"How long are you going to tease me?"

"As long as I feel like it. Tell me it isn't something you'd do yourself." He blew hot air across my pussy again then swirled his tongue around my clit.

Panting, I twisted back and forth, every synapse frayed. "Please lick me. Drive your tongue deep inside."

"That's better. Then what do you want after that? Tell me or face additional punishment."

"Fuck me. Please just fuck me."

His guttural sounds changed, becoming even more intense. Then he rewarded me by pulling my already swollen clit into his mouth, sucking as he dipped a single finger past my swollen folds.

I was mad with need, tossing my head back and forth, incapable of stopping the strangled moans. I could tell he was watching me, studying every reaction, always looking for more. His hunger knew no bounds, the man capable of sparking the electricity between us with a single look.

As he feasted, his needs intensifying, I could no longer think clearly, the pleasure too great. He kept me wide open, pumping several fingers into my tight channel, flexing them open as he plunged them long and hard.

He knew exactly what I liked and had from the first, able to pull me close, so very close, building the excitement to the point I was almost always in a frenzy. Today was no exception. As I continued writhing, his growls increased in volume, drowning out the heavy beating of my heart. How could this man turn me on so much, breaking down every defense mechanism? How had I allowed myself to fall for his methods, derailing my entire life?

And why was it starting to no longer matter?

He licked and finger fucked me for an eternity, until I was breathless, exhaustion rushing through me.

"Please let me come," I finally begged, giving him exactly what he wanted. He'd known it was going to happen, had prepared himself to keep on taunting me until I did. He was that way, demanding full control.

"Then come for me, Sarah. Fill my mouth with your juice." Gabriel buried his face in my pussy, shifting his head back and forth.

My body had been trained to obey his commands and within seconds, an orgasm tore through me, my core exploding.

I gave him the scream he'd wanted, and I would do so again.

And again.

Until there was nothing left.

Which is exactly what he wanted.

He'd once told me he'd break me. I wasn't certain if we weren't shattered together.

CHAPTER 2

arah

Five weeks earlier

I'd watched the bloody scene unfold as if in slow motion. I'd sensed what would happen before it had, a crazy beeping sound going off in the back of my head as if a warning was being sent. I'd backed away from the street corner where I'd been prepared to cross, first in line at the edge of the pavement because that's the kind of woman I was, always pushing myself harder.

Faster.

More.

But the crowd of people wouldn't budge. I was locked at the very edge of the road, a sickening feeling of anticipation making me woozy. I'd glanced at several of their faces in the timestamp that had been dragged into a vacuum, knowing that not one of them was paying attention.

Or cared.

In fact, they'd pushed me off the sidewalk in preparation of the light changing and almost into the line of fire.

Even as the gunshot went off only inches away, the explosive crack reverberating in my ears, no one had stopped going about their daily activities or bothered to look toward the victim and the person responsible.

But I had.

I'd lunged forward, screaming for help although I doubted it was coming. I'd terrified the perpetrator with my loud voice only seconds after blood and brain matter had painted my freshly washed scrubs. And I'd reacted the same as I did every day in the operating room, dropping into action, searching for any sign the man with dilated eyes was alive.

Performing CPR was second nature to me, a course I'd learned when I was twelve, a part of being a Girl Scout. I was told later I'd been the reason he'd remained alive, still breathing when he was rolled into my operating room.

I'd been his savior once.

But the odds hadn't been with me. Perhaps there was a random selector in the heavens, the angel in charge identifying how many saves one person was allowed. Or how many times a person could be a savior.

It had appeared I'd used up my credit for the day, the man dying on the table. His driver's license had provided an identity, a name to be used on the death certificate. But the pictures inside his wallet had told a story about his life. A beautiful wife in her late thirties. Two adorable children and a Golden Retriever with a happy tail. They'd sent him off to work that morning with a coffee cup plastered with similar photographs, the couple likely discussing what they would do that night after he got home from his accounting position.

They'd never thought about the possibility that it could be his last day, or that road rage would be the reason. Maybe they forgot to say they loved each other. Or maybe there'd been an argument the wife would always regret. For a little while his friends would mourn his loss.

Then they'd go about their daily lives because that's what happened.

When I'd received an early morning call from my floor nurse only minutes before alerting me another patient had difficulty breathing, I'd wasted no time heading for my car. It didn't matter it was early or that my car was covered in frost. I didn't listen to the forecast or worry about whether I could get there in one piece.

I jumped into the car, determined to save a life.

"She's crashing," Maggie said, her voice strained.

No, dear God. I wouldn't lose another one.

Cringing, I fiddled with the heater, trying to get the defrost on high. "I'm on my way. Make certain and have the surgical team prepped. We won't have much time." When my main nurse called, I knew the situation was dire. I had minimal time to try to save the woman's life. Angie had fought hard, but the blood loss had been significant, sepsis likely setting in.

"You got it, Doctor. Be careful. It's icy as shit."

"Don't worry, Mags. Careful is my middle name." I ended the call, wrapping my hand around the steering wheel so tightly my knuckles were white almost instantly. I'd prayed the medication I'd prescribed would work, but I had my doubts I'd be able to save Angie's life.

I had to. There was no other choice in my mind.

I made a turn, the back end of my Cruze drifting to the right. Damn it. *Control. Breathe.* I did what I could, leaning forward as I weaved my way through the early morning traffic. Thank God it was lighter than normal, the recent early snowstorm keeping a few die-hard New Yorkers cuddled up in their beds. That's exactly where I wanted to be, but duty called as it did so often. I loved my job, but the recent overload of patients was killing the entire team.

As I made another turn, the windows started to fog. "Come on, you piece of crap. Work!" I fiddled with the blower, turning it on high, but the fog kept sliding across the windshield's surface. No. No. If I had to pull over, it could mean the difference between life and death. As I braked for a stoplight, I could feel the tires losing traction, the salt covering the surface of the crunchy snow not able to work in these temperatures.

Please. Please. Help me get there.

When the light turned green, I wasn't shocked the asshole behind me immediately started honking his horn. Everyone was in a hurry. I carefully pressed on the gas, barely able to see out the window. Panting, I leaned forward as far as possible, rubbing my gloved hand across the surface. The minimal help gave me a three-by-four-inch view of the road. Damn it. The conditions were getting worse. Only four blocks. Four little blocks.

"Come on, baby. You can do it." I kept my speed well under the limit, crawling toward the hospital. When another light turned yellow, I sucked in my breath and pressed on the brake. At that moment it seemed all time stopped, the car skidding to the left. Then to the right.

As my beautiful red car spun in the opposite direction, I noticed approaching headlights, the driver barreling toward me. All I could do was keep my hands on the steering wheel, gently pressing on the brakes.

The car skidded again and I almost panicked, the other car close. So close.

Closer.

Closer...

* * *

Gabriel

Two minutes earlier

"I'm going to kill the motherfucker. That's what I'm going to do," Luciano bellowed.

There was more rage in my brother's voice than I'd heard in a long time. "You can't kill Joseph Moretti." While the Moretti family had been considered our enemy for years, our father had attempted to make a truce, offering one of our sisters as a potential bride for the brutal man's oldest son and the one expected to take the throne when Joseph was killed or died of natural causes. At the point, I knew it would be the former. Yes, the entire Moretti family deserved to be wiped off the face of the earth. I had my personal reasons why, revenge almost all I'd been able to think about for years. However, for my brother to go off the deep end now could be traumatic for the entire family.

There were enemies all around us prepared to swoop in like freaking vultures. I might have been away from the family business for a few years, only recently lured back into the fold, but I knew exactly what we were facing.

The powerful hold the Cosa Nostra had once had on the city was waning, cartels and Russians breathing down our necks. The old methods taught in Sicily didn't work in a technologically advanced city like New York. The various businesses were suffering, my brother concerned a traitor was in the mix providing information to God knew who. It was my job to find that out. I might hate my father and all he stood for, but no one fucked with my brother or sisters.

No one.

Luciano and I had been engaged in a phone conversation minutes earlier, his lack of patience making him refuse to wait until I arrived at his house. Then he'd ended the call, required to take another. Only minutes later he'd called me again, this time from his car, his rage uncontrollable.

"Like fucking hell I can't. Goddamn this weather. I'm sick to death of winter."

I glanced out the windshield, hoping to notice his car. He couldn't be more than a couple of miles in front of me. At least I hoped that was the case, but with Luciano, when he made a decision, nothing would stop him from carrying it through.

No matter the consequences.

He was nuts for taking on the man without backup. I refused to allow that to happen. I only hoped I wouldn't be too late.

"What the fuck happened?" The call had initiated what would end up becoming a war between two powerful entities. My brother had never become this unhinged.

"It doesn't matter. The man will die," he snarled.

Goddamn it. What the hell was wrong with him?

"Don't do anything stupid. Just wait for me, for fuck's sake. You know the kind of security he has in place." I was a goddamn stockbroker, loathing the shit my family continued to undertake. Yes, we were powerful, my father having blackmailed or 'convinced' influential citizens that they would look the other way when business was handled, but I wanted no part of it. Luciano had insisted I take on a role. Up until now, I wasn't interested in getting additional blood on my hands. However, the fact our father continued to insist Theodora marry the fucking pig pissed me off. Nico Moretti was nothing more than a primate who enjoyed breaking a man with his bare hands.

I knew my father well enough to know there was a hidden reason behind the marriage. I planned on finding out what it was. Luciano had been too busy putting out fires, attempting to keep our stronghold on our empire to figure out the great mystery.

"Hell, no, brother. One of my soldiers informed me that Joseph has plans on leaving town today. He's already hiding in an alternate location like the coward he is. But I found him." Luciano laughed maniacally, the sound as damning as what he was about to do. "My guess is he got word how unhappy I was in finding out he invaded our territory. Then the ultimate betrayal. Motherfucker."

I'd already heard Moretti had ordered two of our men killed, which had set the stage for having him eliminated, but whatever Joseph had ordered in addition had set things in motion. I only hoped Luciano was ready for the fallout.

"I'll be there in eight minutes."

"The deed will be done by then," Luciano said, half laughing. He enjoyed the hell out of this.

"Fine." Hissing, I tossed the phone onto the seat. As my chest tightened, I glanced into the rearview mirror. I couldn't recognize myself any longer. I'd spent years distancing myself from the family, pretending I had no responsibilities.

And I'd suffered, wallowing in self-pity like some wounded animal.

"You're worthless," my father had told me several times.

I was furious with myself for all the years that had been lost. Truthfully, I didn't give a crap about the money or clout. I made a damn good living and enjoyed not having to look over my shoulder every two seconds. I slapped my hand on the steering wheel, the crunch of ice under the tires of the Charger another indication the timing couldn't be worse.

That Luciano had managed to convince me to take a leadership position in running Club Rio was a reminder of his influential ability. Granted, he had too much on his plate already and no one outside of the family was allowed to run a single one of our businesses. I'd been given two choices. Take the second in command position over everything or manage the club. I'd chosen the latter, maybe because the corporation was completely legal. Hell, what did I know about running a freaking private men's club? I'd never be king, a position I'd never wanted in the first place.

As I rounded the corner, forced to stop at a light, ugly memories of the past resurfaced. No. I refused to do that to myself. The Morettis had reared their ugly heads again after several years of playing fair in the sandbox, but the truce had obviously been temporary.

Why would they suddenly threaten our family when another deal had been made?

Something didn't add up, but my brother was too embroiled in bloodlust to notice.

A few seconds later, I was far too impatient to wait, speeding through the red light, daring a fucking police officer to stop me. Maybe I was just like my father and brother after all.

With horns blaring, I pressed down on the accelerator until I noticed brake lights in the windshield. Forced to slow down then stop, I craned my neck to find out what the hell was going on. Five seconds passed. Ten. Then a full minute.

A sick feeling jetted into my system. I grabbed my phone, dialing my brother's number. Four rings then his voicemail. Fuck. I leaned back in the seat, taking deep breaths. Nothing was moving.

Another thirty seconds passed, and I threw the gear into park, tossing open the door. I didn't give a shit if I ended up stalling traffic. Something was wrong. I slipped as I jogged forward, people yelling at me from their car windows. As I started to make headway, my feet keeping traction, I heard a siren in the distance.

Oh, hell, no.

An icy chill shifted down my spine, a sixth sense swirling through me like a firestorm. As I moved around a corner, my mind couldn't process what I was seeing.

Two mangled cars.

I moved closer, barely able to breathe.

There was no doubt one of the vehicles was Luciano's. I wasn't the kind of man to pray. I'd known early in my life that there would never be any salvation for a member of the Giordano family. That had been proven several times. Our blood was tainted from generations of evil deeds. Even my mother's devout Catholic faith and her determination to raise decent children who believed in all things good hadn't cracked the surface of our evil coating.

But at that moment I said my first prayer that my brother was still alive.

As I approached, I sensed the other driver had been the cause. Both cars were flipped on their sides, the stench of gasoline filling the air. There were dozens of bystanders, but no one was trying to help. Goddamn them. Goddamn them to hell.

Luciano had been thrown from the windshield, his stupid habit of never wearing his seatbelt to blame. Blood was everywhere, the crunch of shattered glass pinging in my ears. I knelt onto the snow, feeling for his pulse. He was alive.

"Luciano. Help is on its way. Everything will be okay."

He moaned, his eyelids moving. "The woman," he croaked out.

"What woman?"

"Other... vehicle." He continued coughing, blood flowing from his mouth.

I glanced toward the red car, noticing smoke was billowing from under the hood. "So what?" The sirens were closer, but people and cars were blocking them. *Get the fuck out of the way.*

"Save... her."

"Fuck, no. I'm staying right here."

He managed to lift his arm, placing his bloody fingers on my shirt. "Do... it. My... decent... baby... brother."

Damn the man. Was this his last-ditch effort to buy his way into heaven? "Fine." I reacted, stumbling toward the other vehicle, scanning the area. The car would catch fire at any second. Fuck this. I scrambled onto the car, jerking the door handle. It was locked. Fuck. As I peered in, I noticed long blonde hair. Luciano had seen her face before the crash.

She was slumped over the steering wheel, the seatbelt possibly saving her life. How ironic. She'd caused the fucking accident and she might survive. Luciano had known the good side of me, the one he'd often made fun of would never be allowed to walk away from her. I knew all the pressure points to a windshield. Our father had made certain every one of his children had training in weaponry, defense, and knowing how the hell to get out of a damaged vehicle, even one submerged in water.

Enemies had gotten creative in their methods of eliminating their prey.

I jumped off, moving to the other side, a puff of smoke drawing my attention. I'd have one shot at this and with the car being on its side, it would take a miracle of God to get her out. As I started to kick the pressure point on the glass, I almost slipped twice. But I kept going, drowning out the noise of the useless bystanders who were gasping and cheering me on.

Worthless pieces of shit.

When the windshield finally cracked, I wasted no time, punching out as much of the glass as possible. Then I crawled inside, her weak moans indicating she was alive. "I don't know if you can hear me, but I'm getting you out of here." I pressed the button for the seatbelt, not surprised the damn thing was jammed.

She moaned again, suddenly trying to move.

"Don't. Stay right there. I'm going to need to cut you out of this." The flames were already increasing, the stench getting worse. I yanked out my switchblade, wasting no time cutting her free, catching her before she moved. As I gently eased her into my arms, a rattling sound coming from somewhere under the vehicle kicked my adrenaline into overdrive.

I had to wrench my body trying to keep glass from her face. When I finally got out, I held her tightly against my chest, slipping on the ice as I moved as far away from the vehicle as possible.

"Back away," someone yelled. "It's going to blow."

The boom drove me several feet further, dropping us both hard into the snow. At this moment I was grateful for the blanket of white to soften the fall. Panting, I immediately pulled away, lowering her gently onto the surface. "Someone take care of her!" I peered down, noticing her eyes were open. They were the most beautiful shade of blue I'd ever seen. When she blinked, I rubbed her face for no other reason than to give her comfort. "You'll be alright. You're in good hands." Good hands. Hell. She'd just faced the devil and he'd allowed her to live.

As soon as I stood, I noticed EMTs racing in our direction, a fire engine managing to make it through. Then I rushed back to my brother's car. As I peered down, I sensed he was losing his will to live.

Then I threw my head back and roared.

* * *

Beep. Beep. Beep.

I hated hospitals. The smell. The noises. The rush of people when catastrophe struck. And the wails of those left to pick up the pieces.

Today was no different, except my mother and sister were the ones crying. I'd heard my mother cry before, but always softly, as if she was trying to hide her sadness. Everything was different today, the woeful sound unlike anything I'd ever heard.

I stood in the same place I'd been since entering the hospital, trying to breathe while a suffocating weight remained on my chest. When I felt a hand on my shoulder, I bristled.

"It's up to God now."

I was shocked to hear my father say the words. He'd never acted as if he believed. As I tipped my head, I could see tears in his eyes. "Someone is going to pay for this."

"Who, son? Mother Nature? There's no one to blame. Shit happens. It's how we move on that matters in the end, especially in this family. There must be no weakness shown. Ever. Do you understand me?"

My God. My brother hadn't taken his last breath and my father was already returning to business. I gritted my teeth, trying my best to keep from saying something I'd regret. Now wasn't the time to engage in a battle of wills with the harsh man. The single time I'd challenged him just before walking out of his house, he'd broken my nose and injured my pride. I'd sworn to hate him on that day. Up until now, I'd managed. But a broken man was standing in front of me, even if he refused to allow me to see just how weak he'd become.

The four years since I'd left the family fold had taken a toll.

"Listen to our mother. She's bawling her eyes out. Do you plan on telling her the same shit?" Anger continued to build, the kind of rage that could become uncontrollable. The woman I'd saved was to blame. I had to cool down or this would turn into some kind of family brawl.

Fire burned in his eyes as he stared at me. "Revenge is best served cold, Gabriel. And you know I'm a proponent of making all those responsible for a treacherous act pay for their sins, but in this case, the young woman in the other car isn't to blame. Besides, you saved her life. That was your choice."

"What the fuck is that supposed to mean?"

"Stop it. Just stop it, both of you. Our brother is in surgery and you both act as if you can control the damn world!" Theodora's exclamation was louder than normal, her usual demure demeanor coming apart. She was shaking, her makeup smeared.

"You don't understand," I half whispered. *Weakness. Don't show any weakness.* That wasn't allowed in our family. Not for one second.

"Be a man," he'd told me at age twelve. Fine. I would be a man.

"Don't be a fool, Gabe. I love Luciano. He's my rock, a big brother who looks out for me. You're never around. You're too busy sucking up to your wealthy stockholders to give a damn about family any longer. I hate you."

"Don't you dare say that," our mother snapped. "We are family. Period. We will not come apart. Do you hear me?" She looked each one of us in the eyes, finally ending with me, her stare long and cold. "Did anyone contact Maria?"

Our other sister had a modeling gig in Italy. That's all I knew. "I made contact," I told her, although I'd been forced to leave a message. I walked away, guilt riding me hard. Theodora was right. I'd done everything I could to avoid family functions, let alone business meetings where I was listed as one of the stockholders. I'd pretended I was far too busy to engage. I'd tried so hard to shove aside my responsibilities that I hardly knew either one of my sisters any longer.

The ache inside was the most painful thing I'd been through that I could remember. I headed toward surgery, uncertain what to do. What I did know is that the weight of the family's business would fall on my shoulders even if Luciano survived, the recovery time likely long and arduous. I shoved my hands in my pockets after pressing the button for the elevator. Why did I continue to have a feeling there was more to the accident?

My gut was usually right, but in this case, I wasn't certain my thoughts were based on anything but grief, an emotion I knew far too well. As I leaned against the cold wall, I thought about the last conversation I'd had with Luciano prior to this morning. It had ended in an argument after I refused to quit my job. I'd even hung up on him. Then he'd left a terse message regarding the Morettis and something had clicked inside of me.

Family had to stick together.

Shit.

Too little, too late.

As soon as I stepped off onto the surgery floor, I became nauseous. As I walked down the corridor, a set of double doors flew open, two people walking beside a gurney. My heart raced the second I realized the identity of the patient.

The woman I'd saved, the creature who looked like an angel sent from the heavens.

She was alive.

I'd managed to save her.

As she was wheeled by, she opened her eyes and for a few seconds, I allowed myself to be mesmerized by her beauty. She was without a doubt one of the most attractive women I'd ever seen and all sound was blocked out, time ceasing to exist. A strange set of sensations vibrated through, a roar of desire forcing my cock to twitch. There was a shot of electricity, even though I was being pushed back violently. There were four people surrounding her gurney, one straddling her body, performing CPR. She was likely dying and I was aroused. What the hell was wrong with me? I remained

unblinking until I could no longer see or hear the slight creaking of the wheels.

A part of me wanted to possess her.

The other needed her destruction.

The two sides were at odds, but one way or the other, if the woman lived, she would pay for destroying my family.

Either with her body or with her life.

"Mr. Giordano?"

Hearing my name, I slowly turned my head, Luciano's surgeon standing in front of me.

Then he shook his head.

And my world collapsed around me.

As he explained what happened, the words faded into a pool of bloodlust. I made a promise to my brother and one I intended on keeping.

If the woman was responsible for his death, I would kill her with my bare hands.

CHAPTER 3

"*But there was no need to be ashamed of tears, for tears bore witness that a man had the greatest of courage, the courage to suffer.*"

—*Viktor E. Frankl*

Gabriel

Tears.

Far too many had been shed over the last three days. Three fucking days of watching my family suffer, my mother barely functioning given the horrific loss. I'd even found my father in his office, a half-empty bottle of scotch on his desk, tears staining his cheeks.

I'd shed none.

Years before, I'd accused Luciano of being unable to show emotion. He'd advised me that it was best never to become attached to anyone given our line of work because the loss was unbearable. He'd been a hard man, ruthless in every regard, and there wasn't a single person who knew the two of us who hadn't said we were born from the same cloth. We were certainly best friends.

I hadn't realized it until now, but perhaps I'd adopted his philosophy after all. I'd become completely emotionless, except for anger. It burned like the midnight sun, needing a full release. I had my reasons, including the loss of Luciano.

Sighing, I wanted nothing more than to drown out the sounds of organ music. Everything about this hatred was hypocritical.

The day was cloudy, the frigid cold of the recent weather pattern keeping the same ugly snow on the ground that had led to his death. I sensed the cold and ice even standing inside the church, the chill coursing through me like a venomous snake. I stood far removed from my family, incapable of providing any comfort. At least Maria had arrived in time for the funeral, although she'd said few words to me.

There was very little to say between us. I'd lost her trust by shoving aside my heritage.

An accident.

The news had arrived this morning. There was no one to blame for the accident that had stripped my family of a member. What bullshit.

I slid my hand into my pocket, wrapping my palm around the ring Luciano had been wearing when he died. The truth was I had no right to take it from him. I'd yet to earn my place in a separate but equally powerful organization. However, the black onyx piece jeweled with a serpent was a symbol that I intended on honoring.

It stood for a brotherhood that our father considered blasphemous, but Luciano had believed it the way of the future, pitting enemies together under difference circumstances. My brother had teased, associating their quarterly meetings to knights claiming a powerful position at a roundtable. Only they weren't gathering for humanitarian purposes, only to keep bloodshed to a minimum. Maybe joining was the only way to feel close to him.

Maybe I was hungrier for power than I'd wanted to admit to myself.

As my father approached, I stiffened, knowing exactly what he was about to say. I'd prepared myself for the ugliness of the words, the requirement that I could never escape. What he didn't know is that I'd made peace with being forced to take over the helm of our empire. There was a simple reason why.

Bloodlust.

It had consumed me, the hunger for revenge all I could think about since learning the girl's name.

Sarah Washington, daughter of New York Mayor William Washington, the esteemed leader making no bones about the fact he planned on taking down my family. The accident had been no coincidence. There wasn't a single person alive who could convince me otherwise. In my mind, it wasn't supposed to be anything but a minor fender bender, the girl using her feminine wiles to plant drugs or some other evidence in his car. I raked my hand through my hair, fighting to keep air in my lungs.

Whether or not the girl had been used as a pawn mattered very little. Someone had to pay for Luciano's death. Eye for an eye.

The number of politicians and corporate moguls filling the pews repulsed me. They were probably thrilled a member of the Giordano family had lost his life. I was surprised to see almost every member of the Brotherhood was in attendance. I couldn't count on two hands how many times I'd made fun of my older brother for helping organize the group of syndicate leaders. However, I sensed more loyalty than I'd anticipated.

The other man responsible for developing the group, Constantine Thorn, had already made an overture that I might be offered my brother's place on the esteemed council of power. I'd yet to decide whether or not I'd take him up on the invitation if it came. I wasn't in the mood to play politics, even with our own kind.

Huffing, I shook my head. Yes, we were a specialized breed of monsters, men capable of the most heinous activities, crimes that could put us behind bars for life or could mean our death by lethal injection. Somehow, I had a feeling karma would end my life instead. I twisted the ring in my pocket once again. The Sovereign ring was sacred, the right to wear it earned, not given. That only happened with blood spilled and respect earned. I'd done little of either.

But soon that would change.

Maybe I was channeling my dead brother.

Still, I would follow the code of honor that had been established, having at least one conversation with Constantine. He fashioned himself the Don of Dons, unreproachable to almost everyone. I didn't know him, nor did I want to make friends. That wasn't my style.

"I'm sorry, man." The voice was a reminder of my other life, the one in which I'd altered my identity. Not that it was to protect the innocent. I'd wanted to distance myself from the family name and the stigma attached to it. While I hadn't flaunted my identity, I also hadn't attempted to keep my family name or the legacy surrounding it a secret. What good would that do?

"Rick. I appreciate you coming," I said as I shook his hand.

Rick Lyttle worked in the same brokerage, hired only two months after I'd been. He was sharp, a go-getter like me and we'd hit it off from day one. He took a deep breath, studying the crowd.

"Your brother held influence," he said.

"Yeah, he did." Not that he was well liked. People were terrified of what Luciano could do, the brutality that remained deep inside his core. I'd accused him more than once of stepping into our father's shoes instead of leading the Cosa Nostra in another direction.

Luciano had laughed at me, telling me one day I'd understand exactly what was at stake. This was that day and it sickened me. A weight had been placed on my shoulders, but after some soul searching, I'd realized there was no other choice to make.

"I know how much you cared about him."

Nodding, I glanced at Rick's face. He'd had his share of tragedies, including the loss of his sister several years before. "Luciano was the kind of guy you couldn't ignore."

He chuckled and shoved his hands into his pockets. "I hate churches. I've never been to one when it wasn't about death."

Death had weighed heavily on my mind the past few days. I'd never thought much about it beforehand. The family had always seemed invincible. Death was final and the accident that had taken my brother's life was tainted. There was no way around it. "Understood." As my father approached, he grumbled under his breath. My father had made no bones about the fact he didn't like Rick.

"I'll talk to you after the service." With that, Rick walked away, staying clear of the powerful Anthony Giordano, feared by almost everyone who knew him.

My father stood by my side, staring at the priest as he offered the comfort my mother and sisters needed. I'd drowned out the man's voice, constantly scanning those paying their respects. It wasn't unheard of for an enemy to be so callous as to make an attempt during a religious ceremony. Even though my mother had forbidden it, I carried two weapons, ordering Luciano's soldiers to surround the church. Correction. My soldiers.

"You should join your mother," Father said, keeping his voice hushed out of respect.

"Later."

"You're concerned the Morettis will make a strike?"

"Given it was likely they were well aware of Luciano's intentions, I wouldn't put it past them. You shouldn't either. With his death, they will assume the Giordano family can't recover, coming at us with both barrels, no matter the deal you made. They are dead wrong."

Several awkward seconds passed.

"The deal is still on the table," he growled.

"That's for me to decide." Two more of my soldiers had died in a random shooting meant to look like a drug deal gone bad, but in my eyes, someone was sending a message. However, jumping to conclusions when I'd been out of the game for so long was ill advised.

The tension remained high.

"Does that mean you're accepting your position?" he asked, not bothering to look in my direction. What better location to turn over the thorny crown of control than at a funeral. *Business never stopped*, Pops had told me more than once. I was second in line, my two sisters considered incapable of handling the family business, at least to the degree that would be necessary. They'd been kept away from our unscrupulous side, a part of the Italian heritage.

"It means that I will do what's necessary." At this point, I was ready to put a bullet into every Moretti asshole. I'd wanted to do so for years, but Pops had talked me out of it. Now he wouldn't have the right to do so after I accepted the throne.

He gripped my shoulder the same way he'd done at the hospital, only this time his hold wasn't as firm. "I'm proud of you, son, for stepping up to the plate. Your brother would also be. We will make tonight special."

Special. My brother had been dead for three days and it was time to move on.

"Was there any other choice?" I snarked.

"You always have a choice."

I almost laughed. Not in this family. Generations of Giordanos had held whatever home city hostage with money and influence, finding ways to blackmail even the most esteemed individuals. Everyone had a dirty little secret. Even I knew that. Our family wasn't an exception either. We all had things we'd prefer to keep hidden. Luciano had called it a vile game of Russian roulette. Whoever managed to secure the power of the single bullet would be tossed to the top of the food chain.

He'd intended on making certain the Giordanos were the winner in every battle, every small skirmish.

Now I planned on ensuring that happened as well, blood raining in the streets of New York if not.

It didn't matter things had changed over the years, methods used for business different than when my father was my age. The kind of power we wielded was ingrained in the soil under our feet, stained with years of bloodshed.

And it would never change.

"Then I choose revenge." I'd mulled over my anger, searching my blackened soul for what to do. Killing her wouldn't be enough. Both she and her family deserved to suffer in the worst ways for ravaging our family, forcing it into despair. I'd come to that conclusion as the hours had passed. My plans for her would suit my needs for weeks, if not months. Instead of instant gratification, I'd have time to indulge in my darkest needs. That pleased me even more.

Sighing, I knew he had nothing to say. I'd told him of my discovery regarding the woman and he'd said nothing. He was too embroiled in his own guilt for turning his sons into cruel bastards. At least that's what I'd overheard him saying. I felt honored to be placed in the same category since he'd thought of me as disposable.

"What are your intentions?" he finally asked.

"I will be visiting the hospital later today. I'll handle it my way."

He shook his head. "It was an accident, son. Even in our line of work, they do happen. Don't destroy an innocent girl because of your anger."

Our line of work. I wanted to laugh in his face.

"You know exactly who she is, Pops. You can believe that I'm not the only person making this connection. If we don't seek and fulfill our need for revenge, there will be marks against our credibility and our reputation will suffer. With Luciano gone, there isn't a goddamn cartel or syndicate who isn't frothing at the mouth to try and invade our territory. The Morettis might need to get in line."

"I know better than you do how this works, Gabriel. While you've been ignoring your responsibilities, your brother was in the trenches, building wealth as well as our reputation. What I refuse to allow to happen is for you to tarnish it."

I took a deep breath, holding it. The argument wasn't new by any means. There would always be resentment for the decision I'd made, even if I didn't regret it. What it had offered was the ability to look outside the giant palace my father had built without fear of reprimand. Perhaps Pops had no idea just how fragile our position really was.

Or the rose-colored glasses were permanently affixed to his face. I fumed, saying nothing else.

"Be careful, son. People will be watching, and I'm not talking about the girl you're so intent on destroying. You'll need to ask yourself why you saved her life and don't try and tell me it was because of Luciano's request. It's because deep down inside, you're a good man, something that troubled me before but no longer. Use it. Make the organization your own, but heed to the man who exists inside, or mistakes will be made."

"Why the change of heart? You wanted brutality. Bloodshed. You thought I was too soft." I didn't buy he was softening with age.

He eyed me carefully. "Luciano reminded me that one of the joys at having two sons was the ability to have two completely different sides. What I found fascinating is that both of you wanted to change the Cosa Nostra. You told me yourself that things were different in America. I chose not to believe it. I was wrong."

For Pops to admit he was wrong shocked me. That didn't change how I felt. "I know what I need to do. And I never make mistakes. That's something you'll learn about me. If I accept the reign of this family, I will do it my way."

He turned to face me, keeping his voice down, but I could see fire in his eyes of a dragon. I'd rarely known him to act out of anger. At this moment, I was certain he would take out his grief on his only remaining son.

I'd be required to accept out of respect.

Up until today, that would have never happened.

But now, everything was different.

The look in his eyes changed, his demeanor dissolving into the one I'd know the majority of my life. He was Sicilian through and through, waving his fist at me as he spit out ugly words that created instant rage.

"You *are* heir to this goddamn throne whether you like it or not, but you will honor our heritage including the rules that were established long before you were born, or I will kill you with my bare hands," he said between clenched teeth. "I've allowed you to get away with being disrespectful all these years, funding your various hobbies, bailing you of jail because you refused to act like an adult. That ends here. You will learn that your actions, just like anyone else's, have consequences. You will also honor this family by making decent decisions. I don't give a shit whether you like that or not. You are my only son, and you will accept all the responsibilities that come with this position."

With that, he walked away to join the family.

I took a deep breath, realizing there would always be a rift between my father and myself. He would never consider me the rightful heir, even if he had no other choice. As far as the woman, I would do damn well what I wanted.

As the eulogy came to a close, I realized I needed air and headed onto the front walkway, staring out at the snow-covered grounds.

From the day Luciano was born, he'd been waiting to take the helm from my father. As firstborn, he'd been required to follow in our father's footsteps, learning the nuances of the business, the methods used since the beginning of time to keep the wolves at bay. He'd never had the desire to excel in sports or even academics, although somehow he'd managed to do both. Instead of prom night, he'd attended a business meeting with Pops in Chicago, trying to form an alliance with the Callahan Irish mob.

He'd been unsuccessful, but Luciano had built the bridge while in college. That was because of the Brotherhood he'd established by then. My brother was a born leader, whether he'd liked it or not.

At least I'd been allowed to engage in whatever activity suited me. Hell, I'd considered becoming a rockstar, forming a band at fifteen. Snorting, I was surprised Pops hadn't tossed me out of the house then.

Not long after, he'd sat me down, telling me in no uncertain terms that I would find a business application that made him proud. The 'or else' was implied. Or else no money. Or else disowned. Or else my life would be taken if I crossed any lines.

I'd wised up really quickly, deciding right then and there I would have no part of the great Giordano family. He'd made good on most of his threats, cutting me off from my trust fund, eliminating me from any pictures and possible mention of my name in the paper. That's when I'd started to use another name for business, something my mother told me I'd regret later.

Luciano had made the overture only four months before, slowly luring me into the family fold. That didn't mean the various soldiers had instant respect. That would only come with time. If only I'd accepted Luciano's request at helping him with the Morettis earlier he'd still be alive. Guilt was a hard burden to bear.

But here I was, accepting my brother's place. I was blood, which meant something to my father. We were a family steeped in ceremony, both religious and what many would call cult-like behavior. However, it wasn't my choice to break the tradition. I'd accepted the position as leader of our family.

"I don't think I need to tell you how sorry I am."

I'd know Constantine's voice anywhere. He'd been my brother's closest friend, often forgetting they were supposed to be on opposing sides. "I'm glad you were able to be here."

"You're certain it was an accident?" he asked.

I turned to look at him, surprising at seeing the worry lines on his face. "I'm not certain of anything, but his death will not go without punishment."

He nodded, keeping the respect by not asking me any questions. What I did know about the Brotherhood is that if I asked for assistance, Constantine would burn down the city if necessary.

"I wanted to pay you my respects, Don Giordano. And to deliver you this." He retrieved an envelope from his pocket, giving me a respectful nod. I had yet to be proclaimed the Don. Even that had a ceremony of its own. The old traditions Luciano had allowed but hated, doing everything in his power to change things.

I took it from him, offering him my respect as well. The Brotherhood considered themselves kings, rivals in a dangerous game of power, ruthless predators who would stop at nothing to get what they wanted. I'd learned those very words from Luciano years before and it had stuck in my mind as a mantra.

"I'll wait for your decision and do not hesitate if there is anything I or the other brothers can do." Constantine's words were heartfelt.

Even if I accepted the gesture, that did not mean I was automatically provided a seat. I would need to earn the respect of the others, plus perform some secret ceremony that Luciano had refused to mention. I'd thought it was ridiculous, something kids make up. Now I was starting to believe it could be another lifeline.

We could all use more of those.

Out of the corner of my eye, I noticed three of the others standing only thirty feet away. They were watching me. Judging me. Sizing me up in order to be able to make their vote.

My brother's death had placed what I'd considered a curse over my head. The noose around my neck would be next.

Luciano had been born with a cross to bear, his skin seared with the family's crest when he turned eighteen.

After tonight, I would bear the symbol as well, my singed skin and the pain I'd be forced to endure something I'd once feared.

Now I couldn't wait for the ceremony to begin.

Flowers.

I stood outside her hospital room door, holding a damn bouquet as if the girl's health mattered to me. Why I'd purchased them I wasn't certain. Maybe to hide the fact I wanted to look her in the eye. Then I'd know the truth about what happened. At least I could use them as a damn excuse if anyone bothered to challenge my reason for visiting.

I'd also brought a weapon with me, the hatred I had for her remaining. I'd never known the power of grief until recently, but it was almost as powerful as bloodlust or sadistic desires of the flesh.

As I opened the door, I expected she'd have a room full of visitors. Seeing no one, I walked inside, never blinking as I stared at her. Sarah. I repeated her name in my mind several times, even whispering it more than once. The syllables floated across my tongue. They were soft, feminine, and easy to say even if done so in anger.

She seemed so innocent, her long hair splayed out across the thin pillow, her porcelain skin shimmering even in the ugly light hanging over her bed. Sighing, I placed the roses on the small table in front of two other arrangements, moving closer. My muscles tensed as I peered down at her. Jesus Christ, my balls were tight as drums, my arousal an instant reaction just like it had been before. My earlier assessment had been right. She was stunning, her voluptuous lips adding to the intense longing that had occurred the moment I'd laid eyes on her.

Sleeping beauty.

Suddenly, the weapon in my pocket was nothing but an annoyance.

My hunger was off the charts, filthy thoughts sweeping through my mind. I would make her fall in love with me.

Then I'd crush her heart.

Only a twisted man could find a woman lying in a hospital bed attractive.

As I stared down at her, I was surprised that the need to end her life had all but faded away. I'd been right to alter my plans. There was no reason to destroy something so beautiful when I could claim her as my own.

PIPER STONE

I glanced at the beeping machines, a smile crossing my face. The revenge would be the sweetest feeling of all. I took out the plain card I'd grabbed from the flower shop, taking my time writing out a card that she would read later. My eyes never left her as I slid the note into the envelope, carefully placing it in front of the crystal vase.

A slight moan pushed past her sleeping lips and as she twisted, long strands of hair fell across her face. The need to touch her became something I couldn't resist. After brushing the hair from her cheek, I rubbed my knuckle back and forth across her soft skin, no longer shocked by the level of electricity shifting back and forth between us.

Was it possible God himself had put us together? Luciano would laugh at me, suggesting that two figures, one presenting all things good, the other the breath of the devil himself, would likely tear a hole in the cosmic atmosphere. But he'd encourage it.

"My beautiful sleeping beauty. Soon you'll be mine."

She murmured, her eyelids fluttering open briefly. Then she returned to a peaceful slumber.

I thought about my father's wishes, his need for me to prove myself as a capable, but also caring leader. Fine. That I would do in spades.

I would allow her to recover.

Then I would hunt her like prey, seducing her into surrendering to my will.

And I would taste her.

Take her.

Fuck her.

Own her.

Only then would the pain begin to subside. Maybe karma had offered me a gift.

One life for another.

She'd face an eternity with a man she'd learn to hate.

She would beg for her freedom, promising to do anything I asked.

As I rolled the tips of my fingers down her arm, an entirely different ache settled in my system. There was no such thing as freedom in the world of the Giordano family. At least not right away.

Until death do us part.

* * *

Sarah

"Don't worry. You're going to be fine."

The voice was deep and dark, the intense baritone comforting. I could feel his arms around me, the warmth unlike anything I'd ever felt. I'd never felt so protected in my life.

"Where am I?" I asked, unable to see his face.

"Paradise. You're mine now. You never have to worry again." I sensed he was big and strong and as he rolled his fingers down my arm, I knew that he would always take care of me.

Only I didn't know his name.

Beep. Beep. Beep.

I swam up from the vivid dream, slowly opening my eyes. My body was tingling and I could swear whoever I'd been dreaming about was real and that he'd touched me. Whoa. Hold on. What was going on? Where was I? Panting, I tried to move but my body wouldn't cooperate.

Beep. Beep.

What the hell was the sound? "Oh." I couldn't see. What was wrong?

"Oh, my God. You're awake. Thank God."

The voice… Something was wrong. No. No! *Calm down. Breathe.* "Carrie?" I managed, barely recognizing my voice.

"Of course I'm here. Mom and Dad just went to get a bite to eat. I'll call them."

"Wha… wait. What happened?" I blinked again, the light far too bright.

"They said you might not remember." She took my hand into hers and slowly she came into focus. "There you are. You had us worried."

I blinked several times, finally able to look around me. A hospital. "O-kay. Um… How long have I been out?"

"Four days."

"The babies!" I tried to sit up, but pain washed through me.

"Stop. Don't move. I went to your place. The fur babies are just fine," she insisted. "You knew I'd take care of them. You need to worry about you." She narrowed her eyes then smiled. "Lots of people care about you. Look at all the flowers. You have several from work," she pointed. "And the Reynoldses brought the bouquet over there. Even your dog walker brought you a card."

I kept blinking, trying to put the pieces together, the fleeting images in my mind far too fuzzy to put together. Driving. That's right. I was going… to the hospital. Snow. Ice. An accident. My car. "An accident," I managed.

"That's right. Don't try and remember. It's a miracle you're alive."

A miracle. Why couldn't I remember all the details?

Everything was still fuzzy but as my sister lifted her head, I followed her gaze, a strange trickling sensation furrowing in my stomach. "Who sent those?"

"I have no idea. I stepped out for five minutes. They weren't here before."

"There's a card." I tried to point to it but was very weak.

"I'll get it for you." She immediately rose to her feet, moving around the end of the bed. "They're beautiful."

"Yes, they are." Red roses. That seemed like a strange choice for someone recovering from an accident. "I need to get out of this bed. I have a patient who needs me."

She tossed me a look and she didn't need to tell me the woman I'd been rushing to see had died. I closed my eyes, furious with God for doing this. I'd been Angie's only chance. An overwhelming sense of sadness coursed through me. I felt sick inside, ready to throw up. When I tried to move, Carrie stopped me.

"Not yet. You're a doctor. You should know better. You need to regain your strength."

I tried to shift, but the pain in my chest forced a hissing whistle from my throat. "I'm a surgeon, thank you very much."

"At least you're regaining use of your holier than thou attitude," she quipped. "It means you're on the mend."

"Come here so I can smack you." It felt good to banter with her like we'd always done, even if a heavy weight remained on my shoulders. Why couldn't I remember what had happened? I knew all the clinical reasons why. I'd spent collectively hours explaining to families of accidents and violent events why their loved one had trouble remembering anything about what they'd gone through. Yet, I'd always thought if something happened, I'd have no problem remembering every detail.

You're protecting your mind from the truth.

"Let me take it out of the envelope for you." I noticed her eyes glanced from one side of the note to the other.

"What's wrong?"

"Do you have a boyfriend that you didn't tell me about?" She laughed softly as she glanced at me.

"No! Of course not." What was she getting at? I tried to sit up, groaning from discomfort. I yanked on the thin sheets, noticing the bruises on my legs. Thank God I hadn't needed a breathing tube.

"Oh, la la. Then you have a secret admirer. Would you look at those roses? There must be three dozen and they're perfect."

"Let... me see." I was determined to try to get my life back, managing to sit up.

"I'm going to need to get a nurse. You're not ready for this yet."

"Give me the card. Please?"

I barely had time for my friends. I read the card then pulled back, a series of tingling sensations slithering all the way to my toes. It was almost the same feeling as I'd had in the dream.

Or had it been real?

I read it again and this time, a cold chill trickled down my spine.

My sleeping beauty

I will await your recovery. Then it will be our time of exploration, to share in the joys of togetherness. Until then, sleep well...

.   .   .

"There's no signature," I said quietly, turning the plain white card over several times. The words were written in cursive. While I was no expert, I'd say it was a man's handwriting.

"That's what makes it so romantic." When she noticed my expression, she frowned. "Maybe it's one of the people you work with? Hell, your dog walker? He is pretty cute."

The chill remained as I pushed myself to remember. Did this have something to do with the accident? *Think. Think.*

Then I remembered a few details. "Angie. I was rushing to the hospital. I was… Oh, no. There was another car. Oh, God. Wasn't there a fire? What happened?" I could hear the monitors going haywire as my blood pressure rose. Images started to rush into my mind, my stomach twisting from revulsion.

"You need to calm down. Come on. It's going to be okay." Carrie stood, wrapping her hand around my arm.

"What happened? There was another car. Are they alive?"

"You're right. You had an accident. The ice. The conditions were horrible. You're lucky to be alive. The doctors said that. You almost died. We're all so glad you're here."

Wrong. Wrong. Wrong.

Oh, God. I could feel death all around me.

"Tell me!" I was close to being hysterical, but at this point I didn't care. I had to know. "There was one person in the other car. Yes, a man. I saw his face. Is he alive?"

She shook her head, trying to look away from me. I slapped my hand on hers, digging my nails in.

"Tell me what happened."

"I'm sorry, honey. The driver of the other vehicle was killed. It's not your fault," she said softly.

As the air was sucked out of the room, tears slipping past my lashes, I turned my head away, staring at the most beautiful roses I'd ever seen.

It had been my fault. I was certain of it. If only I'd started the car earlier there wouldn't have been any fog. If only I'd paid more attention. If only I'd taken another route.

If only…

CHAPTER 4

"A thousand moments I had taken for granted, mostly because I'd assumed there would be a thousand more."

—Morgan Matson

Sarah

Four weeks later

Death had never been something I'd thought much about even though I was a surgeon. I'd certainly never feared it given my track record, the number of lives I'd saved from the brink of death. Now it was almost all I could think about.

A blackness where there was nothing but silence.

There was a hole inside of me where the ugly shadows were sucked away, allowing me to have steady hands with every surgery. I'd felt blessed that I'd been able to save so many lives. Now I felt as if the accident had evened the score.

Ugh. I hated to think this way, fearful my patients would ultimately suffer. The advice I'd been given by just about everybody was to live my life to the fullest. How the hell was I supposed to do that when I'd taken a man's life? I knew I hadn't been directly responsible, but it still felt the same, the ugliness remaining churning in my stomach.

I'd tried not to wallow in the depths of despair that I'd seen happen to survivors of other horrific tragedies, but now I fully understood what the saying meant of 'the pot calling the kettle black.' At least I'd been able to return to work three weeks after the accident. The only way I'd gotten through the first hours after I'd left the hospital, let alone the first week had been because of Goldie and Shadow, my two incredibly loving dogs who'd refused to leave my side.

At least with work, I was able to lose myself in my duties for long hours, exhausted every night. I'd been reminded by just about everybody that I'd been given a gift, a second chance at life. I'd listened to just how close I'd come to dying, the surgeon who'd not only saved my life but also the use of my legs sitting down with me the very day I'd accosted my poor sister.

I'd also learned I'd had an angel looking out for me that day, a Good Samaritan who'd broken the glass, dragging me to safety. If he hadn't, I would have died in the fire that consumed my poor Cruze. I'd been in shock, although I could swear I remember hearing the person tell me every-thing would be okay.

He'd been able to save my life, a pedestrian who'd stepped up to the plate when a surgeon hadn't been able to save two lives and a third one had been lost because of decisions made, karma stepping in. I remained sick inside, trying to process the constant emotions, but it was growing more difficult every day.

"Live your life," I'd been told more than once.

"Be grateful you're alive," my mother had told me.

"Don't let it get you down," several coworkers had said.

Yes. Yes. And yes, but how did I go about living when I felt dead inside?

What continued to disturb me was the person who'd died in the crash was considered royalty, his family owning half of New York, including all the people in it.

Luciano Giordano had been considered brutal by any standard, his penchant for violence matching his dark moods and sadistic tastes. If the man set his sights on you, then you were as good as dead. I'd never met him, nor had I even paid any attention to pictures on the internet or whatever local television station was touting the fact he was also the city's most eligible bachelor. Even now, I couldn't bring myself to find out anything about him. That would derail everything I was trying to rebuild.

However, the man's death had delighted my father, which continued to make me sick. He hated the Giordano family, had pledged to destroy them. He'd had the audacity to thank me before realizing what he'd done. I hadn't talked to him since. My father had grown up on the rough side of town, learning the hard way that money and clout, as well as utter brutality, were the only ways to make it in New York. My grandparents had been dirt poor, barely making ends meet.

Meanwhile, the Giordano family reeked of opulence. I could understand his hatred of them, but to wish them dead was something I couldn't tolerate. I'd taken an oath that life was sacred. It pissed me off even thinking about it.

Not fixating on the other victim had been at the suggestion of one of the grief counselors the director of the hospital had insisted I talk to. It had also been suggested I take a vacation since I was back to working sixteen-plus-hour days. I'd told them I was fine when I was anything but. However, work was the only time where the demons didn't crawl inside, trying to drag me to hell. Even being with the fur babies had been difficult as of late.

When two days had been forced on me under threat of being suspended, I'd almost launched into the director, but I'd finally agreed. Maybe I did need to get my shit together.

"Hey, I'm going to take off for the day, maybe enjoy a short walk," I told Maggie, trying to keep my mood light.

"You do know it's like twelve degrees out there. Right?" she asked.

"I'm a big girl and the cold air will do me some good."

She shrugged, muttering under her breath. "It's your funeral if you catch cold." She immediately snapped her head up from the papers she was looking at, the flush on her cheeks reddening to a deep crimson. "I'm so… Oh, my God. I mean I just…"

"Relax, Maggie. I know exactly what you meant, and I plan on wearing a coat. The one I came into work in?"

I thought for certain she was going to pass out. Almost everyone in the hospital had treated me with kid gloves at first, fearful I would surrender to my depression. However, I was a hell of a lot stronger than they knew. A nice walk to the best little coffee shop in the world would do me good. Plus, the caffeine would help after the long shift I'd had. At least I'd convinced Carrie to stay with the pups for a few hours today, so I knew they'd be walked and well fed. Maybe I'd even do a little shopping.

After grabbing my purse and coat from the locker room, I headed down the back elevator, tapping my foot to the elevator music. Carrie had even suggested I try to find a date every once in a while. Who, me? Dating? I didn't see it happening. Not since Mr. Three-Timer had turned my world upside down.

Maybe I still had a secret admirer, although the flowers had died, the note tossed, and I'd heard nothing more from him. Oh, well. Who needed a big, strapping man when I had not one but two vibrators? I laughed as I stepped out of the elevator, heading toward the door.

The air hit me like a thunderbolt, the entire winter much colder than the last three years. I yanked the material around me, keeping my head down as I headed into the wind. I'd forgotten my gloves this morning, which wasn't unusual. I'd remained far too rattled.

As I walked into the coffee shop, the scent of fresh pastries made my mouth water. I couldn't remember the last time I'd had a full meal, taking on extra shifts just to keep myself busy. Poor Goldie and Shadow. They hardly knew their Mommy Dog any longer.

As I waited in line, I debated on whether or not to indulge in an ooey gooey Danish. I was trying to be good. I almost laughed at the thought. When it was my turn, I stared at the menu, my gaze constantly shifting to the Danish.

"What would you like?" the girl behind the counter asked.

"A very tall mocha latte and…" I shifted my attention back to the Danish for the third time, chewing on my inner cheek.

"Miss?" the girl asked after at least a full minute had passed.

"That's it. Nothing else."

As she rang up the coffee, I gazed lovingly at the beautiful baked creation underneath the glass. No, it was about five thousand calories. At least. Grinning, I grabbed my coffee, taking a sip then turning around without looking. When the lid popped off, hot liquid splashing on the very tall man behind me, I was mortified.

"Oh, my God. I am so sorry." Holy shit, the man was hot. Not just typical cute in a businessman kind of way but sizzling as if he'd just stepped off the pages of a magazine hot. His jaw was clenched tight, his scent powerful. Seductive. There was no reason for my stomach to be doing flipflops, but it was, a little buzzing sound occurring inside my ears.

I expected him to grumble, to call me names. That was the usual attitude I'd gotten lately. People were disgruntled about life. Instead, when he spoke, the sound was delectable and deep, perfect for the voiceover in the romantic part of an action flick.

"It's just coffee," he said, laughing softly. "There's no harm done." When he reached around me, yanking several napkins off the counter, the light brush of his shoulder against mine sent a wave of electricity straight down my legs. Even worse, it slowly crept up to my pussy. To say the man was gorgeous was an understatement. Tall, dark, and handsome defined in a dictionary with the man's picture as an example was exactly what I was thinking.

"Hot coffee. Scalding coffee to be exact. I've ruined your clothes."

"I have others and maybe I like all things hot, the hotter the better."

The deep rumble of his voice made me instantly light-headed. I hadn't been flirted with in so long, I wasn't capable of handling the attention. I wasn't the kind of woman to be flustered by anything, but I couldn't think of a snappy reply to save my life. "Well, then. Try the mocha latte. It's perfect for you."

With that, I skirted away, heading for the only small table left open. I laughed inwardly at my ridiculous behavior. What was wrong with me? Exhaustion and months without a single date. Wait, what month was it? No, over a year now and the last date had been... no, I wasn't going there. And where had my manners gone? I should have insisted I handle the cost of his dry cleaning.

I sipped my coffee, trying not to look in the man's direction. He was at least six foot three, his suit worth more than the new car I'd finally selected. He was utter perfection wrapped in expensive clothing. Thank God, I couldn't see him.

I was shocked when I felt a presence directly behind me, more so when the Danish I'd been ogling was slid in front of me.

"I think you forgot a part of your order," he half whispered, and my nipples were immediately aroused. "It would be a sin not to enjoy something so indulgent."

"Um... You didn't have to do this." Sin. Pure sin. The words resonated in my mind.

"I assure you that I never do anything I don't want to do."

I glanced up and managed to keep my shit together. "You're very kind. I'll pay for the dry cleaning. I should have made the offer before. I apologize."

He laughed again, the sultry tone oozing of passion. Who was I suddenly, some romance author? "Please, don't continue apologizing for what karma had in mind. And dry cleaning won't be necessary."

"Fate?"

When he narrowed his eyes, a slight tremor sizzled my senses. "Yes. I've always been a firm believer in fate. In fact, some of the best things that have occurred in my life happened when I least expected them; however, these gifts often need to be nurtured. So, in that regard, you can do me a favor."

"I'll try."

"It would seem there's nowhere else to sit. Would you mind if I joined you?"

"Of course you can," I said quickly, without thinking. As he eased into the seat, he continued to smile. Now that I was able to take my time looking at his features, I was wrong about my earlier assessment. He was godlike, his sharp features and strong jaw covered with two-day stubble just the beginning of his incredibly good looks. It was his piercing eyes, so black they held a tinge of iridescent blue. I imagined them glowing in the dark, which was crazy. While the cashmere overcoat hid a good portion of his body, it was easy to see he was muscular, well-toned in all the right places. I noticed his watch and sighed. If I had to guess, I'd say he was rich, the watch at least sixty grand.

I tried to concentrate on the Danish but found myself just picking at it.

"I didn't mean to make you nervous," he breathed.

Don't melt. Don't do it.

"You didn't. I haven't been hungry lately. Perhaps it's all the microwave dinners I've had recently."

"A woman so beautiful should never be forced to eat out of plasticware. That should be a crime in several jurisdictions."

His comment made me laugh, which was something new as of late. I pressed my hand over my mouth, actually snorting, which was my most embarrassing trait. Embarrassment rushed to my face, enough so I grabbed my coffee to hide behind the cup, almost choking on the liquid as I took a sip.

"Well, I must tell you that plasticware is my norm given my profession."

"Which is?" He unfastened his coat, pulling both sides away, leaning back in his chair, his ebony eyes never leaving mine.

"I'm a surgeon."

"Wow."

"Is that a 'wow' because women aren't supposed to able to handle such a demanding field?" I'd heard it before, including from my father, who'd encouraged me to become a lawyer. Then a teacher, both admirable professions but ones he called 'better suited for a woman of stature.' I'd wanted to strangle him.

He laughed and when he did, the sound skittered through me like bottle rockets. So sultry. So... seductive. "I don't see you as the kind of woman who needs to carry a chip on her shoulder or prove herself."

"Interesting. What kind of woman do you see me as?" I leaned forward, darting my eyes down his broad chest. Swooning wasn't something I was used to doing, but it was hard to resist his incredible physique or the exotic after-shave he'd chosen, the deep, rich scent almost intoxicating.

He leaned forward as well, the table small enough we were only three inches apart. After taking a deep breath, he lowered his gaze to my chest as well, a moment of tit for tat that added to the flirtatious moment. "You're the kind of woman who can handle herself in any situation, remaining calm under pressure while providing comfort to those who need it the most. However, you've hidden behind your calling from God, keeping chained the woman buried underneath the angelic layers."

The man could take my breath away, but I wasn't the kind of woman to fall for a line, even if his words seemed heartfelt. "I assure you that there is nothing angelic about me."

A spark in his eye drew my attention and I could almost see his wheels turning. "That is good to hear. Very good indeed."

He remained in the same position, taking several deep breaths before leaning back in his seat, concentrating on sipping his coffee.

I tried to act as if his comments and his presence didn't bother me, but my nipples were swollen, aching and several filthy thoughts continued to travel through my mind. It was hard not to wonder what he'd be like in bed. Would he be dominating, rough around the edges, refusing to allow me any control? I shuddered from the thought.

A few seconds passed, every one of them full of sexual tension.

"And what do you do?" I finally asked.

"I'm a stockbroker."

"I'm certain you're good at what you do given your observational skills."

I was rewarded with another laugh, the sound vibrating into my core. "It's more about attention to detail and never cracking under pressure. I've been... successful, although the hours are grueling."

"Then do something else."

"I just might take your advice." He took another full sip of coffee, slowly placing his cup on the table. Then he grabbed the Danish with one hand, gently tugging off a hunk. As he brought it to my lips, his expression was one of demand, just like I knew he'd be in bed. Jesus. What was I thinking? He was a complete stranger.

"Take a bite for me." There was no suggestion in his voice, just a strong command. I had no reason to follow his order, but everything about him was compelling. I wanted to please him. That wasn't like me in the least. Still, I tilted my chin, determined to challenge him. "No."

He exhaled, the look in his eyes growing fierce, as if he was prepared to require my compliance.

No matter what he needed to do in order to make it happen.

Fine. What the hell would it hurt?

I pursed my lips until he narrowed his eyes. Then I opened my mouth like a good little girl, accepting the bite. The pastry was still warm, a single bead of icing slipping past my lips. When he reached across the table again, swiping the tip of his index finger through the soft goo, I held my breath. Then as he brought the tip to his mouth, pushing it inside then closing his eyes, I was lost in the moment, no other sight or sound capable of getting through.

The second a slight, husky growl rolled up from his throat, I felt weak in the knees.

Get ahold of yourself, for God's sake.

Even the little voice inside my head had a difficult time getting through. I purposely looked away, swallowing several times.

"Extremely tasty, sweet just like I knew it would be."

Why did I have a feeling his words were directed toward me and not the Danish?

"I hate to admit it, but I have a short appointment. I've thoroughly enjoyed my cup of coffee for a change," he said as he rose to his feet. "It's rare that I find such amazing company, and one so beautiful."

I didn't have a chance to say anything before he gave me a single nod and walked away, tossing the almost full cup of coffee into the trash. Exhaling, I brought my cup to my lips again, realizing my hand was shaking.

He was a sexy stranger and nothing else, a one-time blip that allowed me respite from the mental anguish.

And I didn't even know his name.

* * *

The stranger had inspired me to follow through with my plans on picking up a few nice items for myself. He'd been right in that everything I enjoyed doing had taken a back seat. It was time for that to change. I went into my favorite little boutique, a location where the clothes were far too expensive, every piece screaming of decadence. But I could afford it. I spent little money on anything else except dog toys.

I held up dress after dress, trying to decide on just one. What the heck? I'd try on four of them to determine which one I liked. After placing my coat on one of the two leather chairs in front of the three-way mirror, I gathered the items, moving into the dressing room. I was surprised to find I had the store almost to myself, although I didn't mind the quiet, the store owner's selection of music relaxing. I closed the curtain, hanging the items then running my fingers down each dress. For once, shopping made me giddy.

Maybe I was feeling more like a woman than a workaholic.

I stared at myself in the mirror before selecting the first dress, the sleek black silk a direct contrast to my blonde hair. As I removed the scrubs and tennis shoes, my usual attire, I was glad at least I'd worn decent matching under-wear. The thought giving me a wicked smile, I shimmied into the soft material, smoothing down the front before taking a look.

Not bad. Not bad at all.

The dress hugged every curve, accentuating my full breasts and narrow waist. Maybe a little tight in the butt, but not enough to ride up when I walked. I bit my lower lip, twisting and turning. There was no reason a shiver tripped down my spine, but as soon as it did, my breath hitched.

Then he was there, the stranger, opening and closing the curtain, only a few inches away. The immediate heat was oppressive, every thought as naughty as the smile I'd had earlier.

"Beautiful, but the color is too dark," he said in the same husky tone he'd had before. "Try on the green one."

I was stymied for words, another trait I wasn't known for. "Then you need to leave." My voice didn't sound like me at all.

He merely shook his head, his eyes dancing with the same fire I'd seen before. He'd removed both his overcoat and his jacket, rolling up his long sleeves, exposing a gorgeous tattoo on his forearm. His reflection seemed larger than life, his expression carnal.

As if he was prepared to eat me alive.

I'd never been mesmerized by a man, no matter how good looking or powerful. But being around this man dragged at my inner bad girl, the need to let go of my inhibitions strong. I found myself obeying him, which went against everything I stood for. As I eased it over my head, the heat increased, his closeness almost suffocating. While he leaned against the wall, folding his arms, he never blinked as he slid his gaze all the way to my naked feet. I couldn't help but be grateful I'd polished my toenails only the night before, one small luxury I'd kept up with.

He took a deep breath, holding it as he tilted his head. I was nervous, more so than I'd been in my life, but I managed to pull the frock over my shoulders, knotting the slender tie holding the wrap dress in place.

The moment he inched closer, my heart started racing. He issued an elongated growl, the sound pulsing through me, matching the rapid beating of my heart.

"No. The purple one." He slid the tip of his index finger down my arm, and I couldn't seem to stop trembling.

Once again, I obeyed him, this time unable to look at his reflection as I changed clothes. The purple one was tight, far too much so and the second I glanced into the mirror, I noticed his distaste.

"Now, the red one. Scarlet, the perfect color for a stunning woman such as yourself."

The darkness of his tone, the deep vibrations that continued to slide into my overheated core were intense, my panties damp. I could swear the scent of my increasing desire filled the small space. When I was finished getting into the last selection, my face was almost as red as the gorgeous piece of material. He didn't need to tell me that it was perfect in every way, hugging my curves without accentuating everything.

His guttural sounds were a further indication, the look in his eyes drawing me into the strange web he'd already weaved. As he closed the distance, pressing his massive body against mine, I couldn't stop the single whimper. Very gently he removed the hair band, allowing my long hair to fall past my shoulders. "Much better."

My hair had to be a mess, the only style I'd ever bothered with the ponytail, yet his eyes brightened with the intensity of a rocket ready to ignite. The look on his face took my breath away.

He took his time, rolling his fingers over both shoulders, his heated breath tingling my neck. I'd never felt so absorbed in the moment, unable to stop what was happening between us. I'd never had a one-night stand. I'd never allowed myself to get caught up in unbridled passion, especially when I had no clue about the man or his intentions.

At this moment, none of my conservative ways mattered. I craved a man's rough touch, longing to let go if only for a few minutes. When he lowered his head, I closed my eyes, the anticipation of what he was going to do churning through me.

"I thought you had a meeting," I whispered, nerves turning my stomach into knots.

"I did. I'm very efficient."

"Why are you here?"

"Because I wasn't finished with you." He nuzzled into my neck, dragging his tongue up and down my skin.

"What are you doing?"

"Taking what I want."

There was no denying our attraction, the chemistry that coursed through us both like molten lava. He slipped his arm around me, wrapping his hand around my throat and bending my head. When he bit my neck, moans trickled past my lips. I was lightheaded, stars in various colors floating across my field of vision.

He pressed his hips forward, grinding them back and forth. He was rock hard, his cock throbbing against my bottom. Somewhere inside, I knew this was a very bad idea, but I couldn't stop the inertia.

Even if I wanted to.

As he licked the area where he'd bitten me, he slid his other arm around my waist, cupping and squeezing my breast. I palmed his outer thighs, breathless, still trembling as the fire of need tore through us.

His touch screamed of possession, his needs obvious. And I knew he wasn't going to let me go.

He carefully peeled the straps of the dress down my shoulders, exposing the thin lace of my bra. Blinking, I couldn't take my eyes off his, arching my back as he pinched my nipple between his fingers. The pain was instant, the sharp discomfort awakening my senses. Yet the way he touched me was an awakening, as if I was being born at that very moment, naked and open to the world.

When he slid a single finger under the edge of my bra, flicking the tip back and forth across my fully aroused nipple, I felt it deep in my soul. He'd already penetrated the thick walls I'd placed around myself, an armor to prevent caring about anyone ever again.

The moment added strange images in my mind, becoming so profound that I had difficulty breathing. It was as if he'd freed my soul, breaking through the chains locked around me. I obviously wasn't thinking clearly because as he pushed the dress to the floor, I stepped out of it without being asked.

He continued pressing kisses against my neck, growling every few seconds as if he was a beast hunting his prey. I was vaguely aware he'd unfastened my bra, pulling the straps down my arms.

I offered no resistance, the rational side of my mind no longer having a chance to stop the madness of what was happening. I was a doctor, for God's sake. I knew all the risks of unprotected sex, and he could have darker intentions. I didn't care. I needed to feel something again, relishing the fact I was still alive.

"Look at me," he directed, his command not to be denied.

As I'd done before, I obeyed him, watching as he pinched and twisted both nipples, his expression acknowledging the moans of anguish pushing past my lips. Fire tore through me, the need furrowing to the surface becoming insatiable. I longed to touch him, to run my fingers down his chest, wrapping them around his thick cock.

But he was having none of it, totally in control of both my body and my mind.

He slowly lowered his hands, peeling my thong over my hips, pushing it to the floor. There was nothing like the feeling of being totally naked in front of a stranger, allowing him to bask in my wantonness. He seemed pleased, his nostrils flaring as his breathing became ragged.

"You're a very bad girl, aren't you?"

The question would have seemed strange only an hour before, but now, it fit the moment, the answer easy to whisper. "Yes." My panties remained wrapped around my ankles, a shackle that I wouldn't be able to escape from.

When he twisted my nipple painfully, his expression turning dark, I could tell I'd displeased him.

"But you will respect me."

Blinking, a lump formed in my throat, the good girl side of me trying to fight to regain control. But the bad girl won.

"Yes, sir."

"Better." He cracked his hand against my bottom with just enough force I was driven onto my toes. "I'll teach you to surrender." Then he snapped his hand several times, moving from one side to the other.

The pain was terrible, at least at first, my mind a blur from the fact he was spanking me. It was crazy. All I could think about was the noise his hand smacking against my naked skin was making. I held my breath as he continued, realizing quickly that I was hot all over, my skin tingling. Within seconds, I was wet, my thighs slickened.

Growling, he caressed my bottom, his chest heaving. "Yes, you're a very naughty girl who needs a firm hand. Aren't you?"

I had no idea if I was supposed to respond. My mouth was dry, the sound of my hammering heart echoing in my ears. "Yes, sir." Oh, God. What was I doing? Was I losing my mind? If so, I wasn't certain I cared.

As he brought down his palm several additional times, I arched my back, panting as stars floated in front of my eyes. There was a strange feeling of bliss, my body's reaction treacherous.

After several more, he crowded closer, his hot breath cascading over my shoulders.

He fisted my hair at the scalp, yanking back as he took full control of me. Then he eased the flat of his hand down my stomach, sliding his fingers between my legs. "Are you wet for me?"

"Yes, sir."

"Are your thighs burning for my touch, your sweet pussy hungering for my cock?"

I dragged my tongue across my lips, a haze forming over my eyes. "Yes. Yes, sir."

He flicked his finger around my clit, another moan escaping my throat.

"Yes, you're very wet for me, your pussy pink and swollen. Imagine what I can do to you at this moment. What I will do to you."

His voice continued to captivate me, holding me hostage as if I belonged to him. It was strange how desirable the sinful moment was, turning my world momentarily upside down. I didn't care about responsibilities or repercussions.

He kicked off my thong, widening my legs then rolling his finger up and down my pussy lips. "I can't wait to drive my shaft inside. You were a born submissive. Imagine being on your knees, begging for my cock."

When I didn't answer, he pinched my nipple again, the pressure so intense I sucked air through my teeth, biting back a strangled cry.

"But you need to be trained." He kept the pressure on my tender bud, the sting becoming excruciating.

I was blinded by lust, incapable of thinking clearly, but his dirty talk fueled the fire burning brightly. He slipped a single finger into my tight channel and there was no way to keep quiet, the pleasure far too intoxicating. I whimpered as he pumped deep inside, adding a second and third finger after a few seconds. I rolled onto my toes, slapping my hands on the glass to steady myself. Everything about this was a filthy sin, but nothing had ever felt so exciting.

"You're a little slut, aren't you? You need harsh discipline." As if proving his point, he removed his slickened fingers, cracking his hand against my bottom several times. I bucked against the twisted agony, realizing I wanted more.

That didn't make any sense to me. No one had ever spanked me before, but the addition of his full domination set my world on fire.

Panting, I ground my buttocks against his groin, the tingling sensation of his cock coursing through me. He smacked me four additional times then returned his fingers to my pussy, driving them hard and fast, the rhythm matching the rapid beating of my heart. He pressed his thumb against my clit, rolling it back and forth and it was almost all my body could take.

I was writhing in his hold, my mind a complete blur. He twisted my head, the man so tall he was able to lean over my shoulder. As he captured my mouth, immediately thrusting his tongue inside, I pushed hard against him, riding his fingers. Suddenly, I was jerked into a sweet vacuum, an orgasm rushing up the length of my legs, shattering my last resolve. Our lips remained locked in a volatile embrace, the man attempting to devour me with his mouth. He used his tongue in another dominant display, fulfilling a desperate need.

Within seconds, all the oxygen was sucked away, leaving me lightheaded and slightly woozy. His thirst remained unquenched, his tongue delving into every corner of my mouth, searching for satisfaction.

I quivered from his touch, struggling to breathe or think clearly, the moment all consuming.

He continued the rough kiss, dominating my tongue as I came on his fingers, the scent filling the space between us. My muscles were stiff, my legs aching as I remained on my toes, meeting every thrust of his fingers. As he sucked on my tongue, another orgasm swept through me, the tidal wave effect stealing my last breath. Another wave of stars rushed through my periphery of vision, pushing me into sheer ecstasy. Nothing had ever felt so explosive, erasing all thoughts from my mind.

He continued his rough actions, plunging his fingers deep inside, his thumb creating a delicate weave of pain and plea-sure. As the climax finally started to subside, I clawed my fingers down the glass and slumped against him.

I half expected him to disappear, but he wasn't finished with me yet. I was still on an intense high, remaining in a height-ened state when he delivered four additional hard smacks in rapid succession.

"Agony or ecstasy. It's your choice."

"Both. Sir." I wasn't myself any longer. Gone was the highly educated woman who'd earned her medical degree a year early. I was nothing but the naughty girl who would do anything the stranger asked. I was titillated and embarrassed at the same time, but there was no going back. The dam had been broken, my senses ignited.

He chuckled darkly and as I heard his zipper being pulled, I sucked in my breath, trying to focus on the man holding the tight reins. Nothing made any sense, but I was determined to stop trying.

He didn't remove his shirt or tie, or bother lowering his trousers down his legs. He simply freed his cock, slipping it between my thighs. Then he thrust the entire length inside, my muscles screaming from his savagery.

"Oh, God. Yes. Yes."

"So fucking tight, my little slut." Then he pushed me up against the glass, the force he used keeping me pitched against the surface.

Gasping, I arched my back, my actions pulling him in even deeper. He rolled onto the balls of his feet, driving long and hard, every plunge more brutal than the one before.

"Imagine if someone saw us, witnessing our carnal sin." His husky voice invigorated my senses even more, my mind racing at the possibility. Shame tore through me, but only briefly, the carnal need we shared outweighing everything else.

"Yes."

"Would you like that?" He fisted my throat again, holding me close as he bit down on my shoulder, the flash of pain a clear indication a mark would remain. And I didn't care. I wanted to remember the moment.

I purred my response, which only enticed him more, the beast inside of him breaching the surface. No one had ever fucked me so roughly, taking what they wanted without hesitation. I was breathless, panting to try to gather air, but he'd sucked it all out, replacing it with his exotic scent.

The haze remained, every inch of my skin seared from his touch. His cock hit the perfect place, my pussy pulsing as another climax threatened to expose the increasing need. I didn't care what he did to me, how hard he fucked me. I wanted more. And I would give him anything he asked.

He pounded me long and hard, finally jerking me away from the mirror, forcing me to watch our moment of fornication. With one hand wrapped around my throat, the other around my waist, he lifted me off my feet, fucking me like a ragdoll, a possession he would own and play with when he decided.

I was incapable of escaping, his for as long as he craved. His stamina was unlike anything I'd experienced, and I was exhausted from the brutal fucking. When his muscles finally tensed, he nuzzled against my ear, his dark whisper another command that couldn't be ignored.

"Come with me."

"I don't…"

"Do it. Do it now."

His voice was hypnotizing, and my body betrayed me, another powerful climax sweeping through my system. I'd succumbed to him, his commands and needs without question. It was as if he had full control over me. As his cock reached the deepest part of me, I let out a single sharp yell.

It didn't matter how embarrassing the moment or how many people were outside, listening to our savage fucking. All that I cared about was the intensity of the release, my body floating as the sweet wave rolled over me.

He growled in my ear as he exploded deep inside, holding me aloft as he pumped his hips against me.

"Come have dinner with me tonight," he whispered hoarsely.

"Yes. I will," I said without hesitation.

"Good girl. Be prepared to be totally obedient. And remember, no one else can dare ever touch you again."

As he pulled out, I fell against the glass, struggling to make sense of what just happened.

"Where do you live?" he asked.

I muttered the address, still unable to process anything. But as he eased his cock back into his pants, raking his fingers through his hair, I remained unblinking as I watched him.

He rolled his fingers down my spine, slowly trickling them down the crack of my ass. Then his upper lip curled. "Be prepared, my little slut. Tonight I'll claim your ass."

CHAPTER 5

 *abriel*

I fisted my hand as I thought about her, the tingle from having her throat in my fingers something I wouldn't soon forget. For a few seconds, the thought of having her life in my hands had been more powerful than any other experience I'd had. The sick part of me had wanted to crush her larynx, waiting as the light drained from her eyes. The sane man had wanted to take her like an animal, refusing to allow her to say no.

Was any side of me better than the other, or was I nothing more than a twisted fuck who was exactly like my father? In the weeks since accepting the position as head of the family, I'd been forced to see the light, as my mother would say. In other words, I'd learned that all the years I'd tried to pretend I wasn't a part of the Giordano family had been bullshit.

I'd proven that earlier and would do so again, only this time feeding my penchant for blood. It had become a drug to me, much like she could, the need festering until I had no choice but to seek out relief. Fortunately, I'd managed to keep it under control for the most part, trying to maintain status quo with the soldiers and other employees.

I'd allowed the pseudo deal with the Morettis to remain in place, never learning what Luciano had died in order to rectify, but it was only a matter of time. When word that I was taking over had hit the street, it was as if our enemies had taken a pause, waiting to see what I was made of. What I couldn't do at this point was let my guard down. There were issues, but so far they'd been handled. Still, it was only a matter of time. What I couldn't tolerate any longer was the fact certain private information had been used against us. That meant I had at least one traitor within the organization.

The business end had been no problem, the ebb and flow of our legitimate businesses a well-oiled machine. I had to give Luciano credit. He'd turned the corporation into a Fortune 100 company in a few short years. He'd done so with integrity and earned respect.

He'd also gained that with the brutal men who worked under him, controlling the other aspects of our world. I was learning it wasn't as easy as I'd led myself to believe, especially when one of Luciano's most trusted men continued to defy me.

I'd allowed it to happen given my brother's death. No longer. I needed to send a message that everyone in the organization would understand.

Fuck with me and face my wrath.

Still, as I walked into the Club Rio, the shining star of our portfolio, it was difficult to take my mind off Sarah. She'd been completely unexpected, especially the attraction I'd felt instantly. I'd expected to hate her, using that vile, loathsome feeling to begin stripping away her defenses. Instead, I'd fucked her like a wild animal in the middle of a boutique on a busy street.

Since then, I'd craved more.

Perhaps most surprising of all was the fact she'd enjoyed every minute of being fucked by a stranger. By an evil man. Little did she know what she was facing.

I hissed as I studied the sweeping dance floor in the bright light. The club had been my father's brainchild, a location where debauchery and lust feasted on unsuspecting yet powerful clients who could partake in anything they desired to satiate their proclivities.

No matter how depraved.

It was part casino and part sex club, all wrapped around a five-star restaurant and vodka bar. The money made and lost in the establishment was phenomenal.

One lesson my father had taught both my brother and me was that men were weakest when driven to their knees by exposing their sexual secrets. My brother had expounded on the idea, expanding the club, making it by invitation only. Now men from every walk of life begged to be on the waiting list, which was a solid year out. The location was also used for business purposes, paid members allowed to bring a certain number of guests to wine and dine, providing a taste of the forbidden in order to lure them into signing a contract.

Because of all we offered, business was exploding, a second club already in the works. My brainchild. I'd need to deal with the continued animosity and subtle but constant inter-ferences by the Morettis soon.

But not until after my time spent with Sarah.

At the end of seventy-two hours, the simple life she'd led would start to unravel. She would soon be under my lock and key.

My cock ached just thinking about it.

I rolled my thumb across my lips, still able to taste her sweet pussy. She'd awakened the beast inside of me, something I wasn't certain could happen. Sighing, I checked my watch, annoyed the men I'd instructed to meet me here were nowhere in sight.

With the doors opening at noon, the business requiring my expertise had to be dealt with quickly. I thought about how I was going to handle the men's egregious behavior and headed for the darkened kitchen, flicking on the light. The impressive stainless-steel location was enviable by any chef's standards. My brother had spared no expense in renovating the facility.

After opening several drawers, I found what I was looking for. I held the sharp knife into the light, pulling off the guard then enjoying the way the stainless steel shimmered. Then I shoved it into my jacket pocket, not giving a shit if the blade sliced through the material.

I found the group of men in one of the conference rooms, all four acting as if they were bored. They didn't notice me at first as I walked in, one of them powering back an alcoholic beverage. While there were mostly implied rules of our organization, the act seemed blatant given the asshole knew when I'd arrive.

Perhaps I'd been too soft. That would change today.

Dillon noticed me first, suddenly standing taller as he sucked in his breath. He'd been helpful in getting me up to speed, a man I'd known for some time. He pressed his arm against Demarco, who barely shot me a look over his shoulder. Then Demarco slammed down the glass on the expensive coffee table, liquid spilling over the side. The cleaning people had already left, which was something the asshole knew.

Both men had been my brother's Capos, both without a family. But Demarco was considered brutal by any standard.

I'd heard he was loyal, but lately I'd begun to question his behavior. And my instinct was always right.

We'd sparred twice and I'd allowed him to keep his command.

My mistake.

"Tell me something," I said as I walked closer, grabbing the glass from the table. Then I tossed the remains in Demarco's face, staring him straight in the eye as he almost had the nerve to fly over the table.

When I pitched the glass against the wall, the two other soldiers backed away, unused to seeing me like this. The glass shattered, the sound amusing me.

"Now that I have your fucking attention. You will answer my simple question. Do you like working in *my* organization?" I overenunciated the single word for emphasis as I glanced from one man to the other.

Three of the four men looked at each other, uncertain where I was going with this. Only Demarco had the balls or the stupidity to allow a smirk to cross his face.

"What's going on, boss?" Dillon asked.

I barely threw him a glance, keeping my heated gaze on the man I'd come here to punish. "What's going on is that there seems to be some shit going down in my organization. There's talk that information regarding this organization is being fed to one of our enemies. Now, I would have found that hard to believe had it not come from a trusted source. It's also come to my attention that this same individual has tainted our fine reputation enough several of the businesses within the organization are suffering. I'm curious if you've heard anything of this nature?"

As I shoved my hands into my pockets, I wasn't surprised that even Dillon backed away from Demarco. I walked around the table, coming within a few inches. Then I grabbed the big man around the back of the neck, slamming his head onto the table. "You fucked with the wrong man, Demarco."

The bastard reached for his weapon, and I yanked it out of his hand, sliding it down the table. As I pressed his face into the wood, he cursed like a sailor, doing his best to get free from my hold. They had no idea how strong I was or what I was capable of doing.

When the three soldiers backed away, I narrowed my eyes, seeking out Dillon in particular. "Hold him down."

"Yes, boss." Dillon rose to the occasion but not without hesitation. Duly noted.

"What the fuck do you think you're doing?" Demarco snarled.

"That's exactly what I came here to ask you, Demarco. It would seem you've lost sight of who you're working for."

"Don't give me shit." Demarco was a strong man, jerking up from the table by several inches even though the soldiers held him in place.

"Him?" Dillon asked, genuinely surprised at my accusation. "He's the fucking traitor?" I wasn't surprised at his anger. Our father had taken him in off the streets. The one redeeming act my Pops had performed.

"So it would seem. Hold his wrist down."

"You're a crazy motherfucker," Demarco snarled. He was just digging himself a deep hole.

"I might be, but that doesn't really matter. You're required to follow orders, not running off at the mouth." The fact he'd expressed any discord at the change in leadership was reason enough to put a bullet in his brain. Talking smack inside Club Rio was more egregious, but if what I'd heard about him was true in that he'd offered the Morellis information, his punishment should fit the crime.

When I pulled out the knife, it became apparent what I had planned, Demarco bucking even harder.

"You sick son of a bitch. Don't you dare try shit with me."

"Don't dare try it?" I repeated. "I think you have a confused impression of who works for whom. I suggest we get that misunderstanding corrected right now. Keep his fingers spread for me." I waited, neither soldier hesitating before using enough pressure on his hand that Demarco couldn't move it.

"Fuckin' let me go." Demarco's cries would go unheeded. I'd always found it interesting that the largest, most brutal men crumbled first. "You touch me and you die."

He had no idea how threatening me ignited a fire. "I'm not going to do a single thing to you, Demarco. In fact, I won't need to." I moved toward Dillon, handing him the knife. While his eyes opened wide, I sensed he registered I was testing his loyalty. The two men were friends, drinking buddies. If he passed the test, I'd allow both men to live, Demarco only maimed for his insulting behavior. But from here on out, I'd watch Demarco like a hawk. I needed to know how deep the infiltration had gotten before I decided how to handle the Morettis.

If Dillon failed, then the two soldiers would need more time to clean up the mess.

I lifted my eyebrow, allowing a smirk to cross my face. "When you're finished, make certain the room is spotless." As soon as Dillon accepted the blade, I turned around to walk out.

"Wait." Dillon moved in front of me. "How many?"

"I'll leave that up to you." When he seemed confused, I patted him on the shoulder. "I'll let you make the decision just how horrific and damning you believe his actions have been." After squeezing his arm, I walked out.

I knew the man would make the right choice.

* * *

Sarah

Be prepared, my little slut. Tonight I'll claim your ass.

I hadn't been able to get the filthy words out of my mind all day. They'd been crass in comparison to the way he'd spoken to me earlier, but just thinking them kept me aroused. I had to be a sick girl to want more. Claim my ass? It had never happened.

And it never would.

I had scruples after all.

"Are you serious?" my sister asked.

88

And how in the hell had I become turned on by a mysterious man calling me his slut?

Because you've never had a man excite you this way.

Shut up, little voice. I could figure this out for myself.

"I know, crazy, right?" I asked as I tossed the dress on the bed, Shadow immediately jumping on the comforter, his furry butt wiggling as he crawled on top. I gave him a frown, which only caused him to roll over on his back, waiting for me to scratch his tummy. I'd always told my friends, once you have a dog, expect fur everywhere. If they didn't like it, they weren't invited into my home.

Now I tried my best to shoo him off, yanking the hanger into my hand and placing it over the door to my bedroom. Goldie had waddled in, staring up at me with her usual imploring eyes. She hated when Mommy Dog had to go out, even though she was used to my strange work routine.

Carrie exhaled. "I'm really glad you're doing this. What time is he picking you up?"

"Seven. Sharp. So he said."

"A meticulous man."

"Very." I shuddered as I thought about him, still tingling from our intense round of passion. I was crazy for accepting his invitation, especially since I still didn't know his name. I hadn't thought to ask him given everything had happened so fast, the surprise of him following me overpowered by his oppressive actions and the attraction I'd felt from the moment I'd laid eyes on him.

I'd heard about this kind of thing happening to survivors before of course, but not to this degree. Or maybe I was making too much out of it. At this point it didn't matter.

But it should. Who was he?

The nervous voice inside my head had been asking me the same question since he'd disappeared, but not before paying for the dress he'd selected for me. It was all so sudden, his behavior both exciting and terrifying.

"Do you have something to wear?"

I turned to face the dress, exhaling as butterflies formed in my stomach. "He made certain of that."

"What does that mean?"

I was too embarrassed to tell my own sister I'd fucked him in the middle of a dressing room. That wasn't polite conversation. "Let's just say he helped me pick something out."

"Oh, so you spent most of the afternoon together."

Fifteen minutes in the coffee shop, thirty inside the boutique. That could be called an afternoon. "Kind of."

"What's he like?"

"Tall, dark, and handsome with a hint of danger and a touch of arrogance."

"Right," she teased. "Sounds too perfect and you know there are no perfect men."

He might be damn close, the entire package wrapped up in an expensive suit.

"I'm serious." I moved to the closet, opening the door and turning on the light. I had two pairs of heels, one far too scuffed to wear. Thank God the black pair was in good condition, albeit not sexy enough in my mind for the dress. "You are on your way, aren't you?"

"When my baby sister has a date after a bazillion years of celibacy, you bet I'll be on time."

"Thanks for rubbing it in." So I hadn't allowed a man into my bed since... Hell, I couldn't remember at this point. Long enough that it was obvious why I'd foregone the vibrator collection in exchange for a real hunk of a man. I giggled, which was also totally unlike me, but it felt good to do so.

She laughed. "What's a sister for? I'll be there in ten minutes."

I ended the call, tossing the phone on my bed. This was still a crazy idea. For all I knew he could be a serial killer and I was his next victim. The clothes and expensive watch could have been a prop. Hell, he could have stolen it from his last victim.

"Dramatic much?" I asked the other version of myself before plopping down on the bed, allowing my pups to jump on me, plying me with licks and kisses. They'd been my constant friends for years. As they started to get rambunctious, I finally pushed them away, laughing as I scratched first one then the other behind the ear. "Time to get dressed." After a quick shower.

I rushed as much as possible, still struggling into the dress when I heard the knock on my door. As I ran into the living room, the little feet trampling behind me, I started to get anxious. I didn't know how to date. I had no idea how to act. What did I know about anything a stockbroker might be interested in, let alone a man? I growled as I opened the door, cringing from seeing my sister's reaction.

"That is one hot mama of a dress. Your date picked that out? Whew, baby." She fanned her face with her hand before bounding inside.

"Too much?"

"God. It's perfect. What I wouldn't give to have your body. It's funny. I haven't seen you in anything that shows off your hourglass figure in two years."

"That's because I'm always working."

"Who says a surgeon can't be sexy?"

I gave her a hard look and closed the door. I had ten minutes to finish. "You know the drill. Enjoy wine. Food. Whatever I might have."

She lifted a sack I hadn't noticed she'd brought. "Did you really think I'd find anything edible in your kitchen except for dog food? And I've come close to eating it before."

"Very funny." But she was right. So was the mystery man. I'd eaten more cheap frozen dinners in the last two years than I could count. I hurried back to the bathroom, doing my best to apply makeup and style my hair.

I hadn't realized how much time had gone by until Carrie walked to the door of the bathroom, leaning against the doorjamb. "Um, sis. Your date is here."

That shocked the hell out of me. The dogs hadn't barked? They barked at almost everyone except for Carrie. Maybe he had a way with animals. That gave him points on the good side.

"I think he drove up in a Maserati. There's one parked out front." She pointed to the window and my curiosity got the better of me. As I peered outside into the darkness, the sleek sports car positioned under the streetlights glistened. "How do you know it's a Maserati?"

"I know my expensive cars," she teased. "That's like a four-hundred-thousand-dollar automobile."

"And we don't know it belongs to him."

"I have a feeling it does."

After returning to the bathroom and grabbing my fire engine red lipstick, I glanced into the mirror, noticing her reflection. "What's wrong?"

"Oh, nothing's wrong. I'm just wondering if he has a brother. Hot isn't the word for the man. And did you get a load of his muscles?" She leaned in, tossing a look over her shoulder as if he'd followed her. "I know this is a crass thing to say to my sister about her boyfriend, but I bet he has a nice ass and a long cock."

Carrie had always been one to say what was on her mind. That had gotten her a long way in the corporate world, but she'd suck at politics if she was coerced like my father wanted. "First of all, he's not my boyfriend. And second..." *He has the thickest, hardest cock of any man I've ever had.* Oh, yeah, that would go over well. "Second, I don't plan on finding that out. It's a date."

"Uh-huh. Remember what I told you about letting go. Tonight is the night. This weekend in fact. And you look stunning."

I took a deep breath, moving away from the mirror. "It's okay and I can't let go for an entire weekend."

"Yes, you can. You already told me the hospital administrator is forcing you to. God, woman. You do need to get laid."

"Say it louder so he can hear you."

"So, what's his name? I could just call him Stud Muffin."

I moved past her, struggling into my shoes and grabbing my purse. Stud Muffin was all I could tell her myself. At least the name suited him.

"You didn't answer me. Don't keep a secret from your sister."

Sighing, I finally lifted my head, giving her a wicked smile. "I have no idea."

She narrowed her eyes then burst into laughter. "Maybe you do have some wild oats left to sow before you get really old."

"When I return, I'm going to punch you in the face." I steadied myself on the heels, taking a deep breath before walking into the living room.

I'd heard from several people that when you found the right one, the lost part of your heart that you didn't even know was missing suddenly reappeared, then you knew fate had intervened. I'd laughed, being one of many naysayers. There was no such thing as insta-love or finding 'the' one, the single person you were meant to be with.

But as I walked toward the man standing in black jeans, a soft white shirt, and a leather bomber jacket, his eyes full of fire, I could almost believe in anything. He was much more casual than before, but he was just as compelling as he'd been in the suit. Suddenly, I felt overdressed, which is exactly what he wanted.

His nostrils flared and as he stared at me with hooded eyes, there was no doubt he was undressing me with them. I hated the fact he could easily see his heated expression prompted my full arousal, my nipples poking through the thin material of the dress. I could swear he'd purposely selected a style that wouldn't allow me to wear a bra.

There was such a powerful dynamic between us that even without the passion, the air crackled from the electricity dancing through us. There was a confidence about him, a knowing of how his presence was a power in and of itself that I appreciated, but his arrogance remained, as if he knew how powerful he was. I could see it in the way he looked at me, as if I was his possession, a thing to play with and put on a shelf.

I noticed the golden flecks in his irises, and the heated way in which he was looking at me could easily burn me into the ground if that was his intention. There was a rugged-ness about him that differed from what I expected of a stockbroker, muscular without being overpowering. His jaw was chiseled, his cheekbones high, which accentuated his long obsidian eyelashes. I was taken aback by how good looking he really was, grateful the fog from before hadn't returned.

There was something odd about the way he looked at me, almost ominous. There was a darkness to him that threatened to consume everything in its path, a looming desire swirling at the corners of his eyes. I couldn't quite put my finger on why that was the first thing that came to mind. He'd done nothing overt that would suggest he intended on doing me any harm, more as if anyone tried to come between us, he'd crush them beneath his rattlesnake skin boots.

The room was completely silent, except for the same rapidly beating heart I'd had before. That's when I blinked, purposely glancing toward the dogs to hide the warm flush I felt sliding along my jaw.

Goldie was a Sheltie–Golden Retriever and Shadow a black lab and Irish setter mix. In other words, they were hyper, protective dogs who loved attention.

They sat still, staring up at the mystery guest as if he was a god, or maybe a dog whisperer. I couldn't get over it. One thing I knew is that if someone passed the pup test, they were good people. At least that gave me some sense of comfort.

He obviously noticed my intense gaze, chuckling softly. "They're beautiful."

"They like you." I lifted my head, studying his eyes.

"You make that sound like they shouldn't."

"They don't know you. I don't either."

He walked closer, taking my words as a challenge. As he closed the distance, he cocked his head, taking deep breaths. "Then we'll have to rectify that. Won't we?" He cupped my chin, rubbing his thumb so gently back and forth across my skin that I pursed my lips, fearful I'd express the scintillating thoughts rushing into the back of my mind.

"Yes, we will."

He lowered his head and I thought for certain he was going to kiss me. Then he whispered in my ear, "I do have a surprise."

"Another Danish?"

"Something much better. We should get going. Is your sister staying with the dogs?" he asked. Another surprise. He cared about their welfare.

"How do you know she's my sister?" I moved to the closet, grabbing my coat, struggling into it as I watched the way he scanned the room. Was he looking for something or just noticing I lived like a pauper?

"I'm right here. My name is Carrie, Sarah's sister. Yes, I'm staying with them all night long if I need to."

"That's good to hear, Carrie. Don't worry. Your sister will be in good hands." With that, he moved behind me, placing his hand on the small of my back and leading me to the door. "Don't wait up for her, Carrie." His tone was just as commanding with her as he'd been with me.

As he led me into the hallway, a strange feeling settled into my mind as if I'd met him before.

Whether or not that was the truth, I knew one thing so clearly that denying it would be senseless.

Whatever this was between us was about to change my life.

Yet what surprised me about the acknowledgement was that I wasn't certain it would be for the better.

Or that I'd survive.

CHAPTER 6

 abriel

I wasn't normally taken aback by the sight of any woman. That just wasn't my nature, nor had I ever wanted to be consumed by lust or any other emotion associated with the act of passion. The hard shell I'd encased myself in for education, building my brand, and finally for running a billion-dollar corporation with an iron fist precluded romance. But with Sarah, everything was different.

Not that I'd ever claim I had any such desire in my body.

But with her, all I could think about was stripping off her pretty dress, exposing her rock-hard nipples. I wanted to take the time to suck them, pulling them between my sharp teeth then biting down until she cried out in pain. Then I wanted nothing more than for her to beg me to fuck her, screaming my name when I did.

She'd tensed from almost the minute she'd walked into the living room, her eyes narrowing as she looked at me. Perhaps she'd remembered her savior, the only man who'd stepped up to the plate to save her life.

The same one who'd sworn to take it with his bare hands.

I'd told her I would claim her ass and that was just the beginning of my plans.

She'd fixed her cerulean blue eyes on mine, searching for answers. I found it curious that she hadn't asked my name, as if it didn't matter. Perhaps she was fearful of learning it. Whatever the case, I was enjoying toying with her far too much.

She remained on the sidewalk, staring at my Maserati then glancing up toward the window of her bedroom. I reached in front of her, opening the door.

"Get in, Sarah. We have a schedule to keep."

"You mean reservations," she corrected.

"Of sorts." After closing the door, I moved around the front of the car, scanning both sides of the street. After Dillon had proven his loyalty, I had a feeling Demarco had cried bloody murder to the Morettis. I wouldn't put it past them to try to make a hit on either myself or my father. I'd purposely ignored Joseph's two calls, hoping he'd sweat. Even though my father was trying to guide me toward a truce, pushing the marriage between Nico and Theodora, I wasn't inclined to have any connection with the son of a bitch. There would never be a time I could trust him.

As I eased inside, she glanced in my direction, and I didn't need the streetlights to know she was questioning her trust in me. She should. She had no idea she was sitting next to a brutal savage. She'd literally taken my breath away in her dress. While I'd been privileged to see it in the dressing room, she looked entirely different with her hair in curls and makeup on. She was naturally beautiful, no makeup needed, but when she was in a dress and heels, it was easy to sense how formidable she was.

The taste of her had lingered all day, keeping my balls tight and my mind reeling from thoughts of what I would do to her. Taking time away from New York was risky, but I could spend time without the annoyance of business.

And there would be no method for her to escape.

"Where are we going?" she asked after a few minutes.

"You'll see." I could tell she was debating refusing to go with me.

"You should know that I'm not the kind of girl who appreciates surprises or secrecy for that matter."

"I'll keep that in mind."

"But you still have no intention of sharing with me where we're having dinner. I assume you didn't lie to me."

I lifted my eyebrow, surprised her tone had changed, her challenge refreshing. I'd already realized how intelligent she was, but I appreciated the rebellious side as well. That would make breaking her sweeter. "You should know I'm not in the habit of lying. That doesn't suit either my personal life or my business."

"I would assume lying in the world of stockbroking isn't acceptable."

She was testing me, slyly trying to find information. "What is it that you want to know, Sarah?"

"You know my name. I should know yours."

"Fair enough. Gabriel. As far as last names, why don't we keep our tryst a little mysterious." I'd thought about providing a false name in the beginning but finding out now whether she'd learned who her savior had been on that day was valuable.

"Mysterious isn't the word. Reckless is more like it."

"But what's life without taking a few risks?"

"You could be a criminal, a murderer."

She had no idea how right she was. "I could be." The game was getting more challenging by the minute. Now my balls were aching to the point of pain.

"Gabriel," she repeated. "That suits you." As I pulled up to a light, she turned her head to study me, narrowing her eyes. I lifted a single brow, enjoying the quiet tension building between us. It was a stare down, her search continuing. There was a crackling of electricity more intense than there had been before, the air inside the car filled with vibrant current.

As I rolled out of the city, she tensed even more, and I sensed she was uncertain she'd made the right decision.

"You can relax, Sarah. I'm not going to hurt you, at least not in the way you're thinking. We're going to my private plane."

"Whoa. A private plane? Going where?"

"That is the surprise. Are you impressed?"

"I don't impress easily, Gabriel. While I appreciate the attention and the chemistry we've shared, I'm not comfortable with getting on a plane with you. I hope you understand."

I had to think about how to answer her truthfully.

"You've obviously figured out that I've been very successful. I don't usually flaunt it because that serves no purpose. However, when I'd like to enjoy spending time with a beautiful woman far removed from the dirtiness of New York, I am thrilled that I have the opportunity to do so. If that means a plane ride to another destination, then so be it. And it's not something I'd going to feel guilty about."

She thought about what I'd said, holding her breath for a few seconds. "Fair enough."

With that she turned her head, glancing at the passing lights. The tension remained but she was more intrigued than anxious.

"I'll be curious to find out more about you," she said after a full two minutes had passed.

"Are you certain you want to destroy the mirage, or simply enjoy a passionate evening?"

Her slight chuckle was different as with everything else about her. "This afternoon was incredible. I also won't lie to you. However, I'm not the kind of woman to indulge in sex with a stranger."

"I don't believe we're strangers any longer. Do you?"

Her smile was a slight reward, and it also made my cock twitch as the need to be inside of her sweet pussy heightened. Perhaps I was a fool for enjoying the time I'd spent, hungering for more, but as soon as I had her under my full control, I could remove the distraction from my mind. Then I could handle business without thinking about fucking her every second of the day.

I tapped my fingers on the steering wheel, heading off the exit toward the private airstrip. I wondered if she had any idea that she'd just fallen into the clutches of a monster.

I'd planned for every detail, leaving nothing to chance. All the animosity I'd expected to feel hadn't come to pass. She was everything I'd ever wanted and my possession of her was now required.

Whether she agreed or not.

As I guided her onto the plane, I made certain no one had followed us, keeping my hand on my Glock in case we were interrupted. If she noticed my slight action, she didn't outwardly acknowledge it, although I had a sense the woman was very observant. Even cunning. Owning her would be worth every amount of effort I undertook.

Sarah stood in the entranceway, allowing her gaze to sweep the opulent setting. "This is... unreal."

I laughed as I pressed my hand against the small of her back. "My brother had the interior renovated only months before…" I stopped myself before mentioning his death. At any point her memory could resurface, which would accelerate my plan. I was enjoying myself far too much to allow that to happen in the next two days.

"Before?"

"Before he recommissioned another. Naturally, I agreed to take this one off his hands."

She narrowed her eyes, glancing over her shoulder. "The trials and tribulations of the rich and famous."

"Rich, yes. Famous? I hope not. Take your time looking around. We still have a few minutes before we take off." I couldn't take my eyes off her shapely long legs as she moved throughout the cabin, heading toward the bedroom chamber. I continued to keep my promise to her that I wouldn't lie. Luciano had begun renovations. I'd simply had them expedited over the last few weeks. I headed for the bar, selecting a bottle of Krug champagne, chuckling as she shook her head at the sight of the oversized king bed.

Then she closed the door abruptly, taking a deep breath before spinning around to face me. "I meant what I said. I'm not a one-night stand kind of woman."

"Who said anything about a one-night stand? If that had been the case, I wouldn't have asked you to dinner." As I opened the bottle, the slight poofing noise brought a smile to my face. After pouring two glasses, I walked toward her slowly, my hunger nearly off the charts.

"You are a man full of surprises."

"I can be." I lifted my glass in a toast.

"What happens when people don't accept your brand of hospitality?"

"You mean my pushy demeanor."

"Yes."

I waited until she took a sip, her eyelashes fluttering across the shimmer of her cheeks. Goddamn, my cock was still hard as a rock. "Let's just say it's usually in one's best interest to do as I say."

"Why does that sound a little bit like a threat?"

"I don't make threats, Sarah. I simply don't need to. I make promises."

"For a stockbroker, that sounds ominous."

As I headed for one of two leather couches, I expected her to follow. I should have known given her personality that she wanted to continue doing things her way. That would change soon enough. I sat down, leaning back and crossing my legs. "You doubt my profession?"

"No, I believe you could be a stockbroker, but the few I've known are all about crunching numbers, a genius in antici-pating trends, not pushing their clients into a decision."

"It's all about reading the client. There are those who are dead set on challenging the system. Others need coaxing. I've made dozens of men and women extremely wealthy over the years." Which was all true. I wasn't prepared to tell her that I was also a genius at stock manipulation, which should have been a red flag that I was exactly like my father and brother.

She lifted her chin, exposing her long neck, and I envisioned a thick leather collar. She would certainly look beautiful in heels, the collar, and nothing else. I was getting ahead of myself. When she finally sat down, she seemed determined to keep her distance.

Seconds later, the pilot appeared, which was unusual for him to do. "I'm sorry, sir, but I wanted to let you know we may experience turbulence given the approaching storm."

Sighing, I ran the tip of my finger around the rim of the flute. "Will you be able to complete the flight?"

"Absolutely, sir. I've flown in much worse. Try and enjoy the ride."

Sarah frowned as she glanced toward the window. "Does that mean we're flying north? There's an arctic blast coming in from Canada."

"Your deductions are correct. Come here and I'll tell you where we're going." I simply gave her a stern look. There was no need for another gesture. She chewed on her lower lip, debating obeying me, but her hard nipples indicated her desire to follow my command.

She slowly rose to her feet, shifting closer, still too far away. When I wrapped my hand around her arm, dragging her closer, she immediately threw out her hand, pressing it against my chest. "Not so fast. You don't own me."

I fisted her hair at the scalp, ignoring her words. She had no idea what she did to me when she resisted. That only fueled the fire, igniting what was left of embers I'd believed to be ice cold. "Perhaps I don't own you yet, but I will. Very soon." I crushed my mouth over hers, curious as to her reaction.

She stiffened, adding pressure to her hand, pushing with all the force she had. But slowly she parted her lips and I took advantage of it, thrusting my tongue inside. There was no doubt I would devour her several times, bringing her to the heights of ecstasy she didn't know existed. But she would begin to understand my rules.

Her moans filtered past the kiss and her fingers were now clutching my shirt. I kept my firm hold as I swept my tongue throughout her mouth, exploring every inch, every dark crevice. The burst of champagne added to my desire, yet was unable to quench my thirst. As I dominated her tongue, I pulled her even closer, prepared to drag her across my lap. She'd awakened the savage in me, yanking on the vile needs that seemed impossible to fulfill.

When I broke the kiss, our breathing ragged, I bit down on her lower lip until she shuddered in my hold. The chemistry was off the charts, the bolts of electricity threatening to derail a portion of my plans. The plane ride was far too short to satisfy or fulfill my needs.

As she dragged her tongue across her lip, a warm flush crept up on her cheeks.

"Is this how you are with all women?"

"I'll let you in on a little secret. I've been far too busy to enjoy the company of a woman for a very long time."

"Then why me?"

A valid question, the first where I'd need to partially lie to her in order to provide an answer. "The draw to you was captivating. I couldn't stand the thought of not getting to know you."

"Hmm... A charming, good-looking, wealthy man. Why aren't you married?" She scooted away but only a few inches, giving me a sly smile.

"Marriage had never seemed favorable, at least until now."

"Just to be clear. I will never get married."

"Hmmm... What a pity." As the pilot taxied the plane down the runway, I resisted smiling. As the wheels were lifted from the concrete, all the filthy thoughts about what I would do to her continued to play out in my mind. Realizing my heart was thudding rapidly, echoing into my ears almost made me laugh. "We're going to Vermont, to a beautiful cabin I have in the woods. Don't worry, my beautiful creature, we are having dinner." I turned my head toward her, inhaling her exotic perfume. "And you're going to be dessert."

* * *

Sarah

He's going to claim your ass.

I clenched both my pussy and ass muscles at the thought. I had to get my mind off sex, yet given the way we started this… fling, that's almost all I could think about.

Almost.

I only wished the nagging feeling I'd had around him would dissipate.

My mother had always told me that when I liked a boy, I should always study his eyes because they were a true reflection of the kind of man he'd become. I'd followed her suggestion, which had prevented me from dating the captain of the football team in high school. Years later, I'd learned he'd gone to prison for rape. I'd seen the dark, cruel look in his eyes the moment I'd turned him down for the homecoming dance. I'd sensed words he'd never said, but I'd been able to feel the extreme heat resonating from his body. I'd sensed he wanted to threaten me. Instead, he'd smiled, yet from that day forward, I'd done everything I could to stay away from him.

Now, as I stared into the eyes of a man I'd already been intimate with, a strange feeling pooled in my stomach. His dark eyes weren't full of rage or hatred, but there was something underneath the flickering gold surrounding his irises that troubled me.

Or it was because of the way he'd said I was dessert. Or maybe it was because I was sitting on a plane headed to another state and he'd failed to mention I'd be gone for longer than a few hours. What curtailed the fear was the fact my body continued to tingle from the passionate kiss and the way he was looking at me.

Maybe I was being cautious, or maybe because I'd completely lost my inhibitions with a stranger I was chastising myself. Whatever the case, the mixture of apprehension and excitement was powerful.

He didn't attempt to overpower me again, but I sensed the raging beast remained close to the surface. He was ready to devour me and in truth, I wouldn't mind. However, I was thankful we engaged in trivial conversation, both laughing from our choice in our favorite movies. Now I noticed a light in his eyes I hadn't seen before.

And I could breathe easier.

As the engine started to slow, he took my glass from my hand, getting to his feet and refilling for a third time.

"It would appear we're getting ready to land," he said casually as he eased the glass over my shoulder, brushing the outside of his wrist against my cheek. Even the slight touch was enough to create tremors dancing throughout my body. "You should call your sister before we land and ask her if she can stay with your dogs for a couple of days."

"I'm sorry. What did you say?"

He leaned closer, taking a second to slide his finger along my jaw. "I told you I had a surprise."

"Wait a minute. I don't have any clothes and I'm certain not dressed for extreme winter weather and I also have two dogs to take care of. I can't just leave them alone. Maybe you've never had animals before, but dogs need their humans in order to survive. You know, go to the bathroom, food and water?" The fact I was rattling off at the mouth was a clear indication I was suddenly nervous. Who did he think he was assuming I could spend days with him?

His eyes were unreadable, but I could swear he was annoyed that I hadn't agreed readily. "I took the liberty of asking your sister if she would stay, which she seemed happy to do." His admittance was another surprise, one I wasn't certain I liked. He'd planned out everything, his control refusing to be denied.

"Why didn't she say anything to me?"

"Because I told her I was surprising you. If you don't believe me then call her yourself, but you'll need to do it prior to us landing. Where we'll be staying, there is almost nonexistent cell phone coverage."

I could sense he'd issued a challenge. I reached for my purse, ready to make the call when I hesitated.

"You don't trust me," he said.

"I don't know you."

"That's what I hope to change."

"Why?"

"Why?" he repeated.

"Why go to all this trouble? You could get to know me over pizza and a glass of chianti."

He laughed, thoroughly amused. "Yes, you're right, but that doesn't sound enjoyable to me. Call her."

There was a change in him that continued to trouble me. It was as if after one taste, I'd become his possession. The sensations wrapped around the thought kept the butterflies of excitement in my stomach while my rational mind continued to try to process.

"Why is there such a strong connection between us?" I asked, which seemed to catch him off guard.

"Have you asked yourself that question?"

"Several times."

"Did you come to a conclusion?"

I shook my head, although I wasn't being truthful with either him or myself.

"Yes, I think you do know. It's about the darkness," he said gruffly.

As I dragged my tongue across my lips, my throat suddenly parched, he narrowed his eyes. "As in the time of day?"

Of course that's not what he meant.

Gabriel cocked his head, the swirl of gold in his eyes mesmerizing. "As in the agonizing need that continues to build in the darkest catacombs of your mind, the creature hungering for nourishment that hasn't been supplied."

I pulled out my phone, dialing the number. As the phone rang, he glared at me. Why did I have the feeling he was disappointed? I started talking as soon as she answered the phone, the connection already sketchy.

"Carrie. Did Gabriel ask you to stay with the babies for a couple of days?"

"Yes. He said it was a surprise... and... so I..." As soon as the connection died, I took a deep breath, glaring at my phone. "I lost her."

"And how did she answer?"

"Yes. She said yes." The strange feeling in my stomach remained. "As I said, I also have a job."

"You don't need to return for a shift for almost three days."

I snapped my head up, narrowing my eyes. "You planned this? You called my work?"

"That's what men do when they're preparing a surprise."

I glanced at the window just as the plane jerked, a soft moan pushing past my lips. Was he some crazed killer planning on dumping my body at his cabin?

Don't be dramatic. He wouldn't take you there in a private plane.

True, but given the only 'surprise' my only real boyfriend had ever given me was a vivid picture of two of the women he had on the side, I was more than a little skeptical. It was funny how lonely I'd felt over the last few years, even with Goldie and Shadow being such amazing companions. I'd thought death was the worst thing that could happen in a person's life. That's one reason I worked so hard to save every life possible, hoping that it would balance the sense of dread for facing nights alone.

I'd been wrong. Feeling completely empty without sharing time with someone special was crushing, the weight increasing every week and month that passed by. Lately, I'd felt fatigued, but not from lack of sleep or food, but from the lack of human touch. It was crazy to think about that now, other than how alive I'd felt hours earlier.

"A remote cabin." I said the three words as if I needed to confirm what he'd said. I kept my phone in my hand.

"Yes. I'm not talking about camping, Sarah. I obviously appreciate creature comforts. As I said, I do enjoy getting away from the city from time to time, although I've been so infrequently over the years it's a wonder I haven't sold the place. I'm hoping my caretaker has kept up with the maintenance or the chef I hired will likely be in a pissy mood. And yes, I took the liberty of purchasing you a few things."

"Things? Clothes? How did you know my size?"

He cocked one of his sexy eyebrows. "Well, I did spend some quality time with you in a dressing room and happened to notice what size fit you perfectly."

"Right," I half whispered. Could I trust the man? "You hired a chef?" I don't know why the piece of information surprised me. Almost nothing did with the man any longer.

He laughed and returned to his seat, more relaxed than he'd been at the start of the flight. "I doubt you'd want me to try and cook for you, especially when there were only a few cans of food left in the cabinets."

"I thought you could do anything." I shifted on the couch, bristling as the plane was rocked from side to side. When I involuntarily reached out for him, he pulled me so close against him that I was almost sitting on his lap. He wrapped his arm around me, shifting me by the few inches so that I was.

And his cock was hard as a rock, pushing against his trousers. I was momentarily lightheaded, my entire mind foggy as a rush of desire blasted into every cell.

"Don't worry, my little creature. I will always take care of you. Always."

A slight cold chill oozed down my spine to my legs.

As much as the sentiment was meant to be comforting, I had a feeling there was something lurking behind his words.

Something… evil.

CHAPTER 7

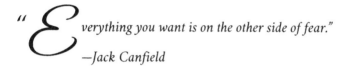

"*Everything you want is on the other side of fear.*"
—*Jack Canfield*

Sarah

The ugliness of my thoughts while still on the plane faded away during the drive. While I'd always adored fresh snow as it fell across the scenic views of New York, it always seemed as if the dirt and grunge from daily life shattered the exquisite beauty within minutes after it stopped falling.

As he drove from the small airport, a four-wheel-drive truck waiting for him as soon as we arrived, the view reminded me what true beauty was like.

Even in the darkness.

Snow had started to fall, the ice crystals pinging against the windshield. Gabriel had no fear of the approaching storm, acting as if he could drive through anything. Oddly enough, I had no fear of him crashing, his total control over everything one of his greatest strengths.

I enjoyed the ride but as he drove down a snow-covered long driveway, I groaned thinking about my high heels.

"What's wrong?" he asked.

"I hate to mention this, but I doubt I can walk in the snow in my heels." There were several lights on inside the cabin, but from the headlights, all I could tell was that the cabin appeared rustic, huge logs encompassing the exterior.

"Don't worry about it." He refused to explain any further, parking and cutting the engine, whistling as he climbed out. After walking around to my side and opening the door, he gathered me into his arms.

"What are you doing?"

"Taking care of the lady I invited to dinner." He said nothing else until after he opened the door, taking long strides inside.

"Whoa," I said quietly. "This is incredible." The cabin was still rustic, but only by standards created from someone with the sizable bank account that Gabriel had. The cathedral ceiling covered in thick wooden beams gave way to twenty-five-foot windows and a stone fireplace just as huge. While the floors were wooden, the color was deep and rich, as if cabernet wine had stained oak floors. The furniture reminded me of the plane, opulent while being completely inviting. The bearskin rug in front of the fire was oversized, adding to the warmth given off by the flickering flames of the fire.

And the aroma flowing through the air made my stomach grumble. I couldn't wait to see the room in the morning light to gawk at the beauty.

"I've often thought about relocating here, but it wouldn't be helpful to a stockbroker if the internet was iffy at best."

"No, it wouldn't." As he eased me down, I shifted in my shoes, faltering enough he had to keep his long fingers wrapped around my arms.

"Be careful, my special creature. I wouldn't want anything to happen to you. I'll stoke the fire and make us both a drink. You can freshen up if you like. The bedroom and bathroom are at the top of the stairs. However, I'd prefer you stay in the dress for now."

"Are you always this dominating?"

He remained silent as he removed his jacket, immediately easing mine from my shoulders. "Since I was the kid most likely to get beaten up. I had to learn very quickly that only the top dog wins. So, I became a top dog. Survival of the fittest."

"Interesting. The bullied becomes the bully."

"It's not necessary to become a bully in order to be in command, although violence is needed at times when conversing has failed. But never with a woman."

"Why does it seem that you would prefer if I was afraid of you?"

"You should be." He turned away from me, moving toward the fire and I held my breath for a few seconds. He was serious. He wanted me to be afraid of him.

Why?

I moved toward the set of stairs, taking my time as I headed to the second floor. He was so certain of himself, acting as if he already owned me. Even if there was a part of me that was flattered by the attention, the money spent on airplane fuel and hiring a chef, the clothes purchased just so I'd feel comfortable here, it all felt far too possessive. As I walked into the bedroom, flicking on the light, the instant I saw the number of shopping bags, not all from the boutique where I'd shopped, the roses and card entered my mind.

Was it possible it was one and the same person? If that was the case, had Gabriel been stalking me for months? Was he some kind of a crazed fan of my surgical work? I'd heard of it before, but I would have remembered if I'd operated on such a fine specimen.

I gritted my teeth, shoving another round of lurid thoughts aside. I had no business acting like a teenager.

Why not? What if this is exactly what the doctor ordered?

Yeah, my little voice could go to hell.

Why was I looking over my shoulder, nervous tension in my stomach? Because I thought he'd be standing there? Would that bother me if he was? Yes. In truth, it would. This was all so much, as if seducing me hadn't been enough.

Only owning me would be.

I opened a few of the bags, fingering the soft sweaters and two pair of jeans. He'd even thought of snow boots, and they were in my correct size. Was it possible he'd gone to greater lengths to learn more about me than he wanted me to believe? With the internet and search engines, anything was possible. I purchased most of my clothing online late at night. A consummate hacker could find every detail of what I liked, including my food deliveries with ease.

For what purpose?

It was crazy that I hadn't demanded his last name. Nowadays, learning a person's name and checking all their social media platforms before accepting a date was responsible.

I'd been reckless, including having unprotected sex.

I shoved the bags aside, unable to pick through any more of them. Although I did want to change out of the dress.

The one he'd selected for me.

The one he'd demanded I wear.

What are you doing, girl? You've lost your mind.

I studied the bedroom for a few seconds, the huge king-size bed covered in pillows. Then I took a sharp turn into the bathroom, noticing candles had been strategically placed on the large whirlpool tub and across the counter. I backed out, moving toward the other room on the floor. The door was locked, which made me curious as to what the man was hiding. As I leaned against the wall and closed my eyes, I could swear I'd seen him somewhere before. He wasn't a patient. I'd remember that. Maybe he'd been in the coffee shop before.

No, my body would have experienced the same reaction.

Why the hell couldn't I remember it?

I was shaking all over, partially from adrenaline. When that happened, it was usually because my mind was working so hard to find an answer to whatever problem I was confronted with. And in most cases, I suddenly remembered the answer or had an epiphany about how to fix the situation. As I walked downstairs, he was nowhere to be seen. I listened for any sounds, but there was only the ebb and flow of the wind starting to howl outside. That alone creeped me out. I peered around the corner then moved to the entrance to another room.

The kitchen was almost as large as the living room, big enough to be considered a commercial kitchen complete with Viking appliances. The man didn't spare any expense. There was a bottle of wine and two half-full glasses sitting on the counter, but no sign of him.

Him.

Now I suddenly had trouble reciting his name in my mind?

Why do you look so familiar? Why?

I felt a presence only seconds before an arm was wrapped around my throat, forcefully dragging me backward and against a hard body. I immediately reacted, trying to twist in order to drive my heel into his foot. It was a reaction I'd trained myself to do in case I was ever attacked. Even though I knew who'd captured me, my natural instinct had been to fight. Did that say something about my distrust or about feeling uneasy of letting go? He chuckled in my ear, jerking me even closer as he ground his cock against my bottom.

"My beautiful little bird. You wouldn't be trying to hurt me now, would you?" he asked, although the husky growl in his voice made the words garbled.

"What do you think you're doing?"

"Taking what belongs to me."

"I don't belong to you." I twisted again, able to duck away from his hold. His look of amusement meant he'd expected me to pull away.

"Yes. You do."

I laughed, darting a quick look over his shoulder. He followed my gaze, his nostrils flaring.

"If you honestly think you're going to find safe passage outside that door, you would be wrong. There are predators everywhere."

There was something enticing about the little game we were playing, but I sensed he'd meant what he said. He truly believed I belonged to him. When he took a step closer, I took two backwards. Then the dance was repeated. I raked my gaze down the front of him, admiring every inch of his muscular body. The man was built like no other.

"Do you like what you see, Sarah?"

"Yes."

"Then you need to trust me."

"How can I do that when you all but abducted me, dragging me to another state?"

"You're free to go anytime." His smirk was far too beguiling. He knew exactly what he was doing to me.

"Maybe I will." I maintained a wide arc as I passed by him, knowing exactly what he would do. When he snagged my arm, twirling me around and fisting me by the hair, stars floated in front of my eyes.

"But you will never be able to get away from me, even if you wanted to."

Somehow, I believed him. He jerked me back, wrapping his arm around me and lowering his head. When he licked the shell of my ear, I dragged my tongue across my lips. His hot breath alone was almost enough to bring me to an orgasm. I fingered his arm, blinking as I studied the colorful design. The red rose was stunning, but the black dagger driven through it was telling. If only I knew what the translation of the Italian words underneath. I had a feeling they were important.

"Why is that?"

He shifted his hips, his actions creating a wave of heat between my legs. I was thrown by the desire roaring through me when I should be doing everything to push him away, at least until I found out everything there was to know about him. Why did he have such an effect on me?

"Because I'm the only man who could provide what you need."

"What do you think I need?"

"Release from the chains you placed around yourself, freedom to let go of your inhibitions. Only I understand the darkness festering inside of you, the wants that drive you crazy, the needs that you can't explain to anyone. I can smell your fear, but it's not me you should be terrified of. It's living the rest of your life never able to feel again, to explore your needs, to satisfy a hunger that gnaws at you every day."

"Who are you?"

"A man cut from the same cloth, longing for the same fulfillment. That begins today. Remove your clothes."

"Not unless you tell me your last name," I demanded.

"I thought you enjoyed our game of remaining strangers."

"I'm no fool, Gabriel. I live in New York, remember."

"But I could easily tell you a lie."

"Yes, you could. But you won't. You have a sense of integrity that will never allow you to lie about who and what you are."

"Very interesting. It would seem my stunning guest has taken several psychology classes."

"It's part of my training. I'll know if you're lying."

He laughed. "Alright. I am Gabriel Riccardo. Since you know my name, it's only fitting that I know yours."

I took a deep breath. At least he'd told me and there was truth in his tone. I was damn good at reading people. It was something that had always helped me in practicing medicine. "Washington."

"Sarah Washington. A perfectly American name."

"Yes, and yours is beautifully Italian."

"If only I'd spent more time in Sicily. My grandparents remain there. Does that satisfy your curiosity, or would you prefer taking a look at my driver's license?"

I allowed myself to laugh, although a shiver remained. "No. I believe you."

"I'm glad to hear that. Now, undress. And Sarah? Do not make me ask you again." He lifted a single eyebrow, his expression commanding.

"I..." Blinking, I wasn't certain why tears had formed in my eyes. Were they out of frustration, fear or the fact he was right about his assessment of me? Was I that transparent? "Wait a minute. How would you know what I need?" I'd never allowed any man to be dominating over me, friend or foe. In fact, I usually ate them for breakfast when they acted as if they were better, faster, or stronger. All the strange sensations about Gabriel I'd felt were coming to a head.

He wasn't just seducing me. He was preparing to dominate me, taking full control.

"So defiant. You have no idea how much that arouses me. To answer your question, because someone of such virtue can't handle the constant possibility of the loss of life. As if by living as a saint instead of a sinner, you'll never lose your ability to save a life, allowing families to thrive and grow. But you're not God, Sarah. You're a woman with needs, desires that burn deep within you. Tell me I'm wrong and I will back away."

Of course he wasn't wrong. The fact he was right was the reason I was terrified.

He kept his firm hold around my neck as he brushed the fingers of his other hand across my arm and down my side. "I've spent far too many years believing there was no one who could ever understand me or the darkness inside. The moment I laid eyes on you, I knew you could handle the sadistic man. Does that mean I may hurt you? Yes. But I will never harm you. Do you understand the difference?"

"Yes," I whispered. The subdued tone of my voice surprised me almost as much as the sensations burning in my thighs, the tightness in my stomach.

"If you don't undress, I will do it for you. Then I'll give you a stern round of punishment for disobeying me that you won't soon forget."

A thrill coursed through me, another shocking moment. Was I possibly excited about the thought of him punishing me again, just like before? The answer sickened me.

He released his hold, backing away and for a few seconds, I was paralyzed, uncertain what to do. If he'd wanted to do harm, that could have happened anywhere on the ride from the airport. That wasn't his intention. Should I rest easy or press further?

"Close your eyes, Sarah."

The way he said my name created an odd thrill, a need that kept my heart pumping and my blood pressure increasing. But I closed my eyes, allowing myself to fall into the sweet abyss that I'd wanted for as long as I could remember, but had never thought to achieve. He'd awakened something inside of me that was difficult for me to comprehend, but he was right in that I could never share it with anyone else. I took several deep breaths then untied the sash, keeping my breathing even as I slowly slid one sleeve over my shoulder then the other.

"So fucking beautiful and all mine."

At that moment, his possessive nature excited me, and I felt beautiful. As soon as I allowed the dress to drop to the floor, I sensed his presence again and shivered.

"Relax. Trust. Remember?"

He gripped me with both hands, and I couldn't help but think about how large they were, his fingers long and broad, his arms muscular. It was a silly thing to think about, but it helped ease some of the tension. As he rubbed them up and down my arms, I started to relax, more so than what little of my rational brain was left could handle. Then he pulled me close once again, wrapping one hand around my throat. His action wasn't about scaring me. That much I sensed. It was about providing comfort that he would keep his promise.

I found it strange I was dissecting the moment, but the reason was obvious. I needed an excuse in order to be able to let go, losing the last vestige of fear before falling head-long into the darkness he'd mentioned. If he was a sadist, did that make me a masochist? I wasn't certain I was prepared for the truthful answer. I'd never been that way. I'd never looked at porn on the internet or gone to BDSM clubs. I'd never asked a boyfriend to spank me for some egregious behavior.

But with him, it seemed I craved exploring something else, something… deeper. Reckless or not, I relaxed completely, my breathing normal.

"I'm going to blindfold you. That will allow you to experience a heightened state of pleasure."

"I don't know."

"I'll take it off whenever you're uncomfortable." The same gruffness to his voice continued, but it added to the excitement. He didn't wait for my reply, sliding a silky mask over my eyes, tying it in such a way I couldn't see even a glimmer of light. Then he rolled his hands over my shoulders, cupping my naked breasts. As he squeezed, I tried to remain calm, knowing he was about to explore every inch of my body. "The chef has prepared several items. However, I enjoy having dessert first."

Tingling sensations slowly drifted down my arms and legs, keeping the adrenaline churning. I had no idea what he had planned, but I sensed his control was just beginning. He pinched my nipples with enough pressure I shuddered audibly, a sudden icy chill flowing into my muscles.

"When I fuck you tonight, you will scream out my name."

He twisted my hardened buds, but the pain was short lived, a moment of bliss scouring my system. I was barely able to breathe, my mind a blur but given my lack of eyesight, every sound he made including his ragged breathing was amplified. So were the prickles popping along every inch of my skin. Then he lowered his hands, sliding them into my thong. I had a feeling he was going to rip it from my body, but he eased it over my hips, which was a hell of a lot more intimate.

The morning session seemed days ago, but it was still the same. I was standing naked in front of a total stranger, one with the most gorgeous body on the planet. The only difference was that I didn't feel as embarrassed as I had before. In fact, I felt exhilarated, more alive than... this morning.

The way his fingers brushed my skin and his hot breath skipped along the back of my neck, I couldn't stop tingling all over. His dominance was a powerful aphrodisiac, keeping me on edge while a small part of me tried to locate my sanity. Maybe everyone who'd given me advice was correct.

Let go.

The darkness obviously helped with what should be another embarrassing moment. I was able to breathe easier, allowing my mind to free itself of the anxiety. After I stepped out of the thong, he pressed his groin against me once again, the light friction stimulating. He rolled his fingers in my hair then slid them down my neck. When he turned me around to face him, only then did I feel at a complete disadvantage. I wanted to bask in his masculinity, catching every nuance of the way he looked at me.

He cupped both sides of my face, rubbing his thumbs back and forth across my lips. I'd long since eaten off the lipstick, but I didn't think he'd care one way or the other. He captured my mouth, but the kiss wasn't rough and controlling this time as he softly parted my lips with his, tenderly sliding his tongue inside. His scent was different, and I wasn't certain why. There was the same hint of spices, the woody fragrance that was entirely too masculine, but there was an added depth I hadn't noticed before. It filled my nostrils, flowing through my veins. The man oozed power and control, but that no longer flagged any concern.

He kept the kiss gentle, rolling my lips open and closed. When he backed away, a tiny whimper escaped. "Put your hands in front of you."

"Why?"

"From here on out, you will not question me, only follow my commands. Is that understood?"

"Yes."

His growl filled in several blanks.

"Yes, sir."

"Better," he said in a husky tone.

I found myself placing my hands in front of me, both fisted with my wrists together. I knew exactly what he was going to do. As I felt the first hint of rope being wound around them, I stiffened. My list of 'nevers' included being tied or shackled in any way.

He tied them quickly, yanking to test their strength. Then he brushed a finger down one arm then up the other. "Arms over your head."

I struggled with the bindings, apprehension pushing me to the edge, my breathing more ragged than before.

"The harder you pull, the tighter they'll become. I wouldn't want you to chafe your lovely wrists."

The sound of his voice was soothing, but there was an underlying tone that heightened my senses, nerves pooling in my stomach. I found myself following his command, my mouth and throat dry from the anticipation.

He turned me around, easing me over the edge of the kitchen table, immediately spreading my legs far apart. "Did you know there's an art to providing just the right amount of pain to entice pleasure?"

"No, sir." I'd never called anyone 'sir' in my life, including my father. Why it didn't feel strange to me now I wasn't certain about, but it intrigued me. He pressed his hand on the small of my back then used the fingers of his other to tease me, rolling them along the insides of my thighs.

I was wet, so much so I gathered a whiff of my desire. As he continued caressing me, disturbing thoughts raced through my mind. What if he left me this way? What if he never allowed me to leave?

The more ridiculous they became, the more current raced through my muscles. I couldn't stop trembling as he rubbed his fingers over almost every inch of my back and legs.

"Perhaps one day you'll wear my mark permanently. For now, we'll begin your lessons in obedience."

His mark? I longed to see his naked body, to touch his heated skin. What little I'd been allowed to do hours before wasn't enough. I needed to explore all of him. After rolling fingers of both hands down my spine, he cupped both ass cheeks, digging his fingers in and lifting my pelvis off the table. Then he issued a growl and within seconds, he slipped his tongue around my clit, swirling the tip in circles.

"Oh..." The angle pressed my face into the cool wood, the tingling sensations incredible.

He spread me wide open, giving him full access. Within seconds, I was in a sweet moment of bliss, panting from the dancing vibrations.

Every sound he made was guttural, amplified more than they should be. He continued for several seconds until my pussy clenched and released. Then he pulled away completely.

Gasping, I lifted my head, longing for him to continue.

"Not yet," he muttered as if knowing what I was prepared to beg. I sensed he took another step away. Then I heard a sound, a moan escaping.

He was unfastening his belt.

"What do you hear?" he asked.

"The rustle of clothes."

"Be specific."

"Your belt."

"Yes. And what am I going to do with it?"

I shuddered from the realization. "Whip me."

"I would never use a whip on your beautiful skin. However, I will spank you as often as necessary both for discipline as well as to heighten your pleasure. Tonight is all about the latter, but I suspect the strap will be used often given you are very disobedient."

"Not true. I've been trained to follow rules."

"I do so like the sound of that. Your compliance will make everything that much easier."

His choice of words seemed strange, enough so my heart thudded several times.

"Easier?"

"For you to accept that there is a fine line where pain and pleasure become so intense that they are no longer distinguishable. I will bring you to both points. Accepting the rules of doing so will enhance the experience." He cracked his belt across my bottom with the very intensity he was talking about.

"Oh, God." I was immediately thrown into a cataclysm of fire and electricity, the anguish having no beginning or end. When he cracked another one in exactly the same place, I jerked up from the table, my body twisting.

Gabriel immediately yanked me back down, once again pressing his hand on the small of my back, rolling what felt like his thumb back and forth.

"Breathe, sweet Sarah. Allow the discomfort to resonate through your muscles."

There was no choice, my entire body spasming.

"Soon, you'll experience pleasure."

I heard the snapping sound of his wrist and bristled, preparing for another series of strikes. They came within seconds, but the sensations were entirely different. Three more and I was wetter than before, juice trickling between my thighs.

He caressed me again then my skin was tickled by his hair as he lowered his head, thrusting his tongue inside my pussy.

"Oh, yes. Yes..." A smile crossed my face as he lapped up the cream, growling like a predatory beast. He pushed at least two fingers inside, the orchestration almost bringing me to an orgasm, the anguish from before all but forgotten. As he'd done before, he brought me close then shifted back to spanking me.

Breathless, I had no idea how long the session lasted or how many times I came close to a climax, but I'd been shoved into raw ecstasy by both experiences. Exhausted, when he fisted my head, lowering his head and crushing his mouth over mine, I kept my eyes closed, unable to move a muscle. He was so forceful in every action, taking exactly what he wanted. There was no option, but I no longer wanted any physical freedom. Only the sweet release that he'd provided for my mind.

After sucking on my tongue for a few seconds, he chuckled darkly then turned me over. He planted his hands on either side of me, leaning over and dragging his tongue beseechingly slowly down my stomach, blowing heated air across my clit.

"Now, I feast, providing pleasure. You were a very good girl." I heard the sound of legs of a chair being scraped across the floor and assumed he'd sat down. He said nothing, almost as if he'd walked away.

I chewed on my lower lip, undulating back and forth on the table.

Then I heard another low-slung growl, the tone so ripe with emotion that it floored me. The man was famished.

As he gathered my legs into his arms, I refused to blink, longing to watch every second of the man devouring me. I fisted my hands, trying to keep my arms in place. I also wanted to touch him, to tangle my fingers in his thick hair.

He raked his fingers along the crack of my ass, teasing me by pressing a single tip against my dark hole. He was telling me without words what he planned on doing. The man was determined to claim me in every way.

Teasing me.

Tasting me.

Fucking me.

The thought excited the hell out of me.

Every move he made was possessive, but all I could concentrate on was the intensity of the sensations, the white-hot heat searing through my system. He sucked on my swollen clit then licked up and down several times.

He took his time, savoring every inch of me, using his finger in conjunction with his tongue. I couldn't stop quivering as he kept me split wide open. He'd been right in that every feeling, every slight touch was magnified, keeping my pulse racing and my mind a fuzzy blur. He knew exactly what he was doing to me, the ecstasy he was dragging me toward.

I lolled my head, trying to catch my breath as he brought me close to sweet release and I was certain he was going to back off just like he'd done before.

After pressing kisses on one inner thigh then the other, he pinched my clit. "Now, you're going to come for me when I tell you to."

"I don't think…" I couldn't come on command. There was no way.

"Yes, you will."

He buried his head in my pussy, his animalistic sounds filtering into my ears. I was more lightheaded than before, panting like some crazed animal. All I could do was concentrate on my breathing as I was brought close. Closer…

"Come for me. Come. Now!"

I was shocked that my body responded to his command, bottle rockets of nirvana stealing my voice. I tossed my head back and forth, bucking hard as he plunged his tongue inside. The sounds he made licking up my cream were raw and filthy, heightening the pure ecstasy. I was thrown by how intense the moment felt, the live wire of electricity shooting from one part of my body to another.

When a single orgasm became a giant wave, I finally let out a ragged moan that filtered throughout the entire kitchen. But there was no time to relax and recover, no rest for the weary.

The predator was hungry for more.

And there was nothing I could do.

CHAPTER 8

 abriel

Sarah remained rebellious, determined not to allow me to have control. While I adored that about her, the limited game of catch and release we'd already engaged in stimulating, I sensed she was getting closer to realizing who I was. She was the kind of woman who wouldn't stop until she learned the answers.

I'd been forced to lie to her by only providing my middle name and not my last. While I'd asked myself why I was bothering with toying with her, a part of the reason was to have her completely under my spell. I could keep her in a locked cage, only allowed out when she behaved, but I preferred her full compliance, her needs becoming unsatiable. Then I could truly control her, using her as a tool against her father as well as other enemies.

There were worse things than being married to the mayor's daughter. I could imagine the talk on the street, the fear that would be put into the other crime syndicates. That would extend endless power to our organization, providing several opportunities.

After I was finished garnering everything I wanted, I could choose to do many things with her.

Right now? All I wanted to do was shove my cock deep inside her tight pussy. I'd been salivating from the moment we'd climbed onto the plane. I'd guessed she'd had second thoughts the moment she'd walked into the kitchen. I'd intended on waiting to fuck her, but my desire to force her submission had overwhelmed me.

Every whimper she'd issued while I'd feasted had added gasoline to the fire. Every glance at her voluptuous body had pushed me closer to losing control. Even now as I yanked her bottom to the edge of the table, spreading her wide open, I could feel a part of myself becoming frayed. That wasn't like me, but I'd never experienced the kind of contemptuous need before this.

For the last several years, women had been nothing special, a method of obtaining satisfaction. In a few short hours, Sarah had rocked my world. I wanted to laugh, to berate myself for taking the forbidden fruit so easily, but I wasn't the kind of man to second guess any decisions. While my father would never approve of the decision I'd made, I was delighted in the way everything was working out.

She was no longer struggling, but I sensed her discord was increasing. Being robbed of a sensual perception was obviously frightening to her. However, I liked placing her on the very edge, pushing her out of her comfort zone. As I unzipped my jeans, the nervous tic on the corner of her mouth was all I could concentrate on. I wanted to kiss her for hours, tasting every inch of her.

What I had to consider was that from here on out she'd be considered my greatest weakness. What I couldn't do was allow my enemies to interfere with my plan, which would mean I'd need to provide twenty-four-hour protection for her once we returned. That would also allow me to keep an eye on her. I couldn't rule out that she already knew who I was, merely playing a game. If that was the case, she'd need to worry about much more than my ability to seduce her.

I took a deep breath and lifted her legs, yanking them back at an awkward angle. She purred a response, tossing her head back and forth. I wasn't a gentle man any more than I was romantic. I wanted to be rough with her in everything, pushing the boundaries to the breaking point.

She was so damn hot, her muscles constricting over my wide girth immediately. I used the anger and sadness I'd felt for weeks against her, dragging her up and down the table. Every sound she made fueled the fire until the open flames threatened to consume me completely.

Panting, I threw my head back, seeking salvation when all I could feel was hatred toward myself. My father. Hell, my own brother for dying. I'd wanted her to suffer and now all I wanted was to make her mine.

"Oh. Oh. Oh. Oh." Her moans escalated and she bucked hard against the table, trying to maintain her position yet her lips twisted from her growing annoyance.

There was something cathartic about fucking her like the brutal animal I was, plunging so deep inside that it had to cause her discomfort. But the only sounds she made were ones in the throes of ecstasy. That made me want more, pushing harder, taking everything I'd craved. This wasn't enough.

I pulled out, taking gasping breaths, jerking the shirt over my head and tossing it. I struggled to get my boots off, pitching them across the room. When I was fully undressed, I issued a husky growl, which put a smile on her face. She undulated her hips, moving back and forth. The glisten of her pussy in the light made me crazy all over again.

I yanked her arms down, fighting with the knot that had tightened in her struggles. When I finally managed to free her arms, I jerked her against me, ripping off her blindfold in the process.

She wrapped her legs around me, blinking several times as a smile curled across her face.

"You like it rough," I gritted out.

"Yes."

"Tell me what you want."

She hesitated, but only briefly, the look in her eyes full of unabashed longing.

"For you to fuck me long and hard. The harder the better."

Goddamn, the woman knew how to turn me on. When she dared to drag her tongue across her lips, I thought I'd lose my shit. I slammed her against the wall, crushing my full body weight against hers.

"Yes. God…" Sarah laughed, still blinking furiously as she stared into my eyes. But as she slid her hands over my shoulders, raking her nails into my skin, the slice of pain was exactly what I was hoping for.

I rolled onto the balls of my feet, jutting my hips forward, and impaled her again.

Her guttural sounds pleased the hell out of me. I pulled almost all the way out, slamming into her again. The angle was entirely different, going even deeper. The way her pussy muscles were clamping down on my cock made me fearful I'd blow my load too soon. I wanted this to last.

"Yes, you do like it, my little slut. Don't you?"

It was hard to believe she was turned on by my filthy words, but I could sense the dark side of her had longed to crawl out of its cave for years. I'd expected a powerful woman given her profession, but she was a powerhouse, which added to the arousal.

"So bad," she whispered breathlessly then tangled her fingers in my hair, giving me a mischievous look.

"You haven't seen anything yet." I pounded into her, my actions unrelenting. Within seconds, beads of sweat formed along my hairline. She dug her knees into me, trying to meet every savage thrust. Every sound we made was primal, beasts and nothing more.

Panting, she tilted her head, gasping for air and I couldn't resist biting down on her neck. She clawed my back hard enough I knew she'd drawn blood. Where had this little hellion come from?

I could tell she was close to climaxing given the way her eyelids were now half closed. I didn't need to command her, but I would just to make certain she knew who owned her.

Even if she wouldn't understand the full totality of that for a few days.

"Come for me, Sarah."

"I don't know," she breathed, lolling her head against my shoulder.

I shoved her hips against the wall, allowing me the leverage to wrap my hand around her throat.

Her eyes opened wide, her mouth pursing as I squeezed.

"You will do as I say. Come for me." My voice was dark, the deep baritone dripping with the lust that I could barely control. She took several shallow breaths, acting as if she'd dare defy me then her pussy muscles spasmed.

"Oh. Yes. Yes. Yes!" Her scream was high pitched, but the lilt was incredible, joyous to hear.

As I kept my hold, she returned her harsh gaze, refusing to give into fear or my dominance. Every part of me wanted to break down her defenses. I refused to stop, needing her to come again.

"That's it, sweet Sarah. I need more." I could no longer recognize the sound of my voice from the strain.

"I can't possibly—"

"Do it!" I interrupted, barking the order.

Even though she fixed her eyes on me for a few seconds, as another orgasm swept through her, I whispered in her ear, "Say my name. Say it, Sarah."

"Gabriel. Yes. Fuck me! Harder."

Most women didn't understand what that meant, but as I fucked her long and hard, I gathered she had a better understanding.

When I slowed down, she panted, her eyes dilated.

I wasn't finished with her yet. I would claim her ass tonight.

The second I removed my cock, she half laughed, allowing her gaze to travel down my chest. Then she took a single finger, tracing it around one of my tattoos.

Somehow, she sensed I would take her again, not fighting me when I yanked her around to face the wall. As I leaned in, she shifted her head, glancing over her shoulder.

"Now, I fuck you in the ass."

I wasn't a patient man, and she would soon learn how true the statement was. I pressed the tip of my cock against her asshole and took a deep breath before slowly easing it inside.

"Oh," she moaned, taking gasping breaths.

Goddamn, she was so tight. I could swear she was an anal virgin. The thought ripped through me like another wildfire. I was mad with the thought of being the only one to take her in her darkest hole.

When I fisted her hair, yanking her neck at an awkward angle, she whimpered. "No man has ever fucked you in the ass. Tell me the truth."

"No. Never."

It was as if the sun had lit up the night sky. I was elated, keeping one hand wrapped around her hair, the other clamping around her hip, pulling her away from the wall. This was where I could finally have relief. Beads of sweat dripped off my face onto her back, my vision muddied.

All I could think about was fucking her, making her mine.

She wiggled in my hold as I fucked her, my balls now aching so badly I could barely see straight. I thrust harder, the force I used driving her into the wall.

"You will never fuck another man. Only me. Do you understand?"

"Yes."

I cracked my hand against her bottom. "Yes?"

"Yes. Sir." There was more defiance in her tone.

"You are mine. Never forget that," I huffed, trying to hold on for a few seconds longer. "If anyone dares to touch you, they will die." I meant what I'd said. She said nothing, still panting as I became more savage.

When I was ready to release, I threw my head back and roared, filling her with my seed.

That's the moment I knew that Sarah Washington hadn't just become my weakness.

She'd become the weapon that would be used to try to destroy me.

* * *

Three days later

The Brotherhood.

I'd heard enough from Luciano regarding the initiation and vote that I knew what to expect. However, I didn't completely understand why the group of brutal men had been formed in the first place. I'd heard a few stories, but my brother had been tight lipped, a requirement of the rules they'd put into place.

As luck would have it, it had been my brother's turn to host the quarterly meeting. I chose Club Rio. I'd taken over Luciano's office, preferring the space on the tenth floor to that of the corporate office building housing the headquarters. The dark woods soothed me.

I'd also learned quickly that it was vital to keep a presence inside the club. With every turnover of management, there were always some employees willing to take advantage of the chaos. I refused to allow that to happen. Luciano had rarely stepped foot inside, spending most of his time in meetings, but when he had, morale had dropped.

I didn't mind that the employees were terrified of me. For now, that could work in my favor. I'd gone through the books, noticing some discrepancies and that would be first on my agenda after securing Sarah. Whether or not Demarco was responsible remained to be seen, although he had zero access to computer files.

I smiled, my balls tightening as I thought about her. Although she didn't know it, I'd given her the gift of maintaining her life for a few additional days.

Then she'd become mine permanently.

I'd already dispatched Dillon and another soldier to keep an eye on her, maintaining a close watch while not invading her space. I'd also asked him to find every scrap of dirt on Mayor Washington. There'd been assumptions made over the years, questionable payments to the man in large sums, but nothing concrete. I needed everything possible against him in his battle against us.

While Sarah's appearance in my life had yet to be made public, I had a feeling Moretti was watching me closely, prepared to strike at the first sign of weakness. The sooner the mayor backed down or played his hand the better.

Especially since I'd sent word that Theodora would never marry Nico. That would push Joseph's buttons, which should allow me to find out why Luciano was so dead set on killing the man. I had to keep my guard up at all times from now on.

The Brotherhood had been instructed to use the private entrance to the executive suite, but I'd chosen to enter by the front door, both bouncers immediately stiffening.

"Any issues?" I asked Bruno. He was not only head of security for the club, he was also considered the general manager. He was brutal, completely without a conscience and had no issue following orders. He was also brilliant with numbers as well as customer service, surprising given his usual demeanor.

"None. A full house. Some special clients, Don Giordano," he answered, grinning. That meant several of the elite members were indulging in gambling or partaking in fulfilling whatever proclivity suited them. I would take full advantage of keeping tabs on all of them, using their indiscretions against them if necessary.

I was surprised how much I'd changed in four short weeks. Tragedy was the reason. I found I enjoyed the role of Don more than I'd thought I would. What did that make me?

As I walked further inside, I sensed eyes were on me from the start. Every employee gave me a nod of respect as I passed by, but I could smell their fear.

For a Tuesday night, the club was very busy. I noticed several politicians as I walked through the main club floor. Before I headed to the elevator, I moved into the casino and was pleasantly surprised at what I found.

Mayor Washington was sitting at a table with friends, indulging in cognac and cigars. That wasn't in any way illegal, the state of New York appreciating the income provided by gambling facilities such as the club, but given his hatred for the Giordano family, his appearance was surprising. Or was it a subtle yet clear threat? I would soon find out.

I grabbed the arm of a cocktail waitress, pulling her aside. "Send a complimentary bottle of our finest cognac to my special guests." I nodded toward their table, watching them intently.

"Yes, sir. Right away."

I waited as she walked away, studying the room. Why Luciano hadn't spent more time here was beyond me. I would enjoy nurturing various… relationships. I waited for a few minutes, studying their actions. I knew for certain the mayor wasn't a member, which meant he'd been invited as a guest. Only yesterday at one of his frequent press conferences, he denounced every crime syndicate, reiterating his commitment to cleaning up the streets. I'd heard he'd recently received threats and had naturally assumed I was to blame.

That wasn't my style, at least not in any traditional method. I laughed and unbuttoned my jacket before heading in his direction. One of the other men at the table noticed me first, his posture becoming tense.

None of the men stood, preferring to act as if my arrival meant nothing, but I could see trepidation in several pairs of eyes.

"Good evening, gentlemen. I'm certain you're enjoying our accommodations," I said, casually glancing from one to the other.

Mayor Washington smirked, purposely blowing a puff of cigar smoke in my direction. "An interesting club, Giordano."

He'd never acknowledged any member of my family with a formal gesture, which had irritated the hell out of Luciano. To me, it was as telling as the slight tic in the corner of his mouth.

Just like so many others, he had no clue how I would handle the leadership position. It was enjoyable to keep everyone guessing. As the waitress approached the table, I remained silent.

"Compliments of the house," she said, placing the bottle in the center.

"I wouldn't want to cut into your profits," Senator Thompson said. He was a burly man in his sixties, once a force to be reckoned with. Now he spent his remaining two years in Congress arguing with anyone who didn't see eye to eye with him. He also had a penchant for underage girls, the photos I'd acquired stored in a safe location. He wasn't a threat, but if he dared cross me, he'd learn what facing my wrath felt like.

"Nonsense," I said with zero inflection. "Anything for our highly esteemed members. I want to ensure that you enjoy every aspect of what Club Rio has to offer. Just be careful that you don't step into quicksand. There is usually no method of rescue." I grinned, shifting my gaze from one man to the other.

"That sounds like a threat, Giordano," Mayor Washington said. "I don't like to be threatened."

"Remember that you are a guest here, Mayor. As such, I could quickly revoke your pass and I don't think that's something you want." I glared at him, daring him to push any harder. There was no doubt by the look in his eyes that he was up to something. It was up to me to find out what before the hammer fell, news regarding his daughter rocking his world. Fortunately, there'd yet to be any photographs in the new media of my face, only a shot of the family leaving the funeral, assumptions made that the younger brother would be taking over.

"Besides," I added. "I never make threats."

Timing was important. I certainly didn't want to hunt my little bird should she decide to flee in fear.

But I would.

Then I'd lock her inside her gilded cage.

"Enjoy your evening," I told them before walking off, heading toward the private elevator. I was certain I'd left a bad taste in his mouth. There would be more.

As I slipped the keycard into the slot, visions of Sarah's face drifted into my mind. She'd become a distraction, which wasn't in my best interest. Soon, she'd be seen as my weakness. I needed to prepare myself for being shoved into the line of fire. Additional security was already being installed at my house in the Hamptons as well as the condo in the city. I'd continue to use both for the time being.

I took long strides down the hallway toward my office, hearing voices just before walking in. When I opened the door, I took my time studying each man. They all came from powerful families across the United States, every syndicate commanding several states near their home base. The fact several inquiries had been made about taking the vacant seat left by my brother's death was a clear indication of how powerful the Brotherhood had become. I couldn't take admittance lightly.

Still, the men stood staring at me in a way that immediately pissed me off. I wasn't here to parade around like some circus freak. If that's what they wanted, they could shove it up their asses.

Constantine grinned as I closed the door, approaching with a drink already in his hand. "I hope you don't mind that we made ourselves at home."

"Of course not. It's my pleasure." Or was it? The Russian known as the Butcher held an icy glare. Maxim Nikitin was formidable. The fact he'd been adopted, thereby receiving his position, had been thrown in his face far too often, which made him an overachiever. Diego Santos was soon to take over from his ailing father, the cartel unlike any others I'd come in contact with. The family was sophisticated, owning a huge percentage of movie production firms and music houses in LA. They'd found a niche outside of illegal drugs, which was impressive. I'd spent time on every member, learning about their various activities. They were all savages.

I half smiled as I headed toward the bar, pouring a tall scotch.

While Phoenix Diamondis was the most jovial of the group, at least from what I'd heard, today he wore a scowl. Commanding Philadelphia was tough under any circumstances. With the Albanians breathing down his neck, he had his hands full with protecting his vast territory.

Brogan Callahan was the most interesting. He was a licensed psychiatrist, his position in the family likely never dragging him to the throne. He had full Irish blood running through his veins, although his accent was slight, but I'd heard he had a vengeful temper. Perhaps we'd get along just fine.

"Allow me to make the introductions," Constantine commented.

I leaned against the edge of my desk, curious as to what he'd say about every man, surprised when there was no glowing review of the person's accomplishments, only a simple matter-of-fact statement about each one. It was the same information I'd secured myself.

"Gentlemen. My brother spoke highly of you," I said, although Maxim was the first to catch the terse tone in my voice.

"But you don't approve," he threw at me.

"It's not for me to approve or disapprove," I said, turning my head in his direction.

"Then what the fuck are you doing here?" he continued.

"Because I invited him," Constantine stated. His voice held the same kind of control as my brother's had, but there was anger in his tone. "Luciano was a valued member of the Brotherhood. You knew his wishes as all of us know each other's. He had a say in who he wanted to be his successor in the case of his death. You will not take that lightly."

The news was a surprise to me. I hadn't realized Luciano had thought of me so highly. Luciano and Constantine had gone to the same college, Brogan a competing university, yet all three men had formed a bond, creating an empire of their own that spanned between the two schools. They were considered bad seeds, men not to be fucked with. The other two had been invited after an extensive search, and a determination that what they had to offer was best served keeping them as 'friends.' I only wondered how far the loyalty would go if push came to shove.

"Constantine is right," Brogan commented. "We will not fuck with that. Gabriel is now the head of the Cosa Nostra. The family is important to all of us, and you know that."

"That all depends on if you plan on making changes," Phoenix piped in.

"There is always room for change. However, the rules and standards of my family will remain the same." What was the man getting at?

He exhaled, giving his nod of approval after a few seconds. "Then so be it. I'm ready for the vote."

"Yeah. I have other issues to attend to," Brogan said in passing.

"Very well. Then cast your vote. You should know, Gabriel, that it requires a one hundred percent approval in order for you to become a member."

I glanced at Constantine, no longer surprised at the level of formality. In a game where all six of us were kings of our own empire, rivals in a dangerous game of power, strict rules would be necessary in order to keep one from feeding off another. That didn't mean we weren't predators, using every method to protect what belonged to us, but it did provide barriers that could not be crossed.

I could only imagine the punishment if one of us did.

"Gabriel Giordano is being offered a seat on the Brotherhood. What is your vote?" Constantine asked.

There was silence in the room for almost a full minute. It was at that moment I was forced to accept that while apart we were formidable, if required to work together, we would be an indestructible force.

Sighing, I took a sip of my drink, watching the ceremonial process with curiosity. One by one the men nodded, except for Maxim.

He walked closer, which instantly made me bristle. He was nothing but a viper, a man who had no emotions other than rage. "Your brother wasn't the kind of man who should have been in the Brotherhood. He was weak. I've heard you are impassive, which makes you nothing but another weak link we do not need." With that, he turned around, his lack of confidence pissing me off, but not nearly as much as what he'd just said about my flesh and blood. No one talked about my family, whether dead or alive, in such a disrespectful way.

Without hesitation, I slammed the drink on the bar, wrapping one arm around his neck while I ripped out my knife with the other, pressing the sharp tip against his jugular.

"I couldn't give a shit about who you are or what the rules of this group. If you ever disrespect a member of my family again, I will cut your nuts off first and feed them to the birds. Then I'll go from there."

The tension in the room was palpable. Then all five men started to laugh.

"Well done," Diego said, half laughing. "Luciano said you were a true savage."

Fuck me. The shit had been a setup to see what I was made of. In response, I dug the tip into Maxim's neck only enough to allow a trickle of blood to flow. Then I backed away, waiting as he turned around, slapping his hand across the slight injury. The expression on his face was priceless, hard as steel, his chest rising and falling from rage.

Then he burst into a grin. "You have balls, my new friend," he said, his accent surprisingly heavy for a man who'd lived a good portion of his life in the States.

"Don't fuck with me and I won't fuck with you," I said in retort.

"I think we all need a drink," Diego said.

"More than one," Brogan added.

While they refilled their glasses, I took a deep breath. There was a hell of a lot I didn't know about my brother. I still wondered what had set him off, leading to the tragic events. Sadly, it was something I might never be able to determine.

"I'm sorry about that. We had to know how committed you were," Constantine said as he flanked my side.

"I can't tell you that I am at this point. I have other issues to contend with."

"The Morettis."

"Yes."

"They've moved into Jersey. Word on the streets is they aren't content with owning the garden state. It would appear Philly is on their radar as well."

Phoenix approached, nodding from overhearing the conversation. "If the Albanians would feed off them, I wouldn't give a shit, but it appears they're working together."

Sighing, I realized it was time to pay Joseph Moretti a visit, if only to find out the reason my brother had flown off the deep end.

"Yes, my brother was determined to put an end to Joseph's reign before he died."

Constantine huffed. "A tall feat. He has security unlike anything I've ever seen."

"Well, I have something he wants," I said as I glanced from one man to the other. "My sister for his son."

"Arranged marriages," Brogan said, half laughing. "They're the mark of an ancient civilization that refuses to die a permanent death."

"Tell me about it. Pops is determined that I marry and provide at least one heir," Constantine said, his laugh boisterous. "Over my dead body."

"Well, if you use women to your benefit and she comes from the right connections, it can prove to be useful." I couldn't help but grin.

"I think wedding bells might be in the future, gentlemen." Constantine held up his glass. "If you need help with the Morettis, call one of us."

"What are the rules of this Brotherhood?"

He looked at me, not surprised I didn't know. "You don't fuck with each other, and the identities of the members and our conversations are private. If you disregard those rules, you won't need to worry about banishment."

"Understood."

"Let's get this over with. Luciano was a man of ceremony," Diego said more to me than anyone else.

"And will continue to honor the traditions he and I set in motion years ago."

Constantine's direction was clear. This was his baby, and it was something else not to be fucked with. I watched as he pulled a knife from his pocket then grabbed a bowl and what appeared to be over the counter alcohol. After pouring a stream over the blade, he lifted his eyebrows. "Blood oath."

I was no longer surprised at the level of seriousness. The commitment Luciano had to the family and to the Brotherhood was evident. I moved closer, placing my drink on my desk.

"Raise your right hand," he told me.

While I'd never been one for what I'd once called ceremonial bullshit, there was a sense of pride that flushed my system for being chosen. Maybe I was more like Luciano than I'd wanted to believe.

"Will you honor this Brotherhood until the day you take your last breath?" he asked.

"Yes, I will."

"And will you come to the aid of each member if necessary?"

"Yes."

He smirked as he placed the edge of the blade against my palm. "Then you are now a full member by giving of your word and your blood. Do not betray the Brotherhood or you'll know what living life in hell is like."

After the blade sliced into my hand, I fisted my fingers, allowing blood to trickle into the bowl. An odd feeling contradicted everything I'd once believed in. I felt like a part of a powerful force.

The strength of family was often considered entirely about blood, but often it became a curse, a toxic weakness that could spiral out of control. However, the blood formed from a bond, an oath not to be broken was sacred.

One thing I'd learned from Luciano that I would never forget.

Love could make you a strong force, but only loyalty could make you invincible.

CHAPTER 9

arah

"Jesus Christ. Who is this secret admirer?" Maggie asked as a gorgeous crystal vase was placed on the nurse's station in front of me by the same delivery driver as the day before. "And why don't you have them in your office?"

I glanced over my shoulder at the one from the day earlier, shaking my head.

"A special guy I know." Special. I wasn't certain that was the term I'd use. In all honesty, there were no adequate words for Gabriel other than dangerous and powerful. And dominating. I couldn't forget about that. The weekend had flown by and not all of it spent in bed. The snow had fallen through the early morning hours, leaving several inches of the most beautiful snow I'd ever seen.

He'd kept the fire going the entire time. We'd enjoyed fabulous food and wine, talking about nothing. And the passion had been off the charts, my entire body aching from the rounds of rough play. It had been a remarkable weekend. I tingled all over, wishing it could be repeated.

"And you know how tiny my office is. I couldn't get any paperwork done if I had them on my desk."

"True. The glamorous life of a surgeon. Well, I don't mind looking at them, pretending to be you."

I rubbed my fingers across my lips, unable to get the thought of him or the vision of his insanely gorgeous body out of my mind. I'd believed him to be carved in all the right places, but he was rock hard, chiseled to the point I'd been forced to blink several times to fully believe what I'd been looking at.

And his kisses had been to die for.

As I moved closer to the roses, this time white in color, the fragrance was almost overpowering. The buds were perfect, not one of them flawed. As I grabbed the card, the scrubs shifted across my bottom, and I was instantly reminded of the spanking he'd given me.

I still had difficulty believing I'd enjoyed being punished like a bad little girl. It was crazy to me, my personality such I'd thought I hated controlling men. But Gabriel made submitting desirable and safe, a contradiction in my mind.

"Honey, that's not from someone you call special. You need to call him a keeper. I've had so many duds lately that I'm beginning to think I'll never find Mr. Right."

"They don't exist, Mags. You need to train a man."

"Uh-huh. Is that what you did with the one you met in a coffee shop? Can you ask him if he has a brother?"

I laughed as I pulled the note from the envelope. There was one word placed directly in the middle in bold, black ink.

Soon...

It was the same as the card from the day before. No signature. No phone call later. Nothing. We hadn't made any plans after he'd driven me back to my apartment. But I'd known he would contact me again. The entire situation was strange, our relationship on the down low. I wasn't entirely certain I wanted that to change. I liked having a little secret tucked away.

Carrie had badgered me upon my return, but I'd said almost nothing. Even Maggie only knew that he was a stockbroker and was well off.

Her question made me realize I had no real clue about his family. "I'll ask if and when I see him again."

"Now, you're being coy. If you don't go out with him again, I'll call you nuts." She shook her head before moving toward the computer, her fingers flying on the keyboard. "Don't forget I'm taking a couple days off."

"I am nuts. Haven't you figured that out? I hope you're doing something kinky." I couldn't believe I'd said the words.

She glared at me, rolling her eyes. "The only kinky thing I'll be doing is going to flea markets with my sister. That's what she wanted for her birthday."

"Ugh."

"I'll say."

I moved to another terminal, checking the rest of the schedule for the day. The two surgeries earlier in the day had gone well, but there were two more scheduled, which could make for a long day. "What happened to the second surgery?" I asked, confused as to why I wasn't notified of a change in schedule.

When Maggie remained quiet, I lifted my head. What the hell was she looking at?

"Maggie?" She seemed to tense then beckoned me closer. I walked closer, narrowing my eyes. "What is it?"

"Keep your voice down. Look at that guy." Her voice was little more than a hoarse whisper.

I glanced at the smaller waiting room, noticing an older couple and a man dressed in black jeans and a dark jacket. "What about him? That's a waiting room."

"He was here yesterday, as in all day."

Half laughing, I twisted my head to look at her. "Some people do spend hours waiting for loved ones. Remember? We're in a hospital?"

"No," she said then turned around. "Yesterday when I was here, I accidentally bumped into him, and I could have sworn I saw a weapon in his pocket. I got busy then by the time I thought about it again, he was gone. I would have said something to you, but you'd left for the day."

There was no reason for there to be a sudden rush of creepy crawlies, but as the hair stood up on the back of my neck, I sucked in my breath. "Maybe you were wrong."

"I'm pretty observant. You know how I am. There's something not right about him being here."

While he wasn't looking in our direction, I did find it curious that he wasn't glancing at his phone or a magazine. Nothing. He was sitting there staring off into space. Granted, I'd seen and experienced what grief did to a person, so I couldn't jump to conclusions. "Look, just keep an eye out. If he does anything strange, let me know. Remember, we have surgery in an hour."

"I know and as far as the second one, I thought you knew."

"Knew what?"

"The man died late last night."

For a few seconds, my throat closed. While I had only spoken with the man and his family for a few minutes discussing his upcoming surgery, there was no indication his health was declining or that he'd become critical. "No, I hadn't heard."

"It was sudden. Cardiac arrest. I'm sorry. I would have told you."

"No, it's fine. I'm headed to my office."

"Hey. What's the hunk's name again?" she asked, her bubbly personality returning.

165

I gave her a stern look then laughed. "You promise you won't spread it around the joint?"

She acted as if she were zipping her lips shut, tossing away the key. "Scout's honor."

When she held up four fingers together, all I could do was laugh. "Now, I know you're lying. You were never a Girl Scout. His name is Gabriel Riccardo."

"Sexy name. What does he look like?"

"Get to work." I started to walk away then glanced back. "Let's just say he could be the next Zorro."

"Holy mother of God. I need one."

We both laughed but I noticed the mystery man had stood, now staring at the wall in front of him. Okay, his behavior was strange. I headed toward the elevator, thankful that as soon as I pressed the button, the doors opened. The steel box empty, as soon as I stepped inside, I turned around. Just seconds before the doors closed, he walked by without looking in my direction.

I found myself breathing a sigh of relief. I grabbed a diet soda from the breakroom before heading into my office. While there was a single window, it wasn't operable and didn't help with the stuffy appearance. I had a feeling the room had once been a broom closet. At least I could close the door and block out most of the usual hospital noises.

As soon as I sat down, I pulled up my files, searching for the man who'd died. As soon as I found his records, I noticed it was listed he had a heart murmur. I wasn't certain I'd remembered that. I sat back, shaking my head. Maybe I wasn't completely healed, at least in my mind. If I continued to second guess myself, it would only lead to serious complications, a need for a leave of absence. I couldn't afford to allow myself to fall into despair. It wouldn't serve me well.

Even though I buried myself in paperwork, I opened the door twice to peer into the hallway. Why? Was I really buying into Maggie's concern? There was no reason to. None. After the second time, I laughed and grabbed a few items to take to the shredder. The second I opened the door, Maggie appeared. We both jumped.

I laughed.

She didn't.

"What's wrong?" I asked. The woman was pale as a ghost.

"You need to come with me."

"What happened? Another patient?"

When she grabbed my arm, I was shocked. "No. I noticed something and thought you should see it." She dragged me into the breakroom, only letting me go to turn on the television.

"What is going on?"

"You'll see. I hope I can find it again. You father is giving another press conference."

"Maggie. You know how I feel about my father's political career." She'd caught me bitching after a phone call from dear old Dad, the man nagging me to come to dinner. I hated the pomp and circumstance around their evening meals, which was why the only time I'd been to the house recently had been Christmas. The four hours had been excruciating. I was nothing like my father and thankful for it. Carrie was the master of handling his pontification and his friends. Even on Christmas Day, he'd had two of his cronies over for drinks.

"Shush. Let me find it."

The moment she pulled the news at noon station on, his face and that of his groupies surrounding him came into view, and I turned away. "I'm not watching this."

"Sarah. Come here."

Groaning, I turned around just as she turned up the volume.

"And I will promise you that by the summer of this year, the beautiful streets of New York will be rid of such monstrous organizations such as the Giordano family, the Moretti clan, and the Pavlov Bratva. All who treat this beloved city like their own private shooting gallery."

My father's voice boomed over the microphones, the crowd of several hundred cheering him on as if he were a god. I was a little sick to my stomach. The fact he'd called the families out by name didn't surprise me. Nothing about my father did any longer. He believed he could walk on water and was bigger than the law.

"Turn it off."

"Wait. Listen."

I noticed it had been prerecorded, which meant Maggie had heard the entire speech before. I folded my arms, doing what she asked.

"And now, we have Gabriel Giordano in charge of the Cosa Nostra." My father stopped to laugh, staring at the adoring faces in the crowd. While the name yanked a red flag into the air, the city was full of Italians. The name Gabriel was nothing special.

When I exhaled, she threw me a look, trying to encourage me to stick around.

"This... kid had the nerve to threaten me last night. Do you believe that? Me, the man who's going to make certain he spends his life behind bars."

"Maggie. Is this about my date?"

Before she had a chance to respond, my father looked directly into the camera. "Now, I know that this boy had big shoes to fill, but the former stockbroker had better come at me with more than a verbal threat."

All time seemed to stop, my father's voice going into slow motion, his words garbled for a few seconds. Was it remotely possible that... No way. Not a chance in hell. But if that was the case, then the man I'd... fucked was the brother of the person who'd died. No. No. I couldn't go down that road. There was no chance it was possible. None. Karma wouldn't be that much of a bitch. "Gabriel is a popular name." My voice was shaky.

"I know that. But you need to see this. They're about to switch back to the newsroom."

I was shaking, my skin crawling all over as the scene in front of my father's office faded, folding into the newsroom. Walking closer, I stared at the screen as the female reporter stood beside various images of the Giordano family, including a photograph of the man who'd been in the accident.

And...

His brother, Gabriel Riccardo Giordano.

As all light faded from my periphery of vision, a strange image popped into my mind. A man carrying me, protecting me from an explosion. His face hovering over me, telling me everything was going to be okay.

His carved features and piercing eyes, the two-day stubble that added to his sensuality, and a well-defined jaw.

The man who'd brought me a Danish.

The man who'd purchased beautiful things.

The man who'd flown me on a private jet to an incredible cabin.

My lover.

My master.

And the man who'd told me he owned me.

As another series of strange sensations trickled down my spine, the door was opened, drawing my attention.

Everything remaining in slow motion, I turned my head, blinking as a nurse walked into the room. But before the door closed, I noticed the man from before standing in the corridor.

There was no doubt he was waiting for me.

To take me to Gabriel.

In order to fulfill a promise made.

* * *

Gabriel

Family.

I'd thought more about family since the Brotherhood meeting than I had in a long time. I stared at the ring on my finger, fisting my hand after doing so. It felt good to have one of my own. Luciano had been seven years older, enough so that I'd been the damn bothersome kid brother trying to tag along. When he'd left for college, I'd buried myself in my education, never athletic enough or a bully like my brother.

Luciano had graduated college, two years later he'd acquired a master's degree. By the time he was summoned home to work with our father, we were different people. He was more polished, yet darker than he'd been, boasting about the posse he'd formed at the university. The smaller facility catered to kids from the rich and famous, including sons and daughters of politicians and crime syndicates. The place at been explosive, at least according to Luciano.

But he and his group of vicious boys had taken full control, using their early training to become monsters against all those who dared cross their paths. Pops had never intended for me to attend the same university, considering it a waste of time.

Now I wondered if I would have turned out differently.

My attention drifted to my other hand and I wondered if the cut would leave a scar. My brother had called them battle wounds. I had several others, most received before I'd graduated high school where I'd grown six inches and gained eighty pounds of muscle.

I made the turn, heading toward the club when my phone rang. The caller wasn't who I'd expected. Maria. My sister almost never called. The fact she'd remained in New York, taking a modeling gig close to home had helped my mother in her grief. While my mother was a strong person, as she'd told me more than once, a child should never go before his or her parents. Since Luciano's death, she'd tried to get me to stop by more often, which I had yet to do.

It always turned out the same, my father telling me everything I was doing wrong. Then as he sucked down more liquor, the conversation always managed to turn nasty. Now that I'd broken the handshake agreement that had been tentatively set in place regarding Theodora and Nico, I was certain my father was livid that I'd overridden one of his decisions. That wouldn't bode well for family get-togethers.

"Maria. What can I do for you?"

"You have no idea what you did. Why? Why the fuck do you have to stick your nose into everything? Why?"

I'd never heard her so upset, her use of language surprising me. She was the demure one, Theodora rough and tumble.

"What are you talking about?"

"You had to make things worse for Theodora. Didn't you? You just had to do it!"

She was borderline hysterical. "Calm the fuck down. What is going on?"

"Don't tell me to calm down! You haven't been a brother to anyone in years. Years! I needed you in Italy and you refused to help me. Now, you sealed her fate. He'll kill her next time."

"Whoa. Hold on. What?" I gritted my teeth, pushing the Maserati to eighty, shifting across six lanes of traffic in order to take an exit off the highway. She'd never expressed this much hatred, her adoration of me something my parents joked about.

"She's hurt. He hurt her!"

"Who are you talking about?"

"Nico. He beat her. Damn you. That wouldn't have happened if you hadn't called off the wedding."

What. The. Fuck? "Where is she?"

"She's here. She came home crying and locked herself in her room. I had to break in." Maria's voice was shaking as she started to sob.

"I'm on my way. Lock the goddamn doors."

"Okay. Okay. Just hurry."

I nearly tossed the phone through the window. If that son of a bitch was responsible, he would be dead by nightfall. I had to concentrate on Theodora. However, it was time to bring Sarah home. If Joseph and Nico came after my sister, it was only a matter of time.

As I raced through the streets, I constantly glanced into the rearview mirror. I also couldn't put it past the Morettis to plan a larger attack. What the hell did the asshole think he was going to accomplish by beating up my sister? I yanked the phone into my hand, dialing Dillon's number.

"Bring her in," I told him as soon as he answered the phone.

"The doc's in surgery. Do you want me to interrupt?"

Shit. Shit. I slammed my hand on the steering wheel. "No, but as soon as she's out, grab her and bring her to my condo for now."

"You got it, Mr. Giordano."

"And make certain security is beefed up around my parents' house."

"Did something happen?"

"Yeah, it did. Tonight we go hunting. Be prepared."

Dillon snorted. "I'm always prepared."

Once again, I ended the call, fuming from everything that had occurred. All I could think about was snapping Nico's neck between my fingers. I would enjoy spending hours with the man, breaking bone after bone.

My heart thudding against my chest, I barreled through an intersection, barely avoiding hitting an oncoming car.

Calm down. Think.

I hadn't gotten this angry since…

Fuck. Karma had manifested itself into pure evil. Maybe that's all the family deserved. Well, to hell with fate or any other spiritual bullshit.

As I pulled into the gated neighborhood, I continued to scan the street. My parents had lived in the same house for thirty years, only recently renovating every room. While the area was secure, there wasn't a single enemy who didn't know where they lived. There were also easy breaches, allowing soldiers to get in on foot without being seen. I would need to rectify that.

Immediately.

I swung into the driveway, still going over twenty miles per hour, slamming on the brakes then barely cutting the engine before I jumped out. I didn't bother pounding on the door, barreling inside and terrifying two of the house employees.

"Mr. Giordano!" one woman squealed.

"I'm sorry, Vanessa."

"Your parents aren't here."

"Good." I rolled up the stairs two at time, storming down the hallway toward Theodora's room. She'd told me recently that she hated being forced to live at home, but the one time she'd threatened to pack up and leave, our father had backhanded her. That wasn't like him at all. He'd never taken a hand to the women in his life. He'd told me more than once that women were the true blessing in the world and deserved to be treated with kindness.

He was one of the few Dons who'd never had a mistress. He'd earned my respect for that if no other reason.

I tried the door, realizing it was barricaded. Then I pounded on it. "Theo, let me in. Unlock this door now."

"Go away!" Theodora bellowed.

I took a deep breath, rubbing my jaw. Then I pressed my hand against the wall, trying to calm my rage. "Honey. Open the door. Please."

"She doesn't want to see you," Maria said.

"I don't care. I will kick down this door if I need to."

I heard their voices and finally footsteps, something being scraped against the floor. As Maria opened the door, she tried to block me. Then she pointed her finger in my face.

She'd grown up since spending time in Italy, becoming a powerful woman in her own right. She was right. I'd ignored her plea of going to Italy with her. She'd been terrified of living in a country she had no knowledge of, even if her grandparents had only been a phone call away.

"Don't you dare upset her any more than she's already been. Do you hear me?" she hissed.

"I don't plan on upsetting her." No, I planned on breaking Nico's neck.

"Fine. I'll be watching you." She backed away, opening the door wider.

Theodora stood by her window, staring down at the gardens. She loved being outside, getting her hands dirty while planting flowers. I'd adored that about her. It was her way of ignoring the family requirements and soldiers parading the grounds. She'd also grown into a beautiful young woman, fierce and protective. Now she needed protection from the same monsters my father had intended her to spend the rest of her life with.

I walked closer, Maria trailing closely behind. When I was within a few inches, her shoulders sagged.

"What happened?" While I tried to keep the anger from my voice, it was almost impossible given the adrenaline coursing through my system.

We'd said a few not so kind things to each other since Luciano's death, all of which I regretted.

"What do you care?" she said curtly, although her voice was breaking up.

"È nostro fratello," Maria snapped. He's our brother.

She'd taken to using more Italian since her years spent in Italy.

"È proprio come nostro padre," Theodora retorted. He's just like our father.

It was cute they believed I couldn't understand them.

"Our father would go ballistic, already burning down the city in order to hunt Nico down. I want to hear it from your lips that he beat you. And I need to see what he did." That last thing I needed to do was to make a decision without learning the truth. Nico's life could depend on it.

She took a deep breath, Maria squeezing her arm. Then she turned around.

I'd experienced bloodlust enough times to know when it was something I would eventually get over.

Not this time.

To see Theodora's beautiful face swollen and with bruises was something that would never be tolerated. Not in my lifetime.

"Did Nico do this to you?" I growled, both hands fisted.

She shook her head. "You know he would never get his hands dirty. He sent one of his henchmen to do it. I was given a message to pass along to you. I will marry him or else."

Son of a bitch. I took a deep breath, resisting touching her. Then I walked toward the window. I couldn't control my anger, slamming my fist into the glass. "He will die."

Both my sisters jumped, yelping from the noise as the force I used cracked the window.

"My God, Gabriel. You can't do this." Maria immediately headed toward me, pulling my hand into hers. It was the same one the blade had been pressed again.

The pain was refreshing, the action keeping my anger from getting out of control.

For now.

But I couldn't allow this to go without retaliation. It was a test, my sister taking the brunt of it. Goddamn my father for promising her hand in marriage.

"Leave him alone," Theodora whispered. "He was just angry."

"Angry?" I repeated. "He doesn't know the meaning of the word."

"You're bleeding," Maria said. "I'll get you a towel."

"I'm fine."

"Bullshit." As she headed for the bathroom, Theodora confronted me.

"What are you going to do?"

"You heard me. You're not marrying the freak if that's what you mean."

"I have to."

"Like hell you do. We don't live in the goddamn dark ages."

"You don't understand," she snapped.

"What don't I understand? That our father wants you to be married to a monster to build some bridge? That Nico is a primate and nothing else? That he will do this to you any time he feels like it? Over my dead body."

"Then they'll force Maria to marry him. I can't let that happen. I won't!"

I took a deep breath, staring into her eyes. "Admirable but neither one of you are going to marry into that family."

As tears trickled down her face, she pursed her lips. "He won't stop. You don't know him like I do because you haven't been around. He's..." She looked away, chewing on her lip.

"I know I haven't and I'm sorry."

She glanced all the way down my torso, noticing the ring. "You took his ring."

I lifted my other hand, shaking my head. "No. I would never do that."

Her eyes opened wide with shock. "You're a member now. The Brotherhood. They asked you to become a member."

"How do you know about the Brotherhood?"

"Luciano used to confide things to me. He treated me like an equal, not like his little sister, something you couldn't understand."

There was so much animosity that an ache formed in my heart. "How many times can I apologize? I can't erase the past. All I can do is promise that the future will be different."

As Maria returned, wrapping my hand in a wet towel, I accepted the fact I'd been a shit for a brother. That didn't make the situation any better or easier to swallow. I need to destroy the Moretti family first. Then I'd work on the relationships.

"Just keep your word, brother. We can't take another tragedy inside this family. Mother cries herself to sleep every night," Maria huffed.

"And I plan on doing something about it."

"By hurting the woman in the accident?" she threw at me.

There were no secrets in this house. "I have no intentions of hurting her."

A wry smile formed on her face. "Let me guess. You plan on marrying her. I know who she is, the mayor's daughter, a man who called you out on national television just this morning."

"What are you talking about?" What the fuck had the mayor done?

"You threatened him? Well, he named you as public enemy number one with a pictorial."

I sucked in my breath. There was more than a remote chance that Sarah had seen the news report. There was a hell of a lot to do in a short period of time. "I want both of you to listen to me. You are not going anywhere without one of my men accompanying with you. Do you understand me?"

"You're not our father, Gabriel, barely our brother," Theodora shot back.

The cut was the kind she was so good at, her sharp tongue something I admired. She refused to play the princess role, which was in her genes. However, she also had no real sense of danger since she'd been protected from the family drama for most of her life.

"No, but I am head of this family now. You will do as I say."

Maria laughed. "I should never have stayed."

"Maybe not, but as long as you're in this country, you will follow the rules." I glanced from one to the other. "My rules."

"The Morettis will retaliate," Theodora said.

"And I'll be ready." My phone rang, the interruption bad timing. As I yanked it into my hand, I sensed Dillon wasn't calling to tell me Sarah was ready and eager to face her destiny. "What is it?"

"The doctor disappeared from the hospital. I checked her apartment. She's not there."

The man had failed me again. That wouldn't happen a third time. "If you've lost her and anything happens, you will pay the price."

"Yes, sir. I'm sorry I failed you."

"Keep hunting. Sarah must be found." As soon as I ended the call, I headed for the door. "I will lock you both in your rooms if you disobey my orders."

"Like father. Like son," Theodora snarked. "You're think you're a king now. Don't you?"

A king. That's what members of the Brotherhood called themselves. Maybe that's how I needed to start acting.

"I will do what it takes to keep you safe." I glanced from one to the other, trying to control my breathing.

"Tell that to the woman whose life you're about to destroy, *brother*."

Even though I opened the door, determined to find Sarah, I took a few seconds to mull over my sisters' words. The weight of my decisions was bearing down, but now wasn't the time to second guess. A war would soon begin.

Then I'd paint the streets in Moretti blood.

CHAPTER 10

 arah

"Carrie. Listen to me. Can I bring the dogs to your house?" I was gasping for air, my voice unrecognizable.

"What's wrong?" she demanded.

"I can't talk right now. Just tell me if I can."

"Look, I have to do—"

"Listen to me!" I snapped, my nerves frazzled.

"Jesus. What the fuck is going on?"

"I'm being stalked."

"By whom?"

"A monster. I don't have time to go into it. Can I bring the dogs to your place?"

"Well, sure. But I need to know what's going on." Carrie was obviously upset, her voice shaking.

I struggled in the seat, twisting so I could look at the traffic behind me. "I don't have time." I'd risked being caught by taking my car, but at least it was in a secured location that the asshole couldn't find. Maybe the bastard didn't know what I drove, although I had a feeling that Gabriel had investigated me, learning everything about my life, including what car I drove. Still, Carrie lived far enough away from my apartment that I couldn't walk the dogs there. Oh, God. What was happening? Why? I'd done nothing wrong.

But you believed you killed his brother.

Fuck the little voice. Yes, I'd had survivor's guilt, but it was an accident. I certainly hadn't planned on losing control, the car spinning.

"I'm leaving work now. I'll meet you there. Whatever is happening, be careful, sis." I had to be worried about Carrie's safety as well. There was no telling what Gabriel would do. What I did know was that the man was powerful. He was also dangerous.

I ended the call, shoving the phone into my pocket as I drove into the parking garage, barely able to catch my breath.

A stalker.

Gabriel was stalking me, hunting his prey. There was no other explanation for what had occurred between us. I'd ditched the surgery by begging another surgeon to handle the simple procedure. After watching the news reel, I'd tried to calm my nerves, even though the terror became paralyzing. The man outside had remained close, hovering like a vulture. I'd finally caught a glimpse of his weapon and there was no doubt he was prepared to capture me.

The reason?

Luciano Giordano's death.

Did his brother blame me for the accident? Was I some pawn in a horrible battle between my father's regime and a powerful syndicate? Whatever the reason, I would be the one to pay in the dangerous, vicious game.

With my life.

I hadn't succumbed to playing a victim my entire life. Not as a kid when I'd been bullied or the assault on the subway years before. I'd fought back both times, one leaving me with bruises and broken bones. And I'd do the same thing again.

I constantly glanced over my shoulder, calculating how much time I had before the end of the surgery. The second another surgeon left the operating room, my ruse and time would be up. As I headed toward the elevators, creeping sensations swept over me. I could barely catch my breath, the fear suffocating. I slapped my hand on the button, dancing from one foot to another. While I had mace in my purse, I was no fool. That wouldn't work for two seconds.

Especially against the big, fat gun.

What had I been thinking, not doing my own investigation of Gabriel before I said yes to a date? I knew better and not just because I was living in New York. There were nut cases everywhere. He'd wowed me, seduced me, and I'd been a willing party. And to think the man had been my hero, saving my life. It was all too crazy. Why save me then plan on killing me?

That's what all mafia guys did. Right?

Now I was thinking crazy, but at least my mind was working.

The elevator rattled, an indication of the age of the building. When it finally pinged, indicating my floor, I almost had a panic attack.

You can't do this.

There was my little voice again. Bitch.

When I stepped into the dimly lit hallway, I held my breath, scanning both sides. There was no one and no noise given the time of day. Most people worked a normal job, which left the building almost empty.

No one will hear you scream.

True enough.

At least I'd grab some kitchen knives, taking them with me. All I needed to do was grab a few things, the pups and I was out of here. Hopefully things would be that simple. My hands were shaking as I unlocked the door, noticing there was no sign of forced entry. Before I opened the door, I glanced at my watch. I had at least another thirty minutes but that was it.

As I walked inside, I remained where I was, listening...

The only thing I heard was the scampering of little paws and the woofs both Goldie and Shadow always did when someone came home. I nearly fell to the floor in relief after closing the door, allowing them to lick my face as tears started to form.

Nope. I wasn't going to do this. It was time to suck it up and get the hell out of here. Should I call my father? And tell him what? Some strange man was hovering in the hospital? That I'd made the mistake of dating then fucking the very man he intended on destroying? Yeah, that would go over well. Besides, if I was wrong and became the reason Gabriel was sent to prison, which is something my father would force to happen, then I would never be able to live with myself.

"Okay, babies. We're going on a little adventure. Okay?"

Woof! Woof!

At least they had no idea what was going on, although Shadow gave me a strange look, as if he knew I was crawling with fear.

"I'm going to grab a few things and some toys." I almost choked on the words, a fog forming in my mind. I dropped my purse then headed for the bedroom, Goldie following. I nearly yanked the shelf off the wall from the force I used grabbing a duffle bag.

Then I stuffed a few items inside before heading to their toybox, snatching a few items that would keep them occupied. I'd buy another bag of dog food later. Perfect. I had everything I needed.

I tossed the bag onto the bed then grabbed a pair of jeans and a sweater, struggling to get into them. Ice ran through my veins, and I did what I could to yank anger from the depths of my being. If I was enraged, I could work faster. Goldie remained by my side and the second I rubbed behind her ear, a horrible sensation jetted through me.

Shadow was never far behind. Never. Especially when I came home. They were constant companions, refusing to leave my side for at least thirty minutes.

Swallowing, I continued to pet Goldie, blinking tears away. "Shadow? Come here, boy."

I heard nothing. No whining. No barking.

"Shadow!"

Oh, God. What was going on? Even my damn phone was in the other room. "Stay here, girl." As soon as I petted Goldie one more time, she took off into the living room, barking three times then stopping.

Now the fear was uncontrollable, my heart racing. I glanced around the room, finally yanking a lamp from the bedside table. As I held it in both hands, I crept slowly toward the door, darting my head around the corner.

"Babies? Come to Mommy."

When I heard a tiny whimper, my mind was too fucked up to know from where. The kitchen? My small study on the other side of the living room? I took several shallow breaths and headed further into the main room, my eyes sweeping from one side to the other. Then I crept closer to the kitchen. There was no one inside. That left one location.

Jesus Christ. The front door was between me and the study. I could bolt out, trying to get help.

Then what would the motherfucker do with my babies? No. I would protect them with my life. I firmed up my grip on the base of the lamp then took long strides toward the room. When I stood a couple of feet outside, I didn't see a thing.

I'd been told I had the courage of a saint. It was time to put that to the test.

I walked inside, prepared for what I'd find.

My eyes were drawn to my furry babies lying comfortably by the small sofa, both with brand new bones in their mouths.

And the intruder sitting in the center with a drink in his one hand, a weapon in the other was the man I'd believed I had an incredible connection with, hoping our budding relationship would turn into more.

He was as gorgeous as ever, the light stubble covering his strong jaw making him appear even more dangerous, the flash of his eyes indicating lust as well as slight amusement. The same electricity crackled in the air, stifling my breath. He appeared comfortable in my home, stroking Shadow's head as he stared at me, his legs crossed, his jacket unbuttoned.

All I wanted to do was wrap my hands around his throat, strangling the life out of him.

But I knew I'd never get the chance.

"Hello, Sarah. I think it's time that you and I got to know each other even better."

"Who the fuck are you?" I shifted from one foot to the other, my muscles tense but I wouldn't hesitate to use the lamp, smashing it against his head. I only hoped it would crack his skull open.

He lowered his gaze to my hands, his smile widening. And he continued to stroke Shadow, who couldn't be happier.

"And what did you do to my dogs?" The anger was finally surfacing, spewing from my mouth.

"I did nothing. I find that with all things precious, you only need to use dark commands while providing reinforcement. Wouldn't you say that to be true, my beautiful submissive?"

"Fuck you. You stalked me. You used me."

"Yes, and I will do it again."

His words no longer stunned me, his arrogance just what I would have expected. But his intentions were what horrified me.

"Get out of my apartment or I will call the police," I snapped.

"And say what, exactly? That I broke into your apartment? There are no signs that I did. That you don't know me? Well, I have a few trinkets I could show them from our time spent together." When he pulled a pair of my panties from his pocket, holding them against his nose, I had to fight to keep a moan from escaping.

"You're a sick fuck."

"You once called me handsome. What did I tell you?"

"That you were a monster."

"And see? I didn't lie to you. I am a monster, a man created from your nightmares." His deep voice penetrated the room, sending a cascade of sizzling vibrations into my core. Every emotion rocked my mind and heart, but it was the hot and wet feeling pooling between my legs that horrified me.

How could I be attracted to a killer?

Should I believe all the horrible things my father had said, his insinuations that the Giordano family were brutal murderers? I didn't know what to believe and couldn't rely on my instincts at this moment. The same dazzling feelings remained even though I was sick to my stomach.

He casually took a sip of his drink then placed the glass on the table in front of him. My glass. My liquor. My house.

He'd invaded my space, as if he had the right to do so.

"Get out," I said again, as if I believed he would comply with my demand.

Laughing, he rose to his feet and all six foot three of him seemed more menacing than before.

"I'm afraid that's not going to happen, at least not without you by my side."

"You're crazy if you think I'd go anywhere with you." I lifted the lamp, daring to take a step closer.

He lifted his eyebrow in response, more amused than ever. "Go ahead, Sarah. If it makes you feel better, take a swing at me, but I assure you that if you miss, you'll regret it."

"You're threatening me?"

"No, as I've told several people as of late," he said in his husky voice as he moved around the table, glancing lovingly down at my fur babies, "I never make threats. Just promises."

"I don't care why you're here; I don't want you to remain."

"Oh, I think you do. In fact, I think you're hungry for what only I can provide."

"Asshole."

"Isn't your pussy aching, longing to have my cock driven inside? Are your nipples hard, fully aroused from the thought of all the filthy things I will do to you? Isn't your heart racing, blood pumping through your veins from the longing to succumb to my needs?"

"Not for a second."

"You're lying to yourself. Now, we can do this the easy way or the hard way. If I'm forced to take you with me, you won't like the punishment you receive. However, if you come with me willingly, then you'll enjoy the start to your new life."

The man was out of his fucking mind. "As I told you, I'm not going anywhere with you." I refused to back away when he took a step closer, fighting the urge to burst into tears. No. It wasn't going to happen.

"Then the hard way it is." With two long strides, he grabbed my arm, trying to swing me around.

I reacted instantly, smashing the lamp against the side of his face, breaking the connection. Then I bolted toward the door. "Babies. Come!" Thank God they listened, scrambling to follow me while Gabriel roared in the background. I had my hand on the doorknob, twisting it when the door was kicked in. The force pummeled me backwards and against the arm of the couch. Gasping, I watched as the man from the hospital entered, slamming the door behind him then heading in my direction.

He managed to grab my arm, jerking me against him then wrapping his arm around my neck after turning me around. He stood like a fucking statue as I struggled, but his hold was tight enough every sound I issued was little more than a strangled gasp.

"Let... me... go."

The dogs were barking, snapping at the man. When he acted as if he was going to kick Shadow, I rammed my elbow into his gut.

"Don't... you dare!" I continued fighting him even as I heard footsteps. The sight of Gabriel walking into the room left me petrified. Blood trickled down the side of his head, his features contorted as rage swept through him. He held the gun in his extended arm, pointing the barrel at my face.

"You shouldn't have done that, Sarah. Now, I will need to punish you." Gabriel cocked his head, dragging his tongue across his lips and it was all I could do not to retch in front of him. As he lifted his gaze toward the man holding me, anger returned.

"You fucking lost her," Gabriel snarled. Then he shifted the weapon toward the man. "That was the last time."

"I'm sorry, boss. I thought she was in surgery," the man said. There was no pleading done, just a dull emptiness, as if he knew his life was over and accepted it. That was crazy. However, he loosened his grip, maybe prepared to toss me aside when the bullet went through his brain.

"Don't you dare kill him. It was my fault. I had another surgeon do a procedure for me." What the hell was I doing defending the bastard? What was wrong with having one less criminal in the world?

Because you're not a killer. You save lives.

The thought was both cathartic and irritating.

Very slowly Gabriel returned his gaze to my eyes. In all the times he'd looked at me, studied me, wanted me, he'd never had such an intense look in them. He was looking into my soul, ripping it apart then putting it back together. Next would be my body.

And he'd dared try with my heart.

Fuck him.

"I'll take his punishment," I added, which shocked the man I'd once thought I cared for.

A smile slowly spread across his angular face. "You'd take punishment for a man you don't even know?"

"Yes," I said without reservation.

"That either makes you a martyr or a woman with a heavy conscience. I wonder which it is." He debated my offer, taking a deep breath then lowering his weapon. "Then so be it, my beautiful bird. But remember the deal you made for his life."

I could no longer swallow, my body trembling as the man held me.

Gabriel placed his weapon in his jacket then walked closer. He gripped my chin painfully, rubbing his thumb across my lips. "You do know who I am."

"Yes. You lied to me."

"No. I did not. I simply didn't tell you my given last name. I've used Riccardo for years."

"Why? Why hide who you are?"

He debated my question. "Because it was necessary. Here's what's going to happen. You're coming with me."

"Why?"

"One life for another. You took my brother's life. Now, I take yours."

"Then go ahead and kill me."

His firm hold remained, and he nodded to the man who instantly released me. Gabriel fisted my hair at my scalp, dragging me into my toes, forcing me against him. I was repulsed, slamming both fists against his chest.

196

"If I'd wanted you dead, your family would be mourning by your gravesite," he stated with utter dominance in his voice.

"You are such a bastard. I didn't kill your brother on purpose. You know that. And why did you save my life? Why? So you could torture me?"

His eyes opened wide for two seconds, long enough for me to realize he was surprised I'd recognized him completely. "Because he asked me to."

There was no reason for the information to hit me hard, but it did. I was still sick inside, my mind foggy as events from that horrible day played out. Suddenly, I felt weak, disgusted with myself even if I knew there was no reason.

He lowered his head, taking several deep breaths. "I've waited patiently for this day to come, to have what belonged to me on the day he died."

"That's insane. I don't want this."

"What you want no longer matters."

"What are you going to do?" Why was I bothering to ask?

"It's simple. You're going to do everything I demand of you. Then you're going to become my wife."

His wife. What? Hold on. Was this some sick kind of joke?

"No. I will not do it."

"You don't have a choice."

As his lips brushed against mine, the same tickling sensations rushed through every cell and muscle just as they'd done before. I wanted to be sickened but desire roared through me, nullifying the fear and hatred. How was that possible?

He crushed his mouth over mine, holding our lips together for several seconds before slipping his tongue inside. He tasted of bourbon and cinnamon, his scent infiltrating every cell. I was lightheaded, butterflies in my stomach, my body betraying me as he explored the darkest parts of my mouth.

I clenched my eyes shut, unable to shove aside the dancing vibrant colors as the hunger increased. While I felt sick inside, I knew the real sickness was how much I remained attracted to him. We'd entered into a toxic tryst that would end badly. Yet my fisted hands clenched around his shirt, my back arching as the kiss became a passionate roar.

I couldn't control myself, my mind a blur even as electricity rocketed through us. How could this be happening? How could I fall into such a dark abyss?

When he broke the kiss, he nuzzled against my neck, nipping my earlobe. "If you disobey me under any circumstances, you will be punished. If you attempt to escape, I will find you." He eased back so I could look into his eyes. "And when I do, the kind of punishment I'll issue will remain with you for a very. Long. Time."

A lump remained in my throat and for some reason, I searched for any sign of humanity in the man. All I witnessed was the dark veil that had replaced the spark in his eyes, something evil and dangerous. I'd fallen for his blatant seduction, giving him my body as well as my trust.

And I'd fallen for the man himself.

"Take her to your car. Make certain she is unable to escape," he directed toward the man.

"What about my babies? I will not leave without them. You will not hurt them, or I will kill you. I will find a way." I was almost hysterical, tears slipping past my lashes.

Gabriel looked over his shoulder at them then sighed. "I may be considered a monster to humans, Sarah, but I will never hurt an animal. Change in plans. Take the dogs with you, Dillon. Make certain they are provided food and water."

"In your house or the condo, Don Giordano?" Dillon asked.

Don Giordano? Panting, I knew I was losing my mind.

"The house. I think absolute privacy will be needed," Gabriel answered, laughing hoarsely. "I will handle Doctor Washington myself."

With that, orders were given, and my world was turned upside down. What would happen from here I couldn't guess.

But I knew he was right.

They would be the things nightmares were made of.

Gabriel

I waited until Dillon had left with the dogs, standing near the window of her study. I'd been subjected to her sobs as she'd hugged them goodbye, insisting Dillon take the bag she'd packed with him. To her credit, she hadn't hurled insults or threatened me. It was as if she was accepting her fate.

A better man would feel guilty for destroying her life. But I wasn't that man. The more time spent accepting my role, the less human I became. That had been my father's hope all along. I took a sip of my drink, finding it odd the taste was now bitter. When I turned to face her, I could smell her continued fear, now stronger than the earlier desire we'd both shared.

She rubbed the wetness from her eyes, turning around to face me, her expression of rebellion returning. "For the record, I will never give into you willingly again. Not once."

"That may be true, but it won't change anything."

"No, of course it won't. You're used to getting what you want. You'll always be a criminal, a murderer."

The fact I had yet to commit murder in any capacity wouldn't matter to her. In her eyes, I'd become an enemy.

"Yes, Sarah. I take what I want."

"You have no right."

"Just like your father has no right to persecute us." Was I going to spend time defending my family? That was bull-shit. I'd never done that with anyone else.

She smiled at me, shaking her head ever so slowly. "You're completely deranged."

"Maybe so."

"I hate you. That will never change no matter what you do to my body."

It was better that she hated me, at least for now. "So be it. Remove your jeans."

Her response was to fold her arms, keeping her glare.

"Do you remember the deal you made, the punishment you offered to accept in exchange for Dillon's life? Or have you forgotten so quickly?"

As her lower lip quivered, I could tell she was having a difficult time maintaining the thick armor she'd placed around herself. She glanced away, blinking several times. The woman standing in front of me was so damn strong, more so than anyone else I'd ever met. I admired that about her.

It also made my balls tighten. I didn't want to take her here. Maybe I was the asshole hoping for a sick fairytale, wanting her to submit by her own free will. That might never happen again. Still, keeping her safe was as important to me as using her to take down her father. The dichotomy was leaving a vast break in my usual way of handling business.

"Or would you prefer to watch as I exact punishment on Dillon instead?"

"Don't you dare. Don't you fucking dare. I don't know why you consider yourself God, but you're nothing but a little man hoping to boost your ego by lording your power over everyone you meet. Whatever you think he did is bullshit."

"How would you know, Sarah? Tell me that? That man could be the reason my sister was beaten by a man she was supposed to marry. That man may be responsible for placing your life and those of your precious dogs in danger. I can't and won't allow that to happen to anyone I care about." I'd raised my voice, my venom shocking her, especially given what I'd just admitted.

Fuck.

Yes, I did care about her, which was damning in and of itself.

She opened her mouth then pressed her fingers across her lips, holding back another moan. "I'm so sorry about your sister. Is she okay?"

I nodded just once, turning my head. "There are dangers in my world you couldn't understand, people who are more abominable than I am."

"You chose this life."

"That's where you're wrong. I chose to walk away from this life. Then my brother was killed."

Now the weight was shoved onto her shoulders. The bright light I'd seen in her eyes so many times suddenly faded. I sucked all the joy and life out of her with a few words said out of spite. After a few seconds, she lowered her head, turning away from me. Then she unfastened her jeans, tugging off her shoes then lowering the dense fabric past her hips.

Then she stopped, shaking her head.

"Do. It. Now."

Shaking, Sarah murmured her hatred once again.

I could tell she was crying again, but I knew the instant she turned to face me, her tears would stop. She was determined never again to cry because of me.

As she finished removing her jeans, I slowly unfastened my belt. I'd wanted to strip her life away a few weeks ago. I'd longed to bring her the kind of pain she'd brought to my family. As I yanked the thick strap from the belt loops, I realized that wasn't what I wanted any longer. The time spent with her had changed everything. She'd become more than just my possession, a method of exacting revenge.

She'd become... important, more so than the air I breathed or the blood pumping through my veins. It disturbed the hell out of me how close I felt to her, more so than anyone else. All I could think about was tasting her.

Burying my face into her sweet pussy.

Driving my cock deep inside her tight channel.

Crushing her with my weight.

And fucking kissing her for hours.

Instead, I was treating her like the captive she'd just become.

Christ. How many hours had I spent thinking about having her luscious mouth wrapped around my cock, sucking me dry?

"Lean over the couch," I told her.

Her final act of defiance was to give me a salute. She walked stiffly to the couch, doing exactly as I commanded. I wanted to get this over with, taking her to safety. Nico's act meant the Morettis were willing to cross whatever line.

However, it was next to impossible not to be fixated on her gorgeous ass, my mind envisioning that way I'd fucked her like an animal only a couple of days before. There had to be a special kind of hell for men like me who could have anyone they wanted but had become determined to sully a perfectly normal woman.

As soon as I approached, she stiffened. When I rubbed my fingers down her spine, she shivered. The marks from before had faded, which made my mouth water at the thought of adding more. I was a sick man to think that dominating a woman was the only method of finding happiness. Why had the time spent with her started to make me question everything about myself?

That in and of itself was dangerous, something I couldn't afford. I took a step away, folding the belt in half. "The punishment I'm about to give you is only about the fact you tried to get away from me. I'll handle your penance for the deal made at a later time."

Sarah said nothing, nor did she make any movement. But I could tell her entire body tensed, the anticipation keeping her breathing ragged. I cracked the belt against her rounded bottom, sucking in my breath from the act. Then I smacked her four times in rapid succession. Today I'd only issue twenty. It was just a taste, a reminder of my power.

I took the time to caress her skin, the heat from my action cutting through the rough pads of my fingers. After a few seconds, I fisted my hand, my eyes drawn to her glistening pussy. She was still enjoying this, the connection between us stronger than ever. However, she flinched when I rolled my hand between her legs.

"You're wet, sweet Sarah. I think you like this even more than before."

"Bastard," she whispered.

"Yes. Who are you trying to convince? Me or yourself?" I swirled the tip of my finger around her clit, expecting her to jerk away. She maintained position, but the moment she shifted her hips back and forth, I could tell she was rapidly losing her ability to fight what had been started the moment we'd locked eyes.

That would make me a romantic, which I wasn't. Besides, she knew it had been a ploy and would never forget how I'd managed to play her.

"Get it over with," she said through gritted teeth.

Chuckling, I couldn't resist sliding a finger inside, thrusting several times. She stiffened once again, pushing up from the couch. I pressed my hand against her back, shoving her down.

"Don't make me start over. I will do anything I want to you."

"How many times are you going to remind me of that?"

"Until it settles in." I took a step away, sliding my slickened finger into my mouth. The taste of her was so damn sweet, pushing my cock against my trousers. It would take every ounce of control not to fuck her.

I delivered six more, stopping only when I heard her moan. I'd finally broken through another layer. After closing my eyes briefly, I realized a single bead of sweat had managed to slide down from my hairline. She did this to me, as well as several other things I couldn't explain. After wiping it away, I continued the round of punishment, my breath catching with every crack of the belt.

She whimpered, shifting back and forth, further igniting an intense fire.

When I was finished, I found breathing strenuous. I glanced down at her hourglass figure and shook my head. This was the very reason I'd end up in hell.

Which was exactly what I deserved.

CHAPTER 11

 abriel

"You won't get away with this," Sarah said, the conviction in her voice still amusing. She obviously had no idea what I was capable of.

As I pulled into the neighborhood, I shifted my gaze, watching as she wrung her hands. I'd used rope, tying her wrists together, but she hadn't bothered to struggle. That didn't mean she wasn't planning to try to escape. The blindfold was a precaution as much as a reminder of the time we'd shared. At least my home was far removed from the ugliness of the city, gated and surrounded by thick trees. The added security was almost in place, but I would keep her under lock and key at least in the beginning. "You believe Daddy dearest will come to your defense, breaking down my doors to claim his baby daughter?"

She half laughed. "I guess you don't understand how important family is." As soon as she said the words, I heard her deep exhale. Her words were biting, but that's not what she'd intended, at least not with regard to Luciano. I'd been able to tell how disturbed she was from my accusation, the tears forming in her eyes genuine.

Her professed innocence didn't matter in the least. Her abduction had gone far beyond the tragedy. Her usefulness would be even greater given her father's blatant and very open threat. There were times I was surprised at William Washington's arrogance, promises made to constituents who adored his verve and his extreme boasts. It was almost laughable in my mind, especially given the dirt I had on the man.

I'd nurture the patience that continued to wane until the time was right.

"And I guess you underestimate mine." She turned her head and even through the blindfold, I could tell her eyes were pinned on me, venom crawling through her system. I did so love a fiery woman. Breaking someone weak had no appeal.

And she would break, bending to my every need.

As I pulled into the driveway, slowing down, she tensed. Her breathing was ragged, her fidgeting increasing. I opened the window only enough to allow the system to recognize my face. The gates swung open almost instantly, the two soldiers I'd dispatched to remain at the front of the house giving me respectful nods. Dillon had already arrived, the dogs brought to their new home.

I'd always wanted a dog, a pet that was all mine, a companion that didn't judge me or need anything other than love and sustenance. My father had refused, reminding me that loving any creature was a weakness and that I had to choose carefully. I found it fascinating her dogs seemed to adore me, enjoying the treats I'd brought without hesitation. Perhaps the best way of breaking her defenses was attaching myself to her beloved animals.

"You promise you won't hurt my babies?" she asked, her voice no longer holding the same edge as before. Perhaps she'd sensed I was thinking about them.

"It would serve no purpose but to further alienate you. That's not my intention."

"Then what is, *Gabriel*?" She used my name out of spite. Little did she know it only shoved another moment of full arousal into my body. "Using me to destroy my father? Is that what this is all about? I'll give you a heads up. He doesn't care for me very much. Whatever you think you have on him won't be enough. He'll never stop until he breaks your empire apart bit by bit." She laughed, as if this was all a game.

At some point her defiance would become an irritant. For now, I'd use it to further my own ends. I parked, cutting the engine and climbing out. The afternoon was already waning, the January day turning frigid in a few hours. As I headed for the passenger side, Dillon walked out of the house, heading in my direction.

Sarah had saved his life, although likely only short term. I would make good on my promise to punish her for his misdeeds more than I already had. That would come later. I still had business to attend to before being able to relax for the evening.

"Again. I'm sorry, Mr. Giordano," Dillon said.

The beating Theodora received continued to weigh heavily on my mind. Someone continued to talk, exposing my activities. I couldn't rule out or trust anyone at this point. However, there were ways of finding the pigeon. It was entirely possible there was more than one. I didn't hesitate, snapping my hand around his throat. Dillon was a large man, outweighing me by a solid thirty pounds, but I had the ability of snapping a man's neck no matter how muscular he was.

His eyes opened wide but to his credit, he didn't react. "You failed me. You were given a reprieve but not by my choice. If you do so again, no one will be able to save you." I dug my fingers in, waiting as he coughed. Then he nodded. When I released his hold, his expression turned sheepish. The truth was he was the only one I could place any amount of trust in at this point. Until I found the leak, I wouldn't rest easily.

He'd done what I'd asked before, Demarco learning to live without two of his fingers. However, if I needed to send another warning to the men employed under my stead, then I had no problem doing so. The last thing I needed was a weak link. "Make some calls. Find Nico Moretti. I don't care what rock you need to turn over. Hunt him down. He and I need to have a discussion."

"Yes, sir." He threw a look toward the car. "Did something happen?"

"Yes, it did. Are the soldiers in place?"

"Yes, sir. All over the grounds. No one will get through the security system. I promise you."

I stared into his eyes for a full ten seconds then looked away. "You have twenty minutes to find him. Have two soldiers meet me at that time. While I'm gone, you will protect Ms. Washington with your life. She has roam of the house, with the exception of my office. If a single thing happens to her, you won't receive a quick death. Do I make myself clear?"

"Yes, sir. No one will touch her." He managed to keep a steady gaze, his jaw clenching. I'd put the fear of God into him. "There's something you should know, a witness."

"What do you mean a witness?"

"A nurse. They were watching some news footage on the television. Your picture appeared and both Doctor Washington and the nurse were staring at it."

Fucking fantastic. If Sarah had told the girl what had happened between us, it wouldn't be long before the police made contact. "After I return, you'll need to find her."

"And do what?"

I rubbed my jaw. "Make certain she doesn't talk, but I don't want her killed. We may need to put her on ice until after I've had a discussion with the mayor."

He exhaled then nodded. "I know a place I can take her."

"Then make it happen. If the woman has already contacted the police, then they'll arrive within the hour. You'll need to lock the good doctor in her room if that happens."

"I'll take care of that as well. You can count on me, Mr. Giordano."

"See that I can." The shit was getting messy. "Anything on our illustrious mayor?"

"He has a hefty offshore bank account with several million dollars. It took me a while to find it."

"Interesting."

"I can't access it yet, but I will."

"As soon as you do, let me know where he got all that money."

"Yes, sir." As he yanked out his phone, I felt more confident that he would watch her like a hawk. Maybe I was testing him again. Maybe I was a goddamn fool.

Only after he moved around the house, his phone in his hand, did I retrieve her from the passenger seat. "Come with me. Watch your step."

Sarah lifted her head, taking a deep breath. "I can smell the ocean."

"I'm sure you can."

"Aren't you going to remove the blindfold?"

"You've yet to earn any privileges, Sarah. I'd keep that in mind. When you learn to respect me and my rules, then you'll enjoy the time you spend with me."

She laughed, the lilt the same subtle yet beautiful chorus of vibrations, only this time hearing the sound made me tense. I guided her toward the stairs, leading her up each step in front of her. When we were inside, I removed the blindfold, waiting as she blinked several times.

"Where are they? Where are my babies?" she demanded once again.

"They're here."

"I need to see them now."

"You're in no position to make a single demand."

She chewed on her inner cheek, before turning her head away from me. I wasn't certain by the slight sound she made whether she was impressed with the house or loathing the fake opulence. "Come with me."

"I'm not going to cooperate with you unless I know the babies are okay. Period. You can beat me all you want."

Beat.

I'd never abused a woman in my life, and I wasn't planning on starting now. Unfortunately, she didn't know that and for tonight, I needed to keep her compliant while I handled Nico. Things would change tomorrow. I backed her against the wall, remaining within a few inches. "You need to remember where you are and who I am. I haven't brought you to a prison, Sarah. I brought you to my house. If it doesn't suit you, I'll hire contractors to change it for you, decorators to make the colors work. I'll purchase whatever furniture you'd like, but this is the only place you're going to be allowed for the unforeseeable future."

She narrowed her eyes, a slight smile curling in the corner of her mouth. "You really are worried. Enemies? I'm certain you have dozens of them."

"My family has had several enemies over the years. This is no different."

"Except you weren't the chosen son to lead nor did you ever desire to. Now, you also have a weakness. Me. You're vulnerable, especially with my father breathing down your neck."

The woman was far too smart for her own good. I planted both hands on either side of her, her shackled wrists now a hindrance. I glared down at her, drinking in her essence. I'd thought about the fact she was an angel of mercy, capable of choosing life over death if she wanted to. I found that ironic given the situation. "Weakness can be found in everyone just like sin. It's how you protect what is most valuable to you that matters. In matters of life and death, choices often need to be made. That's something I'm certain you understand."

Her jaw clenched, the fire in her eyes searing a hole in my heart, her hatred burning bright. "Death can often be the only peace."

"But it will never comfort those left alive."

"No." She finally looked away. Why was I fucking with the anguish she wore like a badge of honor?

"I will take you to your dogs. You are to remain inside the house at all times."

"How long? They'll need to go to the bathroom."

"I can't risk it tonight, not when…" I wasn't ready to explain anything else to her.

"When? What?"

"Nothing. You have some food for them and water. If there is a mess, one of my men will clean it up. Do you understand?"

She nodded, refusing to back down.

"Good." I kept my head hovered over hers, our lips centimeters apart. I took several breaths. Then I led her toward the stairs.

She only tried to pull out of my arms once, giving me a hard look. When I yanked her forward, she almost slipped on the stairs.

"Stop fighting me, Sarah. I don't want you hurt."

"Isn't that exactly what you want? Isn't this about your guilt for not being able to save your brother while you were able to save me? Then you found out who my father is and believed I did it on purpose. Didn't you?"

I allowed a smile to cross my face. Saying nothing, I pulled her up the remainder of the stairs, leading her toward the room I'd equipped specifically for her. The door was closed, the lock in plain sight, although I'd only use it if necessary. She had no idea the amount of guilt riding me, often becoming suffocating.

She swallowed hard then shook her head. "A prison. That's my sentence for trying to save a dying woman on an icy morning. Just so you know. She died because I wasn't able to save her."

I hadn't heard the reason she'd been on the road. Did that change anything? Not at this point. "This can be your prison if you choose to make that way."

"It will always be my prison. Until the day I die."

As soon as I opened the door, the dogs came running and she squealed with delight, dropping to her knees.

"Babies. I thought I'd lost you."

I remained where I was, scanning the room. I knew she'd expected a barren room, devoid of furniture unless I'd placed a cage in the center. It was far from the truth. "Let me untie you. I will not lock you in, but Dillon will be with you at all times."

"Am I really the reason he's still alive? For some crazy reason, he's loyal to you."

The question was loaded. "You managed to keep me from doing something I would ultimately regret." I was surprised I'd admitted it to her.

She seemed pleased with my answer, some of the earlier spark returning to her eyes.

She stood, turning to face me and holding out her hands. Only then did she glance at her surroundings. I'd given her the master bedroom, a location I'd chosen not to stay in the few times I'd been at the house. I'd planned on using it for something else, even if my father had made the selection for me, a college graduation present. There were too many bad memories associated with it, including a personal tragedy that would never allow me to enjoy the building or the surrounding grounds.

My head ached, another reminder that she would do anything possible to seek her freedom.

As I untied her wrists, I noticed a change in her eyes, the sadness that I expected. When her hands were free, she backed away, folding her arms.

"This is… not what I expected," she admitted.

"This is yours. Obviously, I'll need to get you some additional clothes. I'll make certain and purchase whatever dog food you need. For now, this is going to have to do. I have business to attend to." Dillon had already made certain they had water and food bowls in the room, even retrieving the toys she'd shoved into the small bag.

"It's beautiful." I sensed she hated admitting it.

"It will do until you make it your own."

"What are you doing?"

"Handling the son of a bitch who attacked my sister."

She dared walk closer. "An eye for an eye."

"That's always been effective."

"How much blood do you have on your hands?"

"Don't ask questions you don't want the truthful answers to."

"I want the answer. Those hands touched me in passion. Right now, I feel dirty, as if I'm tainted by the blood of so many others. It makes me sick inside."

"Feel free to take a shower. The door is right through there." I heard the terseness in my voice and so did she. I hadn't intended for this to turn into an argument. She would follow my goddamn rules or face the consequences.

As the dogs continued jumping on her legs, she shook her head, her brow furrowed. "How can you live with yourself?"

"Because that's what I'm required to do."

"How very sad. The man I met was a beautiful, decent man with an incredible laugh and a wonderful sense of humor."

"That man doesn't exist."

"Bullshit. Only when you realize that will you never be happy will you allow a change. If that's possible. Maybe your soul is already too black for that to occur."

Happiness. I knew better than to wish for it. The tension was palpable.

"I shouldn't be long. Dillon will be downstairs." I was in the doorway before she said anything else.

"Don't do this, Gabriel. This isn't you. You're a stockbroker, not a monster."

"No, Sarah. I've always been a monster. That's what I was brought up to be. I only successfully disguised it underneath five-thousand-dollar suits and behind expensive sports cars. None of that was who and what I am. The sooner you accept that the better."

As I closed the door, I realized that was likely the most truthful statement I'd made.

* * *

Sarah

A prisoner.

I'd never believed under any circumstances that I'd become one. I'd prided myself for following the rules my entire life. I'd never even gotten a parking ticket. Now I was a bird in a gilded cage, and it terrified me.

I turned around in a full circle, my pulse racing. The bedroom was lavish by any standards, the king-size bed adorned with a deep purple comforter, several pillows nestled on the surface. The hardwood floor was rich in tone, mahogany in hue. There was a leather sofa and a matching chair positioned near a floor-to-ceiling window, a bookcase directly behind filled with various fiction and nonfiction books.

Even the light fixtures were incredible, at least one of them a Tiffany and I doubted it was a reproduction. The stone fireplace on one wall was massive, drawing my attention. I could envision nights of romance, not my wrists being shackled to the bed. I stared down at my arms, noticing a slight chafing from the rope on one of them. I'd struggled, doing everything I could to get out of Gabriel's clutches.

My nerves had gotten the better of me, leaving me exhausted and nauseous. I walked to one of the windows, peering out at the grounds. I'd been right. The house backed up to a beautiful scene of water, an oversized dock perfect for mooring a boat. There was a helipad and a giant pool, although still covered for the winter season. My parents lived in a beautiful house, but not nearly as stunning as the one I'd been locked inside.

Everything was surreal, my mind a blur from everything I'd learned.

Why was he really keeping me? Was he serious about getting married? He couldn't force me. Could he? I'd heard of arranged marriages, but two parties had to agree, especially since I wasn't underage, and this was the United States, for God's sake. Shit like that didn't happen. Somehow, I knew better. I had the distinct feeling that he would force me to sign the marriage license under threat of doing something horrible to my father.

Sighing, I eased to the floor, crossing my legs, allowing the pups to crawl all over me. He was a brutal man. I'd begun to see that, but there was a tenderness to him that allowed him to care for my dogs. He had no reason to do that, unless he was trying to keep me from escaping. He knew exactly how to hold an invisible blade to my throat. I'd never do anything that could potentially cause them harm.

So all three of us were his hostages.

I was so drained I couldn't cry, had no desire to scream because no one would hear me. What in the world could I do? My purse. Had he brought my purse with him? I glanced toward the bag Dillon had dumped on the bed and shifted away from the dogs, crawling closer. When I stood, my hand was shaking as I lifted the duffle bag. No purse. Gabriel's soldier had thought of everything. There was no way to contact anyone. Other than my sister expecting me at her place, no one knew anything was wrong.

And I'd been careless or stupid enough not to tell her what was going on. Wait. Maggie. She knew. Maybe she'd already contacted the police. What could she say to them? My only hope was she'd had the forethought to contact my father. Then I remembered she was going on vacation. Shit. Carrie was the only person who would draw any attention to my absence, but she knew nothing. Oh, God. What had I done?

I backed away, once again glancing at the puppies. "Stay here just for a little while. I'll be right back. Okay?" I'd talked to them like they were human from the day I'd picked them up from two different shelters. They understood enough they didn't barge toward the door.

I walked out tentatively, closing the door behind me, leaving the pups inside. The house was too quiet, as if there'd never been any love inside. I'd seen so many emotions in Gabriel's eyes from hatred to sadness. He was a conflicted man who was doing what was required of him. Was it possible he cared about me?

Don't go down that road. Does it matter if he does?

No. It didn't.

Or at least it shouldn't.

Somehow, I knew my life was forever changed because of the wicked choices I'd made.

PIPER STONE

I quietly walked down the stairs, listening for any sounds. I wasn't certain if I hoped Gabriel would still be in the house. The thought of what he had planned churned my stomach. Killing was a part of his world, so innate that it was just another day at the office. For me, it had been mentally and emotionally destructive, dragging me to the darkest part of myself.

There was no one in sight as I reached the landing, no indication Dillon was close by. I remained as silent as possible as I moved from room to room. The living room was spectacular, the sweeping views to die for. The space was huge, meant for entertaining at least twenty-five people with ease, but the ambiance gave it a cozy feel, the fireplace adding to the expectation of comfort on a quiet winter's day. While there was no fire going, I gathered a slight scent of hickory.

I ran my fingers over the soft camel leather as I walked to the set of back doors, the view overlooking the ocean. I noticed a hot tub and cabana, also large enough to accommodate a party, a perfect place for a band.

There was so much beauty that it took my breath away, but the underlying truth of what the house and ground represented at its core couldn't be shoved aside. Blood and death had provided such lavish surroundings. Yes, I knew the Giordano family had several lucrative legitimate businesses, but the shadow of those involved in criminal activity was the mainstay. Generations of his family had gotten wealthy off destroying others.

Now my family was in a bullseye position. It was only a matter of time before the poisonous dart infested my little world.

222

As I headed to the kitchen, I thought about how my father rose to power. Yes, it was from years of service and hard work, but I was no fool. I knew he'd also used methods of extortion, walking the thin gray line between right and wrong. I'd overheard him telling my mother that it was the only way to get ahead in a city full of vultures. Maybe I was too naïve in that I'd tried to force myself to believe he was a good man deep down.

The ugly truth was that he wasn't that much different than Gabriel, only I wasn't privy to whether he'd killed anyone other than in the line of duty in his years of being a police officer. I had a feeling he was hiding several ugly secrets, which Gabriel would find and use. At this point, my worrying wouldn't solve anything.

The kitchen was just as gorgeous, but so cold that I wondered if a single meal had been prepared in the stacked set of ovens. I couldn't help myself, opening the refrigerator. I should have known. It was fully stocked with fresh fruits and vegetables, poultry and meats, veal and pork. However, the condiments had never been opened or had recently been replaced.

I went through the doorway that led into the dining room, eyeing a door that couldn't lead to the outside. After opening the door and flicking on the light, I walked down the stairs carefully. The steps were crafted out of the finest wood. Still, I had a feeling I'd find a dungeon beneath. To my pleasant surprise, it was a fully stocked wine cellar. There was a small tasting area complete with a beautifully carved cabinet full of crystal wineglasses.

Every bottle of wine was perfectly placed, only some of the various vineyards represented recognizable. But I knew they were expensive. Only the best for the son of the Giordano family.

The only son.

The one who'd survived.

I'd killed the other one.

A cold shiver slammed into my system, so icy that my legs trembled. He'd wanted me to feel guilty, the bastard. I hadn't killed his brother. If Luciano hadn't been exceeding the speed limit, maybe the accident wouldn't have occurred.

If your attention hadn't been on other things, the accident definitely wouldn't have occurred.

"Stop it! Just stop it!" A single sob left my throat, the ugliness inside my mind threatening to take over. I couldn't do this to myself. I wouldn't. Suddenly, I was suffocating. I needed air. I turned quickly, rounding the corner to head to the stairs.

Then I ran smack into a hard body.

Hands grabbed my arms, holding me in place.

"Let go," I said without thinking, struggling with whoever had grabbed me.

"Doctor Washington. Are you alright? Did something happen?" Dillon snarled and immediately scanned the area, pulling me closer.

I sucked in my breath, calming my nerves. Then I jerked away. "I'm fine, Dillon. Today, I don't feel like a doctor, just Sarah. You can call me that."

"Not a chance, Doctor. Don Giordano wouldn't approve."

"You mean the king? Do you honestly think anything can happen inside this fortress?"

He glared at me warily, but unbuttoned his jacket, allowing me to see his weapon. My guess was he had at least two more on his person.

"You would be surprised, Doctor Washington. There are always ways of infiltrating even the most secure facilities."

I half laughed, backing further away and staring at him. He was a very good-looking man, although his face bore the scars of his chosen profession. What troubled me was the lack of any humanity in his eyes. "How can you do this? How can you work for such a... monster?"

There. I'd said the words.

He took a deep breath, still studying me as if I was some kind of specimen, or at least a distraction to his usual duties. "Mr. Giordano is a powerful man with a heavy burden on his shoulders. However, I assure you that he is no monster."

"After what he did to you? After what he *almost* did to you?" I was shocked he still had that kind of loyalty. Had it been beaten into him at an early age?

"You don't understand the way of life, or the dangers involved."

"No, and I don't want to. It's crazy. Inhuman."

"In your world, don't you face difficult issues every day, fear that you'll make the wrong decision?"

"Being a surgeon and a murderer are two entirely different things."

A slight smile curled on his upper lip. "But you get to choose. The work the family does isn't about killing people. It's about business transactions, Doctor Washington."

"Please call me Sarah."

"As I said, out of respect I can't do that."

"For fear Gabriel will beat you. Fabulous."

He shook his head. "Mr. Giordano has a good heart, an even better soul, but he has requirements to the Cosa Nostra that he must accept or face death."

"Meaning what?"

He glanced over his shoulder as if he was telling some trade secret and if caught, he'd be executed. "His father would have him killed."

"Jesus Christ." The news hit me hard. "That's fucking insane." I didn't care I was cursing. *Good girls don't curse.* At this point, I was no longer the same woman I'd been even six hours before.

"It is the way of the organization and has been for centuries."

"That was in Italy," I insisted.

"Yes, but traditions never die."

"How long have you worked for the family?"

"A long time. I was a kid on the street with no future except death or prison. Anthony Giordano took me in. I became a part of the family."

I almost laughed in his face. "But Gabriel was going to kill you without question."

"Because of how much he cares for you."

That was twisted as hell, but I didn't say it to him. "I don't care for him. I don't want to be here. I didn't do anything to the man or his family."

Dillon appeared uncomfortable and pursed his mouth.

"I'm sorry. I know I have no right to say anything to you. I'm certain my conversation with you will make your life more difficult. I'm just…" There were no words that would fit in order to finish the sentence. "Is it true that Gabriel never wanted to take the position he was forced into?"

He nodded and said nothing.

"And his… men resent him."

"Yes."

"Why?"

"Because it is an honor to be made Don of the family and Mr. Giordano ignored the traditions, pretending he wasn't a part of the family."

"He wanted his own life; therefore, he now has to prove himself." I knew Dillon couldn't answer that. I closed my eyes briefly, images of Gabriel's face floating into my line of sight. Goddamn it. Why couldn't I get the man off my mind?

"Can I get anything for you or the dogs?"

"Goldie and Shadow."

"I'm sorry?"

"The golden one is named Goldie, for Goldie Hawn and Shadow because from minute one, he was always by my side."

He smiled for real, his eyes lighting up for the first time. "I like that. They're very nice animals."

"They are family to me, Dillon. I'll let you in on a little secret. I'm only close to my sister, not my parents. We've been at odds for years."

"Then you and Mr. Giordano have more in common than you understand."

Laughing, I shook my head. "You might be right."

"Family is very important. You are now a part of Mr. Giordano's *familia*, which means he will protect you with his life as I will."

Just the way he said the words allowed another cold chill to trickle down my spine. "I can take care of myself."

"Not against the type of people you'll now face."

A part of me wanted to ask him about his experiences, but I knew deep down I didn't want to hear any additional horror stories.

"I will make certain nothing happens to your children. You can count on me," he said quietly.

"Thank you, Dillon. That means a lot."

"I will be upstairs if you need me." He turned to go, and I sensed a sadness in him that troubled me.

"Do you have a family, Dillon?"

He stopped short. "I did."

Did. The word said everything to me. He'd lost everything because of this job.

"I'm so sorry."

Nodding, he remained where he was, his back heaving from his heavy breathing. "He does care for you, Doctor Washington. More than you know. You're the only reason I've seen him happy in a very long time."

Before I had a chance to ask why, he disappeared.

There were many dark secrets inside the Giordano family. I feared that when they were exposed, I'd find myself falling for a man I wanted to hate.

My lover.

My captor.

CHAPTER 12

abriel

I wasn't in the habit of being driven anywhere. It wasn't my style and had never been. My father, although he had a driver's license, had driven few times in his life, always chauffeured by one or more of his most trusted men. I hated the custom, believing it to be self-centered, but there were times that having the added manpower was necessary.

This was one of them.

Both Bruno and Gunner were musclemen as well as performing other duties. Their backup would provide an instant warning not to fuck with me. And, if Nico had soldiers with him, they would run interference as necessary.

Nico Moretti was a barbarian in my eyes and always would be. He was my age, but he'd grown up more or less on the streets, his 'higher' education consisting of being a foot soldier under his father's helm, working his way up to Capo. Now he was poised to take over as Don, which could happen at any day. While by all appearances Joseph Moretti appeared to be in good health, I'd taken the time to discover that he'd been diagnosed with pancreatic cancer a few months before, which was the reason he was pushing hard for the union between my sister and his son.

I understood part of the reason my father believed it to be a good idea. Together, the force would be almost impenetrable, but there could never be any real trust between the families, marriage or not. I'd paid attention to their activities over the years, curious about their methods of operation as well as their future intentions. I'd finally convinced Luciano that the Morettis would try to destroy our family and our organization.

That's one reason he'd begun challenging Joseph, which had led to the unfortunate events. Our conversations had been private, at least enough so my father likely had no idea I'd pushed Luciano into challenging Joseph, denying the union.

I was the one who should feel guilt. I'd brought enough evidence to my brother that he hadn't been able to deny my findings any longer. What I hadn't anticipated was his level of rage. That had never been like him before. I'd still yet to discover who had called him. I'd checked the phone records, the 'unknown' number keeping a red flag in the back of my mind.

The culprit would need to be found, but I had a feeling the caller would only be exposed when a war was set to begin.

Did I think it was Moretti? In truth, I did not. But someone had enraged my brother.

Sighing, as Bruno pulled into a parking lot of a local bar Nico frequented, I inserted a new magazine in my Glock. Confronting him in a public space had both merit and possible issues, but it would send a message loud and clear that no one would ever fuck with a member of my family.

Gunner opened the door for me, and I stepped out onto the pavement, noticing the bright moon already in the sky. I wanted this finished in order to return to my beautiful guest. Even as dirty thoughts entered my mind, I forced myself to contemplate the business at hand. Nico always had one man with him, but usually no more. Although I knew the asshole would be on edge. He'd have to be after what he had ordered. I still found it out of character that he'd order something so drastic. He knew I'd come after him.

Far too many pieces didn't add up.

The crowd was rough, some affiliated with the Moretti clan, but they wouldn't make a scene or dare try to eliminate a member of the Giordano family. That wasn't their style.

Or so I hoped.

I'd been involved in activities of this nature before, usually as a second to Luciano when push came to shove, and extra family muscle was needed. Then I'd put a stop to it, refusing to comply with his requests. That seemed like a lifetime ago. However, I'd honed my skills, the training methods forced on me as a teenager ones that I'd never forget. My father had made certain of that in his usual brutal methods.

I buttoned my jacket and scanned the street before walking inside, both soldiers following me. The crowd was still thin given the hour, which allowed me to see Nico holding court in the back. As soon as I walked in, all eyes were on us, several men backing away not wanting trouble while a few dared to puff up their chests, remaining where they were.

Both Bruno and Gunner paved the way, shoving a few men aside. I glanced at the bartender, who quickly moved to the back. Then I headed straight for Nico, not wasting any time with pleasantries.

I grabbed him around the throat, tossing him against a wall. There were several grunts, glasses shattering on the floor. Then there was nothing but quiet until Nico snarled.

"What the fuck?" He shoved himself away from the wall, instantly fisting his hands. I could see the instant recognition sparked in his eyes. There was also confusion. Then he threw a punch.

I backhanded him then landed a hard kick to his gut. As soon as he reached for his weapon, I ripped out mine, smashing the barrel against the side of his head. Then I rammed him against the wall again, hearing noise indicating both my soldiers were actively keeping bystanders from joining in the melee.

I pressed the barrel against the side of his throat, hissing as I cocked my head. "You beat Theodora. I should kill you on the spot."

For a few seconds his eyes opened wide. Then he snarled again. "You're fucking crazy. I didn't touch her. I would never do that."

I could almost believe him.

"No, you took the cowardly way out, using one of your men." I jammed the weapon against his skin, my finger itching to pull the trigger.

He got off a hard punch to my gut, then another to my jaw. I slammed the pistol against his face, taking a step back and holding the weapon in both hands. When he came at me with both fists flying, I shoved the weapon into my jacket then threw several punches of my own. The fucker wanted this the hard way, I was happy to oblige.

I tossed him back and we both fell to the floor, our bodies twisting. I finally got him down, smashing my fist into his face several times.

"Don't do it!" I heard Bruno grunt to someone. The crowd moved back, giving us room.

"I should kill you right here for what you did," I hissed, lifting my arm to throw another punch.

"I didn't do it, you pig. If I'd wanted your sister hurt, I would have done it myself. She's gonna be my wife. I don't beat women. Ever."

"That's where you're wrong. The deal is off. Scamper back to your rat hole where you belong. But if you dare ever try and touch her again, I won't hesitate to put a bullet in your brain." I squeezed my hand around his throat until he put up his arms in defeat. Only then did I back away. I'd managed to control my anger.

For now.

As I rose to my feet, I snapped my head from one side of the room to the other, challenging anyone to try to come at me. Bruno had one asshole by the throat, Gunner holding his weapon toward another. Satisfied the fucker had gotten my point and would take my message back to his father, I backed away, turning around a few feet later. I knew exactly what Nico would do.

He lunged toward me but I turned around, pointing the barrel toward his forehead.

"Give me an excuse to pull the trigger, Nico. Do it."

His eyes were full of rage, but I sensed he knew I was in the mood to follow through with my threat. He nodded and backed down. Then he said something that surprised me.

"I'll find out who hurt your sister. When I do, I'll send you their remains. No one fucks with my woman."

His woman.

He still didn't get it.

Maybe another message would need to be sent in the future. So be it. As I walked out of the bar, I had a feeling the next day would be stressful.

But I'd set the tone for my reign.

Soon word would be on the street, fear placed in several smaller organizations.

Maybe I was enjoying my new role more than I thought I would.

Now it was time to enjoy what belonged to me.

* * *

"Where is she?" I asked Dillon as soon as I entered the house. His expression was unreadable, but I could swear he had amusement in his eyes. That troubled the hell out of me. "I assume you followed my orders."

"Yes, sir, but Doctor Washington is quite… formidable." It was obvious he'd chosen his words carefully.

"Meaning what?"

"Meaning I see why you like her." He backed away, lowering his gaze. "I meant no disrespect."

"None taken, Dillon." I started to head past him then stopped. "It's possible the Morettis will retaliate given my visit to Nico. Make certain the soldiers are on alert. You're in charge of them now."

"Mr. Giordano?"

"You heard me. I trust you, Dillon, but don't take the position lightly. And don't think that just because you've been around a long time I won't be watching."

"Never, sir. I remember everything your brother told me about you."

"Which is?"

"That you were a fair man but brutal when necessary."

I shook my head. That sounded exactly like something Luciano would say. He'd seen the change in me, the smart, shy kid turning into a sharp, angry man. That's one reason I'd lost my one chance at having a personal life. I'd been too violent, enjoying being second in command. He'd advised me to use the rage for the good of the family. I'd laughed in his face, coming to blows after a few choice words were said. He'd said something similar to me after we'd bloodied each other's noses. "You two were friends."

"I liked to think so, but I worked for him, Mr. Giordano. Just like I work for you. I never crossed the line then and I refuse to now."

I tipped my head. "Understood. You know that I'm not like my brother. Not at all."

"I know, but that doesn't change anything. I will always be loyal to this family for as long as you have me."

"Did you locate the snitch?"

"Not yet, but I will. You can count on me."

Somehow, I knew I could. "Have another man watch the house. Hunt down the witness."

"I'm not certain that is wise."

"I need the element of surprise at this point. Tomorrow will be a new day. We need to be prepared for anything. I want you on your game. Do you understand me?"

He took a deep breath. "I got it. I'll have your back." When he stopped and turned to face me, I could tell something was on his mind.

"What is it?"

"Again, I mean no disrespect, but she's good for you."

"How do you know what's good for me?"

"You forget I was around every time you talked to your brother. I can tell a difference. I know how much you care about her."

Care wasn't the word. I was obsessed with her, refusing to consider letting her go. "She's mine, Dillon. Once she realizes and accepts that, she'll never want another man again. Besides, if anyone dares to touch her, I'll kill them with my bare hands."

He smiled from my words, which made me chuckle.

After he walked out the front door, I armed the security system and headed into the living room. I didn't want to be disturbed, my cravings for Sarah too intense. Soon, I would have her pert lips wrapped around my cock.

Very few things or people surprised me any longer. In fact, the usual actions of people typically pissed me off. It hadn't been any different when becoming a stockbroker. I'd learned quickly that most people took shortcuts, refusing to put in the hard work in order to make money in the profession. Then there were those intent on cheating others. As far as women, sadly, the majority I'd spent time with had been more interested in my name and bank accounts than anything deeper.

I'd made a single connection, one that had altered my point of view at a time in my life when I'd needed it the most. Thoughts of the past and my lack of expectations were ever present when I walked into a house I'd learned to hate.

For several reasons I'd expected quiet, so hearing music provided another surprise. From what I could tell, the sound was coming from the kitchen. When I walked to the doorway, I wasn't anticipating seeing Sarah. The sight of her took my breath away. She was barefoot, swaying back and forth in time to a Spanish vibe. Her two dogs were lounging near the window, the darkest one lifting his head when he noticed me.

She was cooking, preparing a meal. I was shocked enough I remained where I was, admiring her from my position. What the hell? I expected her to fight me. Preparing dinner? Either she was attempting to gain my confidence, or she was fighting through her anxiety and nerves. When the black dog started thumping his tail, she stiffened before turning around.

The look in her eyes was powerful. She was trying to search my mind, pleading for details without asking a question.

I walked in without saying anything, grinning when both dogs scampered toward me. I'd never come home from a long day to find someone greeting me. This was far too... normal.

Woof! Woof!

"What are their names again?" I asked as I hunkered down, laughing when both dogs licked my face.

"Shadow and Goldie." She said the few words quietly, as if I'd caught her in a mischievous act.

Even though she attempted to mask her emotions, there was no hiding how much she cared about her pups. "They're truly adorable."

"I thought you couldn't care about anything but yourself." As soon as she made the curt statement, she grumbled

239

under her breath. "That was a shitty thing to say. I don't know you and shouldn't make assumptions." She lowered her gaze to my bruised hand, sucking in her breath.

"An excellent assumption based on fact. However, it's not true." After standing, I removed my jacket, tossing it over the back of one of the kitchen chairs. Then I took my time rolling up my sleeves as I approached, never taking my eyes off her. She seemed uncomfortable at the way I was looking at her, returning to whatever she was cooking on the stove.

"You're hurt."

"A necessary evil."

Sarah grumbled again but grabbed one of the kitchen towels, yanking open the freezer door and grabbing ice. "How many people did you beat up? Or did you just kill them with your bare hands?"

"They're alive, not worth killing."

She tossed the last few cubes into the towel, folding it closed. "You mean he or she wasn't worth the effort."

I grabbed her by the arm, swinging her around. Startled, she slapped her other hand against my chest, almost dropping the icepack. "I will never hurt a woman in the way you mean. Never. As far as the asshole, he got what he deserved." I was almost blinded from desire, my hunger knowing no bounds. She had no idea how close I was to ripping off her clothes, fucking her in the middle of the kitchen.

When she tilted her head in defiance, our lips were almost touching. "The man who hurt your sister?"

"Yes."

"Then he got what he deserved." Her words surprised her, enough so she frowned, pushing away from me then grabbing my hand. As she gingerly placed the pack on my knuckles, I sensed the same hunger that we'd both felt before, but there was more. She was so uncertain of me that I was pissed at myself.

"In my mind, not enough, but I can't kill him just yet."

"Why?"

"Because it's not good protocol." I laughed after issuing the words. "Which sounds ridiculous."

"No, I understand you had to step in or else."

Or else? She'd talked to Dillon. "Yes, it's required, but you should know by now I'm a rule breaker."

My comment garnered me a single smile, heat rising onto her lovely cheeks. "That makes two of us. Keep the pack on your hand for at least ten minutes. You'll need some aspirin if you have that in your house."

"I'm sure I do. Don't you need help?"

"Pour yourself a glass of wine. I helped myself to a bottle from your unused cellar."

She didn't add that she hoped I didn't mind or make any other apologies. She simply returned to what she was cooking, stirring a pot, the aroma incredible.

I did what she asked, marveling at her choice of wine, refilling her almost empty glass and sliding it in her direction. "My father gave me this house, complete with the wine cellar, when I graduated from college."

"Oh, wow. What a gift," she said with disdain. "I received a two-hundred-dollar gift card to Saks."

"That's it?"

"Yeah," she said, tossing me a look. "He wasn't mayor then, just a police captain. Besides, he told me I didn't need many clothes given I'd opted to become a surgeon and lower my standards."

"You're kidding me?"

"Not something I'd joke about." She grabbed her wine, swirling it before taking a sip. "In case all your investigation didn't find out, my father and I are usually at odds with everything."

"That's not something I could find out."

"Now you know. I'm not sure why you think he'll care that much about the fact you're... insisting we marry. He'll likely say something crass like I made my bed, now I need to wallow in shit."

Huffing, I leaned against the counter. "You're his daughter."

"My sister is the favorite child. I was supposed to be a boy. You know, to carry on the family genes. From what I heard later in life, he blamed my mother for not giving him a boy." She took a gulp of wine, her eyes never leaving me.

"What an asshole."

"Take a number, Gabriel. He's not well liked by anyone. I am curious. What do you have on him? I know you're going to use something against him to leave you alone and it's not just about me."

I thought about her question and in that moment, I realized how vulnerable she was, longing for her father's approval while determined to live her life the way he wanted. She and I were more alike than I'd originally thought. "I'm going to appeal to his common sense."

"You're lying to me. That's something you said you'd never do."

The wine was rich, delicious in its full body. I took several sips before easing my glass to the counter, moving closer and tossing the icepack in the sink.

"Don't, Gabriel," she whispered as she threw her hand out. "Don't take this as anything romantic. I don't know you. You kidnapped me. I didn't know when or if you'd come back and I was hungry. I couldn't just roam your beautiful, cold house any longer."

I took a deep breath, ignoring her wishes. "What do you want to know about me?"

"What do I want to know? Everything."

"What I told you at the cabin was all real, the truth."

"That you like action movies? That you prefer Italian food American style? That you would love to have a family? All bullshit."

"Not bullshit." I crowded her space even more, my heart racing. A swift jolt of current swept into us and her lower lip quivered from the closeness. "What we shared at the cabin was special."

"Stop doing that. You're a bastard."

"If that's what you want to believe then fine."

She sidestepped me, moving to the pantry and grabbing out linguine. "What happened to Dillon's family? They died. Right? They were killed because of this… life."

He had been talking. I wanted to be angry, but I sensed whatever they'd discussed had helped lower her walls, if only to be able to engage in a conversation. I'd indulge her for now, but she would not deny me. "Yes, Sarah. They were caught in crossfire."

"His wife? Kids?"

"His wife and little boy."

"Jesus Christ. And he still works with you?" She slammed the box on the counter, almost dropping her glass. Immediately both dogs raced around the corner, trying to protect her. "Mommy is fine. Just fine, babies. Oh, you little cuties." I heard the anguish in her voice as she bent over, petting both.

"It was his choice to continue working with my brother."

"Yeah, I heard. He considers this family. I don't understand how the hell he could continue working for your family, but I admire him for his loyalty, if that's what you call it."

I shoved my hand into my pocket, uncertain of what to say to her.

"I heard your father was planning on killing you if you didn't take his place as the great Don of this Cosa Nostra. Is that true?"

Her tenacity was enticing.

"Yes, that's true. A tradition that began in the seventeen hundreds or so." What the fuck hadn't Dillon told her?

"Would you do that to your own son if he didn't want to become *you*?"

Her question was something I'd never considered. It hit me hard. "No."

"Really?" she asked with attitude.

"I'm not my father."

"You could have fooled me." She took another gulp then placed the glass on the counter, yanking the box into her hand and ripping off the top. When she dumped the entire box into boiling water, several strands fell to the floor, the dogs scampering to find out what she'd dropped. "Damn it."

"Let me get them." I eased to the floor, trying to grab the pasta before the dogs. When I stood, she was staring at me then almost immediately dropped her gaze.

"If I'm ever lucky enough to have a family, they will be sheltered from this life."

"Then your way of life will die with you. All the traditions. All the pomp and circumstance."

"So be it." I'd obviously surprised her.

"You've probably never been in love." She turned around, stirring the sauce with vigor.

There was no reason for me to admit anything about my past. It no longer mattered, at least to me. Everything about the woman yanked at heartstrings I'd shut down. It had never been my intention. "I deeply cared for someone years ago. We met in college and thought we could make a life when we graduated. Then she found out who I was. She ended the relationship over the phone, telling me she couldn't spend the rest of her life with someone she didn't know."

"Good for her." She dropped her head, tossing the wooden spoon onto a plate. "You bring out the worst in me. I'm sorry that you couldn't work it out. Did you try and contact her later?"

"I did. Once. She was dead." I'd done everything in my power not to think about Mary or the circumstances marking her death. It was a level of guilt that had been a driving force in leaving the family business.

"What?" She turned around to face me, horror on her face. "Did an enemy kill her?"

"I don't think so. She was attacked on the streets of Chicago. That's all I found out."

"That's terrible."

"Yes, it is. However, if you're asking if you'll always be in danger, yes, to some degree; but one thing I've learned is that death can occur at any time for any reason. You should know that given your profession." I did what I could to shut down the memories, although I had a feeling they'd continually surface given the way I felt about Sarah.

"Most people don't tempt fate quite so readily nor do they take the kinds of risks you do every single day."

I couldn't help but laugh. "Do you honestly think I will spend my days hunting down bad guys? I leave that to the cops. My father created a successful business starting from the moment he set foot in America. He worked eighteen-plus-hour days to build the business, including spending a lot of time behind a desk making phones calls, finalizing deals."

Sighing, Sarah shook her head. "Don't sugarcoat what you do. You're a criminal."

"Are some of the businesses crossing a line? I'm still not going to lie to you. Yes, but not the majority and Luciano was dead set on shifting most of our business to the right side of the law."

After staring at me for a full ten seconds, she looked away, closing her eyes. "I want, no, I need to hate you."

"But you can't. Can you?" I walked closer once again.

"No, and that makes me crazy. You act as if I will derail my career for you, tossing everything I've worked for my entire life."

"I never said you had to give up being a doctor."

"A surgeon," she corrected.

"Surgeon," I repeated, chuckling under my breath. When I touched the side of her face, she didn't move or try to pull away. I tightened my grip, pulling her close.

"Don't."

"Don't want you or don't tell you anything about my life?"

"Both. It won't matter."

"Why? Because you'll never feel the same temptation, a connection so strong that we can't stand being away from each other?"

"I don't know."

"Yes, you do. Tell me that's not the case and I'll find a way to end this, to give you back your life."

She narrowed her eyes, taking shallow breaths. "Would you really do that?"

I nodded before answering. "Yes."

"You'll never be able to protect me."

"You have no idea what I'm capable of." There was hesitation in her voice but need was increasing in her eyes.

"I want to believe you, Gabriel. I really do."

"Then do," I growled and lowered my head, crushing her mouth with mine. She pressed her hands against me, acting as if she'd try to break free.

Then she started to relax, yanking on my shirt as she arched her back. My hunger continued to increase, enough so I was blinded with the need to ravage her. I wasn't going to be gentle, but she didn't need romance. She wanted domination.

I gripped the back of her neck, grinding my hips back and forth. I dominated her tongue, my entire body on fire as she slid one hand around my neck, tangling her long fingers in my hair. She bucked against me, moaning through our locked lips. The taste of her was explosive, wine and spicy tomato sauce, an irresistible combination. I was famished, but not for whatever succulent food she was preparing.

When I couldn't take it any longer, I pulled away, both of us gasping for air. I reached around her, turning off the burners then yanking her sweater over her head.

Her smile was an indication of just how aroused she'd become but when I caught sight of her swollen nipples, my mouth watered. I wanted nothing more than to sink my teeth into her tender flesh, but that would come later. I needed the kind of relief that only she could provide.

Growling, I allowed my gaze to sweep down to her feet then back to her eyes. "Take off your jeans and panties."

There was no hesitation, no push back of any kind. As she unfastened and pushed the material past her hips, I unbuckled my belt. She stared at me with glassy eyes, her mouth twitching in anticipation of what I had planned. A part of me wanted to mark her again, but my cock was aching like a son of a bitch, my balls on fire.

When she'd completed her task, I gripped her jaw, rubbing my thumb back and forth across her mouth brutally as she panted. Laughing softly, I could tell my blood pressure was increasing. She always managed to wreck me moments before I consumed every inch of her. I'd promised her freedom if she wanted. I had no intention of keeping that promise. No. She was mine. All fucking mine to do with whatever I wanted.

"Are you going to be a good little slut for me?"

"Yes, sir." She was breathless, her body trembling as I wrapped my belt around her wrists, securing her arms.

"Good girl. Down on your knees." I rubbed my jaw as I backed away, barely able to take my eyes off her. Then I dragged one of the chairs from under the table, planting it in the center of the room. "Be good, babies. Your mama and I are going to have some twisted fun." Whether or not the dogs understood I wasn't certain, but they seemed to obey me without question.

As I sat down, she kept her head held high, her eyes shining with excitement. I twirled the belt, thinking about all the things I used it for. When she teased me by dragging her tongue across her lips, I almost lunged for her, fucking her right there. Control. I had to control myself. "Crawl to me. Be my good girl."

She gave me a heated look then obeyed, only she took her sweet time in doing so, tossing her hair back and forth, lost in the extreme lust. I was almost panting like some goddamn animal by the time she crossed the fifteen feet. When she was close enough, I reached out and grabbed her by the hair, dragging her the rest of the way until she was between my legs.

She peered up at me with a mixture of desire and determination. I adored that about her. The sly smile remained on her face as she rubbed her hands up and down the insides of my legs. When she came dangerously close to my groin, I jerked her head up, shaking mine.

"Not so fast, my sweet slut. You're not in control." I dropped the belt over her shoulder, lightly slapping her on the bottom. She wiggled but remained in position, her guttural sounds matching mine. Fuck, the vile things I could do to her. She hadn't just become my weakness. She'd become my kryptonite.

I only hoped she wouldn't become my noose.

She tugged on the material, and I allowed her to yank it past my hips. "Are you hungry for my cock?"

"Yes," she murmured, laughing softly afterwards. Her cheeks were rosy, partially from the shame she felt about wanting this. "I shouldn't be but I am."

As I cracked the belt again, harder this time, she gasped for air. I could torment her all day, but I'd never survive the onslaught of need burning deep within. I gave her three more as drops of pre-cum trickled from my cockhead.

"Arms behind your back," I instructed.

She did so and I pressed her head down, allowing her to lick the strings of cream while I wrapped my belt around her wrists. Her hot breath cascading across my balls was almost enough to make me come.

"Open your mouth for me, princess, nice and wide."

While she did as commanded, I dug my fingers into her scalp, tugging to keep her head at the correct level. I wanted her to watch my face as I fucked her mouth.

"Suck me. Slap through pretty lips around my cock." As soon as her greedy lips were placed around the tip, it was all I could do not to shove my shaft down her throat. "Fuck. Your mouth is so damn hot."

I couldn't help but stare into her big blue eyes as she used her jaw muscles, sucking my cockhead as if she was dying of thirst. Some women had no clue how to suck a man. This beautiful creature between my legs was an expert. She swirled her tongue back and forth, tiny purrs escaping her mouth, the sound intensifying the moment. I was already struggling to breathe, the need to erupt deep in her throat almost all I could think about. However, I wouldn't finish this way. I needed to fill her sweet pussy, driving my cock as deep inside as humanly possible.

Sarah was the only thing that calmed me, driving away the guilt and anger, the frustration and ugliness.

I pushed on her head for encouragement, my patience waning as she took two more inches. I heard her raspy breath sounds and it turned me on. Panting, I threw my head back while my hips lifted on their own, needing to fill her mouth completely. There was nothing sweeter than the sound of her sucking mixed with her soft moans. I could do this for hours, covering her with my cum.

That would come later. Maybe tonight.

As I rubbed my face, stars floated in front of my eyes, my muscles tense as drums. The fact she couldn't touch me was more stimulating than I'd originally thought. I was in full control, taking what I wanted.

"Yes, my perfect little slut. You like this, don't you?" Her mouth was too filled to answer, but her louder moans filtered into the air around us. I pushed her head down, forcing her to take more. She didn't gag, not once. As I pumped my hips, I could sense I wouldn't last very long if she kept this up.

As she sat further up on her knees, the switch in the angle drove more of my cock inside, the tip sliding down her throat. Now I thought for certain I was going to go mad. I was losing control, ready to spew inside her mouth but I was intent on fucking her, making her come.

Using what restraint I had left, I pushed her away, breaking the connection, half laughing as beads of sweat slid down both sides of my face. "So good. So damn good."

The look on her face was feral as she took several deep breaths, biting her lower lip. Her eyelids were half closed. I realized my body was shaking from a rush of adrenaline, the need for her crushing every other thought out of my mind. She was mine.

Mine.

Mine...

And I would die in order to keep her safe.

"Baby," I growled. "There isn't a time I won't be your protector. If the devil himself comes spewing fire, I'll create a firestorm."

CHAPTER 13

 arah

Gabriel's words rattled my mind, the sight of his need for me calming certain fears yet wanting him the way I did was reckless. Insane. But there was no denying the way I felt around him. He was right. I'd thought of him for hours, pacing the damn house like a rabid creature, bugging Dillon more than once to tell me where he was.

The man remained a good soldier, saying nothing. He'd merely checked on me several times, finally to the point I couldn't take feeling like a hostage any longer. None of my feelings made any sense, but I couldn't stop tingling all over, the taste of his pre-cum expanding all my senses.

I no longer recognized myself, ashamed that his brutal actions aroused me so completely. My nipples ached, the tips swollen. I was so wet my juice had already stained my inner thighs. It was crazy. Nuts. I just...

"Come here," he commanded. "Sit on my cock. I need to fuck you long and hard."

He was panting, the expression on his face primal. He'd been this way at the cabin, like a beast needing to be fed every two hours. I'd complied then just as I was doing now.

It sickened me but I couldn't help myself. He'd become a drug to me, dragging the darkness away. I should be terrified of him, but I knew he'd never hurt me. Whatever vengeance he'd wanted had vanished, replaced with need he could never break free of.

God help us both. We would burn in the fires of hell.

I moved closer, trying to control my breathing. He lifted me from the floor, forcing me to straddle him. He held me aloft, rubbing his fingertips along my hips to my stomach, rolling them from one side to the other. Then he cupped both breasts, squeezing until I moaned. He knew how to keep me fully aroused, enough so my mind was a blur, and I couldn't stop panting.

"So fucking beautiful," he whispered and pulled me closer, pressing his lips against my stomach. There was something different about him tonight, all pretenses about who and what we were tossed aside. That gave him the freedom to use me however he wanted. That was so damn exciting my heart thudded against my chest, his rough actions shoving aside the angry little voice inside my head.

There was also something sinful about the fact he was fully dressed and I was naked. And I adored his dirty talk. My pulse raced and as he pulled me down, he dragged his tongue toward my breasts. With the tip pressing against my pussy lips, my legs tensing, I wiggled back and forth until I managed to slide his cockhead inside.

"My insatiable slut," he murmured then yanked me all the way down.

"Oh, yes. Yes." My scream was ragged, the dogs immediately lifting their heads. All I could do was smile from having an audience.

Gabriel realized my attention had been drawn away and followed my gaze. "Imagine having several people watching me fuck you."

"Uh-huh."

"Would you like that?"

"Yes." How could I want that? The man made me crazy, losing myself in something I didn't seem to have any control over.

"Maybe," he huffed as he swirled his tongue around my nipple several times, "if you're a very good girl, I'll make that come true one day."

When he bit down on my hardened bud, I lifted my head toward the ceiling, gasping for air. My pussy muscles tingled, clamping and releasing several times. The angle was different, his cock going deeper. I was lost in a sweet haze as he shifted to my other nipple, issuing low and husky growls as he sucked on the tip.

Gabriel knew how to drive me to the point of an orgasm quickly, but I knew he planned on dragging me to the edge and pulling back as he'd done before. The man had so much stamina, but I sensed he needed to come inside of me. Still, I squeezed my muscles on purpose, rewarded with another guttural sound like that of a wounded animal.

"Be careful what you do, little girl. I will retaliate." His deep laugh filled the air, and he wrapped his hand around my hair, yanking my head. Then he gripped my hip with the other, using his muscular thighs to lift me off the chair.

I was at his mercy, incapable of doing almost anything. There was something freeing about him being in total control. There was also something terrifying, as if letting go and trusting him was placing my life into his hands. And as if by doing this, I'd set things in motion, no longer able to deny what we shared meant something.

I'd meant what I said to him. I wanted to hate him in order to shut down my feelings, but being here in his world, learning more about him made it impossible.

And he knew that.

I'd fallen into a trap, accepting his demands. Whatever was going to happen was completely out of my control.

He rocked forward, slamming into me with such ferocity it rocked the chair. I pressed my thighs against his, my whimpers becoming louder, matching his barbaric grunts. Lights flashed in front of my eyes, forcing me to blink, but there was no chance I could focus.

"Mine. All mine," he whispered several times, unrelenting in his actions. He was such a complicated man, conflicted about his role as well as mine.

Was it possible we could share a life? Could there be more than just a physical connection or was I losing what was left of my mind? I told myself I was nothing more than his possession, but there was a depth in his eyes that could only be explained by...

Love.

No. No. That wasn't possible. He could never feel that kind of closeness. He could never want me that way. Could he?

What was I thinking?

"Look at me, beautiful slut. Don't take your eyes off me."

I shifted my gaze, biting my lower lip. There was more light to his eyes, so much so he allowed me to catch a glimpse of his soul. And when I did, I knew there was no other man for me.

"That's it, baby girl. Now, you understand. You are mine. For tonight. For tomorrow. And fucking forever. Whether you like it or not."

Another promise made.

Another proclamation.

And I knew he would never let me go.

Seconds later, his body tensed, his eyes now half closed. As he pumped brutally, thrusting deep and hard, I bucked against him, the friction unlike anything I'd ever felt. The electricity swirled around us, jolts like bottle rockets breaching every cell. Our moans became louder, our bodies molding together and as he began to shake, I clamped my muscles one last time.

Just as he erupted, filling me with his seed.

As he released his hold on my hair, allowing me to drop my head, I heard his hoarse whisper and shivered.

"No man will ever touch you again. If they do, they die."

* * *

Gabriel

Morning had come far too early.

As I entered the kitchen, the sight of Sarah took my breath away. I remained in the doorway enjoying the view as she studied the ocean, her hand wrapped around a mug of coffee. I sensed another round of discord, which I couldn't blame her for. She needed more from me that I couldn't provide.

I moved toward the Keurig, surprised to find a second cup waiting for me. As I popped in a pod, I noticed she'd finally turned to look at me, her eyes locked on my injured hand.

"Did you take additional aspirin?" she asked.

"My hand is fine."

"If I had to guess, I'd say you have at least one stress fracture if not more. You're not fine, Gabriel. You're hardheaded."

Chuckling, I flexed my fingers, trying to keep from wincing from the discomfort. "I've been through worse."

"Is that supposed to make me feel any better?" She walked closer, shaking her head, her brow furrowed.

"I'll have you know that the biggest fight I got into was in my office after the stock market plummeted. I ended up with three broken ribs and a black eye, but you should have seen the other guy." It had been Rick who'd been forced to pull me off the asshole, receiving a black eye in the process.

She wasn't impressed.

"Are you prepared to die?" she demanded.

Thankfully, I'd yet to take a sip of coffee. After coughing, I realized she was serious. "I don't fear death if that's what you mean. I'm a firm believer that when it's your time to go, then nothing will prevent it."

"A religious man?"

"Not particularly. However, I do believe in fate and karma."

Half laughing, she rolled her eyes. "But you enjoy tempting fate."

I had to think about her mild accusation. "Not on purpose. I'm not a danger junkie, Sarah. But I will do what's necessary, including beating the shit out of someone if required. You know why and you agreed."

"That doesn't mean I like it or that I won't worry about you." She looked away, chewing on her lower lip.

She'd whispered several words of endearment the night before, but so had I. Another wave of coldness had come between us. Maybe that was necessary for the time being.

"We need to discuss some things."

"I'm certain I won't like what you have to say."

"There are rules that you must follow," I stated. There was no sugarcoating what had to remain in effect, especially over the next few weeks. Dillon had already called, his tone alone indicating word on the street was that the Morettis were intending retaliation. That brought a smile to my face. It was time to finish what my father had started.

"Meaning?"

"I think that's pretty self-explanatory." I took another sip of my coffee, noticing she hadn't touched hers. We'd spent a night full of passion, but as soon as she realized I hadn't planned on staying the night, she'd started shutting down.

She laughed softly and slid her mug onto the counter, walking toward the window. "Fine. Or I'll be spanked like a bad girl. Why don't you tell me what they are? Wait. Let me guess. No leaving the house unless I'm given permission and have a bodyguard. No phone calls to anyone. As of now, I'm taking an extended leave of absence from my job, one that I love more than almost anything. Oh, and of course, I'll obey your every command." Her face flushed, her hard nipples poking through the light cream sweater.

I wanted to rip it off and suck on her hardened buds, biting and pinching until she cried out in pain.

Fuck. The woman could drive me crazy.

There was so much arrogance in her tone, but there was no mistaking the spark in her eyes. Our connection the night before had strengthened our relationship. "You make it sound horrible."

Huffing, she rolled her eyes. "That's because it is. You know what's interesting? I noticed a recent addition to your tattoo collection, only the mark is crude, as if your skin was burned by a white-hot piece of iron. Is that your family crest?"

Nothing escaped her. "Yes."

"And you allowed that to happen?"

"It's a—"

"Requirement of the Cosa Nostra," she interrupted. "How very gauche. Am I to expect such a mark when I'm forced to marry you?"

"The only marks on your skin will be those created from necessary discipline." My balls were aching, my thoughts turning depraved.

"And the ring?"

I lifted my hand, twisting the piece of jewelry several times. "A nod of respect from an organization."

"Wow. You've come a long way in your desire to be king."

As soon as I wrapped my hand around her throat, pulling her close, all I could think about was spending time with her. "One day you'll understand."

"I doubt it." She kept her eyes on mine as I lowered my head, drinking in her essence. When I kissed her cheek, she shuddered. Then I released my hold, hating all that I'd become.

"This doesn't need to be difficult."

"Just confining, like a prison. Right?" She backed away, shaking her head several times.

While I knew she needed answers and I had to have patience with her, it was waning more and more. "Most people wouldn't see living in a house by the ocean with people instructed to provide you with everything you need as a prison."

Sarah threw a glance over her shoulder toward the turbulent ocean outside the window, wrinkling her nose. "No matter how gorgeous the wrapping paper, inside it's still the same."

"I'm doing this for your protection."

"So you've said. I believe you're doing it because you fear I'll run so far away you'll never be able to find me."

I pitched the rest of my coffee, leaving the mug in the sink. As I approached, I shoved my hands into my pockets. "Just for the record. There is nowhere you can run and hide where I won't find you. That's the beauty of who and what I am and the people who respond to my every request."

"Blackmail. Extortion. Of course they'll do what you ask like good little men. How powerful that must make you feel."

She pressed her hand against the glass and the simple act was arousing, my cock already aching to take her again. No matter how many times I was inside of her, it was never enough. "What did last night mean to you?"

There was no doubt I'd surprised her with the question. "What did it mean? Nothing. It was sex. Am I attracted to you? Obviously, you know the answer and I hate myself for it." She closed her eyes, her breathing shallow. "And the worst part of it all is that I never intended on caring about you."

A single tear slipped past her lashes and when I gathered it with my finger, she pulled away, opening her eyes and staring at me. As I brought the salty bead to my mouth, she watched intently. The taste was just like every other, sweet and sinful.

And forbidden.

"I can give you a good life, Sarah. I can provide you with everything you've ever wanted."

"Let me guess. Trips to exotic locations?"

"Yes, if that's what you'd like."

"A shiny brand-new Maserati?"

Chuckling, I nodded.

"How about furs and diamonds?"

"I don't see you as that kind of woman, but if that's what you'd enjoy having, then the sky is the limit."

"Planes. Cars. Houses. Jewels. Don't you understand? They are things, possessions. Just like I am. You live in a gorgeous house overlooking the Atlantic Ocean. You drive a fancy car, and the cost of a single suit could feed an entire family for six months. Yet you're not happy. In fact, you're miserable. Did you ever ask yourself why?"

Her question was justified. When I didn't answer, she continued.

"I don't need things, Gabriel. You saw my apartment. I have the basics. I could lose every piece of clothing, all the books and the furniture tomorrow and I would be just fine. What would crush me for all eternity is if I lost my puppies. They mean the world to me. That's called love. Unbreakable, special love. Did you see the way they look at me? Or the way I look at them? You can't buy that no matter how much money you have. Love is priceless. Love is the feeling you get inside, your stomach rumbling and your heart racing just from the thought of seeing the being you love with all your heart. It's that moment when you walk into a room and see that person or furry baby when everything else fades to black. And it's the last thing you think about at night, the first thing in the morning. That's... love. Priceless."

Her words were haunting and beautiful, and I wanted to give that to her and more. "Do you know what I was thinking on the day my brother died and I was able to save your life?"

After a few seconds, she turned her head toward me. "How could I? All you've expressed is fury that I survived and your brother didn't."

The words cut through me like a knife. "I was thinking that even a bad man could do decent things and that I was the luckiest man alive because I was given the gift of saving the life of the most beautiful creature in the world. That's the real reason I found you, and when I did, I couldn't stop thinking about you. Images of you blocked out everything else. My heart raced every time you crossed my mind. When you smiled and laughed, my world became a little bit brighter. I know I'm not deserving of such goodness, but the gift was the most precious one given to me in my entire life. I'm not certain what you'd call that, Sarah. I'm really not. But in my mind, it's the most powerful feeling I've ever experienced. I'm a better man because I saved your life."

She didn't react at first. Then her features softened, her eyes glistening. With her hand shaking, she reached out, brushing the tips across my cheek. I grabbed her wrist, kissing her palm and for those few seconds, I enjoyed being lost in her essence.

"I'm sorry to interrupt, Mr. Giordano, but your father is here and he's insistent on seeing you."

The sound of Dillon's voice riled me, but the thought of my father dropping in unannounced pissed me off. I held her hand against my face for a few more seconds then let go. "I'll be right back."

She recoiled, the special moment broken. Now I was furious.

"Thank you, Dillon. Put him in my office."

"He found his way already, sir."

I shook my head and touched her arm before heading out of the kitchen. My father's arrival could only mean one thing. He'd heard about my exchange with Nico. As I walked into my office, I wasn't surprised my father had taken a seat in my leather chair, already puffing away on a cigar he'd retrieved from my humidor.

"Those things will eventually kill you." I moved toward my desk, leaning against the outside edge, wrapping my fingers around the smooth wood. This was my office. It was also time he realized that by initiating me to the lifestyle, he had no authority over me any longer.

"I'm certain that a bullet will kill me first, son. Maybe coming from my own flesh and blood."

"Why are you here?"

"Because we need to talk." He took another puff then glared at me. "What the fuck were you doing with Nico?"

"I would think that's fairly obvious. He had Theodora beaten. That's not allowed."

"From what I understand, she is difficult, refusing to accept their impending marriage."

I took a deep breath, trying not to explode. "Wait a fucking minute. Are you trying to suggest that Theodora deserved to be beaten?"

"A woman needs to be kept in line."

Oh, my fucking God. "Is that what you did to our mother when she didn't obey your rules, getting one of your soldiers to rough her up to teach her a lesson?"

"Don't you dare raise your voice to me!" He stubbed out the cigar, climbing out of the chair to confront me.

For the first time, I noticed how much he'd aged. He'd always seemed invincible, larger than life. Today he seemed frail. "How dare you."

"Your mother received punishment twice in her life. Then she learned to obey me, which is what you need to do to that woman you're so determined to keep."

All I could do was laugh. "You disgust me. That woman is…" Why was I bothering to explain myself?

"Someone you care about?" He laughed. "Then you're a fool."

"You don't love my mother?"

"Very much, but it didn't start out that way."

"Yeah, I know. It was all arranged. We're in America now, Pops, in case you hadn't noticed. Arranged marriages are a thing of the past. Your daughter deserves to find someone she can fall in love with, a man who will light her world on fire. Not some thug with an attitude. The deal you made is off. Period."

He came closer, shaking his fist at me. When he reared back, backhanding me, it took everything I had not to toss him across the room. I closed my eyes, concentrating on his heavy breathing.

Several tense seconds rushed by.

"You are not my son," he said with rage in his tone.

"I don't want to be." I stared him in the eyes, daring him to continue this round of bullshit. "It's come to my attention that the Morettis never intended on keeping the deal of peace between the families, marriage or not. They have someone inside our operation, Pops. Did you know that? Were you even aware that they had plans of picking us off one by one?" I was curious to see his reaction. The smug look indicated he had yet he'd ignored it. Why?

"Is that why you believed that woman you're so enamored with had something to do with your brother's death?" He laughed after asking the question.

"That woman has a name, Pops. Her name is Sarah. Yes, initially I believed that her father might have had the same kind of toxic influence on her that you've had over our entire family for years. However, I quickly found that she's a woman who refuses to buy into bullshit, which is what I attempted to do. You called me weak because you couldn't control me. Unfortunately, she has no idea what her father has done or the reason he's intent on taking down our family."

"Which is?"

Interesting. This he had no idea about.

"I'll leave that to your imagination." What Dillon had already been able to find out was enough to confirm my suspicions. The man was dirty as fuck. What concerned me was that he was taking payoffs from someone. The question remained from whom. My father shook his head, puffing his chest, but I could tell by the question in his eyes that he knew I'd bested him at a game I'd wanted no part of.

"Is that the crap you fed your brother? Is that why he was so angry? If so, you were responsible for his death."

I remained frozen, trying to accept once again that I'd never meant anything to my father. For some reason, it hurt more this time. The only reason he'd demanded I take the helm was to ensure he could spend his retirement years just as wealthy and powerful as before. "Don't worry, Pops. I'll already carry the burden of his death like a noose around my neck for the rest of my life."

Another few seconds of awkward silence settled in.

"That woman has already gotten to you. I can tell. And yes, you were always a weak man, more so now than ever. You're also a damn fool. Use her. Fuck her. Lock her away. Marry her. But for God's sake, don't love her during this transition phase. You'll be labeled a fool, all respect stripped away. Is that what you want, to be labeled a pathetic excuse for a leader? Your brother was never that way. He knew what was important."

At that moment I wanted to kill him and that troubled me. Wasn't family supposed to be about love, respect, and support? At least my mother had taught me that. No child of mine would be raised without knowing how much they were loved.

"I'm not my brother," I growled. "It's time you realize that. I will love whoever I want and I refuse to allow anything to happen to her or to any other member of my family. Including you. But get this through your head, old man. My sisters will never be forced into marrying someone they don't love under any circumstances. As far as Moretti? He can go fuck himself. If he comes at me, I will destroy him piece by piece."

He remained shocked that I'd talk to him in such a disrespectful manner, but it felt good. It was long past time I took full control of my life, including loving who I wanted to.

As the revelation that I'd already fallen in love with her slammed into my mind, I was momentarily breathless. Everything Sarah had said was exactly the way I'd felt.

Like a fucking caged animal.

No more.

"Get out, Pops. I have business to attend to."

His smirk was one I'd seen for years, the expression he made when disappointed in whatever choice I'd made. I'd never managed to please him, no matter how hard I'd tried or what I'd done. I'd been considered the bad seed.

Now he was going to find out just how *bad* I could really be.

Whether he liked it or not.

He took a deep breath as I folded my arms, watching every move he made. He'd threatened to kill me and I still wouldn't put it past him. So much for the same blood running through our veins.

He took long strides toward the door, still acting as if this was his choice. When he stopped short, twisting in order to stare me in the eyes, amusement almost crowded out the ugly rage. "When is the wedding?"

"Yet to be determined."

"Since you're so busy starting a war that you won't win, I've taken the liberty to task your sisters to help your... bride to be with the wedding. They should be here in a few minutes. Do let me know what day it is so I can make certain and clear my calendar."

My father, a man of warmth of love. I didn't bother answering. The man could go to hell as far as I was concerned. I dropped my head, half laughing from the confrontation. When I lifted it again, I saw Sarah standing in the doorway. She'd heard every word, her eyes reflecting compassion, something I'd never wanted or received in my life.

She walked closer, the pensive look on her face remaining, moving to within a foot of me. "Did you mean what you said, when you told me you cared about me?"

I reached out, intertwining our fingers together and pulling her between my legs. "You should know by now I say what I mean. Does that change who and what I am? No, it doesn't. This life isn't easy nor am I a patient man."

"What does that mean?"

"That means that I'm not perfect nor am I a good man. That's something you sensed from the very beginning. You are a brilliant surgeon, your instincts almost always right. However, don't take what I'm offering you as a choice. You now belong to me whether you choose to believe it or not. What you heard is a bit unlike anything that occurs inside other families. We all have secrets, tell ourselves lies. The difference between my family and yours is that we accept the fact we walk that thin line between right and wrong, using the mistakes of others for our benefit. We don't lie about who we are whereas your father pretends as if he's the city's salvation."

"What do you have on him? I heard what you said, Gabriel. You think he's dirty."

"And you don't?"

She looked away briefly. "I don't know any longer."

"I think you do, which is why you push against him and his wishes."

"Then tell me the truth."

I thought about the information I'd gathered, adding to what both my brother and father had collected over the years and sighed. "Often the truth won't set you free. It'll only devastate what little hope you had for believing in a fairytale. Besides, there's no reason to burst your bubble. If you want to believe your father is still a decent human being, then so be it."

"I'm no fool, Gabriel, which is also something you figured out about me. I also won't be used as a pawn. Do what you need to do but keep me out of it."

"If only I could." I wrapped my fingers around her neck, the action possessive. She wanted to allow her last defenses to fall but refused to trust me. How could I blame her? "Unfortunately, karma made you a part of a vicious game."

"One you're going to extort."

"As I already told you. I take care of my family and will use any means necessary to do so. Now, you're a part of my family. I care for you deeply. That's something else you can choose to believe or not."

"Mr. Giordano," Dillon interrupted again. "You're going to want to see this. I think I found what you're looking for." Dillon held out his phone. This time, his expression was one of rage.

Proof that we had a leak. Things were heating up.

After I nodded, he backed away, giving me privacy.

"I'm sorry about another interruption," I said quietly.

"What's this about going shopping?"

I cocked my head, lifting an eyebrow. "I was right. You over-heard everything."

"Yes. I need answers and when I heard angry voices, I thought I might learn something."

"And I've given you all the answers I'm comfortable with. My father seems to think he can control my life through you. Unfortunately, you will not be going out today. I will take you at a later time."

"That's not fair. I'm going to be with your family."

She was testing me as she enjoyed doing. "You're in far too much danger at this point. However, I'll consider it at a later time."

"Of course you will."

"We'll continue this conversation later," I told her.

"There's no need. You're right. I don't want to hear anything that might disparage my father. He already sullied our relationship a long time ago. I also realize there's no need to talk to you about anything."

"I'm sorry, Sarah. Life isn't always what you hoped it would be."

"You know what I want. And the truth is I know exactly what you need. I only hope you can find it one day."

With you, I will. I couldn't say the words. All I could do was nod.

She started to turn away then stopped, crowding my space. When she placed her hand on my heart, a significant portion of the anger against my father faded away. "Neither one of us is to blame for your brother's death. I learned a valuable lesson more than once being a surgeon. I believed I could fix anyone with the right skills. I realized during my second surgery how wrong I'd been. A young man who had his entire life ahead of him was in a freak accident. I was certain I could become his savior, but I was wrong. From that day forward, I had to face the fact I wasn't God. Neither are you. Live your life to the fullest, Gabriel. You're a wonderful man who did what he could to escape this life of darkness. That's the only piece of advice I'll give you. Thank you for saving my life. You were my savior, my hero."

As soon as she walked out, I realized I'd been holding my breath. Then I felt a crushing ache in my chest. She had awakened my soul as well as my heart.

There was no way I'd ever be able to let her go.

That solidified the fact I'd always been a monster.

CHAPTER 14

arah

Love versus hate.

What was the old adage about there being a fine line? In my mind, the two were interchangeable.

I whispered hateful words about Gabriel several times only to moan in the throes of passion, screaming out his name from sheer euphoria the next. The back and forth was killing me.

Even now, I couldn't get him off my mind no matter how hard I tried. He'd left without telling me where he was going.

Denial.

I'd always known I was damn good at denying the obvious. That had started at an early age, denying my father was stepping out on my mother. They'd pretended like they were the perfect couple, always allowing me to see them as he kissed her goodbye. However, I'd found his collection of pornographic magazines first. Then I'd discovered love notes from some chick named Ann hidden in a special place in the garage. I'd thought my parents had hidden Christmas presents.

That had continued through the years, even discovering some pretty twisted pictures of him with another woman. I couldn't remember her name. She was in a long line of them by then. At that point, he was police captain, my mother able to fend off her sadness through the purchase of new clothes and jewelry.

By then I'd simply turned a blind eye. However, it was obvious I'd stored away the information, which had added to animosity my father and I shared. He'd caught me once looking at his things, grounding me for two weeks for snooping. That had set the tone. Had I believed he was capable of anything worse? Yes. It was as simple as that. There was no sense in lying to myself. His vendetta against the Giordano family had come out of the blue. At least that's what my mother had told me a long time ago. Up to that point, she rarely complained, so when she did so about his newfound hatred, I'd questioned her.

I don't know why that conversation suddenly came to me. She'd been scared. But of the Giordano family. Hmmm... I stood at the set of French doors in the living room, watching Dillon play with the dogs. He was so good with

Dillon

them, obviously enjoying himself tossing three different balls. And the babies were loving it. They had no clue that Mommy couldn't join them. While I felt more like a bird in a cage, what I'd overheard and what Gabriel had said to me had confused the hell out of me.

Or maybe it hadn't.

Perhaps I was just in another phase of denial.

I'd never believed that an instant attraction could or should go anywhere solid. I'd been led to believe by my mother that it took time to learn about each other in order for there to be real feelings. I also laughed thinking about it now. For all her advice, I wondered if she'd discovered what kind of man my father truly was, would she have married him? It was funny. I'd always wondered why they'd never had another child. Maybe she'd refused to allow him to touch her.

I pressed my hand to the glass, allowing myself to fantasize about what it would be like living in the house under different circumstances. While Dillon had made a fire because he'd refused to allow me to do it myself, I still felt a tremendous chill that I had a feeling wouldn't leave quickly.

Until I was under Gabriel's perfect body.

I rubbed my fingers across my lips, hungering for his kisses when I should be thinking about getting myself out of here. His kisses had been wonderfully dizzying, his tongue twisting in a perfect waltz of domination that he'd won every time. The way he'd touched me, while rough at first, had shifted to being tender and sweet, but his mouth had claimed me so many times, it was as if he needed the very air I breathed.

Just thinking about him was enough to keep me from processing the truth about how I felt about him. It wasn't just physical, although no man had ever ignited a fire that burned so brightly I was certain my skin was singed.

Everything remained in an intense haze, which wasn't like me. The yin and yang of the way he'd treated me over the last twenty-four hours had driven me crazy. One minute he'd acted as if I was a beautiful doll that he could place in a corner, waiting for his arrival and filthy use. The other had been as if he needed to devour me whole. Yet there'd been a spark, his emotions disturbing on so many levels. I'd even seen the look in his eyes change as he'd expressed his remorse and guilt about the woman he'd cared about. But he was still holding something back from me, an ugliness that if exposed could tear him apart.

The kind of love that I'd been searching for my entire life wasn't something he could provide. While I adored how strongly he felt about his sisters, willing to protect them with his life, that was all the love he was capable of. I craved more than just the physicality that we shared, even if the passion was extraordinary. I longed for something special, able to trust and respect the person I was involved with.

Was that even possible with a brutal man like Gabriel?

My inner voice continued to nag me, reminding me that he was still human and that I'd seen a portion of his heart. Would that ever happen again?

I'd also experienced such tenderness in the man during the night, but he could never let himself go, caring enough to let down his guard. He'd shut down his emotions, treating me as nothing but a captive, a woman he could use. At least that's the way I'd felt when he'd walked out of the bedroom.

What are you doing to yourself? Why?

Because I wanted…

I closed my eyes, furious more with myself than with him. I'd let my guard down.

Sadly, that's what he did to me, but it wasn't about the man loving me. At least the kind I was talking about.

Marriage.

Love.

Children.

Groaning, I shoved it all aside. I certainly wasn't going to have the perfect wedding even if he provided everything my heart desired.

When I heard laughter, I realized it had to be Gabriel's sisters. Maybe he'd changed his mind about allowing me out of the house. What a pleasant surprise. *Are you crazy? Are you falling into this arrangement?*

While a part of me was giddy like some damn schoolgirl, I realized this might be my only chance of escaping. Right. Who was I kidding? My guess was we'd have ten men trailing behind us. Was I supposed to act like I cared about their brother, looking forward to getting married to him? I glanced down at my attire and sighed. My guess was they were dressed like Italian princesses and all I'd shoved into the duffle bag had been a few shirts and a single pair of jeans. At least I had shoes.

As soon as I heard footsteps, I turned around. Both girls stopped and stared at me. Why was it that every time one of the people in Gabriel's life met me for the first time, it was as if I was a circus animal locked in a cage? He'd told me about them while at the cabin. Now I wondered if what he'd said was true.

They were both beautiful, one taller than the other by a few inches, her svelte body, long dark hair, and stunning blue eyes screaming of model material just as he'd mentioned. The other one was equally as gorgeous, her hourglass figure close to mine. While she'd used makeup to hide her bruises fairly well, the sight of her split lip riled me, and I didn't even know her. Thankfully, they were both wearing jeans. Just like normal women. Was there any such thing inside this family? The shorter girl approached first and I finally threw out my hand for a shake.

She seemed confused, immediately squealing and grabbing my arms, pulling me into a hug.

"Oh, my God. I never thought our big brother would get married."

They had no clue. None. "Um. It happened fast."

"I'll say," the other girl said, swaggering closer, her grin equally as warm and inviting. "Oh, I'm Maria and this is Theodora."

"Hi." This was awkward as hell. I backed away, trying to find the right words. "I'm Sarah."

"I heard. You're a surgeon. Impressive. Very impressive," Theodora said as she gave me another onceover. "I'm happy to have a job at an investment bank."

"He must adore you," Maria added.

"Ladies, I don't know how to tell you this, but the arrangement isn't... let's just say it wasn't by choice." At least Dillon wasn't in the room. He'd likely tell on me as soon as Gabriel returned. Whatever. I didn't care at this point.

Theodora glanced toward the door and frowned. "We weren't born yesterday, Sarah. Besides, our father spilled the beans about who you are and why the two of you met."

"Then you know this isn't what I want to have happen. And your brother doesn't like me very much." *He simply wants to fuck me like a wild animal.* I certainly couldn't tell them that either. While I might be punished later for telling them the truth, I refused to act like a victim. I also wouldn't be stupid enough to try to get their help.

Do you really want to leave him?

The little voice had already switched sides. The answer was a decided 'I have no clue.'

Maria laughed. "You don't know our brother very well. Let me tell you a secret or two about him. One. Gabriel has always been stubborn, refusing to follow the family edicts. Two. He hasn't touched another woman since his ex-fiancée was murdered. It wouldn't matter if you were the president's daughter. If he didn't adore you, then he'd find another way to destroy his target."

"I called our brother on the carpet when our father told us. I could hear it in Gabriel's voice how much he cares for you."

283

I glanced at Theodora but was concentrating on what Maria had said.

"Fiancée?" I asked. He'd left that part out. No wonder he was so possessive.

"Tragic. He was so in love. It was only a couple weeks before the wedding and she was gunned down." Maria frowned.

"A robbery. Right?"

The two women looked at each other, Theodora doing a terrible job of lying. "They really don't know for certain. Obviously, he's over it now. We're happy for him."

"He wasn't very likeable for a long time. Grumpy all the time," Maria breathed.

"I guess he had his reasons," I said absently.

I heard Maria but wondered why he'd lied about this in particular. Because he didn't want to worry me about my safety? That was a good bet, but there was more. I was certain of it.

"He was supposed to bring her to Italy to see me," Maria half whispered, sadness in her voice.

"How long were you there?"

"Almost five years," she answered.

There was something about the timing that bothered me, not that it mattered any longer.

"You've upset her, Maria. That's not why we're here." Theodora broke the tension. "Look, we understand what's happening here more than you may realize, but whether you want to believe us or not, we have short chains as well. The glory of being a princess in the Giordano family isn't what it's cracked up to be. Our father has yet to leap out of the dark ages."

"She's right," Maria piped in. "There are two soldiers waiting outside for the ride alone. I had constant body-guards while I lived in Italy. I couldn't go anywhere without at least one soldier with me at all times. Why don't we enjoy the limo that dear old Daddy ordered for us and spend the day together? We'll purchase a few things, have a nice lunch, and maybe it will allow you to see that we're not all bad. I think you understand the position we're all in."

"Have either one of you ever been threatened?" I asked as I noticed Dillon walking toward the door.

They glanced at each other again. That answered everything I didn't want to ask.

"A few times." Theodora touched her face.

"I'm sorry about this Nico person. If it makes you feel any better, Gabriel beat the shit out of him."

Her eyes shifted into a moment of fiery anger. Then she looked away. "Gabriel doesn't understand and there's no way of explaining it to him that he'll accept."

"That sounds dangerously close to admitting you like the guy, even if he beat you up," I told her.

"That's just it. I don't think he did it. He called me last night and—"

"Theodora!" Maria snapped. "Are you crazy? You talked to that bastard?"

As the door was opened, the dogs bounding inside, I took a step back, watching as the pups gravitated toward them. Then I noticed how Dillon's eyes lit up when he saw Maria.

"They're adorable," Theodora said with a squeal in her voice. She'd dropped to the floor, crossing her legs. The pups were going nuts.

While Maria fawned over them, she remained standing, unable to keep her eyes off the brooding bodyguard. The pull toward one another was similar to what I felt with Gabriel. It was interesting to see it from the other side.

"Dillon. I didn't know you were still here. I..." Maria couldn't finish.

"Maria, you look amazing," Dillon breathed then caught himself after tossing me a look. "I mean, Ms. Giordano."

"Dillon. I'm not going to say a thing," I said to him. "Take your time getting reacquainted. Then we'll leave." Their interaction gave me a real smile. It was nice to see someone so obviously in love. I sat down next to Theodora, stroking Goldie.

She sighed. "Those two have had a thing for years. I think they had a crush on each other starting when she was sixteen. You know how fabulous that went over. Then they shared a kiss much later and our dad found out. I thought he was going to beat Dillon to death. Luciano stopped him from doing so. That's why Daddy allowed her to go to Italy. That was only a few months after..."

"His wife and child were murdered."

"Gabriel told you."

"Yes. I just don't understand how you can stand to live a life with constant danger surrounding you."

Theodora laughed, the sound bitter. "We were born into it. Dillon has nowhere else to go, at least that's what he's told me before."

"They can be together at this point."

"You don't understand how it works. My father would never allow it."

"What about Gabriel? He's in charge now."

After wrinkling her nose, she smiled. "I'm not sure. He's more like our father than he wants to admit."

"I don't know about that." I thought about the conversation I'd overheard and had to admit that Gabriel was very different than I'd thought only a day before. We allowed them some time, Theodora the one who interrupted them.

"We should get going. We won't make it a long day. I know you don't want to do this," Theodora said loudly enough Dillon glanced in our direction.

"I'll take care of the puppies while you're gone," Dillon said. I knew he would.

Maria blushed then backed away, but there was no doubt about how strongly they felt for each other, their initial reaction a clear indication.

The same way you feel when Gabriel walks into a room.

Shut up, little voice. I certainly didn't need to be reminded how my body had betrayed me. I tugged on Theodora's arm before she had a chance to get up. "What did you mean about Nico? Why don't you think he had anything to do with it?"

She seemed sheepish, darting a glance at her sister before answering. It would seem Nico was her dirty little secret. "Because we've been seeing each other in private for a few months. I don't hate the thought of getting married to him. I was shocked when I was attacked and what the asshole said scared me. Maria assumed it was Nico and I let her think that. Because of it, my brother beat him up."

"Because he cares about you."

"I realize that, but he'll start a war and that can't happen."

"You're certain Nico didn't have it done to make a point?"

She shook her head. "The guy who did it wasn't one of Nico's men. I know all of them. Okay? Please don't tell anyone. Please. I'll be banished or worse."

Christ. The girl was in love with the man. I guess it was true that every family had secrets. "I'm not going to say a thing, but you need to be careful. Gabriel is out for blood."

"I know. He's a good man, Sarah. I know what he did to you was wrong, very wrong. But he and Luciano were so close. I've never seen him so devastated except…"

She didn't need to finish her sentence. Gabriel hadn't allowed himself to get close to anyone outside of the family given what happened to his fiancée. Then his only other true friend was killed. "I think I can handle shopping today."

As I stood, Maria walked closer. "I have an idea," I told her. "We'll go shopping another day as well, but I'll insist I come get you." I threw Dillon a quick look and she immediately figured out what I was saying.

"I think I'm going to like having you as another sister, maybe more than my real one."

"Hey!" Theodora snapped. "Not fair."

As they started laughing, I couldn't help but join in. They had a special bond, just like Carrie and I did.

Just like normal people.

As we headed for the door, I stopped and patted Dillon on the arm. "You're a good man. I'll see what I can do."

A wry smile crossed his face, and he nodded both out of respect as well as if to tell me he'd keep our little secret.

As we walked out, I only wondered what other dark, dangerous secrets were lurking in the shadows.

In both our lives.

* * *

Gabriel

"Fuck," I hissed as I headed toward the private door to the club. There were a few cars in the parking lot, some of which I didn't recognize, but the employees would arrive shortly given the opening time. Bruno walked out, giving me a nod.

"He's not here," he said as he scanned the vehicles.

"You're certain of that?" Dillon had asked Bruno to check the security tapes at the club. Something else I'd give the man credit for.

"Positive. I've been watching the cameras after I got here given Dillon's phone call. Besides, the asshole is always bragging about the old Trans Am like it's worth a million bucks. Piece of shit."

I walked inside, not waiting for the elevator, taking the stairs two at a time. I stormed into my office, my hand on my weapon. Bruno had been the one to open up the club, sending Dillon the short video. I headed for the camera system, pulling up the footage he'd tagged.

"I knew it was an employee or a regular. They must have waited inside until the last person left," he said.

It had to be an employee who'd worked in the club, or the security system would have been activated. Few employees knew I'd installed additional cameras in the private area just in case something exactly like this happened. While no one else had a key to my office, that didn't mean there weren't ways of picking the lock. There wasn't a single one manufactured that couldn't be bypassed. If I remembered correctly, Demarco had been a high-end thief before joining the family.

Bruno stood behind me as the image came into view. As the perpetrator moved toward the computer, he made certain he didn't face the camera, but he didn't have to.

He was missing two fingers on one of his hands.

The bastard had wanted revenge. Or he'd been hired several months before to steal information regarding our businesses. Even though he'd been clandestine in his activities, it was too damn easy pegging him as the leak. I didn't believe in coincidences or matters of convenience. I had a feeling Demarco had sold his soul for a hefty sum of money, or maybe the promise of power. Depending on what had been taken could mean every one of our illegitimate businesses could be exposed, which would allow for territory to be taken from under us.

I continued watching until Demarco pulled out a jump drive, inserting it into my laptop. That's all I needed to see. I moved to the computer, not bothering to sit down as I moved to the security system I'd installed only a few days before. It allowed me to see exactly what had been copied, including the timestamp.

The fucker had taken a membership list, which didn't concern me. However, he'd taken some of the information that I'd stored regarding some of our most prominent members that I could use if necessary.

What the hell was he planning on doing, blackmailing them for money? Or leaking the information to the press? I wasn't in the mood to try to figure that out.

"Was he found?"

"Yeah. I told the stupid asshole his car would get him into trouble one day. He's at a motel just outside of town. I just happen to know the chick who runs the place," he said as he grinned. "So I got his room number."

The man was efficient.

"If you ask me, boss, he's making a drop of some kind," he added.

No, he was selling the information for personal gain. If I had to guess, to the Morettis. Fuck. "What's the name?"

As he provided the address, I took a deep breath.

"Do you want me to go with you, boss?" he asked.

"No. Finish what you're doing. I'll handle it." I didn't waste any time heading to my car. How long had he been providing information? With the marriage between Theodora and Nico, as well as stolen documents, they could simply wait until our organization imploded.

I pressed down on the accelerator, furious I'd allow the fucker to live. That would now be rectified. Then I'd begin the process of annihilating the Morettis piece by piece.

The drive was without incident, Demarco's Trans Am hidden in the back of one of the buildings. I added another clip of ammunition then headed to the stairs located in the back, taking them two at a time. I listened for any sounds coming from the other rooms. Given the time of day, there was almost no one at the shithole, which would make things easier.

I moved to his door, cautiously peering in through the inch crack in the drapes, unable to see anyone. As I pulled the weapon into my hands, I glanced down both sides of the corridor then kicked in the door, closing it behind me, noticing his weapon had been placed on the vanity located outside the shower room.

"What the fuck?" I heard his muffled voice. I refused to give him the opportunity of grabbing the gun, snatching it seconds before he threw open the door, shocked at seeing me standing in front of him.

I grabbed him by the throat, yanking him further away from the toilet, smashing his head against the mirror. As it cracked, he moaned, slamming his hands on the counter, but I was too quick for him, wrapping my hand around his throat with one hand, shoving the barrel of my weapon against his temple with the other.

He held up his hands, panting as he tried to get a good look at me in the smashed mirror. "What are you doing?"

"What do you think? Where is it?"

"What?"

I laughed and squeezed his neck until he wheezed. "The drive."

I noticed he attempted to smile and pulled his head away, preparing to smash it again.

"You're too late."

"I'm curious, Demarco. What did the Morettis offer you to sell out?"

He laughed. "They'll come for you. They know about your bitch." He laughed and I slammed his head into the mirror.

"You're in no position to threaten me." Shit. I hadn't told Dillon that she was to remain in the house. Goddamn it.

"You're a fucking fool."

"I might be but at least I'll be the one walking out of here today. You'll be getting a one-way ticket to hell." As I prepared to fire, he had the most peaceful look on his face.

"He said you would never figure it out. It's funny about betrayal. It comes from somewhere you least expect."

I wanted to laugh. Was he offering advice? "Don't worry. I know exactly where it's coming from."

"Every jungle has a snake."

His last words were interesting but not a deterrent. I pulled the trigger not once but twice, backing away and watching as his body slid to the floor.

As I grabbed my phone dialing Dillon, I started to ransack the place.

"Dillon. Is Sarah safe?"

"I'm certain she is, but she's still out with your sisters, sir. Why?"

I jerked up, snarling as my blood ran cold. "What the hell are you talking about?"

"Theodora said your father had them come to take her shopping."

Fuck. Fuck. Fuck! "She wasn't supposed to leave." I'd neglected to mention I'd gone against my father's orders.

"Shit. I didn't know, sir," Dillon huffed.

"Who was with them?"

"A couple of your father's men I don't know. Did something else happen?"

"Find them. Get them back there. Now!"

"Yes, sir."

"Get the house surrounded with soldiers, my father's house as well. Do it quickly and I don't give a shit what my father says, my orders stand. Do you get it?"

"Absolutely, sir."

Why the hell had Sarah disobeyed me? For spite? To push my boundaries even more?

"Last thing. I need a cleanup crew as soon as possible at a motel in shit town." I gave him the address of the motel, unconcerned if anyone had heard any noise. There was a war on the way, one that could destroy our way of life. No. I couldn't… I would not allow that to happen, no matter what needed to be done.

Hissing, I slid the gun into my pocket, tearing the place apart. When I finally found the drive taped under one of the drawers, I wasted no time. She had to be alive. If anything happened to her, I'd burn down the entire city.

But only after tearing the Morettis apart limb from limb.

No one hurt the people I cared about.

No one would ever touch the woman I loved.

If they dared try, they would face the wrath of a true monster.

CHAPTER 15

 abriel

Rage.

It tore through me like a wildfire. I paced the floor of my office, cursing under my breath.

"They're on their way back, Mr. Giordano," Dillon told me. He sensed the caged lion in me was about to break out, ripping everything and everyone to shreds who dared cross his path.

"That's what I heard thirty minutes ago, and don't you dare tell me it's because of New York traffic." Although that was a part of it.

The women had been gone for at least two hours before I'd learned about it. Fucking hours. Anyone could have fired off a weapon from a vehicle or a close building. Even though Dillon had ordered their return, they were taking their sweet time getting here. My patience was completely gone. As I swept my arm across the desk, I took no comfort in the sound of breaking glass or the hard thudding my laptop made when it smashed against the hardwood floor.

The soldiers were in place, but I knew it was only a matter of time before there would be an attempt to invade the tight security.

The dogs barked for a full minute until Dillon calmed them, issuing soft words that I couldn't understand.

I slammed my fists against the desk's surface, trying to control my breathing.

"She's in good hands, boss. I made certain of that."

Exhaling, I glared at Dillon. He wasn't to blame for Sarah getting out from under my protection. She'd been told she couldn't go. She'd been given the rules. She'd ignored them.

And she could have lost her life.

That wasn't acceptable.

That wasn't going to happen again.

"She damn well better be," I retorted. I'd never been this tense or this angry.

He nodded, knowing that I was almost over the edge. "The nurse is out of town."

"What does that mean?"

"She left for a short vacation, so we don't need to worry about her."

I almost laughed. At least something had gone right in the last few days.

A full two minutes passed and the tension continued to mount. My phone rang and I knew exactly who to expect.

"What the fuck did you do, ordering goddamn soldiers to surround my house? My men do a fine job."

"Yeah? Well, things are about to get dicey, Pops. You'll be thanking me later."

"What the hell is going on?"

After explaining the situation, I noticed Dillon was even more furious. He moved twice to the window, peering out to ensure men were guarding the back. "I want a goddamn meeting with Joseph Moretti tomorrow."

"After what you did, you'll be lucky if he doesn't try and put a bullet in your brain."

"Then we'll know he's the one determined to bring us down." I sucked in my breath before I said anything else. "Which I don't buy."

Pops was thrown by my words. "What are you thinking, son?"

"Just set up the meeting, Pops."

He grunted. "I'll see what I can do. You better be right about this."

Yeah, I better be.

"Fucking bastard," Dillon said under his breath.

"Yeah. There are a lot to go around. You could place me in that category."

Smirking, he shook his head. "Not if I want to live for much longer."

I lifted my eyebrows and grinned. He was a good man to have on my side.

Woof!

Happy noises grabbed my attention.

Goldie and Shadow. As I watched them playing with toys that had been brought into my office, I reminded myself that Sarah had once had a life she enjoyed. Then I'd stripped it away, thinking it was my right. The dogs were proof that I'd missed out on what living really meant. I'd shut down years ago, but it had taken bringing the precocious woman into my life for me to be able to admit it.

Even though I dared not say the words out loud.

Weakness.

The damn word continued to haunt me.

I'd been taught since as early as I could remember that exhibiting any signs of weakness would precipitate my death. I wouldn't know when or how, but enemies had long memories. I'd learned to close myself off, caring about no one with two exceptions. Now they were both gone. Goddamn it. Shadow noticed I was staring at him and ventured forward, his entire backside wiggling, his wagging tail reminding me of a helicopter. I'd never been allowed to have pets. I'd never brought a girl to my parents' house. They were simple, normal things that occurred in almost every household. To me, they were foreign. I leaned over, rubbing behind his ears, the sweet ruffing noises he made allowing me to smile.

"They like you," Dillon said quietly.

"Yeah, they'd like anyone."

"That's not true. Dogs have an innate sense for spotting evil."

I lifted my head, chuckling halfheartedly. "And you're an expert?"

"When I was real young, I had a dog. He was my world." Dillon could be the master of masking his emotions. I'd seen more of them from him in two days that I had the entire time I'd known him.

With a single exception.

After he'd lost his wife, he'd let go, mostly with bouts of uncontrollable rage. Then a quiet calm had enveloped him, his silence a clear indication he could blow at any time. To his credit, he'd yet to do that. But he wasn't a happy man.

That seemed to be the norm in the Giordano household. I thought about Demarco and couldn't put my finger on why the entire interaction bothered the hell out of me. What was I missing?

I took several gasping breaths as I lowered my head, visions of her sweeping through my mind. Jesus Christ. I had to get control of myself. I replayed what Demarco had said and knew I was missing something. What the fuck was going on?

When a drink was slid across my desk, I jerked up my head.

"You need this, Mr. Giordano."

I was so sick of hearing my last name that I couldn't take it any longer. "You can use my first name. We've known each other long enough. I'm not my father." If I continued to repeat it enough times, maybe it would turn out to be true.

"Drink the scotch, Gabriel. You need to calm down."

On any other day I'd be pissed at him, but not today. He was right. That's exactly what I needed to do. Why had she gotten under my skin to the point I couldn't think straight?

Because she broke through that steel barrier you placed around yourself. Because she can handle the beast. Because she wants what you can no longer provide.

Was it true? Was I incapable of being the man she needed, not just the horrible monster I'd allowed her to see?

"You care about her," he offered. There was no question in his voice, no attempt to disrespect me, just a statement that he felt was truthful.

"Yeah, I do." Admitting it was easier than I would have thought.

"Then show her."

I studied him for a few seconds, nodding because I knew he was right. "I think it's a little too late for that."

"No, boss. It's never too late. She cares about you too. Both of you are just too stubborn to admit it. I know why you hunted her down, but you obviously made a strong connection with her. That's the truth beneath what the two of you shared, not the business you were forced to sink yourself into."

Since when had he gotten so damn smart? "Perhaps, but there are things that often can't be changed."

"You rule the Giordano Empire. So do it your way. Make changes. Impose different rules. Cut down your enemies. Your goal should be to do whatever is necessary to make yourself happy. If not, you'll regret it."

Truer words could never have been said. "I will destroy the Morettis."

"You're certain Nico was the man responsible?"

Another truth was that I wasn't certain. I'd seen a look in my sister's eyes that had haunted me. She'd been shocked, emotionally hurt, but she hadn't been angry. I didn't like that one fucking bit. "We will plan on rounding up some of their soldiers as another warning."

His eyes opened wide, and I could tell he wanted to disagree with me. He looked away before answering. "Yes, sir. Whatever you believe is right." He walked toward my desk, retrieving my demolished laptop. Then he grabbed my empty glass, heading toward the bar to refill it.

Right.

The word wasn't typical in the Giordano vocabulary. Here I stood, in a house I'd been determined to hate, drinking expensive scotch as I waited for the woman I'd fallen in love with to be brought safely back to the house. I wore Demarco's blood like another badge of honor, basking from the moment I'd pulled the trigger.

I was a sick, disgusting man.

Dillon was definitely right about one thing. I ran the empire. It was mine to do with however I wanted. Changes would be made.

"However, you need to know that word on the street is that you're vulnerable."

I almost laughed. "Does that surprise you?"

It was obvious he didn't want to answer. "They don't know what you're capable of."

"And what is that?"

I'd also never known the man to appear so uncomfortable. "Killing anyone who gets in your way." He poured the glass two thirds full, hesitating before turning around. No, he had no idea what I was made of. I'd yet to make that known. I'd reacted to issues instead of planning, certainly not a recent trait I was proud of.

What I found interesting was that up until a few days ago, I'd never eliminated anyone. That had been Luciano's call. To realize my reputation had changed so quickly should have been appealing. Instead, it was disturbing as hell.

As soon as he slid the filled glass onto my desk, we both heard laughter coming from the foyer. I rounded the corner, taking long strides toward the front door.

Both Maria and Theodora were chattering and laughing as they eased several bags onto the granite floor. To my surprise, Sarah seemed happy, beaming as she finished whatever story she was telling. The dogs came bounding from my office from hearing the sound of her voice, all three girls fawning over them while the pups woofed and barked, gleeful Sarah was home.

Home.

As if she'd ever be able to consider this her home.

"Oh, babies. I missed you. I might have a treat or two inside one of these bags," Sarah said, still laughing. There was so much joy in her tone, something I thought I'd never hear again.

"And Auntie Maria and Auntie Theodora might have purchased a few toys as well," Theodora added.

She'd been the one to beg our father for a dog. Every Christmas. Every birthday. How many tears had she shed from being told no time and time again?

Maria saw me first, her eyes lighting up as I hadn't seen in a hell of a long time.

"Gabe! Your fiancée is incredible. We adore her," she said. Then her eyes opened wide as she noticed the blood on my shirt. She'd seen it before, although at the point when she'd left for Italy, only on our father. I sensed a few seconds of fear until she masked that emotion.

"Yes, we do. She's hysterical. We laughed for hours," Theodora purred. A single nervous tic appeared in the corner of her mouth as she caught a glimpse of the stain on the front of my shirt. I sensed she was terrified I'd killed Nico. But I knew her. She wouldn't ask in front of Sarah.

Both my sisters seemed oblivious to my building anger. Only Sarah sensed my foul mood, turning toward me, her face pensive.

"What the fuck did you think you were doing?" I snapped, barely controlling my breathing. "Sarah, get into my office."

"What's wrong with you?" Maria snarked. "Father said you wanted us to take her shopping."

"That was his determination, not mine. She was told she couldn't go anywhere. Sarah defied me." I took two steps closer and Theodora moved between us.

"Check yourself, brother. What the fuck is wrong with you? She's not a prisoner." She half laughed after making the statement. "Oh, what a fool am I. You kidnapped her. Right? So she is a prisoner. You expect her to follow your rules when you stole her from her life. You're a fucking repulsive son of a bitch."

I'd never seen her this animated, her words of hatred stronger than any she'd spewed in years.

"Why are there guards outside? There must be ten of them," Sarah asked, her voice shaking in anger.

"There are more than that. At my father's house as well," I shot back at her, rolling my hand through my hair, the relief almost as sickening as the worry had been.

"Why?" Maria asked. "What's going on?"

"Business, sister."

"Damn it, Gabriel. We're not children," Theodora hissed.

"No, but you are in danger, and I'm supposed to protect you. Go to my office, Sarah. Don't make me ask you again." Fuck. I was losing it.

"Leave her alone!" Theodora added.

"It's okay," Sarah said curtly. She allowed her gaze to fall, concern in her eyes. Then she shook her head as if comprehending what I'd done. "I'll do what he asks."

Asks.

She still believed I was asking her?

"No, it's not," Maria joined in.

"I can handle him." Sarah's voice was filled with defiance.

"You shouldn't need to," Theodora retorted. "This isn't who my brother is."

I took a deep breath, holding it for a few seconds before addressing her. "This *is* who I am. This is exactly what I must be. Things have changed. Now I'm in charge and this is the way it's going to be. The two of you need to go back to your father's house and stay there."

"What do you mean stay there?" Maria challenged.

"You heard me. You will not leave the house under any circumstances."

Sarah shook her head. "You started a war."

"Yes, my beautiful creature. I did."

I could see fire in Theodora's eyes and as she lunged at me, able to slap me across the face, I resisted reacting. Dillon pulled her off, holding her flailing body as she spewed words of hatred.

"You are a fucking asshole, Gabriel. You don't rule my life, nor do you rule Maria's or Sarah's. Get a clue. You're not God."

Exhaling, I turned my head in my sister's direction. "Yes. I. Am."

The look in their eyes said it all. They would never forget or forgive. So be it if I could manage to keep them alive.

Maria pressed her hand against Sarah's arm, whispering words that I was able to hear.

"I'm so sorry."

"I'll be fine," Sarah insisted as she walked past me and into the living room, the puppies trailing behind her.

"Dillon. Make certain my sisters arrive safely at their father's house. Follow them inside."

"Yes, sir," he answered. "Come on, ladies."

Theodora stopped before being pushed out the front door, glaring at me as she'd done so many times. "What happened to you, brother? You used to be a different person. Oh, and the last time I checked, he's your father too."

Anger swelled inside, clouding my vision, but the rage was directed toward myself. I'd allowed the situation to get out of hand. I'd fallen into my father's trap of using force to get what I wanted. When the door was closed with a hard thud,

I closed my eyes, rubbing my jaw as I thought about what to say to Sarah.

A flood of emotions jetted through me, most with sharp edges, cutting into my skin. I deserved to feel all the fury and hatred, but my sisters had no idea how much I loathed myself.

As I returned to my office, I noticed how sterile the environment seemed. My beautiful surgeon stood with her arms folded, staring down at the mess I'd created in my fit of rage.

"Who did you kill?" she asked so calmly that it took me aback.

"A traitor."

"Says the judge and jury."

"I caught him on camera at one of my clubs."

That surprised her. As she lifted her gaze to meet mine, another wave of sadness settled in. "Are you hurt?"

I glanced at my shirt and sighed. "No. However, I'm worried. Information was stolen from me that could have proven detrimental."

"You really do believe we're all in danger."

I walked closer, wanting nothing more than to wrap my arms around her, keeping her close.

And safe.

Did I have the ability to do that?

"Yes, I do. I believe you've been made a target."

"Because you care about me." Her words were so cold, so indifferent.

"Yes, my beautiful Sarah, I do. The fact it's known will be used against me."

"The way of your life."

"The way of our life."

She laughed then picked up several papers, shooing the dogs away from the broken glass. Then she grabbed my drink, finishing it off in one gulp. "Do you know what struck me today after spending time with your sisters?"

"What?"

"How normal they seemed. Unaffected. Because they were able to laugh, so was I. I enjoyed spending time with them. Then this. I don't know why I thought maybe you were changing. Isn't that ridiculous."

"I think that's amazing," I said honestly. She studied me for several seconds before speaking again.

"I can't marry you, Gabriel. Even if I said the words and signed the marriage license, which you could force me to do, that won't make us married in God's eyes or mine."

"I assure you that I'll make it worth your interest. You'll have your own bank account, credit cards, whatever you need. And as promised, you can go back to your chosen profession, with limitations of course. You can have the wedding of your dreams. Anything you want, anywhere you want." It was fascinating to me that I would do anything to make her happy.

"Oh, my God. You didn't listen to me before. Fuck the money. Fuck the nice things. I can't marry you because I'm afraid of losing myself in you." She was exasperated, clenching her eyes shut.

"You matter to me, Sarah. I can't risk your safety under any circumstances. By now, there are very few who don't know you belong to me."

"So they'll use me against you."

"Yes."

I had listened to her but in truth, they'd terrified me more than I wanted to admit to myself. She was right. Buying her anything would never matter to her.

Her words were so damn heartfelt that I was blown away. As quickly as love sparkled in her baby blues, the deep emotion was replaced with uncertainty and anger with herself for yet another admittance.

"Plus, I need truthfulness and someone who will share their life, not just try and keep me protected as if I'm too frail to handle the truth."

"You're anything but frail, Sarah. You're the strongest woman I've ever met."

"Then don't keep me in the dark about your life."

"There are things that you won't want to hear."

She laughed. "I assure you that I've heard much worse. Just be truthful with me."

"Have I lied to you? I told you from the beginning that I wasn't trying to be a good man. Maybe that's not possible for me to be. However, whether you choose to believe it or not, I do understand and am capable of love. You might not see it, but I am. I'm not completely inhuman. Sadly, certain decisions I've made have placed myself and my family in a precarious position, but what you don't understand or accept is that I had no choice to enter into this life. Taking over was a requirement."

"You had a choice to leave, and you took it. That took guts."

Guts. She had no idea how much leaving had affected me. "But I was forced back."

"By me."

"No, Sarah. I was wrong in saying that. You caused nothing. Fate intervened. I was too blind to see it before. I was too enraged to think clearly."

Sarah looked away briefly. "You asked me if I believed you ever lied to me. The answer is yes, you have. About your fiancée. She was the love of your life. Since then, you shut down completely. You let not only your family win but whoever killed her. Don't you see that?"

Jesus Christ.

Another knife was jammed into my gut.

"You're right, Sarah. I did shut down. You have no idea what it's like to believe someone died because of you." The words hit us both with the full understanding of what we'd shared and everything we needed.

Each other.

Grimacing, I took several deep breaths. "I'm fucking sorry, Sarah. That was cruel."

She shook her head several times. "Yes, it was, but you didn't intend it to be."

What the fuck was wrong with me?

"By the way, did you ever stop to think that maybe I wanted to learn more about you? This might be a game to you, Gabriel, but for me this is unimaginable, especially how strongly I feel about you." She laughed bitterly, a single tear slipping past her lashes. When I tried to rub it away, she took a step back, refusing to allow me to touch her.

Goddamn it, I hated the tension between us.

"You know enough to hate me and maybe that's the way it should be." The hollowness of my voice was the true measure of the intense ache in my heart.

"The trouble is I can't hate you." She took a deep breath and looked away. "She asked you to distance yourself from your family. Didn't she?"

Reflecting on the past would do no good at this point, but it was difficult not to take a few seconds and remember. "Yes. Mary was insistent. I told her no at first because I enjoyed being the kid of a powerful mafia Don in college. What I told you before was true. I simply left out the final reason we broke up."

"Later you asked if she'd take you back after you'd denounced your family."

"Yes."

"Do you know who killed her?"

She wasn't going to let this alone. "I thought I did."

"Nico's family."

I brushed a strand of hair from her face, taking a few seconds to caress her skin. Just touching her calmed me, creating a bubble around us with impenetrable material. Who was I kidding? The bubble could be burst at any moment. "Yes."

"That's why you hate them so much."

"It's not the only reason. However, I'm beginning to wonder if any of my accusations are correct."

"Then don't continue with the violence."

Huffing, I shook my head. "If only it were that easy."

"Just for the record, I would never ask you to forfeit major aspects of your life." She blew the same piece of hair from her face, which caused me to smile. I took her into my arms and breathed in her perfume, longing to devour every inch of her body.

She pressed her hands against me, darting her eyes across mine. "Just for the record, I would find a way to leave my life for you," I told her.

Her eyes opened wide and her expression softened. "Then you'd be a fool."

"I've been called much worse," I teased. I lowered my head, nipping her earlobe several times, reveling in the way her body shuddered in my hold. As I eased away, the way she was staring at me so intently appeared as if she was looking straight through me. I'd felt like from minute one she'd been able to see through the façade.

"And I'm certain you will be again."

"Including by you. Now, we need to deal with certain things at hand. You disobeyed me."

"I thought you'd changed your mind when your sisters just showed up."

"When I give you a direct order, you will follow it."

"Says God himself."

I forced her against me, refusing to let her go. "I have my reasons, Sarah. Don't you see that by now?"

"What I believe is that you have no clue what's happening around you. Nico didn't order the beating of your sister." As soon as she issued the words, she sucked in her breath.

"Why?"

"I can tell. Okay? She likes him."

I narrowed my eyes, half laughing. "Yes, she does." Was she not telling me something? At this point, I wouldn't push her, but it could become necessary. "Just like Maria and Dillon are in love."

She gasped, a small amount of light returning to her eyes. "You knew that?"

"I didn't want to be involved with the family business, Sarah, but that doesn't mean I allowed myself to have blinders on. Of course I did. He's loved her since before he married a very nice girl after Maria left for Italy. Our father refused to allow their union."

"That's why she left."

"Technically, that's why she was banished."

"Oh, my God," she half whispered. "What is wrong with your father? Your mother? How could she stand for her own children being treated the way they have?"

"My mother knew exactly what she was getting into when she was required to marry him. That's the old ways, that of my grandfather and his father before him. The truth is that my mother managed to soften Pops over the years."

"It makes me sick to think about how he was before. I'm sorry if my words upset you. No one would ever be allowed to treat my children that way."

"Which is another reason I adore you," I told her.

A slight blush swept up from her jaw. "So you know, Maria hates your father for what he did and she'll hate you if you don't break that rule."

I had no idea what to say to her. I'd been forced to face the fact that I'd talked a big game about altering my father's organization. Now I was acting as if that's the only method that could work. "In due time."

"Well, maybe there's a little hope for you after all. I didn't mean to alarm you."

"You did. You worried your babies too."

She allowed herself to smile then glanced down at them. "Unconditional love."

I cupped both sides of her face, bringing her closer. "I could have lost you. That ate me inside, releasing the beast that dwells inside every member of this family."

"You didn't lose me. I'm standing right here."

"You don't understand."

"If you truly believe that then help me to understand. Not about the danger. I get that. In your world, violence can erupt at any time, which is why you always carry a weapon with you. I need to know about you. Why do you care what happens to me?"

I knew exactly what she was looking for. As I lowered my head until our lips were almost touching, the ache inside of me continued to grow. I wanted to deny the way I felt, if for no other reason than to keep her protected, but goddamn it, I couldn't stand the thought of letting her go. "I do love you, Sarah. I don't know if that's enough, but it's how I feel."

She gripped my shirt with both hands, lifting her chin even as I held her fast. The look in her eyes was enough to destroy me, pulling apart all the ugly pieces that had framed my being. She had the ability to look inside the man who'd been hiding for years, refusing to accept the monster. In a way, she'd created a cocoon around me, her smile alone a reminder that not everything had to be masked from the wretchedness of reality.

When I finally captured her mouth, I held her lips open, breathing in the air from her lungs, praying the light from her soul would drive the anger and hatred aside. As she clung to me, I allowed myself to be caught in a web of longing, ignoring the pain and pressure, the anxiety that had plagued me. I might have saved her life, but she was the only one who could save my soul.

As the kiss became a manifestation of our intense longing, she rose onto her tiptoes, wrapping her long fingers around my neck. There was an explosion of sensations, hunger more pronounced than before. I couldn't imagine my life without her, even if I knew there was a chance I'd destroy everything good inside me. I no longer cared. She was mine. I'd claimed her the first moment I'd laid eyes on her. Now there was nothing and no one who would dare try to break us apart.

As I swept my tongue inside, dominating her mouth, she mewed in my hold. Her body trembled, her sweet sounds fueling the raging fire deep within. Every sound was blocked out, allowing only the ragged beating of our hearts. The taste of her was bittersweet, a reminder that our connection was tenuous.

When I finally broke the moment of intimacy, she closed her eyes, dragging her tongue across her lips. "I'm sorry."

"For what?" I breathed.

"For not trusting you before."

As she blinked several times, the sight of tears in her eyes sent a dagger into my heart. How in the fuck could I protect her? Exhaling, I backed away by a few inches, keeping my hand wrapped around her jaw. "You need to learn that I only want the best for you."

"For some crazy reason I believe you."

"I'm glad." That might save her life one day.

She dropped her gaze, chewing on her lip. "Then punish me."

Just the sound of her voice alone was enough to drive the beast living inside me to the surface. I allowed a swath of hot air to cascade across her face then pulled away completely. As I started to finish clearing my desk, she didn't need to be told what to do. Although her eyes never left me, she unfastened her jeans, tugging them over her hips. If only she understood how much I wanted to drive my cock deep inside, fulfilling every single fantasy she'd ever had.

I would do that soon enough. However, she needed to learn a valuable lesson. She'd yet to fully understand just how precarious my position was or how much her presence had changed me. My instincts continued to drive me to an entirely different realization than I'd expected upon taking the helm.

There was another enemy waiting in the wings.

I could list several possibilities, including law enforcement, but whoever it was had bided their time before striking like a snake. Luciano's death had expedited their plans. In my eyes, there was only one way of flushing them out.

Using Sarah as bait.

She'd need to learn to trust me in order to be able to keep her safe. Following my orders without hesitation was the only way to protect her.

I could barely take my eyes off her, my entire system on overdrive as an adrenaline rush tore through me. I'd never wanted to get close to anyone other than family after Mary's death. I'd known the second I heard about her murder that she'd been caught up in the family legacy, taken from me to prove a point. To this day, the person responsible had never stepped up to the plate, bragging as usually happened. It was as if history was repeating itself.

My body tensing, I shifted my attention back to Sarah. She'd removed her clothes, the sight of her naked body stealing my breath. She wasn't looking at me, instead staring out the window as if she could find answers to why she remained attracted to me.

"Stay right where you are," I told her before leaving the room, finding a broom and dustpan. It was time for me to learn to clean up my own messes. I'd walked into plenty of rooms where stunning women had taken the forefront, parading around in whatever designer gown they'd purchased in order to draw attention to themselves. I'd never paid enough attention to get a single name.

Walking into my office had an entirely different effect. Sarah was breathtaking under any circumstances, but today even her skin seemed luminescent. I could sense she was nervous, even though she'd learned about harsh discipline already. Everything about today was different.

She remained in front of the window as I cleaned up the debris, tossing the handful into the trashcan. As I beckoned her with a single finger, I took a deep breath, my mind spinning. As she walked closer, I thought once again about how much alike I was to my father.

Cold.

Brutal.

Unforgiving.

Incapable of providing the kind of love someone special like Sarah needed. I'd said the words and meant them, but there was a difference in being able to issue a statement and following through with it. "Lie across the desk," I told her.

She stared at me for a few seconds then did as I asked. This was a turning point that I hadn't seen coming. I'd neglected to tell her that I wanted a family, a house that wasn't a cold representation of a life I'd been forced to grow up in.

As I unfastened my belt, all I could think about was finding a house in another state, a location where there were no displays of violence in the street or people enshrouded in fear. A location where neighbors spoke to one another on a regular basis, enjoyed cookouts in the summer. A beautiful setting where the grass was always green and the flowers bloomed three hundred days of the year.

The perfect place to raise a family, complete with two adorable dogs.

Where holidays mattered.

Where laughter filled the air.

And where children would be safe without fear of being kidnapped off the street.

A beautiful place called serenity.

If only a place like that existed other than nestled in the darkest regions of my mind.

For Sarah, I'd walk through fire to find her a home worthy of her presence.

Even if it meant passing through streets of blood.

"So you know. Mary wasn't the love of my life."

"Then who?" she asked, her breath skipping.

"You are."

CHAPTER 16

 arah

Love.

The conviction in his voice kept me numb, aching inside. I couldn't care less what he did to me at this point. Hearing the words had shattered the last of my resolve. There was no right or wrong about my feelings, just an actuality that would haunt me forever no matter what happened. He was angry and fearful someone was coming for me. He couldn't care less about himself.

Crack!

I heard the whooshing sound first, the snapping of Gabriel's wrist second. Then I felt the blast of pain coursing down my legs. I jerked up from his desk, gasping for air as tears formed in my eyes. He'd spanked me before, but this time the agony was blinding. I knew he was trying to make a point, to remind me just how much danger I was in.

I'd felt it all day even though I was surrounded by two burly men with guns. While their presence hadn't affected either one of his sisters whatsoever, I'd continually stared at them, waiting for some attack coming from behind every bush. Only after a couple of hours had I finally started to relax.

I adored the two women, their verve and love of life undeniable. They'd made me feel welcome, as if I belonged. They'd insisted on purchasing lovely outfits, teasing me relentlessly until I'd tried them on. Then they'd given me hints about Gabriel, as only sisters could do. It had all been so very normal.

And completely weird.

But I'd enjoyed myself, right up until one of the bodyguards had received a terse phone call. We'd been ushered out of a store to the chagrin and loud voices of both Maria and Theodora. I'd thought they'd be demure given their upbringing. I hadn't expected their raucous behavior and take no shit attitude.

When I shifted on the desk, he pressed his hand against the small of my back. "Stay in position."

I knew the drill. Or he'd start over. I almost laughed, although nothing about this was funny.

I'd realized instantly that Gabriel would be angry but seeing the way he'd acted had floored me. It had also released thousands of butterflies into my stomach just like what had happened in the coffee shop. Maria had caught me thinking about him, or as she'd called it 'swooning' over him, and my instant red face had confirmed it. At least they hadn't been able to read my mind. That would have been awkward.

As he delivered four strikes in rapid succession, I sucked in my breath, stars floating in front of my eyes. I could hear his rapid breathing. The man was under a lot of stress, but the way he'd looked at me a few moments ago had not only stolen my breath but had allowed me to see even deeper inside his psyche.

I understood the way family duty often placed a stranglehold on someone's life, but he was suffering the consequences of acting out on his own. There was no doubt the man was dangerous, even if others had lost track of how brutal he could be. He could also be sweet and tender, caring and exciting, but surrendering to him completely would mean losing my soul and I wasn't prepared to do that. I was unable to fathom the life he'd led, the choices he'd been forced to make over the years. He'd given all of himself to a lifestyle not of his choosing. What kind of family did that to their own children?

And was he truly capable of breaking the cycle?

I gripped the edge of the desk and closed my eyes as he cracked the belt down four more times. When he exhaled, the sound was exaggerated and husky, as if this was adding to his stress. As he slowly rolled his fingers down my spine, I shivered almost uncontrollably. He knew exactly how to keep my blood heated and my skin tingling from a light touch and nothing else.

When he rolled the same fingers in circles on one buttock then the other, I sucked in my breath, the anticipation almost killing me. The heat resonating off my skin was incredible, but as had happened before, I was wet from his rough actions, my pussy aching for what only he could provide.

As he continued the spanking, I lost myself in the sound as well as the rush of thoughts in my mind. And images.

His body naked.

His mouth just before he kissed.

His thick, delicious cock.

God! I'd completely gone off the deep end.

Another two brutal strikes brought me back from fantasy land and I kicked out, moaning so loudly the dogs whined. "Oh, God."

"You've done very well," he said, his voice almost unrecognizable given the extreme lust. I knew exactly what was going to happen from here. He'd fuck me over his desk, completing the punishment.

And I'd enjoy every moment of it.

His breathing was still heavy, the sound raspy. When he tossed the belt several feet away, I braced for the moment of ecstasy. Then he scooped me into his arms, holding me against his chest. As he peered down, I wasn't prepared for the depth of what I witnessed in those few precious seconds. His soul was bared wide open, allowing me to see the anger and hatred, the sadness and remorse. And the guilt.

But I also saw something miraculous. A rebirth. No one would believe me. Perhaps I'd never believe it myself, but for those few incredible moments as he took the stairs two at a time, kicking open the bedroom door and ripping down the covers, nothing else mattered.

Just the two of us.

Two hearts beating in time.

Two damaged souls clinging together.

Two bodies prepared to become one.

I'd already lost myself in him.

He turned on a light next to the bed then flexed his fingers, slowly brushing them down my face to my chest, taking his time to allow them to travel all the way to my stomach, then down one leg.

I was shivering all over, the embers exploding into blue-tinted flames. He was entirely different tonight, as if the fear he'd lost me had shaken him to his very core. His power emanated in every movement, the shimmer in his dark eyes. He was famished, the expression screaming of all the vile things he'd do to me, but there was a slight softness to his usual edge.

His eyes never left me as he undressed, peeling away his clothes as if this was the first time we would be together. In a sense it was. He was enjoying the moment, refusing to allow the danger and treachery of whatever was going on outside of this house to interfere with the here and now.

Desire remained just below the surface, my body tingling from his touch. I could no longer hate myself because of it. There was far too much electricity between us, a raging connection that refused to be denied. He was no longer the animal I'd thought him to be, but a man in search of a soulmate, one he believed he'd found in me.

It was crazy.

It was reckless.

It was amazing.

When he was fully undressed, he crawled onto the bed, straddling my hips and planting his hands on either side of me. The man was utter perfection and the sensations crawling through me were exactly like the ones I'd felt when he'd taken me in the dressing room. Before he'd disrupted my world.

Before I'd known he wasn't my knight in shining armor.

But now, everything was different, the few days feeling more like months of knowing each other. It was difficult to put into well-formed thoughts, but he was the ultimate fantasy, a man who would never let me out of his sight.

Using a single finger, I rolled it down the length of his chest, marveling how the light touch seared me.

I caught the look in his eyes and shuddered all over again. The man was going to eat me alive. He lowered his head, taking a deep breath. Then as he blew the swath of hot air across my face, my nipples hardened, aching as they always did. I turned my head when his lips were only a few centimeters away, teasing him.

His growl was a clear indication he wouldn't tolerate it tonight. He nipped my ear, sliding the tip of his tongue around the shell, his hoarse whisper creating another fire. "I'm going to spend hours making love to you tonight. Then I'll start over in the morning."

His tone was also different, deeper and richer, an example of him being able to let go.

"Mmm…" I slid my hand to his groin, rolling the tip of my finger around his cockhead then across his sensitive slit. He was already hard and the second I wrapped my hand around his thickness, his shaft throbbed in my hand.

"Are you hungry for me?"

"Yes."

"Will you obey me?"

"Never," I huffed.

"I thought you'd say that. You'll spend your nights in a cage." There was something scintillating about the teasing sound of his voice, the words turning me on even more.

"I'll break free."

"Then I'll hunt you down. You know what happens then." He captured my mouth, instantly thrusting his tongue inside.

I rolled my arm around his neck, digging my fingers into his skin. He was so completely different that he took my breath away. There was more depth to his passion, exploding between us like a raging firestorm. I threw one leg over his, trying to pull him down. As expected, he resisted. The man would always need to be in charge.

The thought of relinquishing control had never been tastier, drawing out all my inhibitions. Being lost in the man was special, dangerous, and so exciting my mind was a blur. The kiss was a passionate roar, his tongue sweeping back and forth across mine. It was as if all time had stopped, nothing able to penetrate our defenses.

While my rational mind knew that not to be the truth, at this moment I didn't care. I was protected by a powerful force, a single man capable of shoving aside every demon.

He finally broke the moment of intimacy, pressing one hand under my jaw, lifting my head as he dragged his tongue around my lips then down the side of my neck. My heartbeats skipped, blood racing through my veins as he bit down on the skin around my pulse of life.

Moaning, I could no longer feel my legs but the heat between my thighs continued to build, my pussy clenching and releasing.

"So perfect," he whispered and bit down again, the slice of pain forcing a series of whimpers from my mouth. He kept his firm hold, rubbing his thumb back and forth across my lips as he continued his exploration. With every long drag of his tongue, goosebumps floated across my skin.

"I can't wait to call you my wife."

I wasn't certain why his words thrilled me as much as they did. Marriage and commitment, an honored tradition. While I knew he meant the words, I was still shocked by the sound of them.

We'd take a savage vow to become man and wife. I now knew he would protect me with his life, but would he promise to love and honor? That I wasn't certain of. I guess it no longer mattered. Would we be allowed to enjoy any kind of normalcy or would fate intervene tragically again?

I shuddered from the thought, sickened that it had taken death to bring us together. Would death be the reason to tear us apart?

Stop it. Stop thinking that way.

I closed my eyes, refusing to allow my own personal demons to interfere with this beautiful moment.

"What do you really want, my beautiful Sarah?"

"What do I want?" I breathed as he continued peppering my skin with kisses then swirled his tongue around my nipple, languishing over the simple action.

"Yes," he growled, the deep, husky sound reverberating into every synapse.

"Everything."

"Then that's exactly what I'll give you." He shifted his head to my other nipple, sucking on the tip until I thought I would lose my mind. "Are you wet for me, my bratty girl?"

Bratty. He used the term as one of endearment. No longer was I just his slut or his possession. I was his... everything. "Yes."

"Are you hungry for me?"

"Always." Which was the truth.

"Always?"

When he pinched my nipple, twisting it until I cried out in pain, I knew what he was looking for. "Always, sir."

He laughed, blowing another puff of air across my skin. I couldn't stop shaking as he brushed his lips further down, rimming my navel then kicking my legs apart with his knee. The moment he gathered my legs into his arms, I jerked up from the bed, pressing my palms against the sheet, trying to watch everything he did.

There was a carnal look in his eyes, his pupils dilated. With every swipe of his tongue across my pussy, he growled, the sound like a ravenous beast in the woods.

The electric surge was almost dangerous, the live wire skittering to the edge of all rationality. This shouldn't be happening. I shouldn't want him.

But I did.

Whatever the reason, I never wanted this to end.

He pressed my legs as wide open as possible, burying his face in my wetness, licking up and down as if I was the perfect flavor of ice cream. I was so alive that I wasn't certain I could breathe any longer.

I clamped my fingers around the sheet, tugging at the material. "Oh. Oh. Oh." I licked my lips as stars floated in front of my eyes. How could anything feel so damn good?

There was no way of knowing how long he licked me, thrusting his tongue and several fingers inside. He was a master of manipulation, bringing me close to the edge just like he'd done before, refusing to allow me the satisfaction. I was his toy to play with, his puppet and he was the puppet master, and I didn't care that I'd lost myself in what I'd once called a monster.

He was my everything.

I tossed my head back and forth, the sensations too intense. "Please let me come. Please."

"I don't know. You're such a bad girl."

"I'll be good. I promise. Sir." I laughed wistfully after issuing the words. Maybe he had broken me after all.

"Mmm…" He sucked on my pussy lips then plunged all four of his fingers deep inside, ravaging my pussy until I couldn't take it any longer. "Then come for me. Come…"

There was no stopping my body's response. I shivered all over as the climax tore through me like a tidal wave. I was so out of breath there were no sounds, the stimulation unlike any time before. This man… this amazing man was able to drag me to such ecstasy that I'd never be able to come down from the plateau.

He refused to stop, driving me to the point of another savage orgasm. My entire body shook, my mind one fuzzy mess, and it was without a doubt the most intense experience of my life. Only when it slowly started to fade did I ease back onto the pillows, blinking several times in some worthless, crazy effort to see.

There were no words expressed, no promise of what was to come. He simply moved on top, sliding the tip of his cock against my slickness. Then he crushed me with the full weight of his body as he thrust the entire length of his cock inside.

His thick, beautiful cock.

"Fucking perfect and all mine," he whispered, his voice almost unrecognizable.

I wrapped both legs around his hips, clasping my feet together. He rolled his hips, driving into me with such ferocity all I could do was moan. His actions were brutal, but as he pulled away, his eyes piercing mine, he eased my arms over my head, clasping our fingers together.

And for the next few moments, we rocked together, staring into each other's eyes as we coupled in an entirely different way. This was making love, a feast of the heart as well as the soul. There was such sadness in his eyes, the weight of years of guilt and heartache, but there was also more hope than I could have ever imagined seeing in him.

The seconds passed into moments, the pleasure building to another moment of rapture. Panting, I squeezed my muscles and could sense he was close to coming. I wanted us to do so together.

He ground his hips, trying to hold back, but the bliss and intensity of our heated bodies was too great. As he threw his head back and roared, erupting deep inside, I climaxed again, the electricity between us soaring.

Seconds later, he lowered his head, hid chest heaving.

"You will be my wife, Sarah. Mine to hold and cherish. Mine to protect and honor. Mine. Until the end of time."

As soon as he said the words, I trembled, replacing the last five words with those of my own.

Until death do us part.

* * *

He held me, cuddling my back against his chest, the sheets lightly pulled over both of us. I tenderly rubbed his arm, uncertain whether or not he was asleep, refusing to move for fear of waking him. I marveled at the way the dogs remained just inside the room, giving me a little space while performing their duty of protecting us.

Protection.

The thought still scared me.

He exhaled and cupped my breast, squeezing until I whimpered. "What are you thinking about?" he asked.

Whether or not you're going to die.

Whether the unknown boogeyman will come barging into this house.

Whether I'll ever feel normal again.

"Just wondering what's really going on."

He rolled over onto his back, his exhale an entirely different sound. I shifted directions, staring at him as he placed his arms behind his head. Obviously, he was thinking about whether or not he was going to tell me the truth.

"Let me ask you a question. Did Theodora confide something in you?"

"Don't ask me that," I said. "That's not fair to her."

"It may be the only way to stop a war that seems masterfully created." He turned his head to look at me.

"Created? Are you trying to suggest someone is pitting the two families against each other?"

"That's exactly what I'm trying to say, and I think your father is involved."

With that, I sat up, dragging the sheet around me. "That's what you didn't want to tell me."

"I have a feeling he's on the take. Did you know he has an offshore account?"

I laughed. "That would make sense. That's how he probably wined and dined his mistresses."

His upper lip curled. "Son of a bitch."

"Isn't that what all men do who wield that kind of power, like you?"

He growled on purpose. "I'm not most men and no, that's not what we do. Family is sacred."

335

I offered a smile in response. "Why an offshore account?" I asked but could answer it myself. "So it couldn't be found in a traditional sweep by the Feds."

"Yes, or by an organization such as mine. We have connections. There is little we can't find."

"Jesus. Another crime syndicate?"

"Possibly, but it could be one of a half dozen."

"How are you going to know?"

"By approaching your father."

I shrank back, trying to process what he was telling me. "You're going to use me, our marriage."

"Yes, Sarah. I need to."

With the only light in the room the sliver of moon cascading in through the partially open blinds, I couldn't see his eyes, but I sensed his tension, could see the rise and fall of his chest. He wasn't taking this lightly. Neither would I. Whatever my father had gotten himself involved in, the thought of possibly being his pawn sickened me.

"Then do what you need to do."

He reached over, lightly brushing his fingers across my face. "If only I was a different man."

"You are a different man, at least from what little I've learned about your family. Whatever you do, don't make the decision based on your brother or your father or because of the past. Do so because it's the right thing to do."

Exhaling, he tugged me close, nestling me against his chest. As I pressed my ear to his skin, I heard his rapid heartbeat. It was still difficult for me to understand how he could tolerate this life. Now I understood why he'd tried to distance himself not only for him but for the woman he'd adored long ago. There was nothing left to say that could ease his pain or mine. I only hoped that when this was finished, we'd both survive.

"Theodora is in love with Nico. Yes?" he asked out of the blue.

Shit. I didn't want to betray her confidence, but I had the feeling he wouldn't allow me to skip telling him the truth. "Let's just say they've spent enough time together that she is willing to openly recant her story that she thinks he's responsible for hurting her."

He grumbled, cursing under his breath in Italian. "They've been seeing each other in private. Goddamn it. How long?"

"I don't know. Long enough she doesn't mind the thought of marrying him."

As he rubbed his jaw, his breathing remained ragged. "Fine. You are right in that things need to change. We're moving into the fucking new century even if I need to muzzle my father."

"Does that mean you're going to allow their union?"

"That means that I'm not going to stand in the way of anyone's happiness. Both she and Maria are grown women and deserve a life. Just like you do."

I was surprised, curious as to the reason for his change in heart. "You can be a very loving man."

He chuckled, pinching my nipple. "And I can be a ruthless bastard. Never forget that."

"How could I?" I teased.

"Such a bad girl," he growled.

Laughing, I shifted back in the bed. "I think I'll grab a glass of wine. Is that allowed?"

He chuckled and shifted against the pillows. "I must seem like a monster to you if you need to ask if you can move around the house. Things will change, Sarah. It might take time, but life won't always be this way. That much I can promise you."

"Don't promise things you can't force to happen. Contrary to popular belief, you're not God."

"No, I guess I'm not."

I eased out of bed, grabbing his bloodied shirt and slipping it on. There was something cathartic about doing so, as if I'd come to accept his life and the element of danger. Perhaps that made me a martyr, but when you loved someone, you could look the other way with certain... misgivings. I almost laughed as I fastened a few buttons, padding toward the door. I had to step over the slumbering dogs, their little snores always giving me a smile.

As I walked into the hallway, I listened for any sounds that soldiers had entered the house. I could feel them watching, knew that they would protect us with their lives. I was no one to them, just the woman their leader had determined belonged to him. Yet oddly enough, I'd never felt so secure in my environment. It didn't make any sense to me, but I wasn't capable of making impartial judgments, not given the way I felt about Gabriel.

I headed down the stairs, wondering if there would ever be a time my breath wouldn't catch when someone entered the house or when a shadow appeared behind me. When I was at the bottom of the stairs, I couldn't help but venture into his office, moving toward his desk.

The broken laptop was sitting on top, the cracked screen a reminder that he was volatile, an angry man with far too much ability to take out his wrath on whoever got in his way. But I'd been reminded of his gentleness, his ability to yank back from the demons living inside of him. That was the man I'd fallen so hard for, the one who could heat up my core with a single look.

I glanced over my shoulder before opening his top drawer. There was nothing special inside, just typical items found in any desk in any home. When I peeked in the others, I found some files that were old, and a few notepads. It was obvious he hadn't handled any business from this location in some time.

When I got to the third drawer, the single picture inside gripped my heart instantly. It was of him standing in back of this very house, a woman by his side. She was lovely and the way they were looking at each other was telling.

They were very much in love.

I wasn't jealous, but a tiny ping in my heart served as another reminder that life was fragile. No wonder he didn't like this house. It all made sense now, including his fury that I'd left against his rules.

I carefully placed the photograph exactly as it was, slowly closing the drawer. Could I really do this? I wasn't certain I was strong enough.

Sighing, I held my arms as I headed to the kitchen, retrieving the partially open bottle of merlot and two fresh glasses. Then as I headed back up the stairs, butterflies swarmed my stomach from the thought of seeing him again, of lying next to him in the bed all night long. It was silly, a girl's reaction to the homecoming king, not a woman who'd spent several years pretending she didn't need anyone.

We needed each other.

I walked into the room, biting my lower lip. Then I stopped short, allowing myself to bask in the quiet moment that would shock anyone else.

For me, it was a final nod that I wanted to spend my life with him.

He was in the same position fast asleep, one muscular arm wrapped around Goldie, the other around Shadow. They were peaceful and happy together. A little family.

My little family.

And nothing and no one would ever dare tear us apart.

Hell hath no fury like a woman in love.

CHAPTER 17

"$\mathcal{D}$*eath is not the greatest loss in life. The greatest loss is what dies inside while we live."*

—Norman Cousins

Gabriel

The fact I was contemplating my own death was ridiculous at this point. However, in my mind it was a healing feeling, even though I hated the connotations around it. I didn't want to die. Perhaps there'd been a time in my life when I'd experienced the need, but not now. I had everything to live for. I was a wealthy man with a beautiful woman by my side. However, the loss that was furrowing inside was more about losing myself and my humanity than the physicality of losing two people I'd cared about.

Maybe that was a sick way of looking at it, or selfish. Nevertheless, it was true. My life meant nothing in the scheme of things. Sarah's did. She was innocent, a true angel of mercy. To take her away from her healing powers would be blasphemous. I wasn't going to allow that to happen.

At least sharing most of what had occurred with Mary had stripped some of the other demons away. I'd carried the burden for so long that I had a sense of relief that was almost as powerful as the way I felt about her. I was very much looking forward to sharing the news with her father.

And making him squirm.

Dillon flanked my side as we studied the mayor's fine-looking estate. He'd done well for himself over the years, working his way through being a street cop in Brooklyn to detective, then moving all the way up the ranks as his political career began to take off. However, even the mayor's salary wasn't enough to afford the luxuries I'd discovered he owned. Of course, he'd taken the liberty of hiding them in a dummy corporation, including the partial interest in a gambling facility that I knew for certain catered to backroom illegal internet gambling.

For all his pontification, he was no better than members of my family.

"I wish I'd found out more for you, Mr. Giordano," Dillon said. "I mean Gabriel."

What he'd found was enough that with clear conscience I could enjoy every moment of today's impromptu meeting. It was also the smoking gun with regards to the Morettis. They were just as much victims as we were. The Morettis had lost a few men to random shootings over the last few months, always blaming the Giordano family just like we'd blamed them for several eliminations. Word on the street was that they'd been hacked, their computer systems almost completely destroyed, but not before valued information had been taken.

Some asshole had entered the game of Russian roulette. Had that person goaded Luciano on the infamous morning?

While the thought of working together left a bad taste in my mouth, it would be necessary to extend an olive branch in order to secure our passive working relationship. "You did good, Dillon. Excellent in fact. What you managed to find is exactly what I need. We aren't killing him today, unless he makes an attempt."

"You got it, boss."

As I buttoned my jacket, I thought about Sarah. She'd opened my eyes about so many things. "One more thing. It's perfectly acceptable if you want to ask Maria out on a date."

"Excuse me?" He was genuinely shocked, his tone full of anxiety.

I tipped my head, unable to keep from grinning. "You heard me. However, if you hurt her in any way, you will be required to face me. You got it?"

The smile on his face was genuine, his eyes filled with surprise. "I will guard her with my life."

I knew he would, just like he'd die in order to protect Sarah and me.

Good men were hard to find.

Bruno eased from the SUV, eager to track the asshole who'd sullied the club. He'd done an excellent job of scouring hours of tapes, searching for any other suspicious activity. There'd been nothing out of the ordinary, which meant any other activities had been handled by members enjoying a night of debauchery. My thoughts drifted to the evening I'd seen the mayor at my club. Had the man been so bold as to enter the facility he knew would be compromised at a later date?

That remained to be seen and wasn't the subject of today's meeting. Today was all about setting the tone, dropping the news that I was engaged to his daughter. I'd dealt with enough pompous assholes in my life to know he'd run to whatever source was paying him, sharing the news as if it was a Powerball lottery ticket.

As I walked down the front pathway, I noticed two cameras positioned on the front door. The man wasn't taking any chances. Good for him. He would need protection when I was finished with him.

But not necessarily from me. I knew exactly the kind of man William Washington was. A turncoat and a coward. He would sell his soul and his firstborn if it meant he gained more power. I would use that against him.

I knocked on the door and when I heard footsteps a full two minutes later, I was certain he'd taken the time to check his security system. The moment he opened the door, I knew I was right, his expression one of amusement.

"Well, well. Look what the cat dragged through the muck," he said, snorting as he glared at my two men.

"I think it's time we had a discussion."

"And I think you need to get the fuck off my property before I call my buddy, the police chief."

I took a deep breath, gazing at the flowerpots on the front porch. "I would enjoy sitting down with the man, Will. You don't mind me calling you Will, do you? After all, we're going to be family soon. As far as the police chief, I'll be happy to tell him about your partial ownership of Roxie's. You know, the illegal gambling facility catering to the rich and famous? Then I'll direct him to the offshore account you have set up with well over five million dollars set aside for your... proclivities. If he balks, then I'll be happy to supply him with pictures of the seventeen-year-old mistress he has."

"What the fuck are you talking about?" he snarled. "I've done nothing wrong."

It would seem he didn't care about his good buddy.

I turned toward Dillon, smirking from the wide grin on his face. He reached into his pocket, pulling out the evidence I'd had him provide. When I handed it to the good mayor, I watched in amusement as he glanced from one photograph to the other. "Pictures are priceless. Don't you think?" I watched as his face paled. There was more, but I always like to hold the last cards until absolutely necessary.

"You fucking bastard. What the hell do you mean about us being family? You're a roach, nothing more, and I will crush you under my boot."

Dillon slammed his hand against William's chest, pushing him inside. "You need to respect the man, Mayor. He's going to be your son-in-law."

I wanted to laugh seeing the look on William's face. He was mortified instantly, his face turning white. Then I sensed anger replacing surprise.

"What the fuck are you talking about?" he demanded.

I allowed Dillon to continue pushing him all the way into the foyer, waiting until Bruno closed the door before scanning the spacious room. "You've certainly done well for yourself, William. I dare say putting pressure on my family has turned into a lucrative way of life for you."

"You're crazy. What have you done with my daughter?"

"William. What's wrong?" The female voice came from the stairs, the woman's face pensive as she peered down.

"Nothing!" William barked. "Get back upstairs."

"Your husband and I were having a friendly conversation about your lovely daughter and our upcoming nuptials." I resisted laughing because I knew the woman had suffered at the hands of the son of a bitch standing in front of me. She didn't deserve to live the rest of her life treated like she didn't matter.

"That will never happen!" William shoved his hands against Dillon, pushing him aside. "Get upstairs, Emily. I don't need to tell you again."

"Emily. I'll give you a piece of advice," I said in passing. "Leave this piece of shit before he ruins the rest of your life. Would you prefer to tell your beautiful wife about how often you've cheated as well as the fact you're in the employ of some desperate and unscrupulous people? Or should I?"

I shifted my gaze toward her and the smug look on her face indicated she already knew what levels her own husband had gone to in order to achieve success.

"Do not hurt my daughter," she said with the same conviction in her voice I'd heard in Sarah's.

"I don't plan on it, Emily. Your daughter is very special, although your husband never seemed to care. You don't need to be a part of this. Sarah will contact you later with details."

I wasn't certain if she was happy or felt vindicated that someone finally shattered their glass house. Either way, she gave her husband a nasty look then headed up the stairs, taking them slowly. Perhaps I'd given her an excuse to take back her life.

"I'll kill you for this," William snarled, fisting his hand and taking a step in my direction.

While my two soldiers bristled, prepared to do what was necessary in order to keep him from attacking, they knew I wanted to handle the man and whatever punishment I decided to dole out.

When he threw a punch, I drove him against the wall with enough force a picture crashed to the floor. Then I stood in front of him, staring into his eyes.

"You can try, Mayor, but I assure you that you won't succeed. Now, here's how we're going to play this."

He threw another punch, connecting with my gut. After yanking out my weapon, I took a step back, pointing it at his temple. I doubted anyone in his household, including his staff of four would come to his rescue. He wasn't a well-liked man among those who knew him personally.

"You wouldn't dare," he managed, although his words were clipped.

"Do you really want to push me? My bride to be wouldn't appreciate the gesture, at least not at this point in her life. Would you also like for me to tell her about all the filthy things you've done with women over the years?"

He panted, longing to place his hands on me but to his credit realizing it wasn't in his best interest. "Leave... my daughter... alone."

"No can do, Mayor. She's mine now. All mine. That means you will have no further influence over her. That also means that your family and mine will forever be connected. Imagine the grandchildren you'll have. If you play by the rules."

"What the fuck do you want?"

"It's simple. Stop harassing my family and embrace our connection. That's it."

"That's never going to happen," he hissed.

"Then I'm afraid I'll have to supply everything I've learned about you to the proper authorities. I'm certain they'll find your extracurricular activities of interest. Especially since it's about time for you to run for reelection."

His eyes opened wide and he dropped his arms altogether. I could tell he knew he'd been defeated.

I backed further away, smiling from the look on his face. The seed had been planted. That's all that mattered.

"You won't get away with this," he hissed. Now his face was beet red, his mind spinning with what he had planned.

"Oh, I know I will, Mayor Washington. I'll expect to see you at the wedding." I turned around, enjoying the way he cursed my soul into hell.

Perhaps he hadn't gathered my soul had been spoken for a long time ago.

* * *

Respect and loyalty.

In the Cosa Nostra, they were valued more than wealth or even power, certainly more than love. I was keenly aware that love was not only blind but often stupid, causing great wars over the generations.

I'd heard stories of my great-great-grandfather, a man who'd died by his own sword because of falling in love with his brother's wife. The child born eight months later had been spawned from his loins, something that had been covered up for decades. The dirty little secret had tainted the Giordano blood.

Not that it mattered any longer.

It was a story told over cognac and cigars, my father boasting how brave the man had been to accept his punishment without question.

He'd believed his children to be so bold and brave. While the sentiment and my great-great-grandfather's act had seemed laughable in adolescence, I now understood just how powerful love could be.

It would ultimately condemn me, but I'd enjoy every moment of my life until then.

Two days had passed since giving the ultimatum to the mayor. He'd canceled an appearance on a local morning show, remaining locked inside his house the entire time. Several of my men were paying attention, watching his every move from a distance. He'd yet to make any obvious overtures to anyone, but I knew it was only a matter of time.

I'd allowed Sarah to contact her mother, which had at least calmed my bride's nerves. I also believed it had helped the lovely Emily accept that her husband was a deviant. I was certain she'd mention the call to her husband, which I hoped would push the good mayor into breaching whatever cloak had been forced around the asshole playing the real game.

While I wasn't a man of patience, it was required in order to hunt down the assholes who continued to threaten our livelihood. Several of our businesses had suffered unexplainable losses. Even Club Rio had seen a drop in membership. If I had to guess, I'd say the weakest links had been threatened by the unknown third party.

Even the hushed whispers on the street indicated people were afraid. The tension was mounting but no one was doing any talking. Cartels and syndicates always boasted. That was a method used that would place the proper fear of God into people. The quiet wasn't just deafening. It was outrageous, keeping my blood pressure high.

At least with working alongside the Morettis, there would be a better chance of flushing out the son of a bitch playing games.

I'd returned to Club Rio, wanting the meeting to be on my turf.

What was required today pissed me off but was necessary in order to keep the peace. As I slid my card into the slot, something drew my attention, and I turned my head toward the busy road. There was no reason to believe anyone was watching, but I sensed someone was paying as much attention to my whereabouts as I was to the mayor's.

"What is it?" Dillon asked.

"I don't know exactly. Keep an ear to the streets. I have a feeling the snake will rear its ugly head soon."

"Yeah, I don't like the lack of chatter. I'll break some heads later to find out what's going on."

"Not until the pieces are in place," I told him.

After exhaling, I opened the door, walking inside and taking the stairs toward one of the private conference rooms. When I opened the door, I was surprised to see my father already inside.

He'd made himself a drink and was staring out the window at the passing traffic. I could tell he had something on his mind other than the business meeting at hand.

I'd barely closed the door when he started talking. "Did you know I was supposed to marry someone else?" he asked me casually, as if we were old buddies out for a nightcap.

"No. That's not something you ever told me. In fact, I don't remember the last time we had a decent discussion."

"That needs to change," he said, far too quietly for what I was used to.

"What do you need to get off your conscience, Pops?" I moved toward the bar, uncertain I wanted to hear any more of his bullshit.

"She died because of me."

There was so much pain in his voice that I shifted my attention toward him. The memory seemed to have broken him. "What do you want me to say? That we're the same?"

He threw a hateful look in my direction, snarling like the big bad wolf he'd tried to make himself out to be, but there was a difference this time.

There were tears in his eyes. "She was the love of life, a beautiful flower who was considered forbidden fruit. But I had to have her."

The vehemence in his voice was surprising. I finished making my drink, still uncertain why he was sharing anything from his past. "I'm sorry."

"Just let me finish!" He took several deep breaths, throwing back the rest of his drink then immediately heading for the bar. "We kept it secret for almost a year. She was underage and I wasn't. I was the powerful prince of the Giordano family. She was the daughter of a stable hand. There was no way we could be together. When my father found out, he beat me to within an inch of my life. But it was nothing in comparison to what her father did."

I took a deep breath, remaining quiet. My father's hands were shaking, which never occurred.

"I tried to get to her, but she was gone. I found out later she'd killed herself. Not long after that, my father made arrangements with the Don of the Trevillian syndicate, contracting with the man for his daughter's hand in marriage. There was nothing I could do."

While the story was haunting, I wasn't certain if all he was trying to do was ease his guilty conscience. That mattered nothing to me. "Yet you would insist your daughter be treated the same way."

"I don't know any other way, son. And do you want to know why?" He tipped his head, his eyes rimmed in red. "Because the day I found out she died was the day I died too. Don't get me wrong, I do love your mother, but she's lived with a

PIPER STONE

shell of a man her entire life. My children have suffered because of what I did, the sin I committed. All I wanted was for none of you to ever go through what I did. Somehow, fate forced you, my talented second son, to go through the same thing."

Only Mary didn't kill herself. She was gunned down because of the life I'd been born into. "So you're telling me to toss aside the woman I love, finding someone who could benefit our world and nothing else. Right, Pops?" I tossed back half the scotch, this time the smooth liquor burning my throat.

"No, son. I was wrong. What I'm telling you is that I wasted my life suffering, forcing my family to face consequences of something they had no party to. If you love her, then don't let anything get in the way of sharing joy. You deserve to be happy."

I had no idea what had gotten into him, but before I had a chance to respond, we both heard a knock on the door.

Happiness. There was that word again. I'd been taught that happiness had to be forfeited for the greater good of the family. Now this.

"I need to know this. Does Mother know?"

His exhale was ragged, full of bitterness. "She knows something happened in my past. I spared her the details and I'd prefer if you'd do the same."

Secrets and lies.

They'd been a part of my family my entire life, whether I'd known it or not. What I did know is that my mother deserved to enjoy her life without another burden.

"Yes, Pops. I'll honor your request." I glanced at the door and sighed. "Come," I said, taking a deep breath. My father was never this animated. Something else was wrong.

As Nico and Joseph walked in, one of their soldiers behind them, it was apparent the tension would be palpable. Nico narrowed his eyes, glaring at me as he'd done inside the bar. What I didn't expect was the half-beaten man he dropped onto my conference room table.

"I told you I'd find the asshole who beat up your beautiful sister." Nico snarled and slammed the man's head on the wooden surface. "Tell him what you told me."

While the man's face was almost unrecognizable given the beating he'd already received, I knew he was a low-level player with no particular loyalty. It was all about the cash.

The asshole tried to struggle, and Nico repeated the harsh action. "I'll cut your nuts off one at a time if you don't tell me the same shit you spouted off to me." Nico was red in the face, more so than I'd ever seen him. He jerked the man's head at an awkward angle, forcing him to look me in the eye.

"Fine," the son of a bitch hissed. "I was paid to do it. Okay? Is that what you want?"

I almost flew over the table. "By whom?"

"I don't know. Okay? Some dude with twenty thousand in cash."

Twenty thousand to rough up a woman. That had all the markings of the Bratva, the pigs they were. "Name." I had a feeling the asshole was lying, but not about being paid for the deed. He'd likely been threatened that if he divulged his source, his family would pay the price. It was typical Bratva behavior, something I despised.

"I told you," the dude said then coughed. "I don't know."

"Give me something." I glanced at Nico who wore a smug look on his face.

"I swear to you that I don't know. He talked in riddles. Some shit about jungles. I had no idea what he was talking about. Some jungle, a snake. Just shit."

"Every jungle has a snake." I lowered my gaze, clenching my jaw. Where the fuck had I heard that before other than with Demarco?

"Satisfied?" Nico barked.

"Get him out of here." I glanced at the Morettis' soldier, making certain he would follow command without hesitation.

As the man was dragged out like a ragdoll, I refreshed my drink then moved to the head of the table.

The air was thick with testosterone, but at least the elephant in the room had been eliminated. However, the riddle was far from being solved.

"Make yourself a drink, gentlemen. We need to get this meeting started."

I wasn't surprised after both men prepared their beverages of choice that Joseph allowed Nico to take the other head of the table. This was more about laying down the rules between the two families than anything else.

I waited as my father eased into a seat, and I could tell he was still disturbed by what he'd told me. Remaining standing, I leaned against the wall. "We have a serious problem. Someone is fucking with both of us."

"You want us to believe it's not your twisted family?" Nico threw out.

"Nico!" Joseph hissed. "Respect."

"Our men are being picked off one by one by someone else. It would serve neither one of us to create more bloodshed."

"Fair enough," Joseph stated. "I've thought for months there was someone else involved."

Nico seemed agitated. "Who?"

"I don't know, but whoever it is has been feeding the pockets of our mayor. That I know for certain."

Joseph glanced at his son and laughed. "Something else I suspected. Bratva."

"Possible. I will have my soldiers direct their attention to Brighton Beach." The area had been labeled little Odessa given the huge population of Russians. It housed many of the Bratva as well.

"They don't talk, just grunt," Nico snarked.

"They'll talk," I told him. "In the meantime, we strengthen our businesses by solidifying the alliance."

I could tell neither man had been prepared. After I glanced at my father, he gave me a nod of approval.

"Meaning what exactly?" Nico challenged.

"Meaning there will be upcoming nuptials, but only under one condition." I held up my index finger. Nico looked like he was going to jump out of his skin. For a brutal man, the gleam in his eyes was refreshing.

"Of course there would be," he hissed, returning to his usual demeanor.

"Son. Listen!" Joseph snapped. "Go ahead."

"You will remain engaged for a period of six months. If you both feel the way I already know you do, then I will give my blessing. In the meantime, we find the son of a bitch who's determined to bring us down."

Another moment of tension almost pushed me over the edge. I didn't extend an olive branch very often.

Finally, Nico rose to his feet, walking around the table toward me. He stared into my eyes for a full minute before outstretching his arm. "I don't like you, Sicilian, but I will honor the deal made between our fathers."

"No, Nico. This is the deal we make between the two of us. There's plenty of business for two powerful families in this town, but no more." I gripped his hand.

He snorted then strengthened his hold, a twinkle in his eye. "Then we have a deal."

"I have one question, Joseph. Were you aware that Luciano was on his way to end your life on the day he died?"

The man seemed genuinely surprised. "No, I was not aware. What set him off?"

"That's what I need to find out."

Joseph glanced toward my father. "Luciano was supposed to be killed that day, but Mother Nature got in the way. Is that what you're saying?"

My father lifted his head, staring the man in the eyes. They had an odd friendship of sorts, which I had never noticed before.

"I'm going to venture a guess and say yes, but we may never know what he was told," I said quietly.

"I can't tell you how sorry I am about your brother. He was a good man, a good leader, Gabriel, but I see an entirely different set of strengths in you. You are the epitome of your father," Joseph said in total respect.

While I normally would have bristled, this time I lowered my head to him out of the same level of respect.

They wasted no time leaving, which was fine by me. I had other, equally important things to do. Like spending time with a beautiful woman.

"He and I were friends, you know, when I first came to New York." My father said the words so quietly I almost didn't hear him.

"What changed?" I'd heard that from our mother, finding it tough to believe.

He laughed and swirled his empty glass. "Family obligations. You grandfather still wielded power over me."

I finished off my drink, surprised that it took my Pops a full two minutes to rise from his seat. Whether or not he was proud of me I'd likely never hear. For today, that was just fine. He'd opened up more than he had my entire life.

I started to leave when he cleared his throat.

"You did good, son. I'm very proud of you."

I'd waited my entire life to hear the words from him. Today, I realized they no longer mattered. I wasn't particularly proud of myself.

"I never told you how sorry I was about Mary."

He'd never comforted me given the circumstances. Why now? "It was difficult."

"There was a chain of events that started the situation."

"What do you mean?"

He glanced in my direction. "I made a rash judgment, which resulted in the loss of innocent lives. After that I received threats that I didn't take seriously."

"Threats?"

"To hurt my family."

A strange pinging sensation occurred in my ears. "What are you trying to tell me?"

He kept his eyes locked on mine. "That Mary didn't need to die. My arrogance killed her. My sense of being untouchable. A god."

I was sucked into a vacuum, my mind spinning. "She died because of you? You didn't warn me? I would have kept her safe." Anger swept through me, hatred for the man spiraling. I couldn't do it.

"I didn't think the assholes were serious. By then you weren't a part of the business. They targeted you because of that. Because you wanted to live a normal life."

Exhaling, I was sick inside, enraged that my father would keep something like that all these years. I did what I could to keep from lashing out. I'd been the one to tell him to stay out of my life.

"What else are you hiding, Pops?"

The quiet was overwhelming. Then he laughed softly. "I could never lie to you, son. You had an ability unlike anyone else to see through my bullshit and everyone else's. Your mother was diagnosed with Alzheimer's a few months ago. It's been under control with medication, but she's starting to slip. I plan on spending what time I have taking her around the world. Anywhere she wants to go. All those years I'd promised her we'd go to Europe and Singapore and never kept them. She never complained, never once said anything about the fact I was far too busy to care about my family."

I tipped my head, studying him intently. Now I fully understood why he'd shared the horrible story.

He was terrified I was just like him.

"Don't worry, Pops. Take Mother everywhere you can. I'll make you proud."

And I would.

But not just for him, for the family I'd always wanted.

A beautiful bride and two glorious pups.

CHAPTER 18

 abriel

Until death do us part.

The words had more of a special meaning now that I knew my mother was on borrowed time. Maybe the males in the Giordano family were all fools. We wasted so much time pontificating and hungering for power that we lost sight of what was most important and the people who were right in front of our eyes.

Almost everything was troubling, but not nearly as much as the thought of losing time with my mother, my sisters, and especially the woman I loved.

As I walked inside the house, the scent of something else delicious made my mouth water. When I heard the scampering of the dogs, I shook my head. I didn't deserve happiness, but I would do everything I could to make certain I kept my promises to Sarah.

"Hi there, pups. It's good to be home." I said, laughing as they jumped all over me, barking and woofing. I protected the flowers, wondering if buying her roses had been the right thing to do. Chuckling, I moved toward the kitchen, remaining in the doorway and watching her. The scene was similar, her in bare feet dancing to a song as she prepared whatever awesome dinner I knew we'd have.

When she stiffened and finally turned around, I could see relief in her eyes.

"Did I scare you?" I asked as I walked inside the room.

"That's hard given I have two big dogs to protect me. They announced your arrival." She dragged her tongue across her lips, allowing her gaze to fall to the roses. "What's the occasion?"

"Oh, I just thought I'd provide the most insanely gorgeous woman a token of my appreciation." As I handed them to her, our fingers touched, and the same bolt of electricity rushed into my system.

She took a deep breath as she inhaled the aroma, closing her eyes. I loved the way her eyelashes dashed across her skin.

"They're lovely. Is everything okay?"

"It is. I'm going to grab a bottle of champagne."

"We're celebrating?"

"We are," I said as I winked. "It would appear Theodora is getting married."

She grinned, a warm blush creeping across her skin. "You agreed."

"They're in love. Who am I to keep romance from happening?"

"As if you'd know."

Her teasing voice pushed my cock to full attention. "I'll be right back." As I moved into the wine cellar, selecting a bottle, I pulled the ring from my pocket, placing it on the tasting table. I opened the bottle, selecting two flutes and dropping the ring inside one of them before pouring the bubbly.

As I returned to the kitchen, I was surprised she'd found a vase, already arranging the flowers. It was hard not to watch her, studying her every move. She had delicate but strong fingers, which helped make her such a good surgeon.

I put the bottle on the counter, slowly bringing the glasses toward her. As I handed her one, I took a deep breath. "I won't make any promises I can't keep, but I will never lie to you. Do you believe me?"

"Actually, I do."

"Can you trust me?"

She narrowed her eyes. "With everything I have."

"Good."

"You still don't know who's after you?"

"Not yet." Sighing, I tried to ignore the anger still burning inside.

"I'll be fine. I knew they'd come after me in order to destroy you. I wish I knew why."

"So do I." I lifted my glass, feeling an eagerness inside that I hadn't felt in such a long time.

She brought the glass to her lips then stopped, pulling the flute away. "What did you do?"

"What I thought was right."

Tears formed in her eyes, which surprised me almost more than anything. I would not lose her, no matter what I had to do. She took several gulps, laughing as the bubbles tickled her nose. Then she struggled as she reached into the thin glass, attempting several times to grab the ring. After three attempts, she was successful, holding the diamond encrusted with rubies in front of her face.

"It's gorgeous."

I took it from her hand, trying not to get emotional. "I can't promise you perfect either, but I will do everything in my power to give you a happy life. I hope you'll do me the honor of marrying me."

A single tear slipped past her lashes as she nodded. I eased the ring onto her finger then brought her hand to my lips, rolling them across her knuckles. "You captured my heart."

"I know. I think I knew that the first day I met you." I couldn't help but tease her, something entirely different for me as well.

"You're a bad man."

"Don't you forget it." I pulled her close, trying not to allow her to see the concern, the anxiety that continued to build.

The asshole would try to take her away from me.

No more.

She was mine for all of eternity.

And no one would ever be able to tear us apart.

Even if I had to sell what was left of my soul to the devil.

* * *

Sarah

Two weeks later

Valentine's Day.

I'd hated it for as long as I could remember. I'd been the girl least likely to get one of the cutesy valentine cards in pretty pink or red envelopes when I was in grade school. I wasn't certain they even did that any longer, but it seemed to be all I could think about given my wedding day just happened to fall on what I'd called a sanctimonious holiday.

"You look nervous. This isn't your wedding day," Carrie teased. "Just the rehearsal and dinner, at a fabulous location I might add."

It wasn't that I didn't feel excitement. I just had a strange feeling that had continued to build over the last two weeks.

My father wasn't who he said he was, my mother telling me she'd asked for a divorce. Then there was Gabriel's continued yin and yang behavior. Of course I understood why.

He was waiting for what he'd called the guillotine to drop.

There'd been skirmishes with the Bratva, enough that the press had started hounding him. He was certain the Pakhan was behind the close call with sabotaging the family organization. But I sensed he continued to have questions, as if putting the pieces of the puzzle together.

I was being used as a pawn with my agreement. He expected the hit to happen at the wedding. No expense had been spared, the media and everyone who was anyone invited. He was goading the person, giving them a red-carpet invitation.

And I hated the fact my wedding day, what was supposed to be the best day of my life, was being held hostage by a real monster.

The rehearsal dinner was being held in private, details known by only the closest people to the organization and the few people who were to be a part of the ceremony itself.

There would be dozens of soldiers hiding, waiting for the perpetrator to make his move. Even now, I was more protected than I'd ever been, several of Gabriel's men waiting for me to finish getting dressed.

He'd allowed me to spend some time with Carrie at her house, so few people knowing where she lived. I had ten minutes left before it would be time to go, chauffeured in a bulletproof SUV to the rehearsal itself.

"I know. I'm just thinking about everything."

"You're certain you want to do this?"

The last two weeks had been difficult emotionally, Gabriel trying to hold in his anger at everything that had occurred. He'd worked long hours, requiring my constant surveillance. While I'd been back to work, the tight security had been oppressive. Plus, he was still holding guilt as well as anxiety for his mother's condition. What that had shown me was the depth of his many layers, his personality changing right before my eyes almost every day.

"Yes. Without any shadow of a doubt."

"Are you okay?" Carrie asked.

"Stop worrying. I'm fine." I twisted back and forth as I looked at myself in the mirror. The dress was another one he'd picked out, his taste incredible. I looked like a princess in red, his favorite color.

"Why don't I believe you?"

"Because that's the kind of woman you are."

We laughed and she grabbed our two glasses of wine. "You look beautiful. Do you love him?"

I didn't need to think about the question, but I did. "I know it sounds crazy, but I do." I moved to the table, pulling the knife Gabriel had given me into my hands.

"Who wouldn't love a man who kidnapped you?" she asked then gasped slightly. "Are you taking that?"

"I'm wearing it."

"You're kidding."

I shook my head and eased it into position in the holster strapped around my thigh. Gabriel had insisted since I'd refused to take a gun.

"This is nuts," she whispered.

"Protection."

"I don't care. It's… crazy."

"Relax, sweet sister. Gabriel knows what he's doing. I trust him."

I gave her a hard look in the mirror, and she shrugged. She was only partially teasing. She still couldn't understand everything, mostly because I could only tell her but so much. What I hadn't realized was that she'd already known our father wasn't the decent human being he portrayed himself to be, happy our mother was trying to find a life of her own.

"He's my Prince Charming, in a different package."

"Uh-huh. As long as he's good to you. That's all that matters." I took a sip and twisted my ring. It was gorgeous, a shock when he'd given it to me. We'd had so many nights of passion, including my full surrender. I tingled from the sensations that remained from the night before. The man was a powerhouse in bed.

And out.

That's what concerned me the most. Would I need to worry about him every day? Only time would tell.

As we heard a knock on the door, she smiled. "I think your future husband is waiting. Let me grab my purse and coat."

I gave myself another onceover and touched the necklace he'd given me the night before. He said it was my good luck charm. I knew he'd hidden a tracker in the charm. He couldn't fool me. As I backed away, a series of tingling sensations flowed through me.

Maybe Valentine's Day was the perfect choice.

And no one would dare interrupt such a glorious occasion for fear of facing wrath.

My wrath.

I turned around, heading toward the door as Carrie opened it.

And in those few seconds, I realized just how precious life really was.

Someone would die today.

And I believed it would be me.

Gabriel

"You look nervous," Bruno said as he approached.

"I just want this over with." I hated the pomp and circumstance, including having a rehearsal for a ceremony that I doubted would take place.

Of my design.

It was a dangerous game to play, but the mysterious bastard's hand needed to be forced. We'd faced two weeks of basic silence on the streets, and the business losses were getting out of hand. We'd expedited the wedding in hopes that the bastard would reveal himself. I almost laughed thinking about how Sarah had been involved every step of the way. I'd never thought she'd become my partner in a dangerous scenario, but she'd insisted.

The woman was strong as steel.

He smirked then slipped his hand inside his jacket, pulling out a small flask. "I brought this for you just in case."

Huffing, I glanced at it, starting to refuse, but right now a shot sounded like exactly what I needed. After taking a long pull, I noticed Rick as he approached, a huge smile on his face.

"You're late," I barked.

He held up his hands, giving me the onceover. "Hey, man. Someone has to work around here." When he offered his hand for a shake, I accepted, glad he'd been able to make arrangements to be here, pushing off a well-deserved vacation.

So he'd told me more than once.

When he grabbed the flask out of my hand to take a swig, then returned it, I didn't object. He'd taken on a lion's share of my clients, as if he wasn't getting off doing so.

"Where's the lovely bride?" he asked.

"With her sister." I checked my watch and took another swig. Then another.

"I'll see what I can find out," Bruno told me. "Just try and enjoy this, Don Giordano. This is a special time for you."

He'd stepped up to the plate, allowing Dillon to remain as Sarah's fulltime bodyguard, something she loathed.

"I can't believe you're really going through with this," Rick said in passing.

"Call it karma."

"Call it kismet."

I threw him a look and we both laughed.

As my mother approached, I stiffened. I'd noticed her memory loss in the last few days, the questioning look in her eyes as confusion set in. At least Pops had made good on his promise to her, booking several trips over the next few months.

"I'm proud of you, my beautiful boy," she said as she wrapped her arms around me.

I held her close, kissing the top of her head. "You always wanted me happy."

"People rarely get second chances."

"I know."

She pulled away, gripping my arms, noticing the flask in my hand. Then she winked before walking away. She could tell how nervous I was.

I started pacing, the anxiety increasing. As Rick got a call, I almost snarled for no reason.

"Hey, I gotta take this, man. I'll be right back. Business never stops," he said.

"Just be ready. We're out of here in less than ten minutes after Sarah gets here."

"Stop worrying."

As if I could.

Another five minutes passed.

I glanced at my watch.

Another five minutes and I was finished waiting.

"Where the fuck is she?" I snarled, mostly to myself. I was standing in a church, although it wasn't the one we were to be married in. However, it still made me uncomfortable. I hadn't wanted to let Sarah out of my sight. The fact she'd convinced me to allow her to spend a couple of hours with her sister was a normal request.

However, our lives were anything but normal.

And where the hell had Bruno gone? I took one more swig and shoved the flask into my jacket. I needed to keep a clear head.

"She'll be here. Stop worrying," Maria told me.

"They're late," I shot back, shaking my head after doing so.

"By five minutes."

"No, something is wrong." I pulled out my phone, dialing Dillon's number. When it rang four times, I knew my instincts were right. I immediately headed for Bruno, drawing his attention. While I didn't want to panic, my gut had been telling me all day this was a bad idea. "Why aren't they answering?" I asked my soldier. When he didn't respond, everything seemed to spiral out of control. I slammed my hands against him, shoving him outside.

"What the hell are you doing?" my father demanded as he followed me, several of my soldiers doing so as well.

When I tossed Bruno against the side of the building, he grinned. Without hesitation, I shoved the barrel of my weapon against his temple.

"You can't do this," Theodora yelled. "It's a church."

"Get back inside!" I snapped, returning my attention to a man I thought I could trust. "Where is she? What have you done with her?" Every soldier had their weapons pointed at Bruno. How in the fuck had I missed he'd been the real traitor? I searched my memory, realizing he'd been placed perfectly to provide both business as well as personal information.

"What's going on?" Theodora demanded as she bounded outside.

"Get them inside! Now!" I snapped, two of my soldiers immediately moving in front of my sisters.

"I've done nothing, except supply you with a libation," Bruno said, laughing even in the face of death.

The flask. Fuck. Fuck.

"Get back inside, Theodora. Pops. It's the end game."

My father yanked out his weapon, helping her everyone else inside.

"Now, you have three seconds to tell me where she is or you're going to face your maker," I growled. Whatever the poison in the liquor, I knew it would begin to show at any time. I had to get to her. Where the hell had they taken her? What the fuck was going on?

"No can do, boss. Oh, wait. You're not my boss any longer. You'll be happy to know she will be taken well care of."

What the hell was he talking about?

"And there will be a wedding, only you weren't invited." As Bruno laughed, a strange feeling settled into the pit of my stomach.

Then a knowing that had been blocked by years of anger and guilt, heartache and pain.

I pulled the trigger, not waiting for his body to fall before turning toward my other soldiers.

I heard a voice inside my head, a saying from long ago, but one that finally broke free in my memory.

And my world began to crumble.

Every jungle has a snake…

* * *

Sarah

Darkness.

I'd never feared it before, but as I opened my eyes, the darkness was terrifying. I shifted, trying to remember what happened. Then I realized my hands were bound.

Don't panic. Think. Listen.

I did my best, my heart racing, but even as I blinked several times, my eyes becoming accustomed to the low level of light, I realized I was in danger. Four men had burst inside Carrie's apartment, all carrying weapons. Within seconds, a dark hood was placed over my head and I was carried out, Carrie's muffled screams the last thing I remembered.

Oh, my God. Did they hurt her? Was she even alive? I shivered, doing what I could to keep from becoming frazzled, taking several deep breaths.

What was that smell?

I dared to take a deep breath, realizing the scent was roses. There had to be hundreds of them for the fragrance to be so thick. At first it was intoxicating.

Then it made me sick to my stomach.

What sick bastard had placed me among so many flowers?

Think. Think.

I'd seen nothing, but I'd heard Dillon's voice. Then a gunshot.

As panic started to roll in, I twisted my body until I was able to sit up, trying to make sense of my surroundings. Then I noticed light coming in through a distant source. As I continued to try to breathe, forcing my eyes to focus, a strange feeling settled over me. I was still inside a church, the shimmer several feet above indicating a stained-glass window. Turning my head, I noticed several of them. I knew I was right. But where?

Moaning, I tried to get to my knees, my body aching with every move. At least my hands were bound in front of me but as I struggled with them, the burn from the rope was instant, biting into my skin.

I was going nowhere.

"Help!" I called out, although I knew doing so was as ridiculous as it was dangerous. The silence was deafening. I yelled even louder, finally making it to my feet. Every muscle was shaking, but I managed to take a single step, almost falling. There were steps. I turned around, the shadows looming over me unrecognizable. If this was a church, what the hell was I doing here?

I remembered the knife strapped to my leg, but from the way my wrists were bound, it was impossible to reach it. If I could move enough so it tumbled to the floor, then maybe I could figure out a way to free myself.

Before I had a chance to try, I heard footsteps, a hard thudding sound that echoed all around me. Tensing, I took several shallow breaths, still fighting with the rope.

When a series of lights were switched on, I was blinded, wincing as I blinked several times. Whoever was walking closer took their damn sweet time.

There were more footsteps on both sides, several of them, the heaviness indicating men. I could swear they were walking in formation, as if... soldiers.

My vision cleared, showing me that I'd been right. I was inside a small church, the wooden pews directly in front of me. Jesus. I'd been placed on the altar. As I turned around in a full circle, terror swept through me. There were red roses everywhere, petals strewn about on a white runner. As if a flower girl had carefully dropped them.

I noticed a pink satin pillow with two rings nestled in white ribbon.

There was going to be a wedding after all, only my groom wouldn't be Gabriel.

The single set of footsteps moved closer and I found the courage to turn around, holding my breath. I didn't recognize the person standing in front of me, the man casually holding a gun in his hand, but there was no mistaking the fact he was evil. Even the look on his face sucked away my breath. His smile was crooked, his eyes boring into mine and he had the look of a madman. He was dressed in a dark suit and white shirt, a red rose in his lapel.

Dressed for a wedding.

"What a beautiful bride," he said. "And red is definitely your color. I think it's appropriate for an unholy union. Don't you?"

"Who the hell are you?"

"Does it really matter?"

"Yes," I hissed, still fighting with the ropes. The asshole seemed amused that I was bothering.

"Let's just say over the last few years I've gotten very close to your former fiancé."

"What did you do to him?"

He took a deep breath, holding it in for a few seconds. "Let's just say his muscles should start to shut down right about now. His organs will be next."

Oh, my God. Gabriel had been poisoned. The tracker. Oh, God. I no longer felt the weight of the necklace.

"If you're trying to figure out if your beloved will hunt you down, I had a feeling he'd make certain you were protected in every way possible. You see, I've studied him and his entire family for years. I had nothing else to do since his father killed my family."

"All this for revenge."

What in the hell was he talking about?

"Revenge is the very sweetest when served cold," he said, and I could swear he was unraveling.

I bit my lower lip, scanning the area to see how I could run away from him.

"Anyway, the necklace was tossed. Just in case. I'm a thorough man." He walked even closer. "Have the minister brought in."

One of his men reacted instantly, moving through another door.

"Now, I was simply going to kill you, but then I realized how beautiful you are, even if you destroyed my plans of killing Gabriel's brother. Then it all became clear how to hurt him the most. Through your suffering."

"What are you talking about?"

"The accident. How quickly you forget. Let me refresh your memory. I lured Luciano Giordano out that morning. I told him that Joseph Moretti had placed a hit on his sister. That was all it had taken. Then I was going to have the joy of torturing him before putting a bullet between his eyes. You fucked it up!" His yell was strangled, an indication how deranged he'd become. None of this made any sense.

I remained quiet, uncertain of what to do. His glare remained harsh for a few seconds. Then it became lustful as he dragged his tongue across his lips.

"You're going to be all mine. Imagine all the filthy things I'm going to do to you. I assure you that when I'm finished, you'll beg to die, but I won't allow that to happen. When Gabriel takes his last breath before being dragged to hell, I'm certain he'll think of you. Once wasn't enough. Now, I've found the ultimate revenge."

Through his rambling, I realized what he was admitting.

"You killed his fiancée all those years ago?"

He laughed, the sound echoing. "Yes. Did you know she was pregnant?"

That couldn't be true. Could it?

"Aww. He didn't tell you that? Well, no matter." He moved closer, his heated gaze sweeping down my body.

I was sick inside, barely able to keep standing.

The minister was dragged in, his expression one of terror.

"Good. Now we can get on with the ceremony. With any luck, I can show off my new bride before Gabriel fades into the darkness."

Gabriel. Where are you?

I cried out to the man I loved in my mind, backing away until I hit a railing.

The asshole wagged his finger, making a tsking sound as he closed the distance.

I struggled harder, ignoring the biting pain. The ropes loosened but not enough. Still, I refused to stop fighting.

"Keep struggling. I do prefer a woman with fight in her. However, that won't change anything. Minister, prepare to marry us."

Out of the corner of my eye I noticed a flash, my heart racing. When I caught sight of Gabriel, I almost whimpered, giving his presence away. He shifted his gaze in my direction, narrowing his eyes. I sensed he was telling me to stay exactly where I was. As he came closer, I sucked on my bottom lip to keep from crying out.

"Not so fast, you motherfucker. She's mine." Gabriel had a calm exterior, totally in control, but I sensed his rage was out of control. His hand was firmly wrapped around his weapon, a smile curling across his lips.

The man laughed. "Not for long." He moved toward me and I jerked back.

"You won't survive this, Rick," Gabriel added. His weapon was in both hands, the look on his face full of determination but as he moved forward, I could tell whatever poison he'd been given was starting to work, his gait unsteady.

I bit back a gasp from hearing Gabriel's voice. He'd found me. How? I jerked my arms, shocked that I almost managed to yank one hand free. As Gabriel approached, gunfire erupted, the mystery man's soldiers unable to react in time. As blood was splattered onto the walls, I couldn't keep from yelping.

As I tugged, twisting my arm, Rick grabbed me, wrapping his arm around my throat.

Stay calm. Keep pulling.

I tried to keep my movements to a minimum as Gabriel continued walking forward, fighting the drug with everything he had.

Rick pressed the barrel to my head just as I managed to pull one hand free.

"Why?" Gabriel asked.

"Because your father killed my wife," Rick hissed.

Gabriel's eyes opened wide. "Jesus Christ. All this time you waited for revenge?"

"I wanted every one of you fucking lowlifes to suffer."

"You had my sister beaten."

"Yes. I would have done it myself, but you had to think the Morettis were responsible."

As Gabriel faltered, almost dropping his weapon, several of his soldiers came closer. His chest heaved and there was no doubt his muscles were starting to shut down.

Rick tipped his head, his hold tightening. I risked sliding my hand between my legs, managing to touch the handle of the knife.

"Let her go. You'll never make it out of here alive." Even Gabriel's voice was affected. He needed to get to a hospital, or he would die.

The tension was mounting, the soldiers moving closer.

"Then I'll die knowing your last breath is watching your lovely fiancée take hers." After a few seconds, Rick whistled.

And all hell broke loose, enemy soldiers bursting into the room.

Gunfire blasted from every corner, Gabriel's men dropping and rolling, several falling as soldiers dressed in all black stormed into the church.

Gabriel lunged forward, his roar unlike anything I'd ever hear. It was now or never.

I yanked the knife, twisting and driving the blade into Rick's stomach. He reared back, loosening his hold and I pitched to the floor, the knife still in my hand.

Pop! Pop! Pop!

The shots were closer. Gasping, I crawled away, scrambling to get to my feet.

"Not so fast," Rick snarled, yanking me by the hair. As he swung me around, all I could see was blood oozing from Gabriel's chest. He was on the floor, fighting the drug and the pain, trying to get to me.

The knife was knocked from my hand as Rick took aim.

"No!" My scream was muffled, visions of my life flashing in front of my eyes.

"Sorry, princess. We could have enjoyed spending time together." Rick laughed and all I could do was call out Gabriel's name.

"Gabriel!"

Pop! Pop!

Everything was in slow motion and all I could hear was the echo of gunfire, the ragged thumping of my heart.

And the bellow Gabriel issued as I swung my head. He was on his knees, the gun pointed toward Rick. Additional shots were fired.

Then he pitched forward as Rick tumbled onto his back.

"No. No!" I scrambled across the floor through a stream of blood, my body shaking. As I gathered Gabriel into my arms, cradling his head, the gunfire continued. "Stay with me. I'm right here."

He opened his eyes, managing to lift his arm, brushing his fingers across my cheek. "Safe."

"I'm fine. Just breathe, baby. Breathe. I need help. Please!"

"I... love... you."

As his eyes slowly closed, his arm falling away, I threw my head back and screamed.

CHAPTER 19

 abriel

Six weeks later

Death.

The thought was no longer with me, although on this day, I was reminded just how precious life truly was. Again. Perhaps this time, I'd let it sink into my brain that I couldn't waste another damn day.

As I stood in the doorway, all I could think about was ravaging Sarah's hot little body. My cock was fully aroused, my balls tight and I knew I wouldn't be able to keep from taking her just as I'd done only hours before.

I still had a difficult time processing all that had happened, Rick's scheme of revenge taking him years to perfect. He'd hired several mercenaries to help in his endeavor, able to afford their salaries given his profession.

As well as his family's status within the Bratva.

If only I'd remembered earlier the one saying he used every so often when he lost a deal or a stock crashed, then dozens of lives might have been saved.

Every jungle has a snake.

He'd purposely sent warnings that I'd ignored given my own need for revenge. I'd played into his scheme after Luciano's death. His hatred for my family had been born the day my father had made a mistake, the 'innocent' lives lost including Rick's wife.

The fact he'd killed Mary and our unborn child had been too much to bear, but he'd used the combined tragedies to become close enough to learn far too much information about my family. I'd allowed it. I'd been reckless.

And because I had, my family had been jeopardized. I'd learned since the catastrophic event at the church where he'd been married that his family was powerful, his Russian roots providing access to the soldiers he'd hired. And the Bratva had been behind him, his father considered second in command to the Pakhan.

Rick's need for revenge had parlayed a chain of events, the Bratva using it for their gain, terrorizing anyone who'd gotten in their way. While I'd worked with the Morettis in sweeping the streets of as many of the Bratva as possible, it was only a stopgap and nothing more. They would continue the war, seeking another round of vengeance as well as gains in their territory. What surprised me was how reactive Nico had been in his new role as Don of the family, his father taking a turn for the worse.

The events had been a revelation, pushing me into further acceptance of my new role. I'd lost several good men, but Dillon had been spared, although he'd spent two weeks in the hospital with a bullet wound to his chest.

If I hadn't had my Florence Nightingale by my side, I would have perished, the poison almost ending my life. Rick had planned the events so well, using his patience as the greatest weapon while I'd reacted out of anger and guilt.

A valuable lesson and one I wouldn't forget.

Sarah finally noticed me as she applied the last of her makeup, her eyes sparkling in the bathroom light as she stared at me in the mirror.

"You look stunning," I told her as I walked further inside, crowding her space and pressing the full weight of my body against her.

"You look mighty handsome yourself," she purred.

I rolled my hands down her arms, taking a deep whiff of her perfume. As I ground my groin against her bottom, she trembled, her mouth pursing.

"We don't have time."

"We always have time," I told her then lowered my head, nuzzling against her neck. She was warm and soft, perfect in every way.

And she was all mine.

She tried to push me away and I ripped her dress over her bottom, pressing my hand between her legs. "They can wait."

"No, they can't. Besides, my sister is here."

"Uh-huh. She can wait as well." I shoved aside her thong, driving two fingers inside her tight channel.

Moaning, Sarah pressed her hands on the counter, easing her legs apart. "You're so bad."

"No, you're the very bad girl, remember." I nipped her earlobe and shifted my other hand to my zipper. As I pumped my fingers inside, she wiggled in my hold.

"This is no fair."

"Life isn't fair. Remember? But you're required to do everything I say."

She blushed, biting her lower lip, her eyes now half closed. "Yes, sir."

When my cock was free, I wasted no time driving the entire length into her sweet pussy. Her moan was like music to my ears, the way her body molded against mine dragging the beast from his lair all over again. I pulled her away from the counter, gripping her hips as I thrust hard and deep, her muscles clamping around my shaft.

"Oh, God," she whispered, pressing her hand against the glass and arching her back. She never took her eyes off me as I fucked her, taking my time to fill her completely. I could do this for hours, my needs never satisfied.

Panting, she pushed back against me, her eyes glassy and her mouth twisting.

"What do you want?" I breathed.

"Keep fucking me. Harder."

"Yes, baby. I will." I slammed into her, the force driving her into the edge of the counter. As I rolled onto the balls of my feet, we both became breathless, steam from our combined breaths fogging the mirror. I thrust brutally, barely able to contain myself.

"More. Harder."

Every request drove me to the edge of sanity, my needs only increasing. I adored this woman, would do everything to protect her. Seconds later, I could tell she was close to coming. She threw back her head, her mouth open wide, her moans filling the bathroom.

"That's it. Come for me. Come for me, now!"

Her body began to shake, her breath skipping as her muscles clamped and released several times. There was nothing like seeing the throes of ecstasy on her face. My chest was tight, my pulse racing and I became a wild man, fucking her long and hard as one orgasm swept into another.

"Yes. Yes!"

God, I loved her screams.

"Gabriel. Harder. Please."

My muscles tensed, sweat beading across my forehead as I continued plunging as deep as possible. Only when she sagged against the counter did I allow myself any relief. As my body began to shake, I finally let go, filling her with my seed.

Then I crowded over her lithe body, placing my hands on hers, intertwining our fingers as we both tried to steady our breathing. "Beautiful. Mine. Forever."

The three words were ones she loved to hear.

I kept her in the same position for a few minutes then backed away, grinning as I watched her try to recover. Then I pulled a box from my pocket, easing it around her shoulder.

"You've given me too much already," she said even as she accepted the gift.

"This is something different." I raked my fingers through my hair and adjusted my clothes as she opened it.

"The necklace is beautiful," she whispered, darting a look into the mirror.

I took it from her hand, easing the sterling silver band around her neck, the single jewel a beautiful ruby. "It's not just any necklace, my sweet submissive. It's a collar. Now, everyone will know you are all mine."

"Does that make you my master?" she asked playfully as I fastened the choker.

"That goes without saying. Every infraction will be handled accordingly." To prove my point, I smacked her bottom three times, laughing as she squealed. "Stunning."

"It's gorgeous."

I backed away, holding out my hand. "Time to go. There are guests waiting."

"Oh, no. I need to clean up a bit."

"Not allowed. I want you reeking of my scent."

"You're incorrigible."

"No, just demanding." I grabbed her hand, ignoring her cries as she tried to pull away. She knew better. I would never let her go. Both Shadow and Goldie barked several times, their tails wagging from happiness. They'd become close, refusing to sleep anywhere but in the bed.

I wouldn't have it any other way.

As I pulled her down the stairs, she continued fighting me and all I could do was grin.

The day was warmer than expected, spring flowers blooming in the garden, the storm from the early morning hours giving way to bright sunshine. It was a perfect day for a wedding.

She stopped fighting as soon as we walked out of the house. This would be our last month in the location, her suggestion I sell the estate one that made sense. We'd found a new home together, much smaller but one with enough room to start a family. I'd seen such emotion on Sarah's face when she'd asked me about my unborn child, fighting tears as she'd allowed to me to grieve for only the second time. She'd been my rock, a woman who loved me against the odds.

Maybe karma had finally shifted in my direction.

"This is perfect," she whispered. "Just what Maria wanted."

"All because you made it come to life." The fact my father had blessed the wedding between my baby sister and my second in command was as surprising as the change in his attitude as of late. With my mother's condition stable for the time being, he'd become determined to enjoy his retirement, secure in the fact he had a son with a firm hold on the reins.

"You had a little bit to do with it," she purred and kissed me on the cheek, finally pulling out of my hand. "Maybe one day we could have a wedding this beautiful."

"We'll see."

She had no idea we were flying to Italy ten days from now, a special celebration planned, including our nuptials in front of my grandparents. Our entire family and hers would be in attendance, all expenses paid.

Even her father.

I'd decided not to turn him in to the Feds or to carve him into pieces. It would serve no purpose. His role had been minimal, tasked with heightening his level of persecution in exchange for cash, but his criminal activities in other avenues far outweighed accepting a bribe. However, he was no longer persecuting our family, selecting another victim to spend his time pontificating about. He'd been advised to do so more than once. Besides, he had his own issues to deal with, including his impending divorce.

The event would be cathartic, bringing the past to the present and maybe crushing the demons that had plagued my family for years.

394

As I looked toward the ocean, I could almost feel Luciano's presence. He would have enjoyed this day. Theodora was beaming, Nico her date and they appeared happy, although I'd keep my eye on him until I was certain. My mother was smiling more than I'd seen her do in a long time, her medication keeping her capable of planning the wedding with ease.

Maria was glowing, unable to keep from laughing. At least her marriage would keep her in the States, as well as her unborn child.

Then there was my father, keeping his chest puffed out as he greeted the influential guests one by one.

Today was a good day.

Dillon walked close, nerves consuming his usual gruff expression. As he held out his hand, I pulled him in for a typical familiar bear hug, which shocked the hell out of him.

"Hell, you are considered family now," I told him then backed away.

He grinned, nodding as he turned his head to capture another look at his bride to be. "Thank you for everything."

The man had saved Carrie's life then watched over me at the hospital, even though his doctor had insisted he rest. I owed him many things for his loyalty.

"She loves you," I told him.

"I'm one lucky man."

"Yes, you are. Don't forget it," I teased. "So am I." I noticed Sarah shifting away from the crowd in order to find me again, her smile beaming.

"Don't worry, Don Giordano. If I do, I'm certain you'll remind me," he said as he laughed.

"Gabriel."

"Not today. Today you represent my family."

As I looked into his eyes, I was honored by the level of respect. I didn't deserve a second chance. But I was grateful I'd been given one.

I made one additional promise on this beautiful day. That I wouldn't waste a minute of my life.

"I think it's time," I nudged and grinned as he wiped his hands on his suit.

"I won't let anything happen to her. Ever," he said with conviction.

"I know you won't."

As he walked away, others gathering close to the gazebo, Sarah headed toward me, her grin creating an intense need all over again. She slid her arm around me and lifted her head to the sky.

"Look. There's a rainbow."

I tipped my head and pulled her tightly against me. There would always be enemies and they would be handled. However, they would no longer rule the organization or my family. "It's beautiful. Just like you are."

She laughed as she clung to me. "The rainbow signifies hope, life reborn. I feel like that's what happened. We were reborn and our lives combined as one."

"You're my little dreamer."

"No, I'm just a woman finally finding love."

As the ceremony started, I kept my eyes on the fading colors. I was no romantic, but I took it as a sign.

Everything happened for a reason.

Love had managed to triumph over both evil and death.

And I would never forget the gift of being given a second chance.

The End

AFTERWORD

Stormy Night Publications would like to thank you for your interest in our books.

If you liked this book (or even if you didn't), we would really appreciate you leaving a review on the site where you purchased it. Reviews provide useful feedback for us and our authors, and this feedback (both positive comments and constructive criticism) allows us to work even harder to make sure we provide the content our customers want to read.

If you would like to check out more books from Stormy Night Publications, if you want to learn more about our company, or if you would like to join our mailing list, please visit our website at:

http://www.stormynightpublications.com

BOOKS OF THE SINNERS AND SAINTS SERIES

Beautiful Villain

When I knocked on Kirill Sabatin's door, I didn't know he was the Kozlov Bratva's most feared enforcer. I didn't expect him to be the most terrifyingly sexy man I've ever laid eyes on either…

I told him off for making so much noise in the middle of the night, but if the crack of his palm against my bare bottom didn't wake everyone in the building my screams of climax certainly did.

I shouldn't have let him spank me, let alone seduce me. He's a dangerous man and I could easily end up in way over my head. But the moment I set eyes on those rippling, sweat-slicked muscles I knew I needed that beautiful villain to take me long and hard and savagely right then and there.

And he did.

Now I just have to hope him claiming me doesn't start a mob war…

Beautiful Sinner

When I first screamed his name in shameful surrender, Sevastian Kozlov was the enemy, the heir of a rival family who had just finished spanking me into submission after I dared to defy him.

Though he'd already claimed my body by the time he claimed me as his bride, no matter how desperately I long for his touch I vowed this beautiful sinner would never conquer my heart.

But it wasn't up to me…

Beautiful Seduction

In my late-night hunt for the perfect pastry, I never expected to be the victim of a brutal attack... or for a brooding, blue-eyed stranger to become my savior, tending to my wounds while easing my fears. The electricity exploded between us, turning into a night of incredible passion.

Only later did I learn that Valentin Vincheti is the heir to the New York Italian mafia empire.

Then he came to take me, and this time he wasn't gentle. I shouldn't have surrendered, but with each savage kiss and stinging stroke of his belt his beautiful seduction became more difficult to resist. But when one of his enemies sets his sights on me, will my secrets put our lives at risk?

Beautiful Obsession

After I was left at the altar, I turned what was meant to be the reception into an epic party. But when a handsome stranger asked me to dance, I wasn't prepared for the passion he ignited.

He told me he was a very bad man, but that only made my heart race faster as I lay bare and bound, my dress discarded and my bottom sore from a spanking, waiting for him to ravage me.

It was supposed to be just one night. No strings. Nothing to entangle me in his dangerous world.

But that was before I became his beautiful obsession...

Beautiful Devil

Kostya Baranov is an infamous assassin, a man capable of incredible savagery, but when I witnessed a mafia hit he didn't silence me with a bullet. He decided to make me his instead.

Taken prisoner and forced to obey or feel the sting of his belt, shameful lust for my captor soon wars with fury at what he has done to me... and what he keeps doing to me with every touch.

But though he may be a beautiful devil, it is my own family's secret which may damn us both.

BOOKS OF THE BENEDETTI EMPIRE SERIES

Cruel Prince

Catherine's father conspired to have my father killed, and that debt to the Benedetti family must be settled. Just as he took something from me, I will take something from him.

His daughter.

She will be mine to punish and ravage, but when she suffers it will not be for his sins.

It will be for my pleasure.

She will beg, but it will be for me to claim her in the most shameful ways imaginable.

She will scream, but it will be because she doesn't think she can bear another climax.

But when she surrenders at last, it will not be to her captor.

It will be to her husband.

Ruthless Prince

Alexandra is a senator's daughter, used to mingling in the company of the rich and powerful, but tonight she will learn that there are men who play by different rules.

Men like me.

I could romance her. I could seduce her and then carry her gently to my bed.

But that can wait. Tonight I'm going to wring one ruthless climax after another from her quivering body with her bottom burning from my belt and her throat sore from screaming.

She will know she is mine before she even knows she is my bride.

Savage Prince

Gillian's father may be a powerful Irish mob boss, but he owes a blood debt to my family, and when I came to collect I didn't ask permission before taking his daughter as payment.

It was not up to him… or to her.

I will make her my bride, but I am not the kind of man who will wait until our wedding night to bare her and claim what belongs to me. She will walk down the aisle wet, well-used, and sore.

Her dress will hide the marks from my belt that taught her the consequences of disobeying her husband, but nothing will hide her blushes as her arousal drips down her thighs with each step.

By the time she says her vows she will already be mine.

BOOKS OF THE MERCILESS KINGS SERIES

King's Captive

Emily Porter saw me kill a man who betrayed my family and she helped put me behind bars. But someone with my connections doesn't stay in prison long, and she is about to learn the hard way that there is a price to pay for crossing the boss of the King dynasty. A very, very painful price…

She's going to cry for me as I blister that beautiful bottom, then she's going to scream for me as I ravage her over and over again, taking her in the most shameful ways she can imagine. But leaving her well-punished and well-used is just the beginning of what I have in store for Emily.

I'm going to make her my bride, and then I'm going to make her mine completely.

King's Hostage

When my life was threatened, Michael King didn't just take matters into his own hands.

He took me.

When he carried me off it was partly to protect me, but mostly it was because he wanted me.

I didn't choose to go with him, but it wasn't up to me. That's why I'm naked, wet, and sore in an opulent Swiss chalet with my bottom still burning from the belt of the infuriatingly sexy mafia boss who brought me here, punished me when I fought him, and then savagely made me his.

We'll return when things are safe in New Orleans, but I won't be going back to my old home.

I belong to him now, and he plans to keep me.

King's Possession

Her father had to be taught what happens when you cross a King, but that isn't why Genevieve Rossi is sore, well-used, and waiting for me to claim her in the only way I haven't already.

She's sore because she thought she could embarrass me in public without being punished.

She's well-used because after I spanked her I wanted more, and I take what I want.

She's waiting for me in my bed because she's my bride, and tonight is our wedding night.

I'm not going to be gentle with her, but when she wakes up tomorrow morning wet and blushing her cheeks won't be crimson because of the shameful things I did to her naked, quivering body.

It will be because she begged for all of them.

King's Toy

Vincenzo King thought I knew something about a man who betrayed him, but that isn't why I'm on my way to New Orleans well-used and sore with my backside still burning from his belt.

When he bared and punished me maybe it was just business, but what came after was not.

It was savage, it was shameful, and it was very, very personal.

I'm his toy now, and not the kind you keep in its box on the shelf.

He's going to play rough with me.

He's going to get me all wet and dirty.

Then he's going to do it all again tomorrow.

King's Demands

Julieta Morales hoped to escape an unwanted marriage, but the moment she got into my car her fate was sealed. She will have a husband, but it won't be the cartel boss her father chose for her.

It will be me.

But I'm not the kind of man who takes his bride gently amid rose petals on her wedding night. She'll learn to satisfy her King's demands with her bottom burning and her hair held in my fist.

She'll promise obedience when she speaks her vows, but she'll be mastered long before then.

King's Temptation

I didn't think I needed Dimitri Kristoff's protection, but it wasn't up to me. With a kingpin from a rival family coming after me, he took charge, took off his belt, and then took what he wanted.

He knows I'm not used to doing as I'm told. He just doesn't care.

The stripes seared across my bare bottom left me sore and sorry, but it was what came after that truly left me shaken. The princess of the King family shouldn't be on her knees for anyone, let alone this Bratva brute who has decided to claim for himself what he was meant to safeguard.

Nobody gave me to him, but I'm his anyway.

Now he's going to make sure I know it.

BOOKS OF THE MAFIA MASTERS SERIES

His as Payment

Caroline Hargrove thinks she is mine because her father owed me a debt, but that isn't why she is sitting in my car beside me with her bottom sore inside and out. She's wet, well-used, and coming with me whether she likes it or not because I decided I want her, and I take what I want.

As a senator's daughter, she probably thought no man would dare lay a hand on her, let alone spank her thoroughly and then claim her beautiful body in the most shameful ways possible.

She was wrong. Very, very wrong. She's going to be mastered, and I won't be gentle about it.

Taken as Collateral

Francesca Alessandro was just meant to be collateral, held captive as a warning to her father, but then she tried to fight me. She ended up sore and soaked as I taught her a lesson with my belt and then screaming with every savage climax as I taught her to obey in a much more shameful way.

She's mine now. Mine to keep. Mine to protect. Mine to use as hard and as often as I please.

Forced to Cooperate

Willow Church is not the first person who tried to put a bullet in me. She's just the first I let live. Now she will pay the price in the most shameful way imaginable. The stripes from my belt will teach her to obey, but what happens to her sore, red bottom after that will teach the real lesson.

She will be used mercilessly, over and over, and every brutal climax will remind her of the humiliating truth: she never even had a chance against me. Her body always knew its master.

Claimed as Revenge

Valencia Rivera became mine the moment her father broke the agreement he made with me. She thought she had a say in the matter, but my belt across her beautiful bottom taught her otherwise and a night spent screaming her surrender into the sheets left her in no doubt she belongs to me.

Using her hard and often will not be all it takes to tame her properly, but it will be a good start…

Made to Beg

Sierra Fox showed up at my door to ask for my protection, and I gave it to her… for a price. She belongs to me now, and I'm going to use her beautiful body as thoroughly as I please. The only thing for her to decide is how sore her cute little bottom will be when I'm through claiming her.

She came to me begging for help, but as her moans and screams grow louder with every brutal climax, we both know it won't be long before she begs me for something far more shameful.

BOOKS OF THE EDGE OF DARKNESS SERIES

Dark Stranger

On a dark, rainy night, I received a phone call. I shouldn't have answered it... but I did.

The things he says he'll do to me are far from sweet, this man I know only by his voice.

They're so filthy I blush crimson just hearing them... and yet still I answer, my panties always soaked the moment the phone rings. But this isn't going to end when I decide it's gone too far...

I can tell him to leave me alone, but I know it won't keep him away. He's coming for me, and when he does he's going to make me his in all the rough, shameful ways he promised he would.

And I'll be wet and ready for him... whether I want to be or not.

Dark Predator

She thinks I'm seducing her, but this isn't romance. It's something much more shameful.

Eden tried to leave the mafia behind, but someone far more dangerous has set his sights on her.

Me.

She was meant to be my revenge against an old enemy, but I decided to make her mine instead.

She'll moan as my belt lashes her quivering bottom and writhe as I claim her in the filthiest of ways, but that's just the beginning. When I'm done, it won't be just her body that belongs to me.

I'll own her heart and soul too.

BOOKS OF THE DARK OVERTURE SERIES

Indecent Invitation

I shouldn't be here.

My clothes shouldn't be scattered around the room, my bottom shouldn't be sore, and I certainly shouldn't be screaming into the sheets as a ruthless tycoon takes everything he wants from me.

I shouldn't even know Houston Powers at all, but I was in a bad spot and I was made an offer.

A shameful, indecent offer I couldn't refuse.

I was desperate, I needed the money, and I didn't have a choice. Not a real one, anyway.

I'm here because I signed a contract, but I'm his because he made me his.

Illicit Proposition

I should have known better.

His proposition was shameful. So shameful I threw my drink in his face when I heard it.

Then I saw the look in his eyes, and I knew I'd made a mistake.

I fought as he bared me and begged as he spanked me, but it didn't matter. All I could do was moan, scream, and climax helplessly for him as he took everything he wanted from me.

By the time I signed the contract, I was already his.

Unseemly Entanglement

I was warned about Frederick Duvall. I was told he was dangerous. But I never suspected that meeting the billionaire advertising mogul to discuss a business proposition would end with me bent over a table with my dress up and my panties down for a shameful lesson in obedience.

That should have been it. I should have told him what he could do with his offer and his money.

But I didn't.

I could say it was because two million dollars is a lot of cash, but as I stand before him naked, bound, and awaiting the sting of his cane for daring to displease him, I know that's not the truth.

I'm not here because he pays me. I'm here because he owns me.

BOOKS OF THE CLUB DARKNESS SERIES

Bent to His Will

Even the most powerful men in the world know better than to cross me, but Autumn Sutherland thought she could spy on me in my own club and get away with it. Now she must be punished.

She tried to expose me, so she will be exposed. Bare, bound, and helplessly on display, she'll beg for mercy as my strap lashes her quivering bottom and my crop leaves its burning welts on her most intimate spots. Then she'll scream my name as she takes every inch of me, long and hard.

When I am done with her, she won't just be sore and shamefully broken. She will be mine.

Broken by His Hand

Sophia Russo tried to keep away from me, but just thinking about what I would do to her left her panties drenched. She tried to hide it, but I didn't let her. I tore those soaked panties off, spanked her bare little bottom until she had no doubt who owns her, and then took her long and hard.

She begged and screamed as she came for me over and over, but she didn't learn her lesson…

She didn't just come back for more. She thought she could disobey me and get away with it.

This time I'm not just going to punish her. I'm going to break her.

Bound by His Command

Willow danced for the rich and powerful at the world's most exclusive club… until tonight.

Tonight I told her she belongs to me now, and no other man will touch her again.

Tonight I ripped her soaked panties from her beautiful body and taught her to obey with my belt.

Tonight I took her as mine, and I won't be giving her up.

MORE MAFIA AND BILLIONAIRE ROMANCES BY PIPER STONE

Caught

If you're forced to come to an arrangement with someone as dangerous as Jagger Calduchi, it means he's about to take what he wants, and you'll give it to him... even if it's your body.

I got caught snooping where I didn't belong, and Jagger made me an offer I couldn't refuse. A week with him where his rules are the only rules, or his bought and paid for cops take me to jail.

He's going to punish me, train me, and master me completely. When he's used me so shamefully I blush just to think about it, maybe he'll let me go home... or maybe he'll decide to keep me.

Ruthless

Treating a mobster shot by a rival's goons isn't really my forte, but when a man is powerful enough to have a whole wing of a hospital cleared out for his protection, you do as you're told.

To make matters worse, this isn't first time I've met Giovanni Calduchi. It turns out my newest patient is the stern, sexy brute who all but dragged me back to his hotel room a couple of nights ago so he could use my body as he pleased, then showed up at my house the next day, stripped me bare, and spanked me until I was begging him to take me even more roughly and shamefully.

Now, with his enemies likely to be coming after me in order to get to him, all I can do is hope he's as good at keeping me safe as he is at keeping me blushing, sore, and thoroughly satisfied.

Dangerous

I knew Erik Chenault was dangerous the moment I saw him. Everything about him should have warned me away, from the scar on his face to the fact that mobsters call him Blade. But I was drawn like a moth to a flame, and I ended up burnt... and blushing, sore, and thoroughly used.

Now he's taken it upon himself to protect me from men like the ones we both tried to leave in our past. He's going to make me his whether I like it or not... but I think I'm going to like it.

Prey

Within moments of setting eyes on Sophia Waters, I was certain of two things. She was going to learn what happens to bad girls who cheat at cards, and I was going to be the one to teach her.

But there was one thing I didn't know as I reddened that cute little bottom and then took her long and hard and oh so shamefully: I wasn't the only one who didn't come here for a game of cards.

I came to kill a man. It turns out she came to protect him.

Nobody keeps me from my target, but I'm in no rush. Not when I'm enjoying this game of cat and mouse so much. I'll even let her catch me one day, and as she screams my name with each brutal climax she'll finally realize the truth. She was never the hunter. She was always the prey.

Given

Stephanie Michaelson was given to me, and she is mine. The sooner she learns that, the less often her cute little bottom will end up well-punished and sore as she is reminded of her place.

But even as she promises obedience with tears running down her cheeks, I know it isn't the sting of my belt that will truly tame her. It is what comes next that will leave her in no doubt she belongs to me. That part will be long, hard, and shameful... and I will make her beg for all of it.

Dangerous Stranger

I came to Spain hoping to start a new life away from dangerous men, but then I met Rafael Santiago. Now I'm not just caught up in the affairs of a mafia boss, I'm being forced into his car.

When I saw something I shouldn't have, Rafael took me captive, stripped me bare, and punished me until he felt certain I'd told him everything I knew about his organization... which was nothing at all. Then he offered me his protection in return for the right to use me as he pleases.

Now that I belong to him, his plans for me are more shameful than I could have ever imagined.

Indebted

After her father stole from me, I could have left Alessandra Toro in jail for a crime she didn't commit. But I have plans for her. A deal with the judge—the kind only a man like me can arrange—made her my captive, and she will pay her father's debt with her beautiful body.

She will try to run, of course, but it won't be the law that comes after her. It will be me.

The sting of my belt across her quivering bare bottom will teach Alessandra the price of defiance, but it is the far more shameful penance that follows which will truly tame her.

Taken

When Winter O'Brien was given to me, she thought she had a say in the matter. She was wrong.

She is my bride. Mine to claim, mine to punish, and mine to use as shamefully as I please. The sting of my belt on her bare bottom will teach her to obey, but obedience is just the beginning.

I will demand so much more.

Bratva's Captive

I told Chloe Kingstrom that getting close to me would be dangerous, and she should keep her distance. The moment she disobeyed and followed me into that bar, she became mine.

Now my enemies are after her, but it's not what they would do to her she should worry about.

It's what I'm going to do to her.

My belt across her bare backside will teach her obedience, but what comes after will be different.

She's going to blush, beg, and scream with every climax as she's ravaged more thoroughly than she can imagine. Then I'm going to flip her over and claim her in an even more shameful way.

If she's a good girl, I might even let her enjoy it.

Hunted

Hope Gracen was just another target to be tracked down… until I caught her.

When I discovered I'd been lied to, I carried her off.

She'll tell me the truth with her bottom still burning from my belt, but that isn't why she's here.

I took her to protect her. I'm keeping her because she's mine.

Theirs as Payment

Until mere moments ago, I was a doctor heading home after my shift at the hospital. But that was before I was forced into the back seat of an SUV, then bared and spanked for trying to escape.

Now I'm just leverage for the Cabello brothers to use against my father, but it isn't the thought of being held hostage by these brutes that has my heart racing and my whole body quivering.

It is the way they're looking at me…

Like they're about to tear my clothes off and take turns mounting me like wild beasts.

Like they're going to share me, using me in ways more shameful than I can even imagine.

Like they own me.

Ruthless Acquisition

I knew the shameful stakes when I bet against these bastards. I just didn't expect to lose.

Now they've come to collect their winnings.

But they aren't just planning to take a belt to my bare bottom for trying to run and then claim everything they're owed from my naked, helpless body as I blush, beg, and scream for them.

They've acquired me, and they plan to keep me.

Bound by Contract

I knew I was in trouble the moment Gregory Steele called me into his office, but I wasn't expecting to end up stripped bare and bent over his desk for a painful lesson from his belt.

Taking a little bit of money here and there might have gone unnoticed in another organization, but stealing from one of the most powerful mafia bosses on the West Coast has consequences.

It doesn't matter why I did it. The only thing that matters now is what he's going to do to me.

I have no doubt he will use me shamefully, but he didn't make me sign that contract just to show me off with my cheeks blushing and my bottom sore under the scandalous outfit he chose for me.

Now that I'm his, he plans to keep me.

Dangerous Addiction

I went looking for a man working with my enemies. When I found only her instead, I should have just left her alone… or maybe taken what I wanted from her and then left… but I didn't.

I couldn't.

So I carried her off to keep for myself.

She didn't make it easy for me, and that earned her a lesson in obedience. A shameful one.

But as her bare bottom reddens under my punishing hand I can see her arousal dripping down her quivering thighs, and no matter how much she squirms and sobs and begs we both know exactly what she needs, and we both know as soon as this spanking is over I'm going to give it to her.

Hard.

Auction House

When I went undercover to investigate a series of murders with links to Steele Franklin's auction house operation, I expected to be sold for the humiliating use of one of his fellow billionaires.

But he wanted me for himself.

No contract. No agreed upon terms. No say in the matter at all except whether to surrender to his shameful demands without a fight or make him strip me bare and spank me into submission first.

I chose the second option, but as one devastating climax after another is forced from my naked, quivering body, what scares me isn't the thought of him keeping me locked up in a cage forever.

It's knowing he won't need to.

Interrogated

As Liam McGinty's belt lashes my bare backside, it isn't the burning sting or the humiliating awareness that my body's surrender is on full display for this ruthless mobster that shocks me.

It's the fact that this isn't a scene from one of my books.

I almost can't process the fact that I'm really riding in the back of a luxury SUV belonging to the most powerful Irish mafia boss in New York—the man I've written so much about—with my cheeks blushing, my bottom sore inside and out, and my arousal soaking the seat beneath me.

But whether I can process it or not, I'm his captive now.

Maybe he'll let me go when he's gotten the answers he needs and he's used me as he pleases.

Or maybe he'll keep me…

Vow of Seduction

Alexander Durante, Brogan Lancaster, and Daniel Norwood are powerful, dangerous men, but that won't keep them safe from me. Not after they let my brother take the fall for their crimes.

I spent years preparing for my chance at revenge. But things didn't go as planned…

Now I'm naked, bound, and helpless, waiting to be used and punished as these brutes see fit, and yet what's on my mind isn't how to escape all of the shameful things they're going to do to me.

It's whether I even want to…

Brutal Heir

When I went to an author convention, I didn't expect to find myself enjoying a rooftop meal with the sexiest cover model in the business, let alone screaming his name in bed later that night.

I didn't plan to be targeted by assassins, rushed to a helicopter under cover of armed men, and then spirited away to his home country with my bottom still burning from a spanking either, but it turns out there are some really important things I didn't know about Diavolo Montoya…

Like the fact that he's the heir to a notorious crime syndicate.

I should hate him, but even as his prisoner our connection is too intense to ignore, and I'm beginning to realize that what began as a moment of passion is going to end with me as his.

Forever.

BOOKS OF THE DANGEROUS BUSINESS SERIES

Persuasion

Her father stole something from the mob and they hired me to get it back, but that's not the real reason Giliana Worthington is locked naked in a cage with her bottom well-used and sore.

I brought her here so I could take my time punishing her, mastering her, and ravaging her helpless, quivering body over and over again as she screams and moans and begs for more.

I didn't take her as a hostage. I took her because she is mine.

Bad Men

I thought I could run away from the marriage the mafia arranged for me, but I ended up held prisoner in a foreign country by someone far more dangerous than the man I tried to escape.

Then Jack and Diego came for me.

They didn't ask if I wanted to be theirs. They just took me.

I ran, but they caught me, stripped me bare, and punished me in the most shameful way possible.

Now they're going to share me, and they're not going to be gentle about it.

BOOKS OF THE EAGLE FORCE SERIES

Debt of Honor

Isabella Adams is a brilliant scientist, but her latest discovery has made her a target of Russian assassins. I've been assigned to protect her, and when her reckless behavior puts her in danger she'll learn in the most shameful of ways what it means to be under the command of a Marine.

She can beg and plead as my belt lashes her bare backside, but the only mercy she'll receive is the chance to scream as she climaxes over and over with her well-spanked bottom still burning.

As my past returns to haunt me, it'll take every skill I've mastered to keep her alive.

She may be a national treasure, but she belongs to me now.

Debt of Loyalty

After she was kidnapped in broad daylight, I was hired to bring Willow Cavanaugh home, but as the daughter of a wealthy family she's used to getting what she wants rather than taking orders.

Too bad.

She'll do as she's told or she'll earn herself a stern, shameful reminder of who is in charge, but it will take more than just a well-spanked bare bottom to truly tame this feisty little rich girl.

She'll learn her place over my knee, but it's in my bed that I'll make her mine.

Debt of Sacrifice

When she witnessed a murder, it put Greer McDuff on a brutal cartel's radar… and on mine.

As a former Navy SEAL now serving with the elite Eagle Force, my assignment is to protect her by any means necessary. If that requires a stern reminder of who is in charge with her bottom bare over my knee and then an even more shameful lesson in my bed, then that's what she'll get.

There's just one problem.

The only place I know I can keep her safe is the ranch I left behind and vowed never to return.

BOOKS OF THE MONTANA BAD BOYS SERIES

Hawk

He's a big, angry Marine, and I'm going to be sore when he's done with me.

Hawk Travers is not a man to be trifled with. I learned that lesson in the hardest way possible, first with a painful, humiliating public spanking and then much more shamefully in private.

She came looking for trouble. She got a taste of my belt instead.

Bryce Myers pushed me too far and she ended up with her bottom welted. But as satisfying as it is to hear this feisty little reporter scream my name as I put her in her place, I get the feeling she isn't going to stop snooping around no matter how well-used and sore I leave her cute backside.

She's gotten herself in way over her head, but she's mine now, and I protect what's mine.

Scorpion

He didn't ask if I like it rough. It wasn't up to me.

I thought I could get away with pissing off a big, tough Marine. I ended up with my face planted in the sheets, my burning bottom raised high, and my hair held tightly in his fist as he took me long and hard and taught me the kind of shameful lesson only a man like Scorpion could teach.

She was begging for a taste of my belt. She got much more than that.

Getting so tipsy she thought she could be sassy with me in my own bar earned Caroline a spanking, but it was trying to make off with my truck that sealed the deal. She'll feel my belt across her bare backside, then she'll scream my name as she takes every single inch of me.

This naughty girl needs to be put in her place, and I'm going to enjoy every moment of it.

Mustang

I tried to tell him how to run his ranch. Then he took off his belt.

When I heard a rumor about his ranch, I confronted Mustang about it. I thought I could go toe to toe with the big, tough former Marine, but I ended up blushing, sore, and very thoroughly used.

I told her it was going to hurt. I meant it.

Danni Brexton is a hot little number with a sharp tongue and a chip on her shoulder. She's the kind of trouble that needs to be ridden hard and put away wet, but only after a taste of my belt.

It will take more than just a firm hand and a burning bottom to tame this sassy spitfire, but I plan to keep her safe, sound, and screaming my name in bed whether she likes it or not. By the time I'm through with her, there won't be a shadow of a doubt in her mind that she belongs to me.

Nash

When he caught me on his property, he didn't call the police. He just took off his belt.

Nash caught me breaking into his shed while on the run from the mob, and when he demanded answers and obedience I gave him neither. Then he took off his belt and taught me in the most shameful way possible what happens to naughty girls who play games with a big, rough Marine.

She's mine to protect. That doesn't mean I'm going to be gentle with her.

Michelle doesn't just need a place to hide out. She needs a man who will bare her bottom and spank her until she is sore and sobbing whenever she puts herself at risk with reckless defiance, then shove her face into the sheets and make her scream his name with every savage climax.

She'll get all of that from me, and much, much more.

Austin

I offered this brute a ride. I ended up the one being ridden.

The first time I saw Austin, he was hitchhiking. I stopped to give him a lift, but I didn't end up taking this big, rough former Marine wherever he was heading. He was far too busy taking me.

She thought she was in charge. Then I took off my belt.

When Francesca Montgomery pulled up beside me, I didn't know who she was, but I knew what she needed and I gave it to her. Long, hard, and thoroughly, until she was screaming my name as she climaxed over and over with her quivering bare bottom still sporting the marks from my belt.

But someone wants to hurt her, and when someone tries to hurt what's mine, I take it personally.

BOOKS OF THE ALPHA DYNASTY SERIES

Unchained Beast

As the firstborn of the Dupree family, I have spent my life building the wealth and power of our mafia empire while keeping our dark secret hidden and my savage hunger at bay. But the beast within me cannot be chained forever, and I must claim a mate before I lose control completely…

That is why Coraline LeBlanc is mine.

When I mount and ravage her, it won't be because I want her. It will be because I need her.

But that doesn't mean I won't enjoy stripping her bare and spanking her until she surrenders, then making her beg and scream with every desperate climax as I take what belongs to me.

The beast will claim her, but I will keep her.

Savage Brute

It wasn't his mafia birthright that made Dax Dupree a monster. Years behind bars and a brutal war with a rival organization made him hard as steel, but the beast he can barely control was always there, and without a mate to mark and claim it would soon take hold of him completely.

I didn't know that when he showed up at my bar after closing and spanked me until I was wet and shamefully ready for him to mount and ravage me, or even when I woke the next morning with my throat sore from screaming and his seed still drying on my thighs. But I know it now.

Because I'm his mate.

Ruthless Monster

When Esme Rawlings looks at me, she sees many things. A ruthless mob boss. A key witness to the latest murder in an ongoing turf war. A guardian angel who saved her from a hitman's bullet.

But when I look at her, I see just one thing.

My mate.

She can investigate me as thoroughly as she feels necessary, prying into every aspect of my family's vast mafia empire, but the only truth she really needs to know about me she will learn tonight with her bare bottom burning and her protests drowned out by her screams of climax.

I take what belongs to me.

Ravenous Predator

Suzette Barker thought she could steal from the most powerful mafia boss in Philadelphia. My belt across her naked backside taught her otherwise, but as tears run down her cheeks and her arousal glistens on her bare thighs, there is something more important she will understand soon.

Kneeling at my feet and demonstrating her remorseful surrender in the most shameful way possible won't bring an end to this, nor will her screams of climax as I take her long and hard. She'll be coming with me and I'll be mounting and savagely rutting her as often as I please.

Not just because she owes me.

Because she's my mate.

Merciless Savage

Christoff Dupree doesn't strike me as the kind of man who woos a woman gently, so when I saw the flowers on my kitchen table I knew it wasn't just a gesture of appreciation for saving his life.

This ruthless mafia boss wasn't seducing me. Those roses mean that I belong to him now.

That I'm his to spank into shameful submission before he mounts me and claims me savagely.

That I'm his mate.

BOOKS OF THE ALPHA BEASTS SERIES

King's Mate

Her scent drew me to her, but something deeper and more powerful told me she was mine. Something that would not be denied. Something that demanded I claim her then and there.

I took her the way a beast takes his mate. Roughly. Savagely. Without mercy or remorse.

She will run, and when she does she will be punished, but it is not me that she fears. Every quivering, desperate climax reminds her that her body knows its master, and that terrifies her.

She knows I am not a gentle king, and she will scream for me as she learns her place.

Beast's Claim

Raven is not one of my kind, but the moment I caught her scent I knew she belonged to me.

She is my mate, and when I claim her it will not be gentle. She can fight me, but her pleas for mercy as she is punished will soon give way to screams of climax as she is mounted and rutted.

By the time I am finished with her, the evidence of her body's surrender will be mingled with my seed as it drips down her bare thighs. But she will be more than just sore and utterly spent.

She will be mine.

Alpha's Mate

I didn't ask Nicolina to be my mate. It was not up to her. An alpha takes what belongs to him.

She will plead for mercy as she is bared and punished for daring to run from me, but her screams as she is claimed and rutted will be those of helpless climax as her body surrenders to its master.

She is mine, and I'm going to make sure she knows it.

Claimed by the Beasts

Though she has done her best to run from it, Scarlet Dumane cannot escape what is in store for her. She has known for years that she is destined to belong not just to one savage beast, but to three, and now the time has come for her to be claimed. Soon her mates will own every inch of her beautiful body, and she will be shared and used as roughly and as often as they please.

Scarlet hid from the disturbing truth about herself, her family, and her town for as long as she could, but now her grandmother's death has finally brought her back home to the bayous of Louisiana and at last she must face her fate, no matter how shameful and terrifying.

She will be a queen, but her mates will be her masters, and defiance will be thoroughly punished. Yet even when she is stripped bare and spanked until she is sobbing, her need for them only grows, and every blush, moan, and quivering climax binds her to them more tightly. But with enemies lurking in the shadows, can she trust her mates to protect her from both man and beast?

Millionaire Daddy

Dominick Asbury is not just a handsome millionaire whose deep voice makes Jenna's tummy flutter whenever they are together, nor is he merely the first man bold enough to strip her bare and spank her hard and thoroughly whenever she has been naughty. He is much more than that.

He is her daddy.

He is the one who punishes her when she's been a bad girl, and he is the one who takes her in his arms afterwards and brings her to one climax after another until she is utterly spent and satisfied.

But something shady is going on behind the scenes at Dominick's company, and when Jenna draws the wrong conclusion from a poorly written article about him and creates an embarrassing public scene, will she end up not only costing them both their jobs but losing her daddy as well?

Conquering Their Mate

For years the Cenzans have cast a menacing eye on Earth, but it still came as a shock to be captured, stripped bare, and claimed as a mate by their leader and his most trusted warriors.

It infuriates me to be punished for the slightest defiance and forced to submit to these alien brutes, but as I'm led naked through the corridors of their ship, my well-punished bare bottom and my helpless arousal both fully on display, I cannot help wondering how long it will be until I'm kneeling at the feet of my mates and begging them take me as shamefully as they please.

Captured and Kept

Since her career was knocked off track in retaliation for her efforts to expose a sinister plot by high-ranking government officials, reporter Danielle Carver has been stuck writing puff pieces in a small town in Oregon. Desperate for a serious story, she sets out to investigate the rumors she's been hearing about mysterious men living in the mountains nearby. But when she secretly follows them back to their remote cabin, the ruggedly handsome beasts don't take kindly to her snooping around, and Dani soon finds herself stripped bare for a painful, humiliating spanking.

Their rough dominance arouses her deeply, and before long she is blushing crimson as they take turns using her beautiful body as thoroughly and shamefully as they please. But when Dani uncovers the true reason for their presence in the area, will more than just her career be at risk?

Taming His Brat

It's been years since Cooper Dawson left her small Texas hometown, but after her stubborn defiance gets her fired from two jobs in a row, she knows something definitely needs to change. What she doesn't expect, however, is for her sharp tongue and arrogant attitude to land her over the knee of a stern, ruggedly sexy cowboy for a painful, embarrassing, and very public spanking.

Rex Sullivan cannot deny being smitten by Cooper, and the fact that she is in desperate need of his belt across her bare backside only makes the war-hardened ex-Marine more determined to tame the beautiful, fiery redhead. It isn't long before she's screaming his name as he shows her just how hard and roughly a cowboy can ride a headstrong filly. But Rex and Cooper both have secrets, and when the demons of their past rear their ugly heads, will their romance be torn apart?

Capturing Their Mate

I thought the Cenzan invaders could never find me here, but I was wrong. Three of the alien brutes came to take me, and before I ever set foot aboard their ship I had already been stripped bare, spanked thoroughly, and claimed more shamefully then I would have ever thought possible.

They have decided that a public example must be made of me, and I will be punished and used in the most humiliating ways imaginable as a warning to anyone who might dare to defy them. But I am no ordinary breeder, and the secrets hidden in my past could change their world... or end it.

Rogue

Tracking down cyborgs is my job, but this time I'm the one being hunted. This rogue machine has spent most of his life locked up, and now that he's on the loose he has plans for me...

He isn't just going to strip me, punish me, and use me. He will take me longer and harder than any human ever could, claiming me so thoroughly that I will be left in no doubt who owns me.

No matter how shamefully I beg and plead, my body will be ravaged again and again with pleasure so intense it terrifies me to even imagine, because that is what he was built to do.

Roughneck

When I took a job on an oil rig to escape my scheming stepfather's efforts to set me up with one of his business cronies, I knew I'd be working with rugged men. What I didn't expect is to find myself bent over a desk, my cheeks soaked with tears and my bare thighs wet for a very different reason, as my well-punished bottom is thoroughly used by a stern, infuriatingly sexy roughneck.

Even though I should have known better than to get sassy with a firm-handed cowboy, let alone a tough-as-nails former Marine, there's no denying that learning the hard way was every bit as hot as it was shameful. But a sore, welted backside is just the start of his plans for me, and no matter how much I blush to admit it, I know I'm going to take everything he gives me and beg for more.

Hunting Their Mate

As far as I'm concerned, the Cenzans will always be the enemy, and there can be no peace while they remain on our planet. I planned to make them pay for invading our world, but I was hunted down and captured by two of their warriors with the help of a battle-hardened former Marine. Now I'm the one who is going to pay, as the three of them punish me, shame me, and share me.

Though the thought of a fellow human taking the side of these alien brutes enrages me, that is far from the worst of it. With every searing stroke of the strap that lands across my bare bottom, with every savage thrust as I am claimed over and over, and with every screaming climax, it is made more clear that it is my own quivering, thoroughly used body which has truly betrayed me.

Primitive

I was sent to this world to help build a new Earth, but I was shocked by what I found here. The men of this planet are not just primitive savages. They are predators, and I am now their prey...

The government lied to all of us. Not all of the creatures who hunted and captured me are aliens. Some of them were human once, specimens transformed in labs into little more than feral beasts.

I fought, but I was thrown over a shoulder and carried off. I ran, but I was caught and punished. Now they are going to claim me, share me, and use me so roughly that when the last screaming climax has been wrung from my naked, helpless body, I wonder if I'll still know my own name.

Harvest

The Centurions conquered Earth long before I was born, but they did not come for our land or our resources. They came for mates, women deemed suitable for breeding. Women like me.

Three of the alien brutes decided to claim me, and when I defied them, they made a public example of me, punishing me so thoroughly and shamefully I might never stop blushing.

But now, as my virgin body is used in every way possible, I'm not sure I want them to stop...

Torched

I work alongside firefighters, so I know how to handle musclebound roughnecks, but Blaise Tompkins is in a league of his own. The night we met, I threw a glass of wine in his face, then ended up shoved against the wall with my panties on the floor and my arousal dripping down my thighs, screaming out climax after shameful climax with my well-punished bottom still burning.

I've got a series of arsons to get to the bottom of, and finding out that the infuriatingly sexy brute who spanked me like a naughty little girl will be helping me with the investigation seemed like the last thing I needed, until somebody hurled a rock through my window in an effort to scare me away from the case. Now having a big, strong man around doesn't seem like such a bad idea...

Fertile

The men who hunt me were always brutes, but now lust makes them barely more than beasts.

When they catch me, I know what comes next.

I will fight, but my need to be bred is just as strong as theirs is to breed. When they strip me, punish me, and use me the way I'm meant to be used, my screams will be the screams of climax.

Hostage

I knew going after one of the most powerful mafia bosses in the world would be dangerous, but I didn't anticipate being dragged from my apartment already sore, sorry, and shamefully used.

My captors don't just plan to teach me a lesson and then let me go. They plan to share me, punish me, and claim me so ruthlessly I'll be screaming my submission into the sheets long before they're through with me. They took me as a hostage, but they'll keep me as theirs.

Defiled

I was born to rule, but for her sake I am banished, forced to wander the Earth among mortals. Her virgin body will pay the price for my protection, and it will be a shameful price indeed.

Stripped, punished, and ravaged over and over, she will scream with every savage climax.

She will be defiled, but before I am done with her she will beg to be mine.

Kept

On the run from corrupt men determined to silence me, I sought refuge in his cabin. I ate his food, drank his whiskey, and slept in his bed. But then the big bad bear came home and I learned the hard way that sometimes Goldilocks ends up with her cute little bottom well-used and sore.

He stripped me, spanked me, and ravaged me in the most shameful way possible, but then this rugged brute did something no one else ever has before. He made it clear he plans to keep me…

Auctioned

Twenty years ago the Malzeons saved us when we were at the brink of self-annihilation, but there was a price for their intervention. They demanded humans as servants… and as pets.

Only criminals were supposed to be offered to the aliens for their use, but when I defied Earth's government, asking questions that no one else would dare to ask, I was sold to them at auction.

I was bought by two of their most powerful commanders, rivals who nonetheless plan to share me. I am their property now, and they intend to tame me, train me, and enjoy me thoroughly.

But I have information they need, a secret guarded so zealously that discovering it cost me my freedom, and if they do not act quickly enough both of our worlds will soon be in grave danger.

Hard Ride

When I snuck into Montana Cobalt's house, I was looking for help learning to ride like him, but what I got was his belt across my bare backside. Then with tears still running down my cheeks and arousal dripping onto my thighs, the big brute taught me a much more shameful lesson.

Montana has agreed to train me, but not just for the rodeo. He's going to break me in and put me through my paces, and then he's going to show me what it means to be ridden rough and dirty.

Carnal

For centuries my kind have hidden our feral nature, our brute strength, and our carnal instincts. But this human female is my mate, and nothing will keep me from claiming and ravaging her.

She is mine to tame and protect, and if my belt doesn't teach her to obey then she'll learn in a much more shameful fashion. Either way, her surrender will be as complete as it is inevitable.

Bounty

After I went undercover to take down a mob boss and ended up betrayed, framed, and on the run, Harper Rollins tried to bring me in. But instead of collecting a bounty, she earned herself a hard spanking and then an even rougher lesson that left her cute bottom sore in a very different way.

She's not one to give up without a fight, but that's fine by me. It just means I'll have plenty more chances to welt her beautiful backside and then make her scream her surrender into the sheets.

Beast

Primitive, irresistible need compelled him to claim me, but it was more than mere instinct that drove this alien beast to punish me for my defiance and then ravage me thoroughly and savagely. Every screaming climax was a brand marking me as his, ensuring I never forget who I belong to.

He's strong enough to take what he wants from me, but that's not why I surrendered so easily as he stripped me bare, pushed me up against the wall, and made me his so roughly and shamefully.

It wasn't fear that forced me to submit. It was need.

Gladiator

Xander didn't just win me in the arena. The alien brute claimed me there too, with my punished bottom still burning and my screams of climax almost drowned out by the roar of the crowd.

Almost…

Victory earned him freedom and the right to take me as his mate, but making me truly his will mean more than just spanking me into shameful surrender and then rutting me like a wild beast. Before he carries me off as his prize, the dark truth that brought me here must be exposed at last.

Big Rig

Alexis Harding is used to telling men exactly what she thinks, but she's never had a roughneck like me as a boss before. On my rig, I make the rules and sassy little girls get stripped bare, bent over my desk, and taught their place, first with my belt and then in a much more shameful way.

She'll be sore and sorry long before I'm done with her, but the arousal glistening on her thighs reveals the truth she would rather keep hidden. She needs it rough, and that's how she'll get it.

Warriors

I knew this was a primitive planet when I landed, but nothing could have prepared me for the rough beasts who inhabit it. The sting of their prince's firm hand on my bare bottom taught me my place in his world, but it was what came after that truly demonstrated his mastery over me.

This alien brute has granted me his protection and his help with my mission, but the price was my total submission to both his shameful demands and those of his second in command as well.

But it isn't the savage way they make use of my quivering body that terrifies me the most. What leaves me trembling is the thought that I may never leave this place... because I won't want to.

Owned

With a ruthless, corrupt billionaire after me, Crockett, Dylan, and Wade are just the men I need. Rough men who know how to keep a woman safe... and how to make her scream their names.

But the Hell's Fury MC doesn't do charity work, and their help will come at a price.

A shameful price...

They aren't just going to bare me, punish me, and then do whatever they want with me.

They're going to make me beg for it.

Seized

Delaney Archer got herself mixed up with someone who crossed us, and now she's going to find out just how roughly and shamefully three bad men like us can make use of her beautiful body.

She can plead for mercy, but it won't stop us from stripping her bare and spanking her until she's sore, sobbing, and soaking wet. Our feisty little captive is going to take everything we give her, and she'll be screaming our names with every savage climax long before we're done with her.

Cruel Masters

I thought I understood the risks of going undercover to report on billionaires flaunting their power, but these men didn't send lawyers after me. They're going to deal with me themselves.

Now I'm naked aboard their private plane, my backside already burning from one of their belts, and these three infuriatingly sexy bastards have only just gotten started teaching me my place.

I'm not just going to be punished, shamed, and shared. I'm going to be mastered.

Hard Men

My father's will left his company to me, but the three roughnecks who ran it for him have other ideas. They're owed a debt and they mean to collect on it, but it's not money these brutes want.

It's me.

In return for protection from my father's enemies, I will be theirs to share. But these are hard men, and they don't just intend to punish my defiance and use me as shamefully as they please.

They plan to master me completely.

Rough Ride

As I hear the leather slide through the loops of his pants, I know what comes next. Jake Travers is going to blister my backside. Then he's going to ride me the way only a rodeo champion can.

Plenty of men who thought they could put me in my place have learned the hard way that I was more than they could handle, and when Jake showed up I was sure he would be no different.

I was wrong.

When I pushed him, he bared and spanked me in front of a bar full of people.

I should have let it go at that, but I couldn't.

That's why he's taking off his belt...

Primal Instinct

Ruger Jameson can buy anything he wants, but that's not the reason I'm his to use as he pleases.

He's a former Army Ranger accustomed to having his orders followed, but that's not why I obey him.

He saved my life after our plane crashed, but I'm not on my knees just to thank him properly.

I'm his because my body knows its master.

I do as I'm told because he blisters my bare backside every time I dare to do otherwise.

I'm at his feet because I belong to him and I plan to show it in the most shameful way possible.

Captor

I was supposed to be safe from the lottery. Set apart for a man who would treat me with dignity.

But as I'm probed and examined in the most intimate, shameful ways imaginable while the hulking alien king who just spanked me looks on approvingly, I know one thing for certain.

This brute didn't end up with me by chance. He wanted me, so he found a way to take me.

He'll savor every blush as I stand bare and on display for him, every plea for mercy as he punishes my defiance, and every quivering climax as he slowly masters my virgin body.

I'll be his before he even claims me.

Rough and Dirty

Wrecking my cheating ex's truck with a bat might have made me feel better... if the one I went after had actually belonged to him, instead of to the burly roughneck currently taking off his belt.

Now I'm bent over in a parking lot with my bottom burning as this ruggedly sexy bastard and his two equally brutish friends take turns reddening my ass, and I can tell they're just getting started.

That thought shouldn't excite me, and I certainly shouldn't be imagining all the shameful things these men might do to me. But what I should or shouldn't be thinking doesn't matter anyway.

They can see the arousal glistening on my thighs, and they know I need it rough and dirty...

His to Take

When Zadok Vakan caught me trying to escape his planet with priceless stolen technology, he didn't have me sent to the mines. He made sure I was stripped bare and sold at auction instead.

Then he bought me for himself.

Even as he punishes me for the slightest hint of defiance and then claims me like a beast, indulging every filthy desire his savage nature can conceive, I swear I'll never surrender.

But it doesn't matter.

I'm already his, and we both know it.

Tyrant

When I accepted a lucrative marketing position at his vineyard, Montgomery Wolfe made the terms of my employment clear right from the start. Follow his rules or face the consequences.

That's why I'm bent over his desk, doing my best to hate him as his belt lashes my bare bottom.

I shouldn't give in to this tyrant. I shouldn't yield to his shameful demands.

Yet I can't resist the passion he sets ablaze with every word, every touch, and every brutally possessive kiss, and I know before long my body will surrender to even his darkest needs...

Filthy Rogue

Losing my job to a woman who slept her way to the top was bad enough, and that was before my car broke down as I drove cross country to start over. Having to be rescued by an infuriatingly sexy biker who promptly bared and spanked me for sassing him was just icing on the cake.

After sharing a passionate night, I might have made a teensy mistake in taking cash from his wallet in order to pay the auto mechanic, but I hadn't thought I'd ever see him again…

Then on the first day at my new job, guess who swaggered in with payback on his mind?

He's living proof that the universe really is out to get me… and he's my new boss.

ABOUT PIPER STONE

Amazon Top 150 Internationally Best-Selling Author, Kindle Unlimited All Star Piper Stone writes in several genres. From her worlds of dark mafia, cowboys, and marines to contemporary reverse harem, shifter romance, and science fiction, she attempts to delight readers with a foray into darkness, sensuality, suspense, and always a romantic HEA. When she's not writing, you can find her sipping merlot while she enjoys spending time with her three Golden Retrievers (Indiana Jones, Magnum PI, and Remington Steele) and a husband who relishes creating fabulous food.

Dangerous is Delicious.

* * *

You can find her at:

Website: https://piperstonebooks.com/

Newsletter: https://piperstonebooks.com/newsletter/

Facebook: https://www.facebook.com/authorpiperstone/

Twitter: http://twitter.com/piperstone01

Instagram: http://www.instagram.com/authorpiperstone/

Amazon: http://amazon.com/author/piperstone

BookBub: http://bookbub.com/authors/piper-stone

TikTok: https://www.tiktok.com/@piperstoneauthor

Email: piperstonecreations@gmail.com

Made in the USA
Middletown, DE
22 March 2023